CUTE MUTANTS

VOL 3:

THE DEMON QUEER SAGA

SJ WHITBY

For everyone who's still becoming who they truly are

CHAPTER ONE

So this is my life: I'm sitting in a swanky office with my big fuck-off boots up on a massive wooden desk. The CEO of Jinteki Research Laboratories glares from the imposing leather chair behind it. Her name is Gladdy Quick, aka Fetch, and she's a mutant like me. Except where my power is communicating with ordinary objects—like the desk who's burbling away to itself about the many things it contains—hers is psychically identifying someone's weaknesses and ruthlessly manipulating them. It makes her an excellent CEO and a shitty boss. She regards me from remarkably pretty brown eyes and brushes long, glossy curls out of her face.

"Take your boots off my desk, Dylan."

"The desk likes it."

"I do." The desk is very earnest. "It is perfectly splendid. There's something satisfying about the solid feel of a chunky heel. On the other drawer, I don't like to incur the wrath of the boss, unlike some people of my acquaintance and—"

"Maddy, make her take those boots off," Gladdy says. Her bodyguard leans against the window, looking out at the street below. She has blonde hair in a pixie cut and lips painted a virulent green colour. She's also a mutant, codename Sourpatch, who turns food into a highly toxic stomach acid. Technically, she's also undead, but we don't talk about that because it's rude.

"I'm not getting involved in your dick-measuring contest." Maddy grins at me, because she finds banter endlessly entertaining.

"Just put your boots on the floor." Dani sits beside me, looking irresistibly beautiful. Where I'm slouched to the point of almost collapsing out of my seat, she's sitting perfectly straight. Shouldn't that take away gay points? Dani is codenamed Marvellous and co-leads the Field Team with me. She's a telekinetic with a metal arm, a body that's almost as deadly as Wolverine and, for some unfathomable reason, is in love with the ambulatory trashpile known as Dylan Taylor, aka Chatterbox, aka me.

I sigh theatrically and obey. Dani and I are both dressed in black jeans and navy singlets with our Cute Mutants logo on the front. She looks naturally, effortlessly badass, where I look like an idiot dressing up in some weird quasi-military X-Men cosplay.

"You realise this shit is why Bancroft tried to have you killed." Gladdy is talking about our old boss. He *did*

try to take us out, but it didn't work, and now he's dead. It's a long story, better told elsewhere.

"I did a lot worse to Bancroft than putting my boots on his desk." I hold her gaze until she looks away. She can see my fears written on my face, but I don't know the specifics—presumably they're about losing people. My hand goes automatically to the tattoo on my left bicep with the names Wraith and Reverie.

That's the biggest difference between us and the X-Men. When mutants like us die, we don't come back.

"Now that Dylan's discovered basic courtesy, let's get this meeting started." Gladdy rocks back in her chair. "I've had more interview requests, which I've put off. They've connected the Firestone incident to the Jinteki incident. People are loudly speculating about the existence of extrahumans in New Zealand."

In the months since the Yaxley/Jinteki situation exploded in our faces, things on the extrahuman front have become far less secret. Japan, France, and Russia have official government-affiliated teams, and there are rumours of more. The narrative veers from cautiously optimistic to dire proclamations of the doom we bring. The broad consensus is that *for now* things are tolerable. There aren't many of us, and we're mostly in the care of governments.

All this makes us wary of media attention. They don't need to dig deep to find unpleasant stories.

"Give them Alyse," I say. "She's our resident charmer."

Gladdy leans over the desk. "I'm not giving them her or anyone else. I want you to appreciate that I'm keeping the media off your back. It means you owe me a favour, which I'm about to cash in."

"Why do I not like the sound of this?" Dani asks.

"It's a favour for the Americans." The room falls silent. Bancroft was rather shit-scared of a group called Quietus, who are a private security company based in the US. Emma's investigating them, but they're as secretive as their name suggests.

Our nagging Americans are more official. They're called EMID, which stands for Extrahuman Monitoring and Intelligence Division. It's a new organisation spinning out of the alphabet soup of American intelligence, intended to keep an eye on anyone like us. They're leaning heavily on our government to keep us in line.

"Fucking EMID." I've lost count of how often I've said this.

"Yes." Gladdy shows me her stern face. "They continue to gently remind us of their power and reach, as well as their extreme eagerness to fuck us if we won't play their games."

"Rude," Maddy says. "We don't want to be fucked."

Dani shoots me a look that I understand very well, and okay sure, she's very hot, but now who's being unprofessional?

Our situation here is precarious. When we took over Jinteki, there was a whole massive budget—literally hundreds of millions of dollars—earmarked for continuing research into extrahumans. That's a phrase that here means a whole raft of dodgy shit like medical experimentation, detention facilities, and a hundred euphemisms for torture. None of this is technically illegal. We've seen the international legislation, or at least Emma and Dani summarised it for me when I batted my eyelashes at them. The short form is that we're dangerous creatures and potential enemy combatants. We're not human in the eyes of the law.

Bancroft promised a war was coming. He might be right, but we're trying to avoid it for as long as possible. That means pretending to be tame little mutants and faithful servants.

"Let me guess—they've got an errand for us to run," Dani says.

"Of course."

"And we definitely have to do it?" I'm always arguing this particular point.

"EMID is the biggest fish in the pond, so we need to look like we're toeing the line." Gladdy stares back at me. "Don't give me that look, Dylan."

"What look?" I'm not giving her a look.

Gladdy sighs. "You're not the one talking to EMID, which is probably a good thing. I spend my days stopping this from collapsing on top of us."

"We haven't even done anything yet," I tell her.

"They won't need a reason to come for us." Her lips tighten and she taps a button on her tablet. Everyone's phone vibrates in unison. Emma, our resident technical genius, has completely cleaned down the phones we were given. She's replaced them with a suite of her new apps, which she assures us are far more secure. We trust her. She's our Goddess and the one who gave us powers. How? Why? *That* part is still a mystery, and she's more obsessed with it than anyone.

When we open the file, it's disappointingly thin.

"This is it?" Dani arches an eyebrow at Gladdy. I'm dumbass enough to feel the tiniest flicker of jealousy, because her eyebrow arch should be for me alone.

So soft, Emma says in my head.

Stop fucking eavesdropping, nosy. This is one of Emma's newer powers, the ability to communicate psychically with each of us. More of the mystery that is her. I wonder if EMID has any theories on the why and how and—

Let's hope EMID aren't looking for me. That would be really scary.

I read over Dani's shoulder as she flicks through the file. It's mostly surveillance, pulled from the Five Eyes intelligence network that New Zealand shares with a bunch of other countries, including America. The information is mostly about a series of thefts from a supermarket, and mysterious activity in a block of flats that's supposed to be abandoned. EMID has jumped to the conclusion that it's some mutants they lost track of. To show them that we can play nice and be good global citizens, it's our job to scoop them up. What we're supposed to do after that is unclear.

"We can look into it." Dani glances at me and I give her a tiny nod of assent.

Gladdy snorts. "Thank you so much for your cooperation. Fucking field team, think you're such badasses."

"That's because we are." I grin at her and look over at Maddy, who's still gazing out the window. "Madbae, you want to come play with the cool kids?"

"Who'll look after poor Fetchy?" She mock pouts.

"Fetch is tougher and meaner than any of us," I say.

Maddy laughs and reaches out to ruffle Gladdy's hair. If anyone else on the planet did that, they'd get some hideous psychic torture. "Am I allowed to hang out? Please?"

"It'll give me five minutes peace," Gladdy grumbles.

"We'll get out of your hair then, Mum." I swing myself out of my seat and head for the door. "If you're lucky, we'll bring you home some mutants. Don't wait up."

Gladdy's office is on the top floor of the building that used to belong to our old bosses, Yaxley Technology Solutions. They don't exist anymore, taken over by Jinteki aka Fetch in some complicated corporate shenanigans I didn't bother following. Down the corridor is the big open-plan training room, which should be filled with mutants hard at work at becoming a fabulous fighting team.

Instead, we find two mutants with a pizza box between them, watching a kung fu movie on an iPad.

"This is what you call training." Dani stands over them, looking down disapprovingly.

"It's called fuel." The short girl with the shaved head and eyes that have become an unusual shade of orange is Katie, aka Kacchan, aka Dragon. She has a temper and breathes fire. Yes, it's pretty fucking obvious given the nicknames.

"The movie is inspiration." The boy with the slim, muscly arms, the spiky hair, and the damn cheekbones is my ex-boyfriend Lou, aka Glowstick. He can generate light and heat when he's turned on which yes, is as weird as it sounds.

"We've got a mission soon," I tell them. "If either of you want to come, finish your pizza and get your damn uniforms on. We'll head out in an hour."

Katie gives me the finger, which is generally a sign she's heard me. We jog down the stairs to the living quarters on the next floor. Something smells incredible.

"Dilly." Pear stands in the doorway of our room. There's often a strange, appraising look in their eyes these days when they watch me, like they're not entirely sure what I've become.

"Hey." I lean into them and share a brief moment of contact.

"Hi, Ness," Dani says, hanging back.

"You come here too." Pear holds out their other arm and Dani joins us. "Are you two looking after yourselves, or worrying about everyone else?"

"The second one." I plant a kiss on the side of their shaved head. "I've got you to do the other part."

After things went very badly with our government handlers, our parents were detained in a secret black-site jail in the Canterbury countryside. It was supposed to be a way of controlling us. It didn't precisely work. Once the blood had been shed and our coup was complete, we rescued everyone. As part of the refit of the Yaxley building, we turned the first floor into accommodation. Not all of the parents took us up on the offer to stay close, but Pear likes the idea of being able to keep an eye on me. So does—

"Joo-hyun!" Dani's Mum appears from the kitchen. Her voice is loud, but she's beaming. "Dylan, Ness. You must come for dinner."

The adjustment's been hard on everyone. Mrs. Kim might be chill about her daughter being a lesbian, but less so about the weird superpowers. The point at which a bunch of teenagers took over a thriving med-tech company with aspirations of making it a mutant outreach centre? Definitely less chill. Still, she's making an effort, which involves making us kickass meals. I try to be vegetarian, but Mrs Kim's bulgogi is practically a mutant power of its own.

I slide into my seat and reach for a plate.

Dani taps the back of my hand lightly. "Jal meok-ge-sseum-ni-da."

Mrs. Kim nods, but there's a tiny twist at one corner of her mouth.

Dani rolls her eyes. "Wrong stress again?"

"Jal meok-ge-sseum-ni-da," I mimic, as close as I can. It means something like we will eat well.

"Gosaenghaesseo!" Mrs. Kim beams at me and I beam back.

"Good job." Dani arches an eyebrow at me. "How do you say teacher's pet in Korean?"

"Dylan *has* worked hard. As have you. I expect more from you of course."

"Of course," Dani mutters, as she helps herself to food.

Today, I eat vegetarian bibimbap, while stealing bits of beef from Dani's plate and pretending that's not cheating. Dinner's a fairly noisy affair. Dani's little brother Min-jun constantly pesters us to let him join the team, despite having no powers. The rest of the Cute Mutants also keep arriving, lured in by the smell of cooking. Soon everyone is there aside from Alyse and Emma, all sitting around what was once the boardroom table.

Kacchan loads half a pizza with kimchi from the fridge and reheats it with a burst of warm breath.

"Show-off." Maddy shoves her bowl over to be heated too.

I hold Dani's hand under the table and look around the room. It seems crazy to think dinners used to be Pear and I reheating yesterday's takeaway. Now I have this group of friends that keeps sprawling outwards. My old dream of being in a team like the X-Men has come true. In the nature of *be careful what you wish for* stories, it's been harder and weirder and sadder, but it's been better too.

I lift Dani's hand to my lips, and she turns her head and smiles at me. The first time I saw her smile like this was the day I broke up with my boyfriend, and the day I fell in love. It still has the ability to make my heart knock painfully in my chest. I'm not so scared I'll fuck things up anymore. The fear is still there, because my brain is a gremlin brain and will not be denied, but I've slowly come to accept that she does really love me. This isn't some giant cosmic prank. Now my fear is that I'll lose her. That my dream of being a mutant superhero will take her from me, in the same way it took my friend Wraith and Gladdy's friend Reverie.

The thought of it makes my whole body clench.

Gently, Emma says in my mind. *Everyone's okay. Now can you please come and see me? Lys says to bring food. I've found something you might call mind-blowing.*

CHAPTER TWO

With generous helpings of food, Dani and I head down to what everyone calls Emma's lair, on the ground floor of the building. Back when we were pawns of Yaxley, this was the briefing room. It still has the giant screen at one end, but now it's full of other expensive equipment. I have no idea what most of it does. Emma asks for things, and Gladdy signs them off without question. It's possibly more Goddess powers.

Somewhere behind a bank of monitors, Emma slumps in a massive gaming chair that dwarfs her. Alyse leans over the back, giving her a shoulder massage. Her mutant name is Moodring, because she transforms based on how she's feeling. Given that she's in a cuddly demi relationship with Emma, Alyse is currently a willowy tree-goddess, heavy with blossom.

Hey, you two, Emma says inside my head.

Use your words, I remind her, and she grins at me.

"Sorry. I get used to the mind thing." Emma's petite and pretty, with long black hair that's currently spilled all over the back of her seat and Alyse's hands. "We barely say a word out loud to each other these days."

"Yes." Dani perches on the table near her. "It's very creepy."

Emma sighs and rubs her temple. "Creepy girl with creepy powers. At least the dreams have stopped, haven't they?"

"Yes, no more dreams," Dani confirms.

For a while after we ended things with Yaxley, we had very intense Emma dreams. Not like the ones we used to share, where we were all in each other's heads. In these ones, Emma was lit up like a beacon, floating in the sky and telling us everything would be okay. Despite the reassurance, it was very disconcerting and made it hard to sleep. She seems to have them under control now.

"I still have Emma dreams." Alyse grins at us. "They're a little different."

"Oh, hush." Emma reaches up and squeezes Alyse's hand. "I've locked the dreams away the same way I control my psychic abilities. It's reassuring to know I'm not entirely useless."

"You're not useless at all." Alyse sifts Emma's hair through her fingers in soothing and repetitive motions. "I would say you're trying to do too much, but—"

"There are too many questions." Emma swallows irritation. "I'm still no closer to finding definitive answers. *However*, I've tracked down the Kyoto Cluster." She taps and swipes, bringing up a cascading array of data. Even before the superpowers thing, Emma's been good with tech, and money buys an awful lot of gadgets.

The screen resolves into the image of a girl standing in front of a row of vending machines. She has long blonde hair and wide blue eyes.

"I don't know what this means," I tell her. "Are you talking in your head again?"

"Impatient much?" Emma clicks her tongue. "This was taken eight months ago. Sara Newton was a California girl living in Kyoto and teaching English." She taps the screen and it changes to a shot of the official Japanese super-team, Sakura. Most of them look human, but one is made of rock. Another is a streak of blue fire, with a wild nimbus of flame crackling around the face. Emma taps a couple more times and the face of Sara Newton is overlaid on top of the burning figure.

"I assume that's not just digital magic." Dani leans in and squints at the screen.

"I tweaked the facial recognition algorithm to be a little more flexible," Emma says, as if this is a thing that regular people do every day. "Sara Newton's is the only face that matches."

"So she became a mutant," I say. "She kissed the Japanese equivalent of Emma, or got a blood transfusion from her, or had an organ donated."

"I checked all the medical options." Emma's fingers dance around the screens, bringing up more data that means nothing to me. "None of it checks out. Where we do find something interesting is her very last Instagram post." It's a picture of the same girl, holding a blue and red crystal cupped in her hands. It looks like it's glowing, but it could be a filter. There's a caption underneath.

Look what I found in the park today! Just lying there among the flowers. Isn't it beautiful? I want to do a giant abstract painting of it!

"So then I snatched her GPS tracking data. After the park, she went back to her apartment. Next day, she walks out onto the street and disappears. Nothing, no data anywhere, until four months later she turns up as part of Sakura's official launch."

She swipes the picture of the blonde girl and the crystal back onto the screen.

I look at the image until my eyes unfocus and it all blurs. "This seems dodgy as fuck. Some magic meteor causing mutations sounds like a shitty conspiracy theory."

"No more than you speaking with a networked hive mind via ordinary household objects all because of a kiss."

I roll my eyes. Even though Emma's story matches what my dearly departed baseball bat told me, it's scary.

I prefer to think I talk to random shit and sometimes it talks back. She makes it sound like I'm communicating with something larger and scarier.

"What about the other members of Sakura?" I ask.

"I'm still digging. My next job is to find the satellite footage for the park where Sara Newton found the crystal and work backwards from there."

"That sounds fun." It's a blatant lie.

"It's long and complicated." She grins at me. "You'd hate it. It'll take all the processing power we have, even with my latest spending spree. We'll get there. This might be a real breakthrough, Dilly."

I'm still staring at the picture on the screen. "You never touched any weird crystals before your party, did you?"

She favours me with a stare that makes me feel like a dumbass.

"Someone's got to ask the stupid questions," I protest.

"It's not stupid." She swipes data around. "Not even close. The dream is to find a chunk of this crystal and analyse the makeup of it. Compare it with what's in my blood. Maybe there's a link."

"Fevered brain." Alyse plants a kiss on Emma's forehead, and Dani and I exchange glances.

"Remember when I was the smart one?" Dani says, mock-plaintive.

"And now you're just a thug like me." I give her a nudge.

She wraps her metal arm around my waist and squeezes me unfairly hard until I yelp "Speaking of thuggery, we've got potential mutant weirdness to track down, courtesy of our buddies at EMID. You want to come, Moodring?"

Alyse shakes her head. "I'll keep an eye on this one." Her soft glow fades away, and she turns rumpled and creased. Emma's still tapping, so I tow Alyse out of the room, leaving Dani behind.

It's weird having conversations *about* Emma these days. She says she doesn't snoop, but she has a habit of wandering aimlessly through our heads.

"How's the worry meter?" I ask.

"Eight, maybe seven." Her usual effortless beauty looks faded and greyscale. She's exhausted. "Ems pushes herself so damn hard, wants every answer to every question. I love her, but she's an impossible girl. Hard to keep things from spiralling."

I put one arm around her. "I think she'll be okay. She's just…preoccupied."

"She's not sleeping enough." Alyse rests her head on my shoulder. "I make her eat and drink, but I can't knock her out at night."

"You take good care of her." I smile. "It's one less thing for me to worry about."

"Too many worries these days," Alyse says. "I guess this is growing up. Running a corporation, trying to stay a step ahead of the assholes."

"You worry about your girl," I tell her. "Me and Dan and Gladdy will do the other stuff."

She nods. "Thanks, Dilly. One day we might be able to rest."

"Yeah, we'll have to figure out what everyone's doing for fun these days. Speaking of fun…" I swing the door to Emma's room open again. "Hey, Marvellous. You coming?"

We head upstairs to retrieve the rest of the team. Dragon is always excited for a mission, although her power can be overkill. She has two modes: gently heating a pizza or setting the house on fire. Sourpatch is waiting too, an enormous smile on her bright green lips.

Lou is curled protectively around his phone, to stop us seeing anything. It's not like Emma isn't monitoring it. If he cares about that, he shouldn't use his work phone, the fucking noob. Nobody cares about his ongoing flirty almost-sext thread with some girl, aside from the fact his new friend's a civilian. Lou is under very strict instructions to lie where possible about anything mutant-related, but he is an intense dude. When this whole superpowers thing started, we were together. There were moments where it was tough going, but now we're friends and it's nice and chill.

"You coming?" I ask him. "Or are our missions interfering with your love life?"

"I can come." He shrugs at me. "She's still asking questions about what I do all day."

"Emma gave you the cover story. You work for a tech startup. Top secret IT bullshit. Your boss is very demanding."

Lou sighs and stares down at his phone. "I don't like lying to her."

"Tell him you work for your ex." Dani grins at me and it trips up my heartbeat. "Someone who's half-feral, incredibly hot, and lives to break your balls."

"You're an asshole," Lou says with a smile.

I swallow words about needing to be careful with his power. If he gets turned on and almost sets her on fire, she'll get an abrupt introduction to the *my boyfriend's a mutant* show and it'll be a circus. Ugh, this is what I've become. Worrying about how the fucking media will react to my ex-boyfriend's love life.

"It's good though?" I ask.

"What is?" He's still gazing at his phone.

"The thing with you and what's her name?"

"Yes, it's good. It's new. She's nice. I'm trying to be, like, very chill."

I try to keep a straight face. "That must be hard for you."

He laughs. "It is very hard, but we all must learn and grow."

"Even me," I say wisely.

"Some of us more than others."

I fake a punch at him, and we head into the shower blocks where everyone changes into uniform. We inherited these from Yaxley—all-black ninja-style outfits that go a decent distance towards being bulletproof and stab proof. They light up in fancy designs that we can program so we look like half-decent superheroes, which is a far cry from how we started out. One of the modes Emma's programmed in makes it look like we're wearing regular clothes. Everyone keeps their mask down for now. Mask up means go time.

Properly attired, we meet outside the elevator, where the words Wraith and Reverie are painted on the wall. As everyone leaves, they take a moment to place their palm over the names. It's a tribute to those we lost, and a reminder of the risks we face. For me, it's a promise to do whatever it takes to stop it happening again.

The elevator doors slide closed and I try to regulate my breathing. It's not like a cheesy TV show where you come face to face with your ghosts and speak meaningful monologues to them, but I still imagine Wraith is here.

"You can't go on a mission without your emotional support himbo, Chats," she'd say.

I'd tell her to fuck off. She'd make some crude remark about Dani and we'd laugh the whole way down.

I reach out and take hold of Dani's hand.

We can do this.

Damn fucking right we can, Emma says absently in my head. The girl never used to swear. I'm pretty sure this is all my fault.

CHAPTER THREE

familiar powder-blue electric vehicle waits outside the building. Roxy has been through a lot with us, and saved our asses on more than one occasion. I love her more than I love most people, and as far as I'm concerned, she's a Cute Mutant too.

"No rest for the heroes," she says in her low voice.

"Or the wicked." I slide into the driver's seat. Dani sits beside me, and the others squeeze themselves into the back. I tell the car where we're heading, and she glides comfortably into traffic. I rest my hand on the steering wheel in case of nosy cops, although Roxy has proven she can outrun them in the past. It shouldn't come to that. The complicated dance Gladdy has done with the New Zealand government and EMID means we have some kind of extra-special authority to talk our way past any police. It's still easier to look like teenagers taking Mum's car down to the supermarket to pick up energy drinks and tampons.

Roxy drives out of the central city and over to the south side of town. The address is an empty block of flats at the edge of a new subdivision. According to Gladdy's information, it's the subject of some complicated legal crap that's stalled development. The important part is that it's supposed to be empty, but an intelligence satellite snapped a photo showing heat signatures inside—two humans and at least five animals. Shouldn't be any problem, but I'm theoretically a grown-up now, so let's be cautious.

"Who's picked their Pride costumes?" Dani asks as we drive.

"Um, their what now?" I tap my fingers on Roxy's steering wheel.

"Pride parade. I know you've heard of it."

"Do we go to that?" I feel an unnecessary rush of nervousness. It's parades and crowds and dressing up all at once. "I mean, have you?"

"Of course. I've been every year for ages. I mostly go with my cousin Hye-jin, but sometimes with…other people."

I smirk. "You're allowed to talk about previous girlfriends by name."

"Doesn't Pear go?"

"They're not so much a celebration person. Less than me, even."

"Oh, that's cool. It's fine. We don't have to go." Dani speaks in a rush.

"Of course we're going." A smile spreads across my face. "I have to see what you wear."

"Last year I wore stupid baggy shorts and a teensy-tiny little rainbow bikini top."

I almost choke, even though I'm not eating or drinking anything.

"I thought that might inspire you." Dani laughs. "Don't worry, you can wear an enormous rainbow hoodie. That's still very Pride."

"I invited you to Pride last year, remember?" Lou pokes my shoulder. "With Queer Club. You literally threw a book at me."

"That sounds nothing like me," I say, although it does, and he's right.

The sun has gone down by the time we reach our destination. The city is lighting up, but the subdivision only has a few working poles to mark intersections. The block of flats is in complete darkness.

We put up our masks, because they've got night vision, infrared, and all the fancy cool shit superheroes ought to have. With the building lit up all lurid and green, we sneak over to the door, which turns out to be locked. The building seems dormant to my power, which means I can't talk my way in. Dani could bust it open telekinetically, and Lou could melt it open with his hot hands, but since Maddy's here, we may as well let her play.

"You want to do the honours, Sourpatch?"

She detaches the bottom panel of her mask, leaving her mouth free. Her lips twist as if she's tasted something gross, and she puts one hand delicately to her stomach. With a convulsive heave of her shoulders, she retches a thin stream of drool onto the lock. The metal melts in seconds. Maddy gives the door a nudge with her foot. It swings open silently.

"Sour power!" She pumps her fist and slips into the darkened stairwell.

"Fan out and search?" Dani asks. "Or stick together?"

"There's no rush." It's probably paranoid but I can't help it. "Let's stay together."

"Greetings, Dylan." The deep voice from behind is my friend, Onimaru Kunitsuna. He's a samurai sword who has adopted me as his travelling companion. He's also a priceless stolen artefact but we avoid talking about that by mutual agreement. The sight of him hovering at my shoulder is familiar enough that nobody bats an eyelid.

"Hey, Oni."

"What evil do we seek today?"

"Maybe no evil at all. If we're lucky, it'll be something cute and cuddly that we can adopt, like this baby firebreather here."

"Fuck you, Chatterbox."

"Hush, little Dragon." I pat her shoulder. "We're supposed to be stealthy."

We rescued Katie from a Jinteki research facility when we were breaking Emma out. She had no family to go home to, so she and Pear informally adopted each other. I've grown to like the little shit too, but she has even less chill than me.

Inside the building, it's abandoned and creepy. The apartments have no furniture, and most don't even have front doors. Half the plumbing isn't even attached. We tiptoe through each cold room and determine there's nobody there, then head back to the stairwell. The steps are concrete, but the boots of our Yaxley-made uniforms keep us nice and quiet.

The first floor is empty too.

As soon as we push open the stairwell door on the second floor, we see a bunch of heat signatures through our masks. They're scattered all down the main hall-way, small and close to the ground.

"The fuck?" Dragon advances, dropping the bottom half of her mask, and taking a massive in-drawn breath.

"Hold," Marvellous snaps, before everything burns. "Those are only—"

"Kitty!" Dragon crouches on the floor, holding one hand out and clicking her fingers.

Sourpatch joins her on hands and knees, making an exaggerated purring sound, and twisting her masked head from side to side like she thinks she's a cat herself.

"We can't take you two anywhere," Marvellous sighs.

"Get back up." I flap my hand at them. "We don't know what they are."

"They're kittens." Sourpatch is surrounded by a purring mass of cats, all fighting for the chance to rub their heads against her.

I jump as one curls itself around my left leg and yowls.

"Yeah, what are kitties going to do?" Dragon demands.

Glowstick gets down beside her and starts patting two cats at once.

"Maybe they've got tentacles and pocket dimensions inside them," I say indignantly. "Or maybe they can breathe fire or spit acid like you two assholes. Poison fangs or claws? Maybe they exude some kind of narcotic gas or—"

I find myself crouching too as the cat at my feet stretches up, lifting a paw like it's desperate for the tiniest bit of attention. It presses its head firmly into my palm, and I can hear the scratchy motor of it revving.

"This is fucking weird," Marvellous says, which is true. How the hell are there so many cats? Is it some kind of bizarre defensive strategy where if you put enough in someone's path, they'll be unable to move because of the cuteness?

Marvellous is less easily swayed by cats than the rest of us. She forges her way through the furry tangle, and I scramble after her. The others finally join us, but it takes five verbal prods. Both Sourpatch and Dragon are muttering and sullen.

"We're not here to pat cats," I tell them.

"Maybe we should be." Maddy's still trying. "We came here to pat cats and chew gum."

"Don't make us regret bringing you," Dani says. "This is still a mission."

We proceed down the hallway, and the tide of cats flows with us. None manifest any unnatural ability. I'm starting to relax when I see human heat signatures in an apartment up ahead. One is lying down and the other sits beside them. They don't look alert or defensive, so maybe the cats aren't an early warning system after all. More little points of heat are scattered around the room.

"Candles?" Marvellous asks over our headsets.

"Makes sense," I murmur back. "Let's do this really fucking gently. I'm not getting a big existential threat vibe."

"Agreed. Glowstick, light the place up."

Lou's gloves retract and he makes a half-erotic sound in his throat. I know it's creepy of me, but every time this happens, I wonder what he's thinking about. Is it his new girlfriend? I hope it's not me, but I can't control his thoughts. Omigod, Dylan, how can you assume his erotic imaginings would even include you—oh shit, we're moving.

Glowstick's hands are bright white bulbs that my mask automatically filters out. With a nod from Marvellous, he strides forward and barges through the door. Dragon and Sourpatch flank him, ready to spit flame and acid. Marvellous and I bring up the rear. Oni sings joyfully in my head.

Here come the Cute Mutants, ready for action.

One of the targets screams and drops something on the floor. The other curls into a tight ball and starts crying.

Honestly, I feel like an asshole.

"Easy, easy," Marvellous says over the comm. "Stay calm, but don't stand down yet."

Glowstick raises his hands like a cartoon superhero, flooding the room with light. There's not much to see, aside from even more cats prowling. A pair of futons lie in the corner, as well as a camping stove and a duffel bag spilling clothes. Five bags of garbage are stacked against the wall. A bunch of candles are scattered around, but they're drowned out by Lou.

Our targets still cringe away. The prone figure is dressed in a faded green puffer jacket and baggy sweatpants, and the one sitting up is in blue jeans and a white t-shirt with stars on it.

"It's okay. We come in peace." I hold my hands up, trying to be reassuring. I get that a bunch of people bursting into your room dressed in all-black ninja outfits doesn't give that vibe, so I pop the mask down. The sitting mutant turns and squints. I wonder what she thinks, seeing a teenager with big eyes and scruffy black hair, attempting a normal human smile.

"What do you want? Are we not allowed to be here? We're not hurting anyone!" She looks to be in her thirties. Her eyes are tired and her brown hair is lank.

The other one is still facing away and shaking.

"Mutant outreach." My smile is flagging. "We're here to help."

"What?" Her voice is scratchy. "What are you talking about?" Her accent isn't from here. It sounds American, or maybe Canadian? I can't tell the difference.

The others pop their masks too, but being surrounded by a bunch of teenagers only makes her more nervous. The cats start climbing into her lap, and one little ginger one leaps up onto her shoulder, wrapping its tail around her neck. There's a cat tattoo on her forearm, a black and white Scottish fold with vivid green eyes.

"There's nothing to be afraid of," Marvellous says. "We're—"

She breaks off when the tattoo blinks. It peels itself off her skin to leap down onto the floor. The new cat yawns, showing off its pink tongue, and saunters over to me. It decides to sit on my foot and begin kneading my uniform with its claws.

"*That's* her mutant power?" Marvellous is incredulous. "This is paranormal shit."

"Worry about that later." I gently detach the cat and crouch beside the woman. "Can you please tell me what's going on? It looks like you need help, and believe it or not, we can actually do that."

The cat woman reaches out to the other person. "Can you help with *this*?"

The guy in the puffer jacket rolls over. His skin is pale and waxy and his eyes are closed. His teeth worry at his lip. He pulls the jacket up along with the damp shirt underneath it. There's a jagged wound across his stomach—a thick red line that looks inflamed.

"Medical assistance," Lou says nervously. We do have a bunch of doctors we inherited from Jinteki, which will be a lot stealthier than bowling into the main hospital in town. It's unlikely they'll be able to help with whatever this is.

The red line trembles and gapes open, revealing rows of sharp, yellowed teeth.

Dragon scurries back and hides behind me. "What the fuck is that?"

Sourpatch leans closer, fingers twitching.

"It's so hungry," Cat Lady whispers. "It's never satisfied."

The mouth gapes wider, until the man's whole chest is a hungry, wet hole. I'm freaking out. Surely this can't be what the cats are for. I've seen some terrible shit, but I don't think I can watch what comes next. When

Cat Lady grabs a torn pizza box from the nearby bag of garbage, I almost sag with relief. She lowers it gently into the stomach-mouth, which begins to chew violently. Steve pulls the jacket back down, hiding it from view, although we can still hear the loud sound of thick cardboard being turned into pulp.

Marvellous grimaces. She really doesn't like chewing sounds, even when I'm trying to eat quietly. These are seriously obnoxious. Maybe she'll appreciate my delicate eating from now on.

"That—" I struggle to think of what to say next.

Cat Lady shivers. "You said you could help."

"We can." I take a deep breath. "We have a place to stay and medical facilities. When did you change?"

"It happened last month. We barely knew each other, the two of us, but we were catching the last bus home after night classes in Toronto. There was only one other person in the bus. Just before our stop, he leapt up and sprayed something in our face. I thought it was Mace at first, but it didn't hurt at all."

Emma, are you listening to this? She might be out of range.

Of course. Dani gave me a heads up. It sounds…weird. Someone deliberately creating mutants like this? It doesn't make any sense.

"I felt fine," Cat Lady continues. "I would have ignored the whole thing, but Steve was really out of it, so I took him back to my place. I don't know why I didn't take him to the hospital or call the police, but the whole thing felt really sketchy. I got him home and he slept in my bed. I thought things would be okay. When I woke up on the couch, I had five new cats. Steve was screaming, and I found him feeding my curtains into his stomach."

"Fuck." Dragon is still behind me, clutching my waist. "I'd have ditched the dude."

"We were terrified. Both of us." The cats are drawn to her as she talks, this purring mass of felines surrounding her. "Were we going mad? Were we dying? Then we dreamed of a pretty Asian girl sitting in a park. She had really long hair and another girl was braiding it. She opened her eyes and said *come to Christchurch, New Zealand*. It seemed the only real option we had."

Emma, I say to the remarkably silent voice in my head. *Those dreams of yours?*

I wasn't doing it on purpose, Dylan. I swear.

"I begged money off my parents and we came straight out here. Except by the time I arrived, the dreams were gone, and we had no idea how to find the mysterious girl. We tried, but there was nothing. And then our money ran out and we had to find this place."

"When did you arrive?" I ask.

"Around two weeks ago." Her eyes fill with tears as Steve thrashes around on the futon. She reaches for more trash to feed into his stomach-mouth. This time

Sourpatch takes it for her, and watches with undisguised delight as she drops a pair of empty cans in.

That's when I shut my dreams off, Emma says. *Which means these people were lost. What if there are more searching for me?*

Don't jump to conclusions yet.

"Let's get you somewhere more comfortable," I say. "Sourpatch and Dragon, can you help Hungry Boy here down to the car?"

They obediently help him to his feet. Dragon is holding him very tentatively, like she's scared the mouth has other ideas.

Dani looks slightly vacant while she chats with Emma. I wonder what they're talking about. More mysterious mutant madness, no doubt.

"How many kitties can we take in the car?" Dragon asks me hopefully.

"I don't know," I tell her. "We're already going to need a second vehicle. Roxy, can you send one of the others over this way?"

"Already done," she says.

"You're the best." I turn my attention to Cat Lady, who I'm desperate to codename Kitty Pride because, you know, the pride of kitties. "How do we get the cats out of here?"

"Oh!" She closes her eyes and spreads her arms. The cats climb all over her. They slowly melt into her skin until her arms, neck, and even her cheeks are patterned with an intricate tattoo. As a tear trails down her cheeks, one of the cats extends a pink tongue to lick it away.

"Holy fucking shit," Dragon and I breathe in unison.

"I'm sorry for crying," Kitty sniffles. "I just miss Luna, Raven, Moriarty, and Watts. I had to leave them behind because they couldn't, you know." She gestures feebly with her arms.

"They were your original cats," Dani says. "Real ones."

Kitty nods sadly, but it's not like any of us can pop over to Canada and pick them up. Maybe Keepaway could've, but they bailed. I never really got to know them, but it would have been super helpful having a teleporter on the team. At least we've got Roxy for transport.

"Come on," I say. "Let's hit the road."

The doorway is blocked by Sourpatch, who's busy shoving a variety of stuff into Steve's extra mouth.

"You can feed him on your own time, you weirdo," Glowstick says.

"I think it's cute," she says defensively.

"Yes, but you also think Fetch is cute."

"I have a soft spot for angry things." Sourpatch tosses a broken cup into the stomach mouth and tugs his jacket back down. "It's why I like you, Chatterbox."

She finally tows Steve after her, and we leave the building. Glowstick obediently lights our way through the dark corridors. His girlfriend must be providing him a lot of material.

CHAPTER FOUR

Back at headquarters/home, we unload Kitty and Steve into the care of Pear and Mrs. Kim. Our new arrivals seem relieved to find other adults. It's clear they don't like that everything is run by under-twenty-ones.

Their attitude irritates me, and I'm still grumpy when we get into the elevator up to Gladdy's office. Dani leans against me and runs her thumb over the back of my hand. It goes some small way towards soothing me. I want to take a break from people, but both Emma and Gladdy summoned us via psychic communication and text message respectively, which means it's urgent.

Everyone turns to look at us when we come in. Alyse is shifted into something pointy and aggressive. The silence is awkward. I figure we're walking into an argument. Dani and I take our seats. I resist the temptation to put my feet up on the desk. It'll only make the tension worse.

"They've been arguing a *lot*," the desk tells me. "It's gotten unpleasant."

"Tattletale." I run my fingertips along her surface.

"Are you done?" Gladdy glares at the desk. "I heard from EMID again, who requested we deliver the targets into American custody."

"They're Canadian," Dani points out.

Gladdy frowns. "Yes, but the Canadians don't have a purpose-built facility for housing mutants, so they're working with the Americans."

"Purpose built facility." There's bitterness in Emma's voice. "You're talking about a jail. Like the one where *you* were held, Gladiola."

"Yes, but these mutants…their powers aren't exactly useful. EMID isn't going to weaponise them."

"You don't know what they'll do." Dani's shoulders are tense. She leans forward, biting off every word. "They can still torture them, or pull them apart to see how they work. I can't believe you of all people are arguing this side."

It's good the others are talking, because the desk might explode into splinters if I said how I feel. I can sense Oni turning in circles in the training room, feeding on my agitation. If anyone tries to give these mutants over to—

"I'm trying to help us." Gladdy slams her hands on the desk, who whimpers. "We need to *appear* to co-operate. If we act belligerent, they'll focus on us. Right now, they're watching from a distance, and we want them to stay that way."

As unhappy as I am, she has a point, and I know Dani sees that too. At the same time—

"Then lie," I say. "Tell EMID we couldn't find the mutants. Or they died in transit. The capture turned into a firefight. Any number of stories. You're good at manipulating perception, Fetch, so do your fucking job."

Gladdy glares at me and I hold her gaze. What's she seeing in my face? My friends dead or in jail? Me, helpless in the face of overwhelming odds?

"Fine," she says with a sigh. "I'll make up a story and sell it. It's a good idea. Thanks, Chatterbox."

Jesus, she must have seen something fucking awful to capitulate this quickly.

"There's another problem," Dani says. "Those mutants came here from Canada to find Emma. Who knows how many others came too?"

"I didn't realise." Emma shifts in her seat, looking defensive. "Or know what would happen when they lost me. Do you think I should start my dreams up again, so people can find me?"

"No." The rest of us speak in unison.

"Not all of them are going to have cute powers like creating cats," I say. "There might be ones like we fought with Bancroft." There was a creepy octopus guy, one that could melt and, worst of all, someone who could take over your mind—the person responsible for

Reverie's death, and almost mine as well. "Lighting you up as a mutant beacon is a crazy idea. We want the lost and the helpless, but not the creepy psychos. Currently there's no way to tell them apart."

"We agree on everything then," Gladdy says with a small trace of sarcasm. "I'll stall EMID, and Emma will keep her dreams to herself. If only we could detect mutants to investigate them."

"Definitely agree on that," I murmur.

Emma nods with a faraway look on her face. Presumably she's thinking about the logistical difficulties of tracking down mutants, and how that relates to finding where she came from.

I'm fine, Dylan, Emma says. *You don't need to worry about me. Really.*

This only makes me feel worse.

We head back downstairs to where Steve and Kitty Pride have been squared away. Kitty's real name is apparently Karen, which makes me snort-laugh. Our new arrivals are now fast asleep in the spare sleeping quarters. I stand in the doorway and watch as one of the cats unfolds itself from the skin around Kitty's ankle and curls up at her neck. Steve's extra mouth seems to be finally sated. He snores faintly. There's an empty garbage bag beside the bed.

I close the door quietly and return to the dining room, where Mrs. Kim and Pear are standing around the table. It's a lot louder in here than usual.

"Yut!" Pear shouts, arms above their head.

Mrs. Kim groans as Pear leans over and moves something around, swiping a wooden disc off the table so it bounces onto the floor.

Dani's the only mutant in the room. She's leaning against the wall, dressed in nothing but a long t-shirt.

"What fresh hell is this?" I cross to the table where there's a board set up, with tokens and four wooden sticks lying haphazardly.

Pear collects the sticks and tosses them across the table. Their expression is much less happy this time. "Gae."

"They're drinking and playing Yut." Dani sidles over to me. "It's a Korean board game. I've seen this story before at family gatherings. It usually involves screaming aunties and uncles, and a bad ending for someone."

"Hush, Joo-hyun." Mrs. Kim takes the sticks and scatters them.

"Geol," Pear and Dani say simultaneously.

"Do you know the rules?" I watch Mrs. Kim move her own token.

"Sadly, I do." Dani crosses to the table and pokes at the sticks. "These are kind of like dice, I guess. Different configurations mean you get to move different numbers of spaces. You try and get your tokens around the board and kick other people's off. It pairs well with drinking and gambling."

"We haven't advanced to the gambling stage," Pear says. "And thank fuck for that, because I've lost every fucking game up until this point. Sorry, Ji-woo. Language. Blame the wine."

"Ji-woo?" I mouth at Dani, who shrugs.

"Help me, Dilly." Pear pats the seat beside them. "You're the big strategist here."

"Fuck no. The real strategy is picking the winner. I'm on Ji-woo's team."

Dani lets out a strangled yelp of laughter. Shit. I can't even blame the fucking wine.

"Mrs. Kim." I can't reverse this shit fast enough, so I pick up the sticks and hurl them into the air. "Help me redeem myself," I whisper.

I can't understand what they say, but they rotate obediently and land all with the round, marked sides up. "Is that good?"

The sticks giggle to themselves.

"Mo!" Ji-woo has apparently forgiven me my sins, because she throws her arms around me and kisses me on the cheek. Definitely blaming the fucking wine for that one. She moves a token around the board and sends one of Pear's flying.

Dani's shoulders are shaking.

"Again," Mrs. Kim says. "Another turn!"

"You know the drill," I whisper to the sticks and toss them in the air. They twist and dance and fucking show off, honestly, which makes it super obvious when they land in a perfectly aligned row, round side up.

"Mo! Mo! Mo!" Mrs. Kim chants, fists pumping.

Dani can barely breathe, she's laughing so hard.

On the other side of the table, Pear's arms are folded. "Dylan Jean Taylor, you fucking cheat. I raised you better than this."

"We're mutants. We do what it takes." I grin at them until their stony face cracks.

They snort and gather the sticks. "If the cheating superheroes can take themselves off to bed, we can go back to me losing honestly."

"I'm exhausted anyway." Dani yawns. "Big day."

"Okay." I put one arm around her waist and give her a chaste kiss on the cheek. "Sleep well."

Mrs. Kim snorts. "Oh so subtle."

I pull away from Dani and widen my eyes. "Time to retreat."

"You are both ridiculous. You and Joo-hyun. Do you really think I don't know?"

I glance at Dani and then switch my attention to Pear, giving them the full force of my glare. I'm glad that Pear gets on with Dani's Mum, but having them live together and trade information is not what I signed up for.

"I didn't say a thing." Pear smirks. "Perhaps you're not as stealthy as you think."

Mrs. Kim shakes her head. "Not stealthy at all. Every night, you go off to your separate rooms. Then fifteen minutes later, I hear the door, I hear Joo-hyun tiptoeing down the hallway, I hear Dilly's door." It's a little bit cute that she calls me Dilly, but it's also embarrassing to be caught. "I approve of your relationship, so why would it bother me that you share a bed?"

"At least they can't get pregnant." Pear winks.

"Precisely." Mrs. Kim nods. "They can do what they wish with each other. It is the sneaking that offends me."

"Fuck me," Dani whispers to me. "This is—"

"I think that's what they're giving me permission for." The funny side is revealing itself to me now, especially the horror in Dani's eyes.

She can't take the embarrassment, and tows me down the corridor. We usually sleep in my room. Otherwise Pillow whines like an insufferable baby about how I've rejected her, left her out of my life, and so on. It's better to endure her running commentary on how beautiful Dani is, how lucky I am, and what a joyous thing relationships are.

As soon as the door closes behind us, Dani starts laughing and throws herself down on the bed. I lie beside her and lay my arm over her stomach. I'm very aware of how high her t-shirt has ridden up, but I pretend not to be. Instead, I press my face into her neck and kiss her. Why does she always smell so good?

"My life has reached a weird point," she tells me.

"It was sweet."

"My mother, who I spent my whole life trying to gain the approval of, and then desperately hiding my queerness from, simply gives a wave of her hand and says I can do whatever I want with you."

I lever myself up on one elbow and look down at her. "You can, you know." I can feel my pulse in my teeth. "Do whatever you want with me."

Her breathing changes. She reaches up to tangle her metal hand in my hair. Her lips part, and she pulls me down to her. This is one of the few things that can quiet my racing brain and my insecurities. Her skin is soft and her kisses are warm, and nothing speaks to me aside from her.

Later, when we're quiet and tangled together, reality comes back in like the tide washing over our beached bodies.

"May you sleep on the breast of your delicate friend," I whisper. We'd been together for a while before I found her Instagram page. She didn't have many posts, but they were all beautiful and moody landscape shots with Sappho quotes scrawled over them. When I read that line, it made me catch my breath. Now that I've done it with Dani, I can confirm one hundred percent that Sappho knew her shit.

She strokes my cheek and tips my chin upwards with two metal fingers. Her eyes meet mine. This simple action is a tiny miracle that opens up the wild vista of her love, a beautiful landscape I hang over like the moody sun in a dazzling sky. How can she make me feel this way?

Every part of me is a combination of flushed and tired and numb. I wish Dani was a bath I could sink into. I'm feeling sleepy, but my brain fidgets around a particular worry. Words slip out of my mouth before I mean them to. "You like girls, right?"

Her mouth twitches. "Up until this point I've only ever liked girls. But I like what you are. You don't need to worry about that."

"I'm not *not* a girl," I say. "I don't really know what I am."

"You're Dylan." She kisses me. "And I love you. I don't think of you as a girl, but I do think of you as my girlfriend. And I still think of myself as a lesbian."

I nuzzle into her neck. "Gender is complicated and confusing. It's never made sense to me, but I still want to fit with you."

"You do." She brushes her hand down my side, tracing lines across my skin that transmute me from a block of ice into a steaming pool of water.

"I still can't pick a box," I tell her, in amongst kisses. "So I'm, like, genderfluid, I guess. That's what I'm trying to say."

"You're coming out to me." Her smile dazzles me.

"I guess. Is that what this is?" I squirm in half-delight, half-awkward. "Like Alyse has said stuff, and Emma probably reads it out of my brain, the nosy brat. I'm pretty sure Pear's known for years, but I've never come right out and *said it* before."

"I'm glad you chose me." Her mouth tastes mine, and I swoon all the way down.

"And it's honestly not a problem for you?" My eyes are anxious, I know it.

"Woman is a very wide box, with space for so many different people to fit," Dani says. "But there's room for people who dance between the boxes too. Shit, I'm terrible at explaining things, but I know this." She looks into my eyes. I am hopelessly lost in them, tumbling and happily adrift. "You are very precisely and specifically what I like. Right from the moment I saw you across the classroom. When my icy-cold heart turned into a warm gooshy fountain of rainbows and glitter."

"Whether I'm a she or a they or a he."

"I love Dylan," Dani says. "He makes me so happy I sometimes lose my train of thought. She makes my heart skip beats. They make me tingle and lose my breath." She gives me another flash of her gorgeous smile. I am forced to kiss her again, helpless against this surge of feeling. "So you let me know what you'd like me to call you, and I'll use that. Even if it's Dillyweed."

My heart peals like delirious thunder. I'm genderfluid, and Dani still clings to me, and her love is a tangible part of my world.

"You can call me anything *except* Dillyweed," I say with a smile. "I'm actually very easy to please."

That makes her laugh way too much. I tickle her until she bites her tongue really hard and throws me off the bed telekinetically.

Pillow breathlessly hurtles over to break my fall. "Human love is a bizarre thing," she says. "I find it impossible to understand. Yet it fills me with such intense longing when I look at you, this desperate urge to comprehend what binds you together."

"Oh, Pillow." I impulsively hug her tight. "You are the president and founding member of soft bitch club."

I position Pillow on the bed so both Dani and I rest on her, which is her favourite place to be. Then I nestle in close and watch Dani. She should be falling asleep, but her eyes flicker. Her busy brain is in analysis mode.

"Are you happy?"

"With you?" Her mouth curves again. "Extremely. With everything else?" She sighs. "I don't know. I'm constantly worried about Emma. What's she becoming? We've been friends for years, ever since the teacher first put us together in class because we were the two Asian girls, but now when I look at her, it's like—"

I say nothing, which is hard for me. I wait and wait and count the gentle rhythm of Dani's heart under my hand.

"She's changing, and I know we all are, but with her it's more…mysterious. And if I'm not worrying about Emma, I'm thinking about the future, or the phrase *the extrahuman species*. Ever since I read it in that stupid document, I see it every night like it's written on the inside of my eyelids."

"People in Japan becoming mutants from weird crystals," I say. "People in Canada becoming mutants from being sprayed by weird substances."

"People in New Zealand becoming mutants by kissing a girl. There are more around the world every day. And the more of us that have dangerous powers, the closer we get to—"

"Genosha," I whisper against her skin. In the comics, it's the mutant nation, where sixteen million were murdered in one of many attempts to wipe out mutantkind. It's only a story. We both know this, but at the same time—

"Genosha," she says, just a breath, and her beautiful eyes are full of worry.

"We'll fight them," I promise her, because I know how to do that. We fought our way to being a team, and we fought our way out from under Yaxley's thumb, and we'll fight for survival. There's a part of me deep down—or maybe not so deep—that relishes the idea of continuing the fight. It's one of the handful of thoughts that I don't tell Dani. There's still a part of me that wonders how far love can stretch, and I don't want to risk breaking it over the burning, reckless core of me.

CHAPTER FIVE

I sleep terribly. It's not an uncommon occurrence, because of my dreams. Tonight, I wander barefoot in the snow—a naked and genderless figure carved from ice. Snowflakes alight on me and shatter into crystal fragments. I leave no footprints, because this world of unfeeling winter is my true home. Finally, I stumble out onto a rocky, frozen shore. The world is entirely white, aside from the charcoal smear of a burned-out dinghy. I find the bloody and broken form of Wraith sprawled among it, charred and shaking.

"You didn't save me." Her plaintive voice shatters my arctic skin.

I sit up in bed, wide awake. My teeth are chattering so badly I have to hold my jaw closed with both hands. Dani is sprawled soft and warm beside me. All I want is to wake her but I can't disturb her for every emotion that streaks through my head.

I lie back down and try to sleep. My fists clench and I tell my stupid brain to think about something else. No snow, no Wraith, no burning boat. It's pointless and I'll never get back to sleep because—

Hey, lovebirds. Put some clothes on and get upstairs.

I jolt awake again. My phone is within arm's reach. I spin it around to see it's just after five in the morning.

Dani's got her head buried in Pillow, but I nudge her until she responds. Once she's finally awake, she snaps into business mode. She's dressed and waiting by the door while I'm standing almost naked in the middle of the room, my eyes unable to focus on anything that looks like clothes.

"I was asleep," I complain blearily.

"I know, Dills." Dani finds a hoodie and tugs it over my head for me, and yeah sure, I could do it myself, but I like it when she does it.

I yawn my way up to the top floor and am still dazed as we stagger into Gladdy's office. I feel vindicated to see that Dani's the only one in a proper outfit. Emma's wearing an old-fashioned nightgown. Alyse is in a baggy Powerpuff Girls t-shirt that's slipping dangerously down one shoulder. Maddy's wearing an enormous plaid shirt that's barely buttoned up enough to cover anything and, most surprisingly of all, Gladdy's wearing a bright yellow sweatshirt with a picture of a cartoon mouse on it. The others must still be asleep.

"I like your little mouse." Obviously I'm too sleepy to have self-preservation turned on.

"Shut up, or I'll strangle you with it." Gladdy scowls. "It's Maddy's, and it was the first thing I found lying on the floor, because the brat cannot clean up after herself."

I shoot a meaningful glance at Dani, because there is much speculation on the Maddy/Gladdy relationship. Are they just super close bros or something romantic? It's very difficult to make sense of the vibes. They share a room, but we've never seen them kiss or anything. It wouldn't surprise me either way.

"I'm assuming there's a reason for the wakeup call?" Dani asks.

"Yes." Gladdy perches on the edge of her desk, which annoys me because of the double standard. "A high priority alert from EMID. There's a video. I figured we should assemble the Brains Trust and Dylan to go through it."

"Very funny, Mousie. Show us the fucking thing." I fold my arms and stare at the TV on the wall, while Emma fiddles with her phone to get the streaming set up.

The screen lights up to show cellphone footage of a recording booth. There's a pretty Māori girl inside singing. The audio quality isn't great, but she's got a nice voice.

"She looks familiar," Maddy says.

Alyse snaps her fingers. "It's the actress, what's her name."

"Super helpful," Dani smirks.

I have no idea who she is, but I doubt we were woken up to watch a girl singing. It goes on for a couple of minutes until my eyes droop. They snap open when something unfolds from the wall behind the singer. At first I think it's a glitch, but it's part of a person, appearing through what looks like a cut in the world. The face is a pale circle with two enormous black holes for eyes. Hair falls around their face in scribbled strands. It flickers, becoming a complex smear of colour, as if hazy light is reflecting through a stained-glass window onto them. I make out wavering shapes of a cross, a snake, twinned daggers.

The phone shakes. Someone bangs on the window.

"Nika! Nika! Turn around."

"Yeah, that's her name," Alyse says. "Nika Pearson."

The shapes on the creature's face turn darker, red shading to black. One hand extends, revealing long fingers in a black glove that stretches halfway up a pale arm. A door bangs and the singer looks up, eyes wide. The backing track cuts off abruptly.

"What the fuck?" She sounds indignant.

The black-gloved hand flickers out and back, a stuttering wave to the camera.

A second figure joins Nika in frame—a big guy in a singlet, with complex tattoos on his biceps. He runs over but it's too late. The singer is falling in slow motion, the bottom half of her face awash in blood. Before she hits the ground, the video ends.

"I think that was a mutant," Maddy says in a ridiculous stage whisper.

"Some kind of creepy mutant." Alyse shivers, becoming almost as pale and pointed as the person in the video.

"We're all creepy." I ask Emma to wind the video back.

She steps frame by frame through the first appearance. At first there's only a tiny rectangle of pale skin with a single blinking eye. In a series of rippling motions, each frame reveals more. The shapes on their face are clear in each individual image—crosses sharpened to daggers, a palm bleeding red and gold, a child lying on a large flat stone.

The arm unfolds in stop motion. Emma skims ahead to the attack itself. It's almost too quick to be captured on film. In one frame the hand is normal size, in the next the fingers are unnaturally elongated, at least a meter in length. The tips are barbed projectiles at the end of five long black spears. In the next frame, the hand is retracted, collapsing back in on itself. It's another few frames before blood appears on the singer's face.

I can't repress a shudder. "Definitely fucking creepy."

Emma runs the movement forward and backward. "It's like they unfold parts of themself. Like they're invisible until they strike."

"Interesting idea." Dani walks over and peers up at the giant image on the screen. The face is frozen with a pattern of a golden sword piercing a bloody heart. "Makes for a damn good assassin. If they come for us—"

"Oni's faster." I hope he is, at least.

Emma plays the video through at full speed again. "Another mutant. I wonder where they came from."

"What else did EMID say?" I turn to Gladdy, who chews on her thumbnail and sneaks glances at her phone.

"They sent that video and a demand to have our field team investigate. The Yaxplane is already standing by at the airport, waiting to take you to Auckland."

I grimace. "That means I have to put pants on, doesn't it?"

"It means you're going to have to act like a professional, yes." Gladdy does not appreciate my joke. She appreciates very few of my jokes. Maybe I'm not as funny as I think I am? "You'll be representing Jinteki and interacting with police."

"And how do we keep EMID happy?" Dani asks.

"They want information and, in a perfect world, this mutant served up on a platter."

"I bet," I mutter. "So they can use them as a pet assassin. And we run off to do their bidding."

"Fucking hell, Dylan, this isn't a shitty movie," Gladdy says to me. "I'm not the grumpy old white dude and you're not the maverick asshole. Okay, so maybe you are the loose cannon, but we're both trying to keep everyone safe."

She looks a lot less scary than usual in her bright yellow sweatshirt, enough that I pull her in for an impulsive hug. It's probably a miscalculation, but I'm surprised when her arms go around me too.

"Omigod, isn't it the cutest thing?" Maddy leaps into us, which is apparently the cue for a whole group hug. My friends are the cheesiest assholes, but if you're about to go and crash a crime scene to investigate a creepy mutant murder, there are worse send offs.

Alyse transforms into something fire-resistant to wake Katie up, but once the grumpy little dragon hears we're off to a crime scene, she perks up and doesn't roast anyone. Gladdy stays behind with Maddy as bodyguard, and the rest of us head off, with one notable exception. Lou isn't in his quarters, and when Emma pings his phone, he's at a suburban house on the other side of town.

"Aka bone city," Katie says, which causes at least two of us to spit coffee over Roxy, for which we have to profusely apologise.

"Hopefully he hasn't set the poor girl on fire." Alyse mops at the back of the passenger seat. "That'll be a hard thing to explain away."

I feel weird turning up at some random's house to take Lou, so instead I send him a sternly worded text and leave him behind.

The flight up is uneventful, but at least in a private jet we can nap on the plane. We land in Auckland to find it's overcast and rainy. Alyse proclaims this the city's natural state, as we stand in the wet waiting for our expensive corporate Uber to arrive. It's annoying not having Roxy. Oni is slung in a case over my shoulder. I don't know how likely it is we'll be able to walk into a crime scene with him.

We're not in superhero costumes, but in our creepy corporate uniform of dark pants and Jinteki-branded jackets. It makes me feel like we're going door to door selling religion. I'd rather be wearing Gladdy's crappy yellow sweatshirt.

Slightly less professionally, Dani is wearing dangly earrings that say UGH. It's such a mood that I'm jealous of them, and I wish I hadn't let my piercings grow over.

The driver finally turns up, somewhat surprised to see a bunch of teenagers, including one with a sword, but he says nothing. Before long, we're stuck in traffic with every other asshole in the city.

It takes us longer than Google promises to reach our destination, and we find it crawling with people in uniform. It's a round building shaped like a tin, with hardly any windows aside from a glassed-in reception area. Apparently it's full of studio space for recording artists.

We get out of the car. The driver leans his seat back and pulls out his Kindle. He's obviously used to this. On the other hand, I am not remotely used to turning up at a crime scene. I am fidgety and awkward. Not even Dani can soothe me.

"What do we say?" I can already feel my throat closing up.

A tall redhead in uniform has noticed our arrival and is on a tangent toward us.

"Help. Dani." I'm no good with people, especially strangers and authority figures. I consider climbing back inside the car like a child, but thankfully I now associate with competent people.

Dani takes a confident stride forward and extends her hand. "Danielle Kim. I'm with Jinteki." She holds out her phone, showing the security information that Gladdy provided.

"Excuse me?" The cop frowns. "I'm not sure I—"

"Jinteki Research Laboratories. We've been asked to consult on this case."

"I've never heard of you." The voice shifts a couple of degrees more stern. "I'll have to ask you to leave."

Dani exhales a slight trace of contempt. "I'm sorry. We don't have time to perform some jurisdictional dance. Can you please find someone in charge?"

Dani might be unfeasibly attractive by human—or extrahuman—standards, but the cop is unmoved. What a pro.

"Are you fans of Ms. Pearson? I understand a lot of people want to pass on their condolences or understand what's happened here but—"

Dani walks right around the cop, and the rest of us follow.

The woman stalks after us and grabs Dani's arm. "If you insist on trespassing, we'll have you removed."

For a second I think Dani's going to hurl her away telekinetically, which even I know would be a Bad Move, but she leans into ice queen mode instead. "I've asked to speak with someone in charge. We're the consultants from Jinteki. I'll keep saying it until we get access."

The woman makes a disgruntled sound, but leads us to an exhausted looking old dude. He actually brightens from his extra-rumpled demeanour when Dani waves her phone at him.

"Finally," he grunts. "McLachlan, why didn't you bring them straight to me?"

"Nobody informed me, sir," she says, back straight despite the shit being dumped on her head.

He shakes his head slightly and looks at Dani. "Someone very high up has given you the keys to the kingdom. You've got access to the crime scene, but please don't bloody well touch anything. McLachlan, don't let them fuck anything up."

The redheaded cop says nothing aloud, but her expression says she's had enough bullshit. Unluckily for her, we're just getting started.

CHAPTER SIX

McLachlan strides off toward the building without a backward glance. Inside, there's an outer and inner ring of studio rooms with a corridor between. We wander through while Emma glances up at the ceilings.

"Are there any other cameras?"

"At the entrance and the main corridors. We've had techs going over them without any luck."

"We'll need a copy," Dani says. We still don't have any idea how this mutant works, so who knows what we might find. Any clue would be useful.

"Hey, everyone." I extend my senses outward. I've gotten better at tuning out the ramblings of random objects but they're always eager to talk with the tiniest prompting. "Did anyone see anything interesting last night?"

I should have been a *lot* less open-ended with this question, because I'm overwhelmed by a lot of lukewarm tea. There was drug use, some sexual encounters, a lot of tedious arguments about music and...

There. Someone quiet and sobbing in the distance.

"Poor wee thing," a catering cart tells me. "Saw the whole thing. All the blood."

"Did *you* see anything though? Nobody getting in or out?"

"Did you not hear? It was a demon who materialised out of thin air!" It carries on ranting about monsters and hell and redemption, but we're already leaving.

It's a short walk to the room where the murder took place. Three guys stand around, all in different uniforms. One has a fancy camera around his neck. They start muttering when they see us. Nobody introduces anyone. We're either not important enough or too important.

McLachlan stands in the doorway and watches with fascination.

The body is still there, and we seem to be the hold-up for it being processed. Dani and I crouch beside her, trying to give some impression we know what we're doing. The bottom half of the victim's face is a mess, her jaw almost severed.

I poke my fingers at the back of my own neck awkwardly. "Either her fingers are really sharp, or the nature of the movement means they can stab right through without any weapon." I make a squelching noise and accidentally catch a cop's eye, who seems unimpressed with my deductive reasoning.

Emma, can you pick anything up at all? I ask.

No, but I got no real sense of those new Canadian mutants either. It's only you lot I have the connection to.

"Unhelpful," Dani murmurs with a faint smile.

"What did you see?" I ask the witness, who is a bulbous silver microphone. She's spattered with blood that's congealed in drips on her shining surface.

"Horrible. Terrible. Ghastly." Before she can work her way through the thesaurus, I brush my fingers gently up and down the stand.

"I know, sweetheart. You're very brave."

"That thing was unnatural. A monster. It shouldn't be allowed."

We're veering a little close to ew, *mutants* for my liking, but I soldier on. "Did you see what happened?"

"Blood and death. It got *on* me and now I shall be forever unclean." The microphone tails off into sobs. "It came back, you know. Later on, after the commotion."

"They did?" The others are standing around the body looking almost official, and here I am draped over the microphone like a drunk singer at the end of a long show. "What did they do?"

"It left a message. I didn't read it, but it's probably in *blood*." She lets out a tragic wail.

I glance around the room, but can't see anything. "Whereabouts?"

It takes a few moments for the tears to subside. "On the wall, over behind the piano."

The piano is giant and shiny, like it should be at the bottom of a spiral staircase. I duck behind it and see something scratched on the wall: *Romans 1:26*. I snap a photo of it. "Code." I cross back to the others. "Something to do with history maybe?"

"It's a Bible verse," Alyse says with a slight gurgle of laughter.

"Ugh." Emma taps on her phone and wrinkles her nose. "It's one about lesbians being unnatural. God, I hate it here."

"Got any great insights, girlies?" It's the cop whose eye I caught. "Are you going to tell us what the murder weapon was?"

"You saw the video?" I ask.

"I saw some messed up garbage they're passing off as evidence. I think it was one of those bastards that did it and doctored it up to look like weird ghost shit. What do they call it? Deep fakes? All to try and distract us from linking this one to the other one."

"Other one?" Dani asks casually.

"Oh, don't tell me you girls don't know?" The cop's enjoying this. "You're the great genius specialists and you don't even know there were two murders?"

Seems weird EMID didn't tell us, unless it's new news.

Emma's already tapping away. "Yes. It took place fifteen minutes later at a location ninety minutes from here. So they can't have been done by the same person."

Unless their mutant powers mean they can travel faster, she says in the privacy of my head, where the cops can't overhear.

Some kind of teleportation?

Too many unknowns.

Emma swipes through crime scene photos. There's even more blood—a great gory stain spilling across an oatmeal coloured carpet. This victim has a ragged hole torn in her chest. It's hard to look at, but the message left behind is far more obvious. The word SIN has been splashed on the wall in big bloody letters.

I have no idea how Emma got hold of the photos, and I don't want to ask, because I'm sure the answer is illegal.

"So, who's the second victim?" Dani asks.

None of the three men will answer.

"Ariana Howard," McLachlan says, still lurking in the doorway.

"Wait, what?" Alyse shoots a glance at me. "Ariana Howard and Nika Pearson played characters who were girlfriends on *Shortland Street*."

"I don't know what that is," I say.

"It's a TV show," she explains patiently. "It's not on Netflix or Animelab so you won't have heard of it."

"And these two actors played girlfriends?"

"That's literally what I just said, if you would listen."

Dani sounds furious. "And now we have a Bible verse about lesbians, and this other message about sin. But they were only gay on TV, right?"

"Everything's always gay on TV these days," our least favourite cop says. "Like every damn show you watch pushes it down your throat. Even that one on *Billions* that can't even decide if she's a man or a woman or—"

"Non-binary." I'm so angry that Oni is vibrating against my back. "And you call them they."

The guy gives a short laugh. "Of course, love, and you look just like one. No offence, but it's true. Doesn't she, Mike? Sorry, you probably don't like being called she, do you? Got one of those other stupid words to use. What is it? Zeem? Hoom?"

This is a situation I don't know how to deal with. I can't throw my sword at some prick for being a bigot. Adulting doesn't work that way. Yet I don't think I could sit him down and change his mind, even if he wanted to have a conversation in the first place.

He gets the force of many glares, and puts his hands up in mock surrender.

"I've figured out who this lot are," he says, with a roar of laughter. "It's the PC police. They're here to

ʜɪᴛʙʏ

take us away for thought crimes. Look at them. You all like to fuck other girls, do you? Or whatever this one is." He points at me and laughs.

"I think you need to shut your mouth." Katie's breath is hot. "You don't need to know who we want to fuck. Just like none of us care who you want to shove your tiny, stinking—" A haze spreads in the air. Something glows at the back of her throat.

"Katie," I put a hand on her shoulder. "It's not worth it. We're done here."

"I can do it," the camera says. "It won't be flash, but I can give him a decent whack in the eye."

Old Dylan would for sure. Break his nose with a chunk of plastic and pretend I had nothing to do with it. Now there are too many strings on me, tugging in different directions. Dancing one step ahead of everyone who wants to drag us down. Trying to be a fucking hero. We graduated from high school recently, or the others did. I just dropped out. It's been a lot to keep things afloat. I missed the bit in the X-Men comics where everything seems like *work*. There's so much responsibility, and everything's a hell of a lot more complex. You can't just punch everything until it's fixed. I've killed a man in cold blood and now everything seems harder. Bancroft doesn't haunt me in the traditional way. I don't see his face when I close my eyes. That honour is reserved for Bianca. I do worry about becoming *like* Bancroft though, always counting costs and compromising, making deals with various devils. It's giving up, not growing up, and I'm honestly not ready for either.

"Yes," Dani says, still simmering. "We're done."

We're not actually crime scene investigators. None of us have any idea what to do next. We're here for mutant spookiness, and if there are no spooky mutants lurking around, we're out of options. The group of us pushes past the cops without anyone getting their nose broken.

We make our way out of the building without speaking. The rain has disappeared, the clouds are gone, and the sun is shining down. It's like we walked out into a parallel universe, the weather turned so quickly.

McLachlan shoots us nervous glances. "I'm sorry about that. Detective Pocock is... well, he's one of those—"

"He's a prick and a relic," Dani snaps. "And people keep letting him get away with it. We're all waiting for the bigots to die out and pretending they're not infecting the next generation."

"He's good at his job." McLachlan acts like that excuses the other shit.

"And I suppose he treats you well?" Dani asks. "As a subordinate and a woman."

The cop looks at her sharply and then looks away. "I made a complaint. Nothing came of it. There's no point. Not for just words."

Dani makes the same contemptuous noise from before, but at twice the volume. We reach the car, and McLachlan leaves us without any farewell. Her responsibility has been discharged.

"He was an asshole," I say.

"I know." Dani's metal fist is clenched so tight I'm scared it'll break. "I'm so fucking *tired* of assholes, and of having to prove myself all the time. At best I'm a joke. At worst…well, you end up like Nika."

I put an arm around Dani. Her body is rigid, but I hold her anyway, in the hope she can bleed some of that tension off into me.

"You don't *really* think they were killed for being pretend lesbian, do you?" Alyse asks. "I'm pretty sure Nika Pearson has a boyfriend irl and—"

"What other explanation is there?" Dani steps out of the curve of my arm and towards Alyse. "You saw what the Bible verse said. You think they were killed because someone hated the show they were in? There's a long history of people being attacked for being queer or trans or—"

"I thought the world was changing." Emma's voice is soft but it cuts across Dani even so.

"Not fast enough, and not while people like that asshole cop are around." Dani turns to me, and I think I see tears glistening in her eyes. "I hate this. They don't deserve to make me feel this way."

I wish there was something I could do, but I'm helpless. In the comic world that still plays in my head, we'd rush back inside the building. Dani would throw the cop into the wall with her powers and hold him there until he apologised. Katie might roast someone. I'd accidentally break someone's face.

Instead, I stand and watch Dani clench her jaw.

"There's nothing here," she says. "We need a lead on this mutant, Emma."

Emma hooks her hair behind her ear. "Our best lead on anything is still the crystals. The data's being analysed. If we can find any kind of signal—"

"Who would do it?" Alyse's voice cracks. "Kill people like that, for no real reason at all."

"Maybe they're working for someone," Dani says. "Something like a new Yaxley, running a mutant team of their own. Except why would you use them to kill *actresses*? I can't find any logic that applies. It's more likely someone doing it out of hate, and that is—"

"It's terrifying." Alyse shudders. She's not wrong.

CHAPTER SEVEN

Once we're in the car and moving again, Dani reports to Gladdy. She talks in a flat voice about the double murder, and the depressing fact that we have no leads at all. Gladdy is clearly disappointed.

"What did EMID expect?" Dani's still wound super tight. "It's a locked room mystery with a mutant murderer."

"They hoped I could find something." Emma's switching between a phone and a tablet. "They're convinced I've got some psychic connection to all mutants, not just our cluster, and that they can use me as some kind of location and detection system." She sees we're all staring at her. "What? I got hold of some of their emails. There's a bunch of cryptic code word shit in there I can't figure out, but they definitely want to use me as—"

"You're their Cerebro." I nudge Alyse. "It's the mutant detection machine in the comics. Powered by a psychic so the X-Men can locate mutants all over the world and help them."

"Except I don't think EMID has any benign intentions," Emma says, and that's something we all agree on.

Dani stares out the window. She seems unreachable, locked away inside her own head. It's super lame and cliche, but I used to think I was alone with my special, self-loathing pain. I could sit there outwardly stoic, while inside I'd be chasing myself down a rabbit hole of spiralling misery. Everything back at the crime scene, from the dead woman to the sneering cops, sent Dani down a hole of her own. She won't find an answer to the world's bullshit at the bottom of it. She'll only feel worse about herself.

I have to find a way to break her out.

I'm curled up with my feet on the seat, tapping away on my phone. Once I find something promising, I lean forward and show it to the driver. "I want to go here."

"Dylan, what are you up to?" Alyse asks.

"I'm half-leader of this group, aren't I? So in honour of that, you're going to go along with my dumb shit."

The driver is obviously paid enough not to ask any questions, so he veers from our planned route and into the city. Traffic is shit again, but we finally stop at the harbour. I jog over to the ticket booth. Most of the trips are sold out, except for super expensive tickets that come with a tour guide and champagne. I tell the woman we don't need the extras.

Back at the car, I brandish the tickets and make everyone get out.

"Are we doing something exciting?" Katie looks out at the water.

"We're trusting Dylan." Alyse grins at me over Katie's head. I think she's figured it out.

Dani's still distracted and quiet. "We should get back to Fetch."

"It's a little detour, that's all." I take her hand and drag her toward the dock we're supposed to leave from. "Trust me."

Before long, we're all on a fancy boat that noses its way through a whole bunch of other fancy boats and onto the open water.

Our expensive tickets give us a deck all of our own, and everyone takes advantage of it by being moody and quiet. Alyse and Emma sit together and rest their heads against each other. Katie is at the bow, sending up little burps of flame into the air. Dani stands at the railing and stares at the ocean as if it holds something other than water. I can't break into the tangle of her thoughts. The sun is high and makes the water sparkle so bright I need to shade my eyes.

The boat reaches a smaller dock and we disembark. Without explaining anything, I head for a trail I found on my phone. We walk for nearly an hour through bush. It's beautiful, in amongst all that dappled green, with the lazy buzz of insects and the slight smell of honey from the trees. Alyse and Emma seem quite happy to wander. I shoot glances back at Dani. She has her head down, walking at the back of the group.

"What are we doing here?" Katie skips up alongside me.

"*Trust Dylan* is so hard, is it?"

"Not when it comes to punching shit, but what the hell is this for?"

I give a jerk of my head towards Dani.

"*Oh.*"

"Yes, very good. Oh."

"Sometimes you're a lot like Pear." She grins at me.

"Gross." I poke her in the side. Even though I'm flattered, there are some things you can't admit. Maybe when I'm twenty and old.

The bush finally clears and we come out on top of a ridge. I stop dead. The land slopes steeply down to a bay that's an unreal blue, like something out of a video game.

I was always bad at creative writing in school. I have no flowery words. All I can say is that it nearly hurts to look at. When Dani takes my hand and kisses it, I feel like the bowl of the sky and the dazzling weight of the landscape are conspiring together to crush me with their beauty. Even that doesn't hold a candle to her.

I lean in and put my mouth to her ear. "You will remember, for we in our youth did these things. Yes, many and beautiful things."

She turns to me, and it's like the view—this unreal beauty of *how can something this perfect exist in the same world as everything else*. Her arms go around my neck and her mouth is on mine. I'm aware of the warmth of the sun on my back, but the world recedes like it's all background blur and we're the only two things in perfect, vibrant focus.

"Not one girl I think, who looks on the light of the sun, will ever have wisdom like this." Her lips move against mine as she speaks. "And her light stretches over salt sea equally and flowerdeep fields." Her smile breaks my heart and forges it back together, lighter and airier and with more space in every bloody chamber of it for her.

"Beautiful."

"You love me," she whispers.

"I really do. I know the world is shit and people are assholes, but there's also this." I gesture with one arm.

She takes my face in her hands and kisses me again, so impossibly soft and delicious that my swoon must be measurable from orbit.

"There's also you," she says. "The person I love."

It suddenly gets a lot warmer as a tongue of flame goes scorching over our heads.

"Okay, enough smooching." Katie has her hands on her hips. "If you made a fucking pie chart of *time Dylan spends as a mutant*, by far the biggest piece would be making out with Dani."

"It's called priorities," I tell her. "But I'm sorry for making you suffer through a boat ride, a walk, and a beautiful view."

It's meant to be sarcastic, but she's nodding like it's not. "Where's something for the rest of us?"

"I'll buy you an ice-cream at the dock," I tell her.

"It better be a big one."

Alyse makes the mistake of sending a shot of the landscape to Gladdy, as if we exist in some reality where Fetch would be happy for the Field Team to be roaming about looking at pretty things. Three seconds later, all of our phones buzz.

Fetch: Okay, where the actual fuck are you?

Chatterbox: omg chill

Chatterbox: we took a detour

Fetch: You're supposed to be here

Marvellous: We will be

Marvellous: We don't exist at your beck and call, Fetch

Fetch: I don't have time to debate this

Fetch: You need to get back here asap

Glowstick: wow and yeah thanks for leaving me behind u guys

Dragon: hahaha well we didn't want to raid bone town lmao

Glowstick: fuck off kacchan

Glowstick: personal business is personal business!!!

Fetch: JUST GET BACK HERE

Moodring: ok whats ur damage now, fetchy

Chatterbox: yeah whats the hubbub bub

Fetch: we've got visitors

Marvellous: Who?

Fetch: Take a guess

Chatterbox: ok so we dont have time to see a view

Chatterbox: but u have time for guessing games

Fetch: EMID

Fetch: Do I need to spell it out?

Marvellous: Are you serious?

Fetch: Entirely

Marvellous: What the hell are they doing there?

Fetch: I'm stalling

Fetch: Please stop sightseeing and get your asses on the plane

Moodring: pics plz

Chatterbox: yeah pics or it didnt happen haha

Fetch: I fucking swear, you all drive me mad

> Sourpatch: omg so many notifications you guys!!
>
> Sourpatch: it really is them tho
>
> Sourpatch: the muricans
>
> Sourpatch: they're kinda cute idk
>
> Sourpatch: lemme sneak pics lol

We then get a series of pictures taken on a weird angle. They show a brunette who's pretty in an interchangeable way. Her hair is short and neat. She's wearing all black with a black coat that looks like it's billowing around her.

"Hello, Maleficent," Alyse smirks.

Next to her is a tall white guy with broad shoulders and shaved head. He's not super muscly, but he definitely looks tough. He's pretty in the same sort of TV-casting way as the woman. The most curious feature is a metal collar, like someone's wrapped a chunky black octagon around his throat.

"Fuck is that?" I ask, but I have a sinking feeling.

"Hard to say." Emma zooms in until the photo is a blur. "If I had to guess, I'd say it was Leash 2.0." When we were first scooped up by Yaxley, we all got an implant put in our brains that was supposed to control us in dire circumstances. Thanks to whatever weird connection we have with Emma, we didn't die when Bancroft threw the kill switch. I wonder if they tried to cater for that design flaw with the new version.

"On a leash like a hound." Dani throws me a *dun dun dun* look.

"It's an X-Men thing, isn't it?" Alyse says. "I recognise the nerdy looks on your faces."

I can't help but start babbling. "There's a dark potential future—which is hilariously only 2013 in the original comics—where mutants are hunted almost to extinction. Some are brainwashed to track down other mutants for the bad guys. They're called hounds."

"Why are all the comics about mutants so scary?" Alyse asks.

"Because they know too well what people are like." Emma looks grim as we leave the beautiful view and head back to the docks. I wish I knew what she was thinking, but she's not sharing.

"Genosha," Dani says.

Back at Jinteki HQ, we find Lou and Maddy lounging in the empty reception area. We built it on the ground floor so we look halfass like a real place of business. They spring off the wall like they've been caught.

"About time, slowpokes." Maddy links arms with Dani and I.

"Gladdy's freaking out," Lou tells me. "I didn't think she was scared of anything."

"She'll be fine." I think her fears are the same as mine—that our people will be hurt or worse. We're playing Aladdin's game, keeping one jump ahead of everyone chasing us. It's not much if you slip.

I don't want to meet EMID in our dumbass preppy clothes, so we make a quick uniform change. It doesn't hurt to be prepared and bulletproof.

When the elevator dings open at the top floor, Gladdy and the Americans are waiting.

"The Cute Mutants," the woman says, in this drawling voice that sounds made for saying *y'all*. "I've heard a lot about y'all." Well, shit, there it goes. "My name is Tanner, and this is my associate, Jackson. He's one of you—an extrahuman—with abilities of strength and short-range flight."

Pssh, I say to Emma. *How boring. It's like your most basic bitch ability.*

The tall dude nods. None of us nod back, which is probably rude, but we're all in watchful and wary mode.

"I'm sure y'all want to know why we're here, so let's get that out of the way. It seems New Zealand is becoming a hotspot of mutant activity. First there was your original cluster, then the Jinteki experiments, and now it seems we have multiple unrelated mutants appearing." Okay, when she says it like that, it does sound hella dodgy. "And the latest twist is these suspicious murders."

The unspoken statement is that they're here to take over. It feels inevitable. People don't like teenagers, especially if they're in charge.

"We have things under control," Gladdy says. "As I reiterated multiple times."

"Sure, y'all might see it that way." Tanner's got this easy, comfortable manner like we're all having a lovely chat. All we're missing is some iced tea. "Thing is, our bosses talked to your bosses, and the agreement is EMID should provide oversight, given y'all's lack of experience."

"Oversight," Dani says.

"All it means is we're here to help. Guidance and training. Friendly advice." Tanner smiles wide, showing off all her white teeth like she's the big bad wolf. "Y'all will still run the show, but missions will be subject to my approval. I'll also be receiving all your intel."

"We appreciate this," Gladdy says in tones so glacial you'd think our planet wasn't heating like mad. "And while I'm not entirely sure that——"

"First agenda item." Tanner cuts Fetch off like she didn't even speak. "We need to discuss the Canadian citizens you recently acquired. They fall under EMID jurisdiction, but Ms. Quick here has been less than forthcoming about…well, everything really."

Don't trust them, Emma says in my head, and while I don't need any encouragement, I wonder why she says it. Stalling too long is going to look suspicious and—

"They're dead." I know Dani hates it when I blurt shit out, but nobody else is saying anything.

"Really." Tanner looks me up and down. She shifts position slightly, leaning in towards me. Jackson unclasps his hands from behind his back and lets them rest at his sides. The dude has big hands.

"I don't like being this far away," Oni whispers from the elevator.

"It was a shitshow," I say, trying to appear even more inept than I am. "They were holed up in this abandoned building that was full of cats. We walk in the door and this guy comes at us out of the dark with this fucking red hole in his stomach." I pause, wondering if it's dramatic enough. "We've had bad experiences with other mutants in the Bancroft mess. Some of us overreacted."

"Yes, the Bancroft incident was unfortunate," Tanner says. It's just fucking double-speak. We know that someone in EMID approved us being taken out. How high is this woman on the food chain? Is the 'unfortunate' part that we survived? "We'll take the bodies off your hands though. They're still useful."

"We don't have the bodies," I sneer. "We're not going to leave evidence like that lying around. Besides, they weren't in great condition."

"What happened to them?"

"Cremated." Dragon lets a delicate curl of flame trickle from her lips. "I'm what you might call the attack dog."

Oh my god, the dramatic little brat. Emma sounds delighted. *I don't think we can avoid accepting their help here, unless we want to get in a fight.*

Probably not the time, no.

Is there a 'yet' at the end of that sentence?

Let's wait and see.

Tanner glares at the stocky figure of Katie and then transfers the weight of her attention to Gladdy, almost as physical as a slap. "So two innocent people are dead, the mutants you claim to care about, and y'all are acting like you don't need our help."

"It was self-defense," I say defiantly. The elevator doors slide open. Oni glides out to hover at my shoulder. "You sent us into a situation with shitty intel and it went sideways. And then today we got sent after another psychotic mutant, this time with *zero* information."

"We all wish we had better intelligence." Tanner's back to staring at me. "We're doing what we can, but the mutant situation is evolving, if you'll pardon the pun."

Nobody laughs, although Jackson cracks his knuckles like punctuation.

"We do come with *some* intelligence," Tanner says. "And news of another big bad in town. A man named

Matthias Fisher, responsible for over two hundred and forty deaths on American soil. Now he's here, presumably sniffing after your little beacon." She snaps one hand out to point at Emma, who lowers her head. "Yes, we heard about that. Every mutant in our facilities was talking about you for a couple of weeks."

"I didn't know," Emma says quietly.

"Regardless, we didn't expect Fisher to jump in this direction, but it's an opportunity we can't pass up."

"What's his deal?" I ask. "Why is he so dangerous and why haven't you stopped him already?"

"We tried." Tanner looks uncomfortable for the first time. "Believe me. We had him in custody but he escaped. The facility he was in isn't there anymore. Hell, we don't even know what power he has, because everyone who's seen him use it is dead. He's possibly the most dangerous person alive, human or extrahuman."

"How many mutants have you sent after him?" Dani asks.

"Our government's policy on extrahumans is to involve them as little as possible. We gave you a chance, but send a mutie to catch a mutie tends to fail dramatically in my experience. So now we're here. Oversight." She has the nerve to fucking grimace at us, as if we're all in the same boat.

I want to tell her to stop saying *mutie*. Even more, I want her to know that if we *were* in the same boat, I'd cut her damn hands off and throw her overboard.

"So how do we find this most dangerous mutant alive?" I pluck Oni from the air before he gets carried away, feeling him tremble lightly.

"With Leash," Tanner pulls out her phone. "There's something wrong in his brain which cuts off the pain trigger, but it works as a lojack. He's currently a hair over two klicks away."

"You leave a mass murderer to wander the streets while you come here and trade barbs with us." Gladdy stares at Tanner, eyes narrowed. Reading her fears. "He's never killed any civilians, has he? All the deaths have happened while trying to capture him, which increases your government's desire to bring him down. And every time you've tried there have been more deaths which… Jesus, Tanner."

"It's become something of a point of pride among our organisation about bringing him in alive." Tanner gives us all her best death stare. "It's very important to understand what makes a man like this tick."

I bet it is, Emma says. *We can't let them get their hands on him. If they find a way to control or replicate him?*

So we have to find him, not die, and also somehow keep him out of the hands of the Americans? Sounds like a dangerous game.

It is. You know I'm right though.

As usual.

"Okay, Tanner." I look her in the eye. She's taller than me and I have to tilt my head slightly. "Let's try this the soft way first. Rather than starting a clusterfuck in the city, we'll try to talk."

"I don't think you know what you're dealing with," Tanner says.

"He wants to talk to me." Emma's got calm-and-determined face on. "Let's see if we can lure him in."

Are you sure about this? I ask her.

Not even close. But it's better than risking everyone else's lives, isn't it?

Tanner's grimace shifts into something more predatory. Her eyes seem to light up when she looks at Emma. "Now *that* is an interesting option. If he can come with you willingly and walk into a trap…"

I'm worried. If they want Matthias Fisher for what he can do, they want Emma even worse. We're going to have to be really fucking careful not to slip.

CHAPTER EIGHT

In the end, only Emma and I approach the deadly mutant. Tanner and Jackson take some super fucking suspicious black SUV that screams *shadowy government assholes*—not literally, but Roxy does call them that in a super bitchy voice. We park around the corner from the cafe. Dani is pacing and clenching her fists. Alyse is almost dissolved with worry, turning into a cloud of Alyse-particles that smell of cherry lipgloss. Tanner is entirely made of threats and dire promises. I tell everyone to fuck off and that we'll be fine.

It doesn't stop Dani. "I don't even bother saying the word reckless any more." Her forehead is pressed to mine and her hands are on my shoulders. "Please be careful and tell Oni that if he doesn't protect you I'll—"

"Tell your lady-love I would give my life for you."

"She knows," I tell him. "She's only being dramatic."

"I'm not being dramatic *enough*." Her lips find mine, but briefly, because she's humming with too much energy. "Dilly, you are going to talk to someone who's very dangerous."

"As long as we can keep things chill, it'll be fine."

"Be alert, be aware, be paranoid. Call for me if you need anything."

"Yes. Professional Dylan reporting for duty."

Emma and I are dressed in casual clothes. For me, that means a giant Todoroki jacket, jeans and skate shoes. If I look like I rolled out of bed and grabbed the first thing I found, that would be accurate. Emma is in extremely tight pants and a baggy man's shirt which is sending Alyse into an adorable half-lust, half-protecc transformation.

"Everyone needs to keep their distance." I say this to Dani, Alyse, and Tanner equally. "If he thinks for a second that he's at risk, that's when we'll be in danger." For all the ongoing discussion about how I am the Reckless Child, I'm not the only one who's been known to go ham if their best bb is in trouble. "Let's go before he finishes his flat white."

Emma nods. There's no point delaying it. We leave Roxy and walk around the corner. The day is warm but with enough breeze to take the edge off. Fisher's seated at a cafe table, looking content. He has a muffin and a tall glass of something with ice in it. There's even an old-fashioned physical newspaper spread open on the table.

We approach without him noticing. I point out a chair for Emma and take one for myself. We arrange them on the opposite side of the table. I sit backwards on mine because it looks badass, but instantly regret it because it's uncomfortable. The sun is hot and I'm already sweating.

Fisher glances up, and places his cup very carefully on the table. His forehead wrinkles.

"Mr. Fisher," I say. "I believe you were looking for my friend here."

He's in an open-necked polo shirt and wearing sunglasses. When he takes the glasses off, I'm worried he'll unleash concussive force beams like Cyclops. Instead, pale blue eyes regard us calmly. He holds out his hand to shake ours, and the angle of the sun turns his fingers into long tendrils. His eyes find Emma. "I felt you from a long distance." For some reason it's creepy when he says it. "Yet when I arrived, your candle was snuffed out."

"I'm here now." I can hear the shiver in Emma's voice. *This guy's freaking me out, Dilly.*

No shit. Be ready.

"You're really her daughter." He leans across the table and we both shift backwards. "It's uncanny."

This is not what I expected. I narrow my eyes. "What are you talking about? Whose daughter?"

"Teen Spirit. I dug and dug and I found her. Behind the veil. There are shadows cast by other worlds, and among the dance of possibilities, the truth is revealed. My brain wouldn't accept it at first. Bounced off like a rubber ball. The ghost in the world."

Emma, what the fuck is he talking about?

I have no idea.

Sweat prickles on my neck. "You're not making any sense. Start from the beginning."

"There is no beginning. Not anymore. Once there was a before, but now there's only an after. It's a splinter driven into everyone's brain, driving us all mad. They want to kill me because I know too much."

I think this guy is crazy, Ems.

"You said something about Teen Spirit?" I try one last time. "What's that?"

"It can't happen again. You sit with her daughter and have no idea what she is. The world can't sustain another fracture. She cannot be allowed to exist. Her mother was a monster, and this girl contains the seed of the same. I'm so sorry, because I believe she's genuinely innocent but—"

His shadow, Emma screams, so loud it stabs into my brain.

I look at the ground. The vague outline of a person twists into thick lines that spill across the concrete.

"Time to fucking move." I chose the chairs we're sitting in because they greeted me when we arrived. At my command, they screech down the footpath away from Fisher. Mine smacks into a woman with a stroller, but Emma's continues until it runs out of steam and sits there panting. I make apologies, but the woman screams and drags her crying baby into the doorway of the closest shop.

Fisher is on his feet, him and his goddamn shadow. They stalk down the street towards me. He's pale and slender, but his shadow is a rolling grey mess of tentacles that billow around him.

Oni howls out of the sky, a silver missile arrowing towards Fisher's head. He screams something in Japanese, but one dark flourish of the shadow snatches at him.

"Does this belong to you?" Fisher smiles.

"It has me held fast." Oni sounds shocked.

I can't believe it either. This isn't supposed to happen.

"Dylan, I cannot escape the clutches of this demon. He is an entity rooted in both spirit and physical realms."

"This isn't helping, Oni," I snap. "We need another plan." I tap the side of my head. "Guess what? Massive fucking surprise, things have turned to shit. Fisher wants to kill Emma and now he's attacked us with his—"

I don't even finish the sentence, because a massive shape thunders around the corner. The overall impression is of stone and sinew and thorns, a patchwork naturalist Hulk. Alyse is shrouded in the centre.

She heads straight for Fisher.

Before she can reach him, three figures stagger out of the cafe. Each has a loop of shadow around their neck like a noose. Their faces are taut and terrified.

Alyse comes to a halt, scanning for Emma, who's safely down the street for now.

"Give me the girl," Fisher says calmly, as if it's an entirely reasonable demand. "I must have her. Otherwise these people will die."

"You don't get the girl." Alyse reaches with her claws, but they sink into the tentacles that surround him like boiling fog. She's snagged, and can't pull herself free. The more she struggles, the deeper she's dragged in.

"Shift forms," Dani snaps over the comm, but Alyse is either too upset or unable to change.

Fisher drags his captives closer. They gasp for air. When they clutch at the tendrils that have them bound, their fingers come away sticky with blood. I have no idea what you're supposed to do in a hostage crisis.

"Emma's not going anywhere," I say. "Let's negotiate."

"There's no alternative. Once I saw her in my mind, I knew she had to die before the world breaks again."

I try to match his calmness. "Nobody's breaking the world. And you're not getting Emma."

"Then you're responsible for the deaths of these three people." Fisher sounds resigned. "And then I will execute more and more innocents until you give in. It's simple arithmetic, and somewhat of a rather cruel game. How many deaths do you think you can tolerate before you give in and hand over the girl?"

Enough. Emma starts walking back down the street towards us. *I won't let people die for me.*

Giving you to him is not an option. "We need a better plan," I say over the comm.

"It's lucky you've got me." Dani strides around the corner. She's in pain. I can see it in the way she carries herself. Except I can't see what she's moving. What the hell is she up to?

Tentacles of shadow fly towards both Emma and me.

"Bad news. I can't affect his shadow with my lowers," Dani says through gritted teeth, and isn't that just fucking great.

"Can you please take Emma to safety?" I ask the chair that carried me. It gives a little wriggle and obediently rams itself into Emma. She collapses down, and the chair speeds away in a wide arc, dodging the tentacle entirely.

Unfortunately, that leaves a long and crooked shadow coming for me. It zigzags across the ground, leaping up like an optical illusion to wrap a cold tendril around my neck. The pain is so intense I seize up both physically and mentally. My lungs won't take in air. Even though half my brain is telling me I shouldn't, the other half is screaming to rip this thing off my neck. The pain spreads to my hand, overwhelming in its intensity. Why do I keep ending up in situations where people hurt me?

The pain keeps getting worse. It's like there's no upper limit and that's terrifying. I can't even speak or think to call an object to my side. At some point, my body won't be able to take it anymore. Why can't I simply black out and stop feeling this agony?

I remember standing around Wraith's body in the Jinteki facility. I'll be the next one they surround. Dani will blame herself, and so will Emma and Alyse. They'll all be wrong. It's not even my fault, although I can take some of the blame. It's mostly this shadowy asshole, and Tanner for sending us in. All I need is the others to live through this so they can—

"Now," Dani shouts.

The world is obliterated with light. I can't see a thing. The sun just rose in front of my face. I close my eyes involuntarily and feel a slight lessening of the pain at my neck.

"Oh, there you are." Oni's voice is soft and lonely in my head. "And there he is. No shadow in all this light. Perhaps I should— no, wait. It seems your friend has it."

There's a sound of something heavy impacting something soft, and then a visceral squelching. A high-pitched sound of shock cuts off almost instantly.

It takes a few minutes for my eyes to readjust. The first thing I see is the light-speckled form of Alyse, cradling what used to be Matthias Fisher in massive claws. She's gnarled and hooded, made of bloody shadows. He's clearly dead, his body pierced and bleeding. His head hangs limp and one of his arms is shredded.

I take a single trembling breath and something barrels into me—a figure that's warm and soft aside from a metal arm. Dani kisses me hard and then tilts my head up to check the wound at my neck.

"You're hurt," she says with the shadow of a sob in her voice.

Oni spins in a protective circle around us.

Even though the pain is still there, I can't stop smiling at Dani, because she's a beautiful genius who saved all our lives.

It was Glowstick, obviously. Marvellous used her telekinesis to float him above Fisher and light him up. It seems obvious in hindsight, given how shadows work, but I'm relieved Dani was smart enough to figure it out.

As more of the world resolves itself, I can see the three hostages Fisher took lying on the ground. They've all got people checking on them. In fact, the whole street is full. A decent number of cellphones are pointed in our direction.

Dani has her mask down, and Emma and I are wearing civilian clothes. We might have survived to fight another day, but our cover's well and truly blown.

CHAPTER NINE

Tanner comes bulldozing in, accompanied by a bunch of random thugs with Kiwi accents. I wonder what local assholerie she borrowed them from. They close the street down, organise the injured into ambulances, and even confiscate cellphones. It's ridiculous overkill. Do they not fucking understand half these people were streaming their footage? It's already out there.

Once the street is cleared of civilians and everything is blocked off, Tanner starts shouting at us.

"What in the heck was that?" Her coat flaps in the breeze and her fists are tight at her sides. I'm sitting on the ground while a paramedic dresses my neck. Two other goons load the remains of Fisher into a bodybag.

"It all got fucked up." I wince as the guy prods me. "Did you really not know about his shadow powers?"

"I told you." Her expression is impossible to read behind aviators. "Everyone who tried to stop Fisher in the past is dead."

"Yet we're still alive." Dani's tone is sharp. She's still wired and hovering protectively. "You could try being impressed with the fact we took him off the board."

"I'd take less of the high ground," Tanner snaps back. "Unless you want me to dig into how you mysteriously lost comms when you approached him?"

"Maybe it's his secondary mutation." I brush my fingers across the rough surface of the bandage. "His creepy shadow powers interfering."

Tanner is super unimpressed. I think she wants to punch me. "I don't suppose you'll tell me what he said."

"Couldn't understand a word of it," I shrug. "I don't even think it was English."

"There's no record of him speaking another language." She looks in my direction. "We could co-operate, you know."

"This is what co-operation looks like." For once, Dani sounds more belligerent than me. "Us risking our lives in service to EMID."

"Let's get off the street," Tanner says in disgust. "We don't need more attention."

Thanks for not telling her what he said, Emma says.

I don't understand the first fucking thing about it, but I have zero desire for Tanner to get any idea about breaking worlds.

Do you think it was true?

He sounded like a crazy person. I hope he was. We don't need something horrific at the centre of the mysteries surrounding Emma.

No, we really don't. Sorry for eavesdropping, but I'm terrified.

It's okay. I cross to Emma and put an arm around her, even though Alyse is holding her close. *You know we've got you, right?*

Some days it's the only thing that keeps me going.

Back at HQ, Emma finds the stories all over Twitter and YouTube. The conspiracy theorists are loudly proclaiming their rightness and extrapolating in wild directions. The most common story is that we're in the pay of the Americans, which is too close to the truth for my liking. Then there are the patriots-slash-xenophobes who are glad New Zealand has a superhero team to stop international takeovers. Others are terrified and think we should be sent to America, where they have proper jails capable of holding extrahumans.

It's exhausting and depressing.

The fan videos are more fun—various shots of cellphone footage spliced together with superhero movies. A lot of people have made the Alyse and Hulk connection. Even more have put Dani with Bucky Barnes or

Edward Elric. The shot that gets circulated most is the one of Dani and I kissing with Oni flying around us.

You can see a flash of her tongue, the way her hand tangles in the short hair at the base of my neck, and my delighted smile as I pull back and look at her. I barely recognise myself. I look older and sharper, with blood seeping down my neck and staining the top of my jacket. Yet when I see Dani's face, I light up. My innermost thoughts are projected, as if the whole world has a Gladdy-like insight into my heart. It's too intimate and makes me uncomfortable. It's also the first time I've ever thought I'm beautiful.

"You fucking muppets," Gladdy says, when she finally slams out of her long meeting with Tanner. "You really fucked me this time."

"And we usually leave that for Maddy." I'm lying on a mat in the training room with my head in Dani's lap. She's doing my hair in many tiny braids. Nobody feels like doing much of anything, except for Emma, who's back with her computers.

"Do you ever give it a rest? This is serious."

I lever myself upright. I'm sure I look stupid with half my hair braided, but I don't care. "I know it's serious. Emma could have died today, or Alyse, or me. Maybe Lou if Dani had crashed him."

"She almost banged me into the corner of a building," Lou says lazily from the next mat over.

"Did not." Dani gives him the finger.

"I can deal with Tanner," Gladdy says. "I know she wanted him alive, but we've taken their biggest threat off the board. My problem is we can't hide anymore. Everyone wants to know about us."

"Just tell them all to fuck off." I lie back down in Dani's lap. "Say that we're a top secret badass organisation of murderous Wolverine types, and we'll kill them all if they poke their noses in. Send out Katie and have her do her King Explosion Murder dance, maybe roast a camera or two."

"You're not remotely funny." Gladdy glares down at me.

"She's a little bit funny." Dani tugs on my braids. "Not as funny as she thinks she is, maybe—"

"Hey." I take her hand and bite the end of her middle finger lightly. "Fucking traitor."

Gladdy storms back towards her office. I feel a little sorry for her, having to deal with phone calls but hey, she wanted the damn job.

Are you sure you're okay? I ask Emma.

Why does everyone keep asking me that? I didn't get injured at all and—

It's me, I say gently. I was there. *The whole Teen Spirit thing. Have you talked to your Mum?*

There's no point! The exasperation in her voice comes through loud and clear. *My mother is not any kind of mutant or—or—or anything. I can't find any search results for Teen Spirit, aside from the song.*

Oh yeah, that one. Pear loves that song. I can't see how it has any connection.

Nor do I, but there's nothing else I can find. Not even in the EMID network, although I don't have full access to that.

I sigh. *You could just talk to her.*

And say what? I'm making good progress on the crystal thing, which is far more important than the ramblings of a crazy murderer.

I leave her to it. Emma can be as stubborn as any of us. She'll come around on her own time.

I'm thirsty, so I head down to get something to drink. In the hallway, I run into a desolate, drifting shape, more the outline of a person than anything.

"Alyse." I reach for her, but there's very little there. It's cool and tingly, like touching a ghost.

I can't make out her response.

"I don't know what all this is in honour of. You saved everyone, so we should be throwing you a parade."

"I killed someone." Her voice drifts to me. "I crushed him in my hands because I was scared."

I reach for the diffuse outline of Alyse's face and turn it towards me. "So many would've died if it wasn't for you."

She solidifies somewhat, until she's a vague and liquid creature with dark eyes and a watery chest that ripples when she breathes. "This is terrible, but I always thought only some of us could kill. You know, like you and Dani and Katie."

I never intended to be this ice-cold person. I'd rather be about redemption than killing, but the world keeps forcing me into these corners. It's very on brand for me to be a failure, but we need to focus on survival.

"We're the best at what we do," I murmur.

"I thought I could scare people or save people. *Protect* people, you know? And there I was with someone bleeding all over my hands." She looks down, but her hands are soft and there's no sign of blood on them. "I'm a murderer, Dylan."

She's crying, but she's taken a normal Alyse form, so it's easy to take her in my arms.

"It sucks, but it was the right thing in the moment. He would've killed those people, and he wouldn't have stopped."

"There must have been a better way," she sniffles.

"Maybe there was. But I was dying and Emma was next. You did what you had to."

She doesn't say anything, just clings tight and cries until the shoulder of my t-shirt is wet and streaked with mascara.

"I love you," I tell her, because it's true.

She says something back which I assume is reciprocal. I hold her and let her cry. All this talk of killing and guilt brings back what happened with Bancroft. That wasn't some heat of the moment combat decision. I took his life at my coldest, and I have no regrets. It was to keep the team safe, but now we find EMID and Tanner in line behind him. I don't know if I'm capable of killing every threat until we're safe. I don't know if safe is even possible.

I take Alyse through to the kitchen and make her a cup of the soothing tea that Emma swears by. She sits at the table and shivers, with her hands wrapped around the cup. I make myself some, but it smells way better than it tastes.

Soon Emma appears. She looks tired. Alyse starts crying again and they end up in each other's arms. Alyse shifts into something soft, encompassing both of them in comfort and warmth.

I leave them to it. My brain is racing in circles, around Tanner and Bancroft and Fisher and every other asshole that wants to take a shot. I go find Dani, who's reading a big thick book in one of the offices. She makes a big show of using a bookmark rather than dog-earing the pages like you're supposed to.

"The Reaper's Revenge." I frown at the cover. "Isn't that a little too close to home?"

"Fabulous queer people kicking several kinds of ass against a tyrant?" She raises an eyebrow. "It's inspiration."

"Come with me." I take her hand and lead her downstairs. "We can re-enact all the sexy parts. I skip to them anyway."

"You're a fucking disaster, Dylan Taylor."

"And you're the one who loves me."

She leaps onto my back, and I stagger down the hallway to bed.

In the morning, everything is worse, at least in terms of media coverage. For one thing, our names are out there. There are hastily written profiles on each of us. I'm described as *a mediocre student with a history of discipline problems* which okay, fair, but it seems a remarkably underwhelming summary of my existence. What happened to badass superhero, mutant leader, and friend to objects everywhere?

We're all sitting in the dining room together, not that anyone's really eating. Katie has a small mountain of toast and Lou is drinking a protein shake, but the rest of us are all on coffee. Everyone's head down and looking at their phones.

The story has gone international. There are plenty of countries weighing in on New Zealand's super-team. It's a cue for serious-looking people to stand and make statements about us.

"While we welcome new extrahumans, we wish to stress that this is an ongoing situation and there are expectations that must be met. Rogue behaviour on the part of extrahumans cannot and will not be tolerated. Therefore, we will be working closely with the New Zealand government and law enforcement to investigate the events that happened in Christchurch yesterday."

"Turn it off," I tell Lou, who's watching clip after clip on his phone. "Or at least put some damn headphones in. There are only so many ways I can feel judged and threatened before eight am."

Dani's waving her own phone at me. She's loaded up a website for an American magazine that covers LGBT issues. It's got a picture of us kissing, with the words *Queer Kiwi Heroes* emblazoned across it. Someone's edited the photo so the background is blurred and monochrome but we're perfectly clear and lit in rainbow light.

"I like it," Dani says softly.

"Out and proud." I nudge her with my shoulder.

"Yeah." She zooms the photo in so it's just our faces, to show that dual look of delight.

I know that seeing us paired like this is beautiful, but I don't necessarily want the *whole world* to watch us. It's our private joy exposed.

"You look super hot," I tell her.

"So do you. And I look proud." I actually think there might be a tear in her eye. Mine involuntarily start to water, because I am a big emo idiot. "*We* look proud. This is good, Dilly. If we're going to have our secrets spilled to the world, I want it to include this. I want queer kids to see us."

I hunch over my coffee, trying to ride out the wave of awkwardness. "There are plenty of gay and lesbian role models already."

"Not everywhere. And not superheroes. And even still, not everyone's cool with it. If I can make even one single person feel happier with who they are, then I'm glad. We'll be icons at the pride parade."

"I'm not an icon." My fingers trace the lines of her face on the screen.

"Accidental icons are still icons."

I look up at her. "I don't know. I don't feel ready for this. It's just…"

She smoothes the anxious crease in my brow with her thumb and I lean in and kiss her. My coffee breath mingles with her coffee breath.

"I *do* want people to feel happy," I say.

"I know, and it's a very good photo."

"Yes, you love it. I get it. I'll ask Emma to print out a big copy. We can frame it and put it up in the common area like people have their wedding photos."

"Shut up," she says, but she's laughing and there's that same look of delight on her face. I know the others are looking at us. I want to take her back to our room where we can share everything in private. I've gotten a lot better at being around other people—at least this weird group of friends—but I still feel an overwhelming urge to flee. Being known and seen is scary, even when you get more used to yourself.

Everyone else is talking and eating, while I sit on one of the news sites, flicking through the top stories. They're all about us with one notable exception.

"Dani, did you see this?" I send the page to her phone.

I watch as her frown gets deeper.

"Prominent LGBT activist. Stabbed to death in their own home in Wellington. No sign of forced entry. Some kind of locked room mystery. You think this is—?"

"An unfolding mutant who can appear out of nowhere and stab someone with their creepy extending fingers?" I stare at the picture of the victim. They've got close-cropped hair and stubble and a rainbow scarf. They're smiling almost as wide as me and Dani in our photo. "Seems a great time to be a high-profile queer, doesn't it? Just our luck."

"Some kind of vendetta against—"

"Against us," I say grimly. "And people like us. I think Shadowweaver and Stabbyhands are unrelated, right?"

"I mean they're both creepy murderers, but I'd say they're different threats." Dani sighs. "Which means we still need to find this other killer. Do you know if Emma's made any progress?"

Perfect timing, Emma says. *You should come downstairs, because I've found the next piece of the puzzle.*

CHAPTER TEN

Down in Emma's lair, she's spun a couple of monitors around to face the room. One shows a world map with a lot of glowing dots. The other is zoomed in on a single location.

"The crystals?" I ask.

"The sites I've identified globally." She taps the world map, and the majority of the dots shift to grey. "Most are gone."

"Which means lots of mutants," I say.

"Not necessarily." Emma spins a third screen toward us, showing an image of an empty field. She taps a rocky outcropping. "This is a crystal, which sat here for weeks untouched. We can't see everything, because the satellite only takes a single image each day. But it's a boring empty field until..." The next image has a whole bunch of vehicles spilled haphazardly across it, like a toy box has been emptied. The next shows makeshift scaffolding and for a few days, we watch it grow. Finally, the building is complete and for a whole twenty-two taps, nothing changes aside from the arrangement of the vehicles. Then, over only two days, the building is torn down and the field is empty and the crystals are gone.

"They came, they researched, they left," Dani says.

"Uh huh," Emma taps again, and some of the grey dots change to a variety of colours. "These are sites where crystals were found. I couldn't always figure out who, but we've definitely got America, Japan, the UN, China, Russia, and Israel."

"Fucking brilliant." I scowl at the screen. "Mutants worldwide, in the care of governments. We've seen how trustworthy they can be."

"What they're doing with the crystals, I can't tell," Emma says. "But there's less than fifty mutants that we know of across the various super-teams, so the math doesn't work."

"Not all the spots have been found," Alyse points at the other map.

"No." Emma lifts her hair away from her neck. "And I don't even know if this is all of them. Maybe there's a bunch I've missed and—"

"What you've done is incredible," I say, before she can start spiralling too far.

"It's wild." Dani's even more impressed than me, but she speaks science. "How did you do it?"

"First I focussed on the Sara Newton site in Kyoto," Emma said. "I tracked the original back and—" She catches my eyeroll and closes her mouth. "Shall I hand-wave the science for now?"

"Yes," I say with no small relief. "Let's assume it all runs on narrative magic or whatever. We wouldn't understand it anyway."

"I might," Dani says defensively.

"Sure." I put my hand to my mouth and yawn. "I'll go for a nap. Wake me when it's over."

"Fine, handwave the science." Dani nudges me, as if it's my fault I didn't pay attention in class.

"This bit you'll want to hear." Emma says. "A mutant planted the crystals. Here's live footage of the park in Kyoto."

The screen changes to show grainy security video of a park—people walking, sitting on benches, even a kid flying a kite. There's an enormous flower garden in the background. Everything looks normal until a glitch enters the frame. It's a swirl in the shape of a person, showing up in all the colours of the rainbow despite the footage being black and white. Nobody in the park pays attention to the strange appearance, even when they detour into the garden. They pause among the flowers for a full five minutes before disappearing into thin air.

"You can't really see it that well," Emma says. "But if you compare the before and after frames, there's a difference. Plus it's the identical spot where Sara finds her crystal."

"Fuck." Everyone turns to look at me. "I thought this would *explain* things, but it's even more confusing. Why is this rainbow blur person trying to make mutants in the most obscure way possible? Who is it? What do they want? And how does any of this link to you?"

Emma shakes her head. "I've got no answers, although we're finally on the trail. Our glitchy friend was at every site I found footage of."

Dani pokes at the other map. "Mysteriously and coincidentally, there's an undiscovered site right here in Christchurch within driving distance from where we sit."

"Is this a joke?" I'm scowling, because there's a sense of things being *orchestrated*.

"Coincidence or not, we go find it, right?" Dani asks.

"We have to." Even if this is some weird game, it's one made by a mutant and we'll only find more if we keep playing. "I'll let Roxy know."

It's only around twenty minutes' drive from our home base to Victoria Park. Emma's dropped a GPS pin on her phone, and we wander through the woods to find the spot. It's way off the beaten track, which is maybe why nobody else has discovered it. Oni is enjoying the outing. He even makes up a haiku about it, in both Japanese and English.

These trees outlive me
I am forged, a mutant tool
My friends change with me

I call him a cliche and he threatens to poke me.

We find the location from the map. It looks like nothing's there, until Emma spots a drift of leaves with glowing edges. I take a stick and gingerly brush them away. Everyone else keeps their distance. Once the crystal is revealed, it's a chunk of pink and purple rock, partly translucent and lit from within. It's pretty.

We form an unnecessarily large circle around it.

"Surely we can't mutate again?" Alyse looks nauseated at the thought.

"Hank McCoy used to be an agile dude with big feet before he was a big blue kitty cat," I tell her.

"Yes, but that's *comic books*."

"Name the way our lives are different." I pat the sword floating in front of me. "Better to be safe than sorry."

"We can't leave it here," Dani says.

"Maybe Oni can pick it up," I suggest. "If it's got mutating powers, I doubt they'll work on him."

"Perhaps I shall transform into a metal man like your friend Piotr Rasputin, known as Colossus," Oni says. I've told him too many X-Men stories. "Wouldn't that be splendid?"

"Well, yes, but—"

"Do you hear it singing?" Emma asks.

We all stare at her. I'm the least weirded out because I'm used to random things communicating. Sure, the magic mutant rock isn't serenading me right now, but I did hear a haiku from my sword.

"I think it's calling to me."

I hold out my hand. "Emma, don't do anything—"

"Reckless?" She steps into the middle of the circle. "What's it going to do?"

"That's exactly it." Dani looks ready to leap in after her. "We don't know. You wouldn't let any of *us* experiment."

"It's like me. We both change people."

Alyse looks to me beseechingly, but what am I going to do? "It's a fucking rock, Emma. It's nothing like you."

"Perhaps our essence is the same." Emma crouches beside it.

"You better be sure about this." I glare at her as she picks up the crystal.

"Look." She holds her hand out, the crystal nestled in her palm. It's definitely glowing brighter, and I have to shade my eyes with my hand. The crystal emits one long high note—this one I *can* hear—and shatters, as if the exterior is a fragile candy shell.

"Emma," Alyse shouts.

Brightly coloured water drips from Emma's hands and soaks into the soil. Her hands are stained with it, swirling patterns that highlight the creases in her palms.

She looks at us with wide eyes, hair falling over her face.

"Are you okay?" Alyse asks nervously.

Her eyes flutter rapidly. "This is weird. I feel like my head is accelerating through space and I'm standing right here."

"Fuck. It's a drug rock. We need to wash that shit off her hands." Alyse is on the verge of panic, but Emma smiles.

"It's not like that. Things are changing, that's all. I can sense you." She sees my frown and waves a faintly purple hand at me. "No, this is different. Go and spread out, quietly as you can." Emma closes her eyes while we all tiptoe in different directions.

"Dani, Alyse, Dylan," she says, stabbing her finger unerringly to where we are.

"What the fuck does this mean?" I ask. "Now you have mutant GPS, the way we have Emma GPS?"

She frowns. "That's an excellent analogy, Dylan. This is amazing." She opens her eyes and stalks off through the trees. We follow in her wake, trading glances and wishing we had the ability to speak among ourselves in our minds.

Honestly, Dilly, can you not trust me?

I do. It's just—

More comic book weirdness, yes. You're supposed to be the expert in this.

We come out of the trees and walk along the ridge until a rather spectacular view of the city is laid out below us. I find it hard to orient myself from up here, aside from major landmarks like the ocean to the east, and Hagley Park sitting leafy in the middle of the city.

"There are other mutants out there," Emma says. "I can sense the others back home, but—" She snaps a glance at me. "The numbers aren't right. Maybe Shadowweaver wasn't telling lies after all."

"Holy shit." It's all I can think of to say. Does she really mean that—?

"It's not just her. There's more." She reaches for Alyse. "I want to get back."

The rest of us are left to trade confused looks, even though I know Emma can pick up every thought in our heads. She doesn't seem interested in explaining, but heads back to Roxy.

Alyse is in the back seat, transformed into something remarkably soft. Emma is nestled in with her eyes closed.

"Someone's playing games," Dani says to me.

"You think someone lured us there with the express purpose of levelling up our Goddess?" I want Dani to tell me I'm being paranoid.

"Maybe, but it's so damn tortuous," she sighs. "At the same time, what are the odds we find that crystal still intact and it sings to Emma specifically before giving her new powers?”

“If someone did that…” I stroke my fingers around the outside of the steering wheel. Roxy makes a soft noise of enjoyment. “They’re scary *and* powerful. What if it’s some sinister organisation who wants to tinker with mutants? Maybe the plan is to ascend us to higher and higher levels.”

Dani sighs. “That’s a theory. You think that would be better or worse than the ones who want to eradicate or leash us?”

I make a non-committal sound and take her hand. It would be nice to be left in peace for five minutes.

Back at Jinteki, Emma marches up to the living quarters.

“Mother,” she calls. “Where are you?”

The Halls don’t live here all the time. I think they’re having issues. When she’s here, Mrs. Hall spends a lot of time in her room, and even the combined efforts of Mrs. Kim and Pear can’t drag her out. It’s one of the things I've kicked off the bottom of my Shit Dylan Worries About list, because it's not my fucking business.

I start following Emma, but Alyse grabs hold of my arm and detours into the dining room. Dani follows obediently.

"What the fuck?" I hiss at Alyse.

"No eavesdropping," she says.

I slouch over to the bench and start making coffee. I try to ignore Emma banging around down the hallway.

"Mother, get your ass out here."

If I'd finished making my coffee, I would have spat that shit everywhere. Emma barely talks like that to me, who can't fucking breathe without swearing, let alone her mother who's beautiful and gentle.

Alyse grimaces at me, as if this is my fault. We stand awkwardly, pretending we can't hear.

"Emmaline Jing, why do you shout so rudely?" Her mother sounds almost as irritable.

"How could you hide this from me?" Emma sounds livid. "This whole time, you acted so confused and bewildered, but you're a mutant too."

"Emma's Mum is a mutant?" Dani mouths, and I remember I never explained the Matthias Fisher conversation. It's a bad girlfriend moment, but we've had a lot going on.

"What are you talking about?" Mrs Hall sounds incredulous.

"I know you're a mutant, Mum. I can *sense* it."

"I don't know what you're talking about. It's a ridiculous accusation. I have gone along with this madness at every turn, and now you throw this nonsense in my face?"

There's silence. We're all looking at each other. Even Alyse wants to hear better.

"You can't hide it anymore." Emma's on the verge of tears. "Why won't you just *admit* it? What's the big secret? You can explain where I come from—explain my *powers*. Why would you keep this from me?"

"Please stop this. What have I done to make you think this could be true?"

There's a long pause.

"Fine," Emma says flatly. "Keep it a secret. You've kept it this long."

A door slams and a few moments later she bursts into the room. We're all frozen like statues, but she busies herself at the bench preparing tea as if nothing is wrong. Alyse helps get the teapot and cups ready, while Emma stands with the tea canister shaking in her hands.

"My mother *is* a mutant, although she refuses to admit it. Teen Spirit, I gather, from what Matthias Fisher said. The one who broke the world. Perhaps that's why she won't tell me." She presses her lips together tightly. Alyse pulls her in close.

I go to the fridge and search for something to eat. Anything to distract us.

"It's fine." Emma's eyes are red. "Whatever Fisher said, I don't really believe Mum's a threat. Maybe she genuinely doesn't know." She slams her palm down on the bench and takes a deep breath. "It doesn't matter."

There's a weird echo of it in my head as she speaks, and it's there I can sense the lie. Of course it fucking matters. This is all tied in with the mystery of her, and she's run up against a barrier she doesn't want to breach. I get not wanting to talk about it. She wants some mental privacy, like we all used to have.

It's okay, I tell her gently. *We can leave it.*

She shakes her head slightly. "It *doesn't* matter," she repeats more firmly, but it sounds even more like a lie. "Besides, there are other mutants out there. In Christchurch, and further afield too. I have a map in my mind."

"How many nearby?" I ask.

"Twenty-three, if you don't count the ones we know about."

"That's quite a few mutants," Dani says.

I nod. "We need to talk to Gladdy about finding these people and offering them sanctuary." When we first took over Jinteki, this was the dream—making a place where mutants are safe. This could be the first glimpse of it coming true.

"It's important to know if they're dangerous," Dani points out. "We've already run up against Shadowweaver, and Stabbyhands is still out there killing queer people."

Emma shakes her head. "I can't tell individual people or powers apart, but you're right. We need to find as many as we can. And we somehow need to keep it secret from Tanner. It's going to be a nice little dance, isn't it?" She gives us a watery smile. "On the bright side, it'll keep my mind off this shit with Mum."

CHAPTER ELEVEN

Dani and I head up to talk to Gladdy, while Emma goes to bed with a headache and Alyse to take care of her. I hope this isn't the trope where someone gets increased powers, and is immediately struck down by a mysterious illness.

I'm fine, Emma tells me. *People do get headaches, especially after having a shouting match with their mothers in front of everyone.*

You better be okay.

Yes, because that's how life works.

"Stop blathering to Emma," Gladdy says irritably. "I hate that vacant look on your face."

We fill her in on the situation. Her face goes from irritated to intrigued to shocked as we get through the story, especially at the part where there are a bunch of mutants out there and how we want to save them all.

"I get it," Gladdy says, once we're done. "In a perfect world, I'd agree completely."

"Why is there always a *but* with you?" I scowl.

"She has a decent butt." Maddy gives one of her weird winks.

"This but is Tanner's," Gladdy says. "Our government might pay lip service to the idea of protecting its people, but I spoke to some sad man in a suit. He told me they're trying to rule that extrahumans can't be New Zealand citizens."

"Genosha," Dani says with a sigh.

Gladdy scowls at the interruption. "I'm not predicting genocide, but I do expect Tanner to take over. I presume we don't want her getting hold of these new mutants."

"Definitely not, which is why we need to figure out a way to save them under her nose," Dani says. "I mean theoretically we have lives outside of this mutant business, right? Friends, family, higher learning. We can do stuff under cover of that."

I try not to grimace, because literally all my friends and family are here, unless you count Pear's girlfriend and her kids who haven't moved in yet. I think their conversations about me are awkward, and I hope I'm not something they fight about. I wonder if they've seen my picture in the paper.

"I can try using my powers to push Tanner around a little," Gladdy says.

"Will that work?" I ask.

"She's got no idea about our spare mutants hidden away in the living quarters, does she?"

I feel a twinge of guilt. I haven't checked on those two since we brought them back. Pear and Mrs. Kim have been looking after them, so they'll be fine. Tanner's shown no interest in the living quarters at all, which is apparently Gladdy's doing. As creepy as psychics are, sometimes they're useful.

"So we have permission to go on the mutant rescue mission?" I'm slightly sceptical.

"If you're sensible and careful. And even as I say those words, I realise how ridiculous they sound. Dani, I sort of trust you to not fly off the handle, so please keep Chatterbox in line."

"So rude," I mutter.

Gladdy smirks at me. "I do appreciate you pretending I'm in charge."

I give her the finger, but she's not exactly wrong.

Maddy leans forward and puts her green lips right beside Gladdy's ear. "Would you trust me not to fly off the handle?"

"No," Gladdy says firmly. "I even trust Dylan more than you."

"She *is* rude," Maddy says to me. "Maybe I'll quit bodyguarding and come hang out on the cool squad with you."

"All feral girls welcome," I tell her.

"Yay." Her green lips stretch into a smile. "I hereby quit, Gladiola Quick. I'm going to go have fun."

"You can't just quit," Gladdy grumbles.

Maddy tries to wink at me again. "It looks like I quit. And it *sounds* like I quit…"

"Dylan, you can't just take my bodyguard!"

"Field Team has autonomy to select operatives," I say coolly.

Dani flashes a smile. "We did agree on that right at the start. Field Team takes precedence."

I watch Gladdy's teeth clench. "But not Maddy."

"Awww." Maddy leans in and presses her lips hard against Gladdy's cheek. "I think she likes me after all. Her love language is being mean."

"Maybe she loves all of us then," I say with a laugh.

"But me especially!" Maddy smacks another kiss.

Gladdy scowls and rubs her cheek furiously. "I only have three things to say. Stop kissing me. I hate you all. And Maddy's not allowed to quit."

"Young love," I say to Dani with a sigh. "Ain't it fucking grand?"

The next day is Sunday, which is supposed to be for binge watching shows and making out. Except Emma senses two mutants nearby at the same location, which is too good an opportunity to pass up. We give Tanner some excuse about Alyse's family which she doesn't blink at. To look more legit, it's only Dani, Alyse and I who accompany Emma a couple of blocks through town. We end up at a giant white building covered with all these slogans about—

"This is a church." I scowl up at it, feeling like a vampire in front of a cross.

"I didn't know." Emma looks up at the red and gold sign proclaiming this building The First Church of the Crucified Christ. "I'm only following the trail of the mutants."

"I know this place." Alyse strides towards the entrance. The doors are big and tinted glass, but they slide open as we approach, revealing a smiling couple. The dude is in a blue suit and the lady's in a wild floral print dress.

"Welcome, sisters." They even speak in unison. "Are you new to our congregation?"

"No." Alyse smiles radiantly, before I get a chance to correct the word *sisters*. "I'm Alyse Sefo. My parents have attended here for years."

"Ah, the Sefos!" Alyse's parents are some big deal people that go around talking about parenting. I didn't know they were also church people. "Welcome and find a seat. The worship service is still going. God bless you all."

The lobby is enormous, with thick carpets. The walls are blindingly white with slogans and pictures to do with Jesus, God, and the Lord. I can't figure out the relationship between them all. Either way, they've very popular. The faint sound of music is audible, something upbeat with a bunch of people singing.

"Your family goes here?" I ask Alyse.

"I used to as well, when I was younger. Before I figured out I was a heathen, and before my parents figured out I was a little bit bi and tried to keep me out of sight."

"This isn't your Mum's church?" I ask Dani.

"No, Mum dragged Minnie and I to the Korean church. I think this is one of the weird ones. No offense, Lys."

Alyse grins over her shoulder as she heads up a carpeted staircase to the right. "No, you're correct. Weird *and* creepy." The stairs end at a set of big double doors. Another smiling guy pulls one open for us, and the music becomes overwhelming.

We slink into empty spaces at the back of a bank of raised seating that's about three-quarters full. Below, there are even more people sitting in rows that lead up to a stage. There's a band wearing suits and beaming as they play. Everyone in the crowd sings along like the set list is all the hits.

The creepiest thing is any sentient objects in here are singing along. They don't even want to listen to me. I've met very few objects that don't like me—most notably Alyse's coffee table—but these few pews and the big wooden pulpit up the front have zero interest in my opinions.

"This shit's a fucking cult," I whisper to Dani.

"We're in a church so maybe less of the f-word."

A woman who's maybe twenty stands at the front of the stage. She's short and petite, with pale skin and a halo of dark curls. Her slinky black dress looks sexy even though it doesn't show any skin. The main thing she's showing off is her voice, because she can really sing.

"She's one of them," Emma says.

Alyse peers down at the stage. "She's the mutant?"

Emma nods.

"Is her power singing?" Alyse frowns.

"Like Dazzler." Dani puts her head close to mine.

"Dazzler's power isn't singing. It's light generation. You know this."

"I'd still love a Dazzler record. I stan Dazzler so hard."

"I bet you do," I say with a grin.

"Especially badass Bendis-era Dazzler, holy crap. Maybe we can paint a star on your face, and I'll dress up as Magik, then we'll—"

"Dani, we are in a church." My heart is beating so fast I think a hummingbird would pass out.

"Fine, I'll behave." She flashes the smile at me. I want to drag her out of the church to fill in that pie chart of Katie's, but we're here on business. Yawn, I hate being a grown up.

The singing mutant finishes with a wildly overdone high note that makes me roll my eyes. Everyone else in the church goes fucking nuts for it, like it's proof of the existence of God rather than mutation. The band go off to more applause and an older dude bounds up onto the stage in their place. He's dressed in a suit that looks as expensive as one of Gladdy's i.e. if you added up the cost of every piece of clothing I've ever brought in my life, even my ReVe tour hoodie I special-ordered from Seoul, it would not be nearly as much.

The crowd applauds and cheers. Is this guy Jesus? Is that what all the fuss is about?

"That's the other mutant," Emma says under cover of the general hullabaloo.

What's his power? Making people love him? The guy holds his hands out and finally everyone calms down.

"Welcome, brethren." He's got a good voice, I'll give him that. It's like the voiceover guy. Some combination of warm, deep, and confident. "My daughter and the band. Aren't they amazing testaments to God's power and grace?"

"His daughter?" I mouth at Emma, who shrugs.

There's a big round of applause and at least that seems fair enough, because the band were pretty good for a bunch of religious fanatics.

"It's wonderful to see you all here today in the light of God's love." The preacher holds out his hands as if he's waiting to catch someone. "Isn't he a great God? A majestic and awesome God?"

People say yes to this. The dude carries on in this vein for some time. People don't lose their enthusiasm. I never knew God was so fucking needy, I swear. In the bitter ashes of my parents' relationship ending, my Dad made a dumb joke about women existing on compliments. Turns out it's really God who's a slut for them.

The congregation finally quiets, and the preacher begins talking. "I have a story to share with you today. A couple came to me this week with heavy hearts. One of their precious children, a young boy who I've known since he was born—a boy who was baptised in this church—had confessed to them that he was homosexual."

People aren't such fans of this, and I feel a prickle between my shoulders as the murmurs of discontent spread.

"They asked me if God's love would stretch to encompass this sin."

The unhappiness grows. Dani sits hunched and sour beside me. I long to soothe her with my touch, but it doesn't seem the time or place.

"I told them no," the preacher shouts. "God cannot tolerate sin. I told these poor people that this is one of the most insidious lies of the devil. There are so-called Christians who would have you believe this *lifestyle* is acceptable!"

A bunch of people shout no. I want to get up and punch every single one of them. Even better, I could jump down onto the stage and make out with Dani. Oni can stab anyone who disagrees. Except instead I slump in my seat, jiggle my knee, and fidget restlessly with the cords of my hoodie.

The preacher isn't close to done. "I tell you this today—as it has always been, this remains a sin most abhorrent. I told those people they must force their son to see the error of his ways. If he cannot turn from his vile acts, they must cast him out into darkness, to show the Lord they will not tolerate sin."

I hear some woman in front of us say "yes, Lord."

Applause ripples through the crowd. I hope this poor kid isn't here. It's so goddamn hot in here. My vision swims briefly.

"Jesus," I say, and it's not a prayer of any kind.

The preacher closes his eyes and raises his hands.

"Lord," he says. "We pledge ourselves to you and renew our commitment to righteousness. We shall no longer tolerate those who promote or justify this sin. We shall condemn it wherever we see it and—"

I get to my feet awkwardly and barge my way out of the doors. It's a few degrees cooler in the stairwell.

I stop halfway down because I'm shaking, and I don't want to fall. The lobby is entirely empty now.

A few seconds later, Dani crouches beside me. "Dilly, what's wrong?"

"Didn't you hear him?" I turn my head slightly so I can see the curve of her cheek. "He's standing up there saying kids should be kicked out of home for being gay."

"I don't like it any more than you."

"You know people feel this way," Alyse says at my other side. "Like Lou's parents and—"

"Not so many!" I feel lightheaded. "There are hundreds of people in there listening and they're all like yes, Lord, let's throw the kids out into the fucking darkness."

Emma trots a few steps further down and turns to look at me. "I'm really sorry," she says.

"It's the preacher." I feel like I'll throw up or faint. "I don't know how, but you heard him. No longer tolerating those who promote this fucking *lifestyle*. Two actresses playing a lesbian couple on TV, a guy who literally promotes rainbow festivals. He's not just saying it—he's *doing something* about it."

"I don't think he's the one stabbing people." Dani frowns. "It could be the singing girl from the start?"

There's silence as we all compare the unfolding person from the video to the vibrant and gorgeous singer.

"It's closer than the pastor," Alyse says doubtfully.

"I don't care." I get to my feet. "This guy—we need to do something about him first. He's the real problem. We'll put surveillance on him and find out what he's up to."

"You're right," Emma says. "I'll get onto that."

"If he's the one who's doing this—" There's something dark in Dani's voice that I'm not used to.

I reach out for her. It's an involuntary action. My arm snakes around her waist.

"Vile. An abomination in the eyes of the Lord." A face hangs in the air. The hazy pale oval fills with fractured patterns of light. A cross, a malevolent red sun, an ocean of blood. Seen from this angle, I realise it's a mask. A disguise she wears when she strikes.

Dani presses on one of the plates on the inside of her metal arm, sending pain signals shooting through her nerves. She winces as one of the Jesus tapestries on the wall whips across the room. It's hardly the best weapon, but we didn't come prepared. We didn't expect to find Stabbyhands live in concert.

The assassin folds herself away, a writhing motion where she shrinks to a dot and reappears across the room. Only her head is visible, as if she's poked it up over an invisible barrier.

The tapestry flies past and smacks into the wall.

I'm very aware of where her hands might be and how fast they can move.

"You're the extrahuman girls." Her voice is distorted and crackling, but I can still hear the disgust. "I saw that revolting picture of you. Parading your unnatural lusts for the world to see."

Alyse shifts into protective mode. I don't know if her thorny carapace is enough to stop this mutant. I hope we don't have to find out.

"People should be free to love who they wish." Dani stays eerily calm, while I'm bouncing between fury and panic.

"It's not love," the girl snaps. "You cannot give that name to something so aberrant."

Dani kisses me right in front of the assassin which, okay, I love kissing Dani, but this does *not* seem like the right time. It's probably meant to be a gay rights statement, which again I am down with, but context, dude. Usually I'd close my eyes and surrender myself to the joys of young love but I'm pretty fucking terrified that I'll be stabbed by her weird unfoldy fingers, so it's hardly one of our top ten kisses.

An enormous crash startles me, and I break the kiss to see a big cabinet has shattered against the wall. The girl has gone, presumably dodging the new attack

"Kissing makes the telekinesis hurt less." Dani grins at me. "Maybe I scared her off or—"

Right behind her head, something dark flickers, fingers reaching from thin air for her throat.

A silver flash slices through my peripheral vision and crashes into the darkness with a shower of sparks.

Dani throws herself forward into my arms.

"Never fear," Oni says.

"Where the fuck were you?"

"I was waiting out of sight—"

The girl twists in on herself and disappears. The top part of her face pops out of the air right beside us. Her hand flashes out, but is met with steel.

"—and attempting to remain under cover. It seems—"

The assassin appears low to the ground, at knee height. Oni stabs down brutally between us. Even Dani lets out something that might be a scream.

"—to have worked—"

From far across the room, her hand unrolls, her fingers like outflung streamers that narrow to wicked points. It's pretty fucking kung-fu but Oni is there to intercept with an almost casual flick of his blade.

"—does it not?"

"Once again, Oni, we are in your debt."

He swings back to circle me cautiously. I keep tight hold of Dani.

The girl hangs in the air, dark eyes blinking. She makes no further attempt to move, which proves she's smart enough to learn from experience.

"Be sure your sin will find you out," she hisses, and then vanishes again.

We wait a handful of seconds, but when she doesn't reappear, we bolt for the door.

Our trip back to the office is slow, because we're all on edge in case she reappears. My heartbeat is loud in my ears, and my palms are slippery against Dani's. Oni hovers warily overhead, but we get back without further incident.

It seems like a terrible omen that the first two mutants we find are an anti-gay preacher and his psychotic assassin daughter, but so fucking on brand for us that I want to cry.

CHAPTER TWELVE

The first thing we do is report to Gladdy like naughty schoolchildren.

"I can't *believe* you managed to get into a fight on your very first outing. No, of course I can, but I *asked* you to be subtle."

"She was the one who attacked." Alyse's eyes glow briefly red.

"You said Dani kissed Dylan in a church." Gladdy glares right back. "That's not what I meant by subtle."

"She turned up before the kiss." I happily join the glarefest. "I *touched* Dani and she popped out of thin air talking about how vile it was. You should be thanking us, really. It's a massive lead to find this girl. We had no idea who she was before now."

Gladdy makes this noise that I choose to believe is begrudging acceptance. "This is actually true, if unintentional. Are you sure the assassin is the preacher's daughter?"

Emma nods. "I don't have proof to show Tanner, but there were only ever two mutants in that building."

The Aladdin feeling of staying one jump ahead is very strong, except it's getting increasingly complex to avoid the pitfalls. It's like we've reached a new level of the Cute Mutants video game and I'm too shit to complete it.

"We can't let Tanner know about your power upgrade." Alyse is still fairly Hulk-like and standing close to Emma. "If they knew we had our very own mutant detector—"

Gladdy runs her hands through her hair. "I'll handle it as usual. Find a halfway believable story and lean on Tanner. Did you see the preacher doing anything suspicious?"

I shake my head. If it hadn't been for Emma, I wouldn't have any idea. He might not know either. Does he know about his daughter? Given what he was saying to the crowd, all signs point to yes. He's using her to punish people in God's name. It makes me want to scream, and I can see Dani's upset by it too. I want to shut this fucking guy down by any means necessary.

Tanner swaggers into the office with a grin. "Looks like y'all have been discussing things without me." She takes a seat. "It'd be nice if we could all trust each other. Y'all could invite me to your slumber parties. We could braid each other's hair and shit."

"We've got work to do, Tanner," Gladdy says. "No time to play spin the bottle. We've got a report of a face hanging in the air at a local church. Scared the shit out of some kids. Nobody dead, which is a nice change, but the description sounds a lot like our friend from the Auckland video."

Tanner sits back with her legs kicked out in front and her arms folded. "Sounds like a weak-sauce lead. It'll be kids who've seen the video of y'all online and are making shit up."

"Weirdest thing is, the report said the girl looked a lot like the preacher's daughter." Gladdy leans forward with her eyes narrowed. There's a weird emphasis on her words. "You don't want to leave a lead like this hanging. Imagine if this assassin girl carved up a few more people. That would *not* look good to the bosses. A dangerous mutant on the loose while you sat on your hands, having a pissing contest with a nineteen-year-old."

Tanner sighs and fidgets in her seat. "I guess there's no harm in checking it out. It'll just be me and Jackson. Don't want to take any of your lot after the Fisher situation."

"And you said we're supposed to trust each other." Gladdy tilts her head. The rest of us aren't even fidgeting in case we break the spell. "What happens if this girl attacks? I suppose if you're dead then they can't fire your ass." Gladdy looks at the ceiling and sighs. "You should at least take a couple of Field Team. They'll be under strict instructions to behave."

It's lucky we have Gladdy's power, because I don't think Tanner's in any kind of mood to fold. Instead, she gives a little nod. "I'll take the telekinetic and the weird girl with the sword."

"Not a girl," I say.

"Oh it's that way, is it? What? You identify as genderfluid or whatever?"

It's too good a setup. Oh, Tanner. "No, I *am* genderfluid. I *identify* as a bitch."

Dani smirks and Gladdy rolls her eyes.

"I like you." Tanner smiles at me. "I used to be similar." The grin gets wider. "Then they beat that shit out of me in basic training."

Oni glides up alongside her and I hold her gaze until she winks and looks away.

"Marvellous and Chatterbox," Gladdy says. "I'm sure I can spare them."

"All I ask is that y'all follow orders. None of this smartass shit. I know you have a problem with that, but you really don't want our relationship getting worse. We clear?"

"Clear." I grin right back. I'm not scared of her. We've beaten worse.

Dani and I are in full uniform when we head back to the church. It's masks and all, although we leave them blank. It makes us look alien and menacing, which is not the worst thing when you're confronting at least one dangerous mutant. I've got Oni slung over my back as if he's a regular sword. How badass do I look? Extremely, and Dani keeps checking me out, or at least turning her blank mask in my direction, which I'm taking as a compliment. Isn't that personal growth?

Oni hasn't left my side since we first ran into Stabbyhands. He takes his job as defender very seriously. I'm a little worried that he's not back at HQ keeping an eye on the others, but let's hope our assassin is still focused on the two of us.

The smiley welcome party has been replaced by a big security dude. "Do you have an appointment?" His voice is suitably rumbly.

"No, but this is urgent business." Tanner acts easygoing, despite the looming figure of Jackson and our blank shadows. "I work for the Extrahuman Monitoring and Intelligence Division in the American government."

The guy switches to flustered. "Um, right. Well, ok. That's, well, that's very unusual. And you're here to see Pastor Michael?"

"That's right," Tanner says.

"About extrahumans?"

"That would be the logical conclusion." Her wide mouth moves into a smirk.

"Please wait here." The guy disappears behind the tinted doors, which don't open when Tanner shuffles around in front of them.

"He's waiting inside," a voice says. "He's talking to the thing in his ear. Telling it all about *you*." It's the building alarm system. "Pastor Parker is a very important man. He does such incredible work for the Lord."

"Who is the Lord exactly?" I ask, because I'm still confused.

"That's…a very good question. Some sort of magical figure who provides power. Perhaps someone like yourself. You appear to be a creature of might and majesty."

Um, wow. Flattery. "Somehow I don't think Pastor Parker worships *me*."

Tanner gives me a very weird look.

"It's the Dylan effect," Dani says.

"Oh, look!" The alarm system sounds very cheerful. "He's going to let you in. Isn't this delightful. My Lord and his Lord in the same room perhaps?"

"Just call me Chatterbox," I tell the alarm. "Tanner, they're going to let us in."

She frowns at me as the door slides open.

"Ta-da," I spread my arms wide.

Tanner makes an irritated noise and walks into the foyer. We cross to one end where there's a door semi-hidden behind a fabric screen. The guy leads us over and taps a code into a keypad. He's big enough that none of us can see around him.

"The combination is one-four-seven-eight-one-two-four," the alarm system says in a loud whisper. I try to make a note in case we need it in future.

We follow the dude into a block of offices, all glass and black furniture and recessed lighting. At the end of the corridor, we reach a big wooden door. It has a gold plaque that says *Pastor*, like we should all bow down.

The security guard taps respectfully. "Mrs. Tanner from EMID."

"Come in."

The door swings wide, revealing an office with lush carpet and a big desk with a massive Mac on it. There's not a lot on the walls. The main feature is an ornate cross with a disturbingly realistic model of someone bleeding to death on it. Whoever the fuck it is, they don't look happy. What's it for? Intimidation? It's mostly just creeping me out.

The pastor looks less impressive sitting behind a desk rather than in front of a crowd. He's probably late forties, kind of handsome in a vaguely chunky way. He's got a nice smile, I guess, but the killer thing is the voice.

"Extrahuman Intelligence. Not who I expected to find at my door today."

"Abigail Tanner." She holds out her hand. He pauses a moment before shaking it. Tanner doesn't bother to introduce the rest of us, although the pastor's gaze travels over everyone. If he's unnerved by having soldier types in his office, he doesn't give any indication.

"It's good to meet you. It's possible we have some colleagues in common. I'm currently working with Quietus around setting up a New Zealand branch of that organisation."

That word is like a fucking sledgehammer to the brain. Bancroft mentioned them in our final conversation as the religious organisation that he was terrified of. How this fits with a mutant preacher and his mutant daughter running around killing queer people is not something my brain is equipped to calculate. It just screams VERY, VERY BAD at me until I realise Tanner is talking.

"We're here on the trail of a mysterious woman. Reports say she appears to be a mutant." Tanner spouts Gladdy's fake story. The lenses in our masks have optical zoom, so I have it toggled way up to watch the preacher's face. "There was speculation it might be your daughter."

The preacher's twitch needs no zoom to be detected. Looks like we have a guilty party. Let's lock him up—or better yet, use him as bait for dear sweet Stabbyhands.

"Ah, yes." He folds his hands on the desk as if he's about to pray and regards them reverently. "A rather unfortunate tale, I'm afraid. For a number of months, my daughter Violet has been having increasing emotional difficulties."

I almost laugh. It's the most ridiculous explanation. *My daughter became a murdery mutant, and she's been all sad ever since.* Mind you, not *every* mutant takes so easily to the change, so perhaps…

"She's been increasingly erratic, culminating in this morning's church service where she had a breakdown after leading the worship. We took her to one of our small breakout rooms after her collapse, but when my wife went to check on her, she was simply gone."

I didn't see any breakdown, but I *did* leave the church in a huff. It must have happened after we left. Seems a tiny bit suspicious, but not raising a million red flags.

"Were you aware your daughter had extrahuman powers?" Tanner asks.

"No." The preacher looks somber, as if he's conveying bad news. "I think you have been misinformed. She has none of those freakish abilities like those awful young people on the news. Her issues are entirely mental health related, and we continue to uplift her in our prayers."

I feel embarrassed to have gotten it so wrong. It's awkward, and I want to get out of here before I dig myself a deeper hole. The guy obviously cares a lot for his daughter, who is going through some shit. It's sweet in a way.

The preacher sits back in his chair, totally relaxed. "We thank you for your concern. If we find anything else, we will contact you as soon as possible. Do you have a way for us to reach you?"

He's being pretty chill about the whole thing, given that we busted in here and basically accused him of having a mutant daughter. We must have been way off. It's annoying, going back to square one, but what else can we do? I glance at Dani, who gives a brief nod.

Tanner produces a business card from an inner pocket of her jacket and slides it across the desk.

"Thank you," she says. "We appreciate your time and co-operation."

"Anytime. It was lovely to meet you. All God's blessings on you and your important work." The preacher nods to the security guard, who escorts us back out of the building.

"A dead end," Tanner says.

"It's a shame." Dani sighs, and we pile into the Jinteki van to head back to the office.

I lean my head against the seat and close my eyes, feeling a brief rush of gratitude that the Lord is looking after poor Violet, and hoping he'll keep her cradled in the palm of his hand.

CHAPTER THIRTEEN

When we fill everyone in back at the office, it doesn't go the way we expected.

"Are you fucking insane?" Gladdy glares at all of us, not just Tanner. "That story doesn't make any sense. She has mental health issues and they're uplifting her in their prayers?"

"I don't think you understand," Tanner says. "She's not an extrahuman. She's had increasing emotional difficulties. You must have misunderstood the reports."

The reports? Emma asks me. *You were right there. You saw her.*

It's mental health issues. She's not an extrahuman. They're uplifting her in their prayers.

"It makes perfect sense." I slouch in my chair and roll my eyes. "You're all being unreasonable."

Gladdy looks at me in shock. Her hands are tangled in her hair. "Marvellous?"

Dani spreads her arms wide. She's as confused by everyone's lack of chill as me. "What are you not getting? She had a breakdown after the service. There's nothing more to it than that."

"*Obviously* there's something more." Emma shakes her head. "It's the preacher's mutant power. It's something similar to yours, Fetch. He has the ability to convince people."

"What the fuck?" I glare at Emma. "Where the hell is this coming from? You're supposed to be on *our side*."

"He put a whammy on you." She shrugs. "You've been Professor X'd."

It's completely ridiculous. I want to shout at Emma and tell her so. Except it's hard to arrange any kind of coherent argument. I know what happened, but the words aren't there to explain it. I try to join all the dots, but they're scattered like someone's spilled them in my brain. "Holy crap. Maybe he did fuck with our heads."

"No." Tanner holds firm. "The daughter, she has mental health issues. She collapsed after the church service. They're praying for her and—"

Dani shivers beside me. "It's like my thoughts are slipping on ice from one thing to another. It's supposed to be everything following together, neatly ordered like a path, but now there are chasms and—" She breaks off and clutches me. "I hate it, Dylan. I know it's wrong but it makes sense in my head. Like it still *feels right*."

I've never felt so pleased to be kinda dumb. So someone suckered me into believing something wrong. It's happened before, and it'll probably happen again. Smart people can do that shit with words where they turn you around, and somehow, you're agreeing with them even though you don't really. For Dani, this is something more fundamental. She likes to be able to break ideas apart and see how they fit together. For a moment here, the language of thought doesn't make sense anymore.

Tanner still refuses to believe it. I think she's mostly pissed off that the smarmy preacher with the soothing voice put one over on us. It's not until nearly three hours later that she storms into the training room where we're all half-heartedly sparring.

"It was bullshit! All of it." She glares at Dani and me.

"Welcome to the party, pal," I mutter.

"This guy." Her fist clenches at her side. "We're going back and I'm not going to listen to a word he says. I'm going to grab him by the neck and throw him in a cell. Then we'll cut him open and figure out how his brain works."

This is a terrible idea, Emma says. *Think of those powers in the hands of someone like the President.*

On the same page there. We have to do something to stop her.

"I'm going back to the church." Tanner shrugs on her ridiculous coat. "Are you two coming with me?"

"This is the world's dumbest idea, Tanny." I'm leaning against the wall. "What happens when he tells me to shoot you in the face?"

"You've got noise cancelling in your suit. Use it."

"We don't know how his power works," Emma says sharply. "Maybe you don't need to hear it directly. Mutant abilities aren't always straightforward."

Tanner cracks her knuckles. "We'll do a chain. I'll go in with noise-cancelling and take him into custody. If I don't come out quickly enough, then Chatterbox comes in and takes us both out. If they fail, their girlfriend can do it. And so on until the preacher's all bundled up." She gives us the lazy smile. "Either that or I can get on the phone to my bosses at EMID, and see how hard I get to screw y'all."

I don't like being backed into a corner, I tell Emma.

Be very, very careful. This has got to be a reckless-free zone, Dilly. The way you were when you came back was—

Yes, it was very fucking creepy. I hear you. EMID won't get their hands on the preacher.

Dylan, I don't mean…

That's why you pay me the big bucks. I'm the weird one with the sword. I'll do what's necessary.

Dani and I head down to the van along with Tanner and Jackson. We're all as silent as the big guy. I'm hoping for some magical get out of jail free card, like the thing that sometimes happens in a TV show when something comes out of left field and solves everything.

Not much chance of that in real life.

We're pulling out of the basement carpark when Emma's voice appears in my head. *They're gone. Both of them.*

I try not to give a physical reaction, but it's hard. *Did you do something?*

No, this wasn't me. Presumably they've gone somewhere but I can't tell individual mutants apart. All I know is there are none in the church.

Well, fuck.

You were always good at summing things up, Dilly.

It's both good and bad, I guess. We've lost him, but EMID can't get him. We've got to act this out anyway. Can't give Tanner any indication we know anything.

The van pulls up outside the silent church. There's nobody waiting at the door.

"Get us in, Marvellous." Tanner says. "Let's see your powers at work."

Dani never likes doing it on command, but she begrudgingly hits the pain sensor on her metal arm. The doors fly inwards with a crash. Almost immediately, the alarm starts blaring, whooping at full volume.

"Don't be so loud," I complain. "You're giving me a headache."

"We're so worried," the alarm system gabbles. "Everyone left in such a hurry. It was very disconcerting."

"Do you know where they went?"

"They wouldn't say! The Pastor was angry and shouting at everyone. All the servants ran around and did his bidding. Now they've abandoned the ship and I'm worried we're heading for disaster."

I place my hand against the door. "If you just quiet down and stop shouting, we can figure something out."

"Are you sure?"

"Yes, you poor thing. You've been through a lot. Now shhh, and we'll have a nice quiet look through and see if anything's wrong."

The alarm system cuts off with a gurgle.

Tanner gives me a thoughtful look. "Some useful powers in this team of yours. I know you're all loyal to that hellion, but if you ever want alternative employment—"

"I didn't think the US government was interested in sending muties to catch muties," I say, because I never know when to shut up.

"There are other opportunities," Tanner says, "like Jackson here."

Yeah, like Jackson with a big collar around his neck, who's never said a fucking word to us. He's exactly who I want to emulate.

"How you doing, big guy?"

He gives me a sad eyed puppy dog look. I can't tell whether it's because I called him *big guy* like a fucking asshole, or because he's under orders, or whether he can't speak at all.

"Me too," I say, and I'm rewarded by the surprise of a smile. It's not like a good morning sunshine kind of smile, but it's acknowledgement. I give him a nod and we fan out through the church.

As the alarm system promised me, it's abandoned. I stand on the massive stage and look out at the empty rows of seats. I think about all those people in the congregation listening to the preacher.

Do you think he was influencing them all? I ask Emma. *Making them hate people like us?*

I don't know. The cynical part of me thinks people need no encouragement to hate. Perhaps he makes it worse though. Infecting them, making them virulent.

Cheerful girl.

What worries me most is what he might have said to his daughter, Emma says. *Think of how you and Dani felt with only a small nudge to ignore something. What if he's put a deeper compulsion on her? What would it feel like in her mind?*

I shudder involuntarily. *Jesus, that's dark.*

Even if it's true, it doesn't make her less dangerous.

We can't kill her if she's brainwashed, Emma.

There's another pause. I wonder if she's talking to Dani or Alyse. *I know you can't, Dilly. That's why I'm glad Oni's with you.*

It always surprises me when you turn ferocious.

I have the same tattoo on my skin as you. Wraith and Reverie. I don't want any more names there.

One step ahead of the assholes. I'm trying to lighten the mood, but I don't think it works.

Dani finds me and we catch up with Tanner, who's carrying a laptop under her arm.

"We'll find this fucker. He says he's with Quietus, and EMID have a thick file on those psychos, so I'll pull that string and see what pops up. All you lot need to do is what you're told. Sit back and wait for orders."

Yes, because we're so fucking good at that. I scowl at Tanner's back.

"How did you really find him?" Tanner asks over her shoulder. "Bullshit aside. I don't buy this phone call explanation."

"We're foot soldiers." I grin at her. "Fetch says go check out a church, we go."

"Talk to her about it." Dani shrugs.

"I know all about Ms. Quick's power." Tanner shakes her head. "There's something going on. I'll figure it out, I promise you."

I can't sleep properly after the combination of being mind-poked by a mutant preacher and attacked by his assassin daughter. I get into a shouting match with Pillow over whether it's a sane reaction to trauma, then spend the next hour apologising. Now it's five in the morning and I'm wide awake. I decide to go for a run to burn off some energy. Except when I get downstairs in my old Cute Mutants uniform, I see that someone got to our building in the night.

Spray painted in massive letters across the front is the word *extrahuman*. It's been crossed out and *Earth for Humans* written underneath. There's some other shit about *muties go home* and *fuck muties* as well. It's not even interesting street art graffiti—just ugly drippy letters all over our home.

"I'm really sorry." There's a discarded can in the gutter. He rolls amongst damp leaves. "I find the sentiment awful, but I have little control over what they say with me. Perhaps I could rally my brethren and seek out the malefactors. We could make them eat their words, quite literally."

It would probably work, and the idea sparks something in me, but I'm so exhausted that it gutters and dies. Having sentient spray cans give the vandals a mouth full of paint isn't going to stop these people feeling the way they do.

Instead, I go inside and talk some painting supplies into helping me, then we work together to start cleaning the building. Naturally, the brush is much better than me, although it keeps up a running commentary the whole way.

"I understand I am built for a specialised purpose, but I am *far* more efficient than you."

"I already told you I'm grateful," I tell it.

"Oh, and I appreciate your compliments. I am simply commenting—"

"For the tenth time," I point out.

"—that I'm really exceptionally good at this."

"Is that paintbrush moving on its own?" I turn to see two kids and their Dad. There's a boy about ten or so and a younger girl. The boy's in school uniform and the girl has a headscarf on and cute little round glasses. The Dad's dressed like he's on his way to work. They're all watching me. I don't know how long they've been there.

"Yes, and it's very proud of itself."

The brush executes a number of fancy-pants swirls over the front of the building.

"See." I grin at the kids. "It's a showoff."

"How's it doing that?" It's a very good question from the boy. If I only knew the answer.

"What's a mutie?" Another good question from the girl, which gives me a chance to not answer the first one.

"I'm a mutie." I spread my arms wide. "Although it's a nasty word meant to hurt us. I prefer mutant. And that's how I'm making the paintbrush move. It's like superpowers, I guess."

"Like *Teen Titans*," the girl says. "Raven's my favourite."

"Something like that."

"Come on, kids." The Dad reaches out for the girl, who sidles away. "We've got places to be."

"But why do they say *fuck* muties?" The girl's dragging her feet.

"Leila, you know not to use that word." Dad frowns.

"Probably should've painted over that part first." I give a half-guilty smile. "Some people don't like us. They think we're scary and bad. They want us to go away."

The girl nods. "People don't always like differences. That's what Dad says."

Behind me the brush is enthusiastically slopping paint all over the word *fuck*.

"No, they don't. It doesn't make differences wrong though, does it? I think differences make the world more interesting."

"Me too!" The girl beams at me with gappy teeth. "I like your brush, and mutants too."

"We're not so scary. Some of us are pretty cool. You should see my girlfriend. She's got a metal arm."

"Ah." The Dad nods. "You're the two from the news. I think you're very brave."

"I don't know about brave. We're ourselves, and we don't know how to be anything else."

"Sometimes that's brave enough." He gives me a little half-bow. "Now come on, you two, or we'll be late."

"Bye, Mrs Mutant," the girl says.

"Fancy pants people call me Mx," I say, "but friends like you call me Chatterbox."

She laughs in delight. "My Mum calls me a chatterbox!"

Dad finally convinces her to walk away, except she keeps looking over her shoulder until she's around the corner and gone.

"There you go," the brush says. "The world isn't entirely full of villains, is it?"

CHAPTER FOURTEEN

’m sleep-deprived, paint spattered, and irritable when Emma bursts into the dining room. I'm alone and cradling my third coffee.

"The hotline," she says, breathless.

"I don't know what you're talking about."

"The new hotline, the one Gladdy announced yesterday." She looks at me. "You weren't paying any attention, were you?"

I sip coffee and scowl. "I was mind-controlled yesterday."

"As part of us being approachable, friendly, and there to support the community, Gladdy set up a hotline people can call to report suspicious mutant activity."

"*Fuck*." My coffee cup vibrates with indignation and slops hot liquid over the table.

"Fuck," I say in unwitting echo. "You may as well call us X-Factor. Mutants catching mutants."

"It's a way for us to get there first, before the cops or anyone who wants to take the law into their hands."

"It *also* encourages people to see us as suspicious. You can draw a line between X-Factor and Genosha, you know."

"I wish you and Dani would stop talking about that," Emma says quietly. Of all the group, she's the only one that's joined us in reading X-Men. She finds the inevitable conclusions terrifying. When I grew up, I loved the crazy powers and the found family. Now, when I read it as a literal mutant, I feel the sting on a deeper level.

"It scares me."

"Me too." She shakes her head, as if to dispel images in her mind. "Today's problem is a little more mundane. There are some girls causing problems at the mall."

I frown. "Mutant girls?"

Emma slides a tablet across the table. "Either that, or identical triplets. I *do* sense a mutant in that general direction."

On the screen is a snippet of video from inside one of the big clothing stores. A girl holds a metal rod and swings it around her head like a staff. She's got warm brown skin and a thick braid of hair that flies out behind her. Someone I would have sworn is the same person sits on the ground with a McDonald's shake. She lifts her head and sprays a glob of it at the person holding the camera.

A third, identical girl leaps into frame. "Fuck your Earth for humans, *assholes*." She slaps the phone away. The video ends with a blur.

"Someone graffitied that over our building today." I show Emma the photos I took before cleaning up.

"Ugh. Gross, but not entirely surprising. It's all over Facebook. It's a rallying cry for certain people. Obviously, some harassment like that has sent these girls over the edge. We need to deal with this."

"I don't want to go in heavy. No costumes, no Tanner."

"Agreed." Emma takes the seat beside me. Her eyes are serious. "Except you still need to be careful."

"Emma, you know me."

"Exactly." The ghost of a smile is on her face. "That's why we need to wake Dani and the others up."

In the end, the whole field team goes in: Marvellous, Moodring, Glowstick, Dragon, and me. By the time we get to the mall, tensions have escalated. The cops have arrived, and two officers shoulder their way through the growing crowd.

"Officers, wait," Marvellous calls.

They turn, but there's no flicker of recognition. It slightly annoys me, because how many smoking hot Korean women with metal arms are wandering around the city?

"We're with Jinteki." Marvellous shows the officer her phone, but gets a blank look in return. "The mutants from the news?"

"Ah, the one with the arm." The woman officer is taller than us, but I think she'd look down at us from any height.

"Yes." I grin like a smartass. "And I'm the one with the sword."

Her eyes narrow slightly as she looks at me, and her mouth twists in a little sneer. Sure, I'm not an impressive sight at the best of times, but I actually did my fucking hair today and have a light amount of makeup on. I'm semi-presentable, so fuck her.

"We need to call this in," her partner says. "We've only got a report of a disturbance, not a—"

"She's an extrahuman, which gives us jurisdiction." Dani's such a badass and can pull this off so much better than me.

"I'm still calling it in," the cop says stubbornly.

We walk around him and carve our way through the crowd. Nobody's noticed Oni flying overhead. Eventually, there's bound to be an international incident when someone figures out he's a priceless artefact, but I don't think anyone can *make* Onimari Kunitsuna do anything, not me and not the Emperor of Japan.

We hear the shouting first.

"Fuck you all! I'm a fuckering, no, fuckerting, no, *fucking* dangerous what's it called. Dead dead deadly!"

We reach the front and come to an abrupt halt because the girl from the video is there. She's taking wild swipes with the horror-movie kitchen knives she holds in each hand. Her eyes are unfocused, with huge pupils. I have no idea what she's on, but it's not good. She's dressed in the same clothes as the girls in the video, but they're more tattered and torn.

Behind her, two more identical girls have a security guard on the ground. One stands over him, swearing furiously, while another takes occasional wild kicks. These two look even more drunk and incoherent. Their clothes make them look like they've been on a ride in a tornado.

Further back, two more of the same girl are loading up shopping carts full of clothes. These don't seem as wasted, although their movements are frantic. In the doorway to the store, a sixth girl stands and watches. Her gaze darts around, as if she's looking for a way out.

"Back," the knife girl screams. "Stay the fuck back."

"Hey," I hold up my hands in the most unthreatening way possible. If she lunges at me with a knife, Oni will stop her.

"Oh, thank God you're here," one of the knives says. "This is a nightmare."

"Shh," I say. "Everything's going to be fine."

"This is nowhere fucking close to fine," the girl snarls. She briefly looks over her shoulder at the others. I suppress the urge to lunge at her, because we still have no idea what's going on. "Not fucking fine!" She turns back to me and puts one of the knives to her cheek.

"Listen, you don't need to—" I reach out to knife girl.

The girl in the doorway shudders violently and now two of her stand there. One's the original, and one is a wild-eyed version with hair in a prickly tangle and her jeans shredded.

"Not fine," the new girl says. She staggers across and clutches onto the knife girl. "Not fine."

"A copy, of a copy, of a copy," Marvellous says. "She's like Shitty Madrox."

"Who's Shitty Madrox?" Lou asks, because he never goddamn reads the comics, no matter how many of them I shove in his face.

"Madrox the Multiple Man." Marvellous slaps herself in the chest. "Every time he hits himself, he generates a duplicate. They can roam off and have their own lives. Except they're all pretty much identical, which is not the case here."

"I think these ones get crazier every time," Moodring adds, which seems a decent summary.

"So where's Madrox Prime?" I ask. "It's gotta be the most sane-looking one right?"

"Take out the first one and the others might disappear," Lou suggests. "Maybe she's animating them all."

"Or it might piss them all off to see their source destroyed," Marvellous says. "Maybe take out one of the clones first or—"

A loud squawk comes over our earpieces, making us wince in unison.

"The Cute Mutants," Tanner drawls. "Running around off the leash."

"Fuck off, Tanner." I say. "We're busy in the field."

"Yes, I figured that out. I'm not as dumb as you wish I was. You're out *without approval*. I don't think y'all really know what oversight is. It means you brats don't jump unless you've asked permission."

Marvellous scowls. "We're here now. So let's resolve this situation and then figure out—"

"You'll shut up and listen to orders. Do you know what those are? This situation will be resolved by executing the target. In public if you have to, but preferably in private."

"I hope execute is some kind of double-speak," Marvellous snaps. "This girl is confused more than anything."

"The reports I'm seeing have her brandishing weapons in a public place. Based on our experience back home, mutants only get more radicalised." There's a brief silence. "Regardless, you're going to do as you're told and put this mutie down. It's not the first one you've killed in public, is it?"

I watch Dani's jaw clench and reach up to turn my comm off. "Fuck Tanner. I'm going to talk to this girl first. Only do something if a clone attacks me. Dragon, Moodring, you're on crowd control."

Moodring shifts into one of her hulking forms. It's definitely easier for her than it used to be. I have a vague theory it's around closeness to Goddess, but I don't know how to test it without spending a lot of time cuddling Emma. I'm not totally averse to that, but—

"Stay back," Dragon roars and jets a blast of fire over the crowd. It's classic Katie overkill, but it sends them scurrying away.

It also freaks out the clones, and our Madrox Prime spits out another couple of bodies. The first makes it a few steps before collapsing. The other does nothing but stare into space.

The original girl puts her hands over her face. She slides down the wall until she's sitting in a heap.

"I just want to talk." I raise my hands over my head, talking to all the clones. "No tricks. You can keep the knives if you want, but don't use them. I'm coming over."

"Careful, you fucking *thing*," the knife one says, but makes no move.

I walk slowly in the direction of Prime, trying to appear as mild-mannered as possible. It's hard for me, because I've been told more than once I have the worst resting bitch face. I'm pretty sure what I'm doing is called leering rather than smiling, but nobody's freaking out so it must be okay.

The collapsed clone drags herself towards me.

I crouch beside her. "Hey. You doing ok?"

"Not fine," she whispers.

"I know." I want to touch her, but I know not everyone likes it. "Everything's shitty right now, but we're here to help." I pitch my voice loudly enough that Prime can hear.

"Help," the collapsed clone says. "Here to help."

"I'm a mutant too. An extrahuman. I'm here with my friends."

"Earth for humans," Prime says.

The clone on the floor reaches out, her shaking fingers touching mine.

"Come on." I get to my feet and help the clone up. Her skin is fever-hot to the touch and she's trembling lightly. Together we limp over to the wall and collapse down beside Prime. The other clone leans against me. There are tears in her lashes.

"They hate us," Prime whispers.

"I know." I glance over at her.

She bites at her bottom lip and her fingers worry at the cuffs of her shiny green jacket. There's a weird blurring of her whole body, and the stationary clone beside her disappears.

"We're not a superteam," I tell her. "Not really. We're best friends who can do weird shit."

Another blurring, and the poor girl leaning against me is gone too.

This is working. I sit beside her and keep my voice calm. "There are always going to be people who hate us. We can't change that, but being together makes it easier."

"How did you—" Her voice hitches. "How did you find that?"

"We started by adopting any stray mutants we find." I gesture at the others on crowd control. "Sometimes it's annoying, like Katie eats all the leftovers and Alyse leaves clothes all over the bathroom floor. I'm pretty much insufferable too, but if you want to come with us, we have plenty of room and Dani's Mum is a kickass cook."

"Really?" There are tears on her cheeks.

"Yeah, if you want to."

Prime blurs as if she's moving really fast in place, and when I look around there are no more clones. Dragon is still yelling at everyone to stay the fuck back. Glowstick and Moodring rush over to the security guard to check if he's okay.

I help the remaining girl to her feet.

"I'm Dylan," I say. "My mutant name is Chatterbox. It's nice to meet you."

"Skye." She fiddles with the end of her braid. "I don't have a mutant name."

"Don't worry. You'll get one. Inevitably, it'll be one you hate because everyone here has a troll streak." I link my arm through hers and take her back towards the others. "This is Dani, my girlfriend."

"You're the two from the picture!" Skye says.

"That's us." Dani smiles at her. "Mutantkind's queer ambassadors." She extends her metal arm and Skye shakes it, a tiny bit tentative.

"I'm bi," Skye blurts. "Like I've only ever dated guys but—"

"You're bi," I say. "We get it. It's cool. Do you have a boyfriend at the moment?"

She shakes her head vigorously and a copy of her pops into existence behind us. "I did, but he didn't like it when there were more of me. He made a joke about it at first, but he hated the other versions. They're angrier than me and they're—"

"It's cool." I pat her shoulder awkwardly. "Try to relax and keep the clones under control until we get somewhere quieter."

Alyse comes bounding over like the human incarnation of the *ooh, friend* gif.

"Alyse, this is Skye," I say. "And vice versa."

"You joining the gang?" Alyse asks.

"I don't know? I guess maybe? If you want me? But Dylan kind of said it was a place to crash and, um, well, I just don't know?"

"You can do whatever you want." Alyse leans in close. "Some of us are lazier than others, and some of us, like Dylan, are always wanting to run around and fight things."

Skye blushes and murmurs something I don't hear. The crowd is still growing, which means we should probably get out of here. Dragon leads the way, letting out a few curls of flame to ensure people stay back. It doesn't seem like necessarily the best way to conduct mutant-human relations, but it's badass.

"That was impressive, Chatterbox," Dani murmurs to me. "Ending that whole scenario without drama."

"Sometimes talking is the best weapon," I say, in an attempt at demure.

"I almost don't recognise you." She looks sideways at me with a smile.

"Is that a bad thing?"

"Not even the tiniest bit."

"What did you say to Tanner?"

"I told her we'd resolve the situation to her satisfaction." Dani pulls a face. "So now we have to find somewhere to stash Skye that's under Tanner's radar. I was thinking maybe with Pear's girlfriend Sarah? Although that's putting her family at risk, which isn't fair."

I turn to face her. "Or we do this the other way."

"What way?"

I raise one eyebrow.

"*Oh.*" A pause. "Well, I like *that.*"

CHAPTER FIFTEEN

"The situation's dealt with," Dani tells Tanner, when we're in Roxy about a block away from home. "Nice and quiet. Nobody'll ever find her. We'll be back in about thirty."

Skye shivers in the back seat, looking at us with big eyes.

"You wait here," I tell her. "Roxy will look after you."

The rest of us get out and Roxy makes a U-turn to drive away. I'm starting to regret not wearing our uniforms. Bulletproof and stab proof would be super helpful right about now. We're going to have to resolve this quickly.

"I am ready," Oni reassures me.

We approach the building fast when a hollow bang makes me pause. The reinforced front door is slightly bent outwards, as if someone slammed into it from the inside. I have an unpleasant suspicion that I'm exactly right.

Emma? What's going on?

There's no answer in my head.

I shift from worry to panic.

Another series of bangs comes from the door. It flies open, revealing Jackson framed inside. There's no expression on his face, although he's breathing hard. The skin on one arm is blistered and swollen, as if he got acid sprayed on him. Shit, I hope Maddy is okay.

We're all in a straggling incoherent line because once again I wasn't fucking prepared for different eventualities. I thought we'd get inside the building. I thought we had some time. How did Tanner know?

Katie leaps forward, opening her mouth.

Oni shoots through the air.

"Keep your goddamn sword away." Tanner appears behind Jackson. She's holding a tall figure in her strong arms, a long knife pressed against the line of a throat.

"Gladdy." Alyse growls. She's back in Woodland Hulk form but with even bigger thorny claws that drag on the ground. We're about twenty meters away from Jackson and Tanner. Oni falls back to hover beside me. I could try talking to the knife, but it's risky. If Tanner gets a second of warning, Fetch will wind up dead. We need to buy time.

Tanner looks smug, completely in control. "Take another step and watch your precious Fetch die. If Marvellous touches that magic arm of hers, or that wicked sword of Chatterbox's makes a twitch, it's all over. And Dragon, keep your damn mouth closed."

"Can you do it?" I whisper to Oni.

"I cannot guarantee it."

"It's your turn then, buddy," I whisper, barely more than a breath. "Pick your moment."

"You don't need to do this, Tanner." Dani keeps her arms by her sides. "We did what you asked."

Tanner gives a short laugh. "No, you didn't. First you left without telling me, and then you kept the clone girl alive against orders. Worst of all, you thought you could sneak back early and get the drop on me." She laughs. "Goddess was quite forthcoming when we had a gun to Ness Taylor's head."

I can't speak. My vision narrows to a point. Pear, I'm so fucking sorry. I didn't think this would—

"She's fine," Tanner says. "Sorry, they. They'll have a headache when they wake up. I see where you get that dirty mouth from, Chatterbox."

"You'll fucking die," I croak.

"Won't we all? Although you might meet your sticky end before I do. Now I'd like you to all back way the hell up. Jackson, go and get the package."

We obey, splitting into two groups and backing away like a retreating pincer movement.

"Be ready," I whisper to Marvellous.

Tanner strides forward, dragging Fetch with her. She glances back to check on Jackson, and that's when the spray can strikes. He leaps up from the gutter and discharges the rest of his contents right into Tanner's face. It covers her in a black mist. She recoils.

At the same time, Marvellous hits her pain sensor. Tanner's arms fly outwards, the knife twisting wildly in her grip and soaring free. Another hit on Dani's arm, and Tanner sails backwards through the open door like a rag doll.

Moodring sprints in, racing for Goddess, who we're all assuming is *the package.*

"Oni, don't kill Tanner. I want to talk to her first. Glowstick, Dragon, you look after Fetch."

I make it into the building just in time to see Jackson backhand Alyse across the face. The cracking sound makes me wince. The giant form of Hulk-Alyse flies across the room. Her claws scrape the ground, and she collapses in a whimpering heap. She's curled in on herself, a prickly ball. Hurt, but alive.

Jackson holds Emma in his other hand. She's hanging limp.

At least Tanner is down, sprawled by the elevator. One fucking problem solved.

"Oni, knock the big guy down."

The sword swings through the air but Jackson catches him by the blade and throws him into the elevator door with one whiplike movement.

"I appear to be stuck," Oni groans. He's buried up to the hilt. "Perhaps I underestimated this monstrosity."

"Fucking *perhaps*, Onimaru. Get your ass out of the damn door and do it properly." I reverse direction to get away from Jackson. I can fight, but not against something like this. I need another goddamn object to help me.

Jackson tosses Emma into the corner and leaps towards me, scary fast.

I fall on my ass. "Anyone fucking listening?" I screech. I have this brilliant flash of an idea that I need to leave objects lying around everywhere, like that kid in the old movie who fights off robbers with toys. I'm not going to get a chance to do it because this super-strength asshole is about to smash my head into a fucking—

Jackson stops in the air above me, almost close enough to kiss. He pauses there for a second or two, then slowly flies across the room. He lands below Oni with a crash.

I scramble to my feet to find Dani beside me. She's breathing hard.

"Ouch. Hurts a lot to move him."

Jackson struggles back onto his feet. There's still no expression on his face as he marches relentlessly towards us.

Dani's face twists. A ragged scream spills out of her mouth. She collapses forward, her metal arm braced on the floor and her other hand digging into the pain receptor.

Jackson is thrown backwards again, but with less force than before. As soon as he lands, he leaps up. He roars. I can't make out words, but he looks in almost as much pain as Dani. He struggles forward with each step as if he's walking into a powerful wind. Sweat beads on his forehead. His fists clench. The muscles on his arms stand out.

"You want me to roast him?" Katie calls from behind me.

"Let's try and find another way first. He's got Leash on him."

Katie's practically roaring. "Wow. Forgive me for trying to save your asses! There's such a thing as being too damn soft, Chatty."

"I'll show you fucking soft, Dragon, you asshole," Dani rasps. "I can do this all day."

"Yeah, fine." Dragon laughs and I feel the heat from it. "Tough bitches club. How's that?"

Dani grins and blood drips from her mouth onto the floor. "Better. A lot better."

It seems to spur her on, and Jackson slides back across the floor.

"Oh, that works does it?" I laugh and tangle my hand in the back of her hair. "You run this motherfucking world."

"Look who's woken up." Glowstick joins on my other side.

Fetch hangs off him, looking woozy. "Holy shit," she whispers. "This… Don't hurt him, Marvellous."

"Trying not to, but he's making it difficult." Dani spits more blood.

"I've never seen anything like this. He's been hurt so badly, but another mind has been overlaid. We need to get that leash off him. Chatterbox, can you talk it off?"

I've never picked up even the faintest glimmer of awareness from the odd metal construct around Jackson's neck. Still, I need to try. "Hey, is there anyone in there at all?"

Usually I can sense a tendril, even if it's closed to me or asleep. This is completely inert. We've talked before about figuring out the pattern of which objects are receptive, but a) I always find myself in insane situations like this and b) when I'm not, I mostly want to watch TV and make out instead, because fucking *priorities*.

"It's not alive." I feel an old familiar pulse of shame, like I've failed again. I push it down. Feeling sorry for myself won't get us anywhere. "You're going to have to do it, Dani."

"Dilly, I—"

"I know you can't slow him down and remove the leash at the same time. You won't have to."

This time, Oni doesn't hold back. He hits Jackson so hard on the back of the head, I'm worried we've killed him. The big guy crashes to the ground. Hopefully his super strength means he's got a hard skull.

"I feel great shame," Oni tells me. "Perhaps your cavalier attitude to life has rubbed off on me. I have acted in a way that is ill-fitting of one of my age and stature."

"Wow. Nice job blaming me. Everyone makes mistakes, buddy, and you came through in the end."

"Okay, let's see." Dani grits her teeth and closes her eyes. A few seconds tick past. "It's too complicated. I could tear it right out of his neck but that'll probably—"

"Rest," I say. "He's out for the count. We'll try again when you've recovered."

Dani limps over to Emma, who's blinking and looking around. I join her, and soon we're tangled up with the warm and soft figure of Moodring.

"I'm sorry," Alyse sobs. "It hurt so bad."

"Hush." Emma kisses Alyse's forehead. "Everything is okay. We're safe. We're together."

I don't know which of us is holding the others up. Katie throws her arms around me and then Lou joins in too.

After a moment even Gladdy is there, with the indignant figure of Maddy. "It's so unfair I missed the fight. I tried to spit at Jackson but—"

"Hush," Emma says. "We're hugging."

"This is the cheesiest fucking thing," Gladdy grumbles.

She's not wrong, but these moments feel special. It's not only a hug, it's something more.

You're right. It's beautiful, Emma tells me. *I wish you could see it the way I do. We're all connected, like there are tangles of light between us. Some of them are smaller threads, like between Katie and Gladdy. Then some are great tangled rivers, like the one between you and Dani.*

"Um," Dani says. "I feel weird. No, don't freak out, Dylan. This is a good weird. Some extra energy, like I'm fizzing."

I close my eyes. I can sense more objects around me at a greater distance. If I reached out—

"No." Dani taps my hand. "Let me do this. Keep your powers to yourself."

"This does explain why Alyse keeps getting more and more powerful," I blurt. "She spends so much time in proximity to Emma and—"

"Stop talking, please." Dani nestles her head into my neck. "I'm taking apart the leash. I can see every part of it and unlock the mechanisms."

I look over at Jackson, where the complex octagon shape around his neck unfolds like an origami construction. It spreads into a many-petalled thing and then detaches to collapse on the floor in a shower of metal shards.

"Done." Dani smiles through bloody teeth.

The rest of the group crosses to Jackson, but I stay holding Dani up.

Katie feels for a pulse. "He's alive."

"It might take me a while to recover too." Dani's face is unnaturally pale. "I feel exhausted, like I've been exercising for days."

"We pushed your powers too far."

"Need to see if he's okay," she murmurs, but her eyes are already closing.

I get Dani installed in bed and leave the others to deal with our prisoners. I need to hunt for Pear. I bang in and out of rooms until I find them in a spare room with their girlfriend looking after them.

"Hey, Sarah. You got here fast."

"Dylan Jean." Sarah looks up at me. "What the bloody hell has been going on?"

I reach out to stroke Pear's shaved head. "I wasn't here. This American asshole made a power play. I should've accounted for it and left someone else back. Is this one okay?"

"They're fine," Sarah says. "They were asking after you."

"Of course they were." I lean in to kiss Pear's cheek.

"This life of yours…"

"I thought they were safe here," I say bitterly. "Safer than in their house where anyone could find them, or with you where you might get dragged into my shit." I blink rapidly, trying to fend off tears. "How are your kids anyway?"

"They're fine." She makes a see-saw motion with her hand. "Annoying sometimes, as kids can be, but they're doing well overall. I think they're happy. Hazel has the picture of you and Dani on her wall. Tells all her friends that it's her step-sib and their girlfriend."

I raise an eyebrow at *their*, but I can't keep the smile off my face. "Sorry, but it's cute."

"Perhaps it is, but I'll be quite happy if she never gets caught up in your madness," Sarah says calmly.

My cheeks are hot. "I wouldn't want her in all this." I gesture wildly. "But I never intended to be here either. It just sort of…happened."

"Ness worries. They lie awake at three in the morning, covered in sweat because they dream of you dying."

"And I dream of my *friends* dying." There's ice in my voice involuntarily. "I'm trying to fight for a world where we can survive. And yes, I understand I'm not fucking there yet, and I get that Pear had a gun to their head. I know that's fucking inexcusable and shitty but I have to keep fighting or—" Words dissolve into something else.

Sarah puts her arms around me and strokes my back.

"Kid, what the hell are you crying for?" Their voice is croakier than usual, but I'd recognise it anywhere.

"I'll leave you to it," Sarah whispers, and pads out of the room.

I collapse down on the bed beside them. "I'm not fucking crying," I tell Pear, with what shreds of dignity I can muster. "You decided to wake your lazy ass up, did you?"

"Figured I'd milked being held hostage at gunpoint for long enough," they deadpan.

"She's not dead. Tanner, I mean."

"I'm glad. You're not a killer, Dilly."

Wrong. The gap between Dylan Taylor and Chatterbox grows wider every day. I'm worried that one day I'll look back and won't be able to bridge that anymore. Or maybe it would be easier that way. I'm still not ready to shatter the last of Pear's illusions about me, so I smile.

"Was it scary?" I ask.

"I was terrified." Their eyes meet mine and I flinch away. "Emma wouldn't stop talking and giving you away. Worrying too much about me, the silly girl. I tried to stop Tanner, but the next thing I knew Katie was waking me up."

I curl my knees up to my chest. "I'm sorry, Pear."

"I'm a tough old creature. I'll survive. I'm more worried about you. I don't want this to make you angry. Angrier."

"There's a whole world out there to do that," I say, but I remember the little girl in the headscarf smiling at me while I cleaned up graffiti. I think about Hazel having a poster of Dani and me up in her room. Not everything is terrible, and at least Pear's alive. We all are. There are bright sides after all.

"I'm glad you're okay." They pat my hand.

"I came out the other day," I tell them. "As genderfluid, I mean. To Dani. I haven't told anyone else yet, but I thought you'd like to know."

"A bit of everything then." They look at me fondly, almost too much love in their eyes to take.

"I don't know. It feels right for now. You said this thing once about how we're always becoming. I like that. Mutant doesn't mean changing once. We're always in flux."

Pear grunts assent. "Even me, taking on Tanner while armed only with a shitty attitude."

"Fucking badass."

Their eyes flutter closed again, and I sit for a while longer and watch them. Sometimes I try to map the lines of genetics and see where I came from. I'm a weird mix of my parents. I wonder where the susceptibility to having mutant abilities comes from. I wonder if we injected Pear with Emma's blood whether they'd transform too.

Listen to you, thinking about heritable traits.

It's you and Dani rubbing off on me.

We could try mutating your Pear if you want? I have to admit I'm curious about susceptibility and whether they'd have the same or similar powers as you.

This wouldn't have anything to do with determining what powers Teen Spirit might have? I ask and there's a brief silence between us.

Sometimes I preferred it when I couldn't read your thoughts.

Said anything more to your Mum yet?

We had an entirely pointless conversation where I apologised for accusing her of being a mutant. She seems happy to let the entire thing rest. Her confusion seems real so…

You think Fisher lied?

I have no idea, and I don't know how to find out the truth. One more mystery to solve, I suppose.

Sarah comes back in to watch Pear, so I wander off to find Dani. I end up in bed, curled around her body like I'm attempting to merge forms. Her breathing is shallow, and her skin is waxy. Emma's called in an ex-Jinteki doctor to check her out. The doc said Dani's fine and just needs rest, fluids, monitoring, and all that boring shit. Except I can't quite believe it. It's like the *Buffy* episode where they combine their powers and then a dream demon tries to murder them.

I'm exhausted myself, but sleep evades me. My eyes snap open every time they droop closed. I feel Dani's forehead and neck and wrist, looking for all the evidence she's going to survive.

At some point, there's a warm body turning in my arms and a mouth searching for mine.

"You're alive," I whisper.

"Even if I wasn't," Dani says. "I'd come back for you. Death can't stop true love, can it?"

"Cheeseball." I kiss her lips. "You think this happens every day?"

She pulls me tighter against her. I can barely breathe, but that's all secondary. We're both alive and all I can think of is making sure every part of her is still exactly the way I like it.

Unfortunately, the world has other plans.

"I thought you were supposed to be recovering," Gladdy says from the doorway.

"This is how I recover." Dani stretches her arms above her head and arches her back.

"Put some clothes on and get out here. Tanner's awake."

CHAPTER SIXTEEN

Dani and I end up talking to Tanner dressed in voluminous hoodies, because Gladdy was in too much of a hurry for us to get properly dressed. It feels phenomenally on brand for me, like ok sure, let's interrogate the woman who works for American Extrahuman Intelligence like two barely dressed urchins.

Gladdy, on the other hand, is impeccably dressed as always, in incredibly tight pants and a shirt that hugs her figure. She's made up and has her hair done. Is she trying to rub it in or what?

The room is empty aside from the bed that Tanner's handcuffed to. We did leave the mattress on at least.

"You killed Jackson." Tanner rattles the restraints like an angry ghost. "You stupid, stupid children. My government won't accept that."

"Guess again," I say.

"You've imprisoned him." She snorts. "Possibly even stupider. He won't stop until he's killed all of you. He may be pretending now, but he's biding his time." She tilts her head. "I'm listening for the sound of screaming."

"Maybe third time's lucky." I shrug inside my hoodie.

Her eyes dart from face to face. "There's no way you could remove the leash. Not even with your freakish powers, *Chatterbox*. And Marvellous is a large-scale telepath. You would have killed him trying to take it off."

"You're out of guesses," Dani says. "Let's talk about you and your mistakes instead."

"Also known as Tanner being a great big tactical dumbass," I chime in.

"Why did you do it?" Dani perches on the edge of the bed. "Why force the issue and demand we kill Skye?"

"Orders." Tanner sighs. "Not that you teenage disasters know what those are. Some of us who've been trained properly understand a little thing called the chain of command. My bosses told me that I needed to get you under control or terminate the programme. You may have noticed I don't like to fuck around."

"Didn't you read Dilly's file?" Dani asks. "Apparently they're not so good with authority."

Tanner sneers. "The whole situation with Bancroft and Jinteki stank. Things get out of control and when the smoke clears, everyone's dead but you. There was a lot of argument about whether it was accidental or deliberate."

"Somewhere in the middle," Dani says. It's true enough.

"You should have heard the arguments." Tanner's laughs sounds genuine. "A few of us said you were a dangerous global threat. The vast majority said there could be nothing to fear from a bunch of teenage girls."

"And what did you think?" I ask.

She flops back down. "Most of them have never been teenage girls."

I stretch out my hand and Oni floats into the room. He lands lightly in my palm and I swing him through the air. "So now you're our prisoner. Chain of command may be intact, but you failed fucking *spectacularly*. I'm guessing your bosses won't like that."

"She's scared of Quietus," Gladdy says from her position against the wall. "There's all sorts of fears in there. They call themselves God's warriors. The shields of the angels."

"The quiet ones," Tanner says.

"Bancroft wasn't a fan either." I frown down at the woman in the bed, who looks too comfortable for my liking. "What's the big deal about them anyway?"

Tanner looks from me to Gladdy and back again. "Quick's not in charge at all, is she? It's you, the feral one."

"The weird one with the sword." I go for a Dani eyebrow raise. "No, I'm not in charge. We work together. Sometimes we shout a bit, but it's a group effort."

"EMID thinks you're all under the sway of your psychic Fetch here." Tanner eyeballs Gladdy. "Why the hell do you call her Fetch anyway?"

"She's a mean girl." Dani smirks at Gladdy, who's glowering at both of us.

Tanner bursts out laughing again.

"Nice distraction," I say. "Why don't we get back to Quietus? They've got you and Bancroft scared, but our mutant preacher is in bed with them."

"They're fanatics," Tanner says. "Mutants are evil tools of Satan, sent to dethrone God and destroy His works. They'll do anything to destroy the abominations. I'd write them off as crazy people, but they've got far too much money. There are rumours that high-up EMID people are involved with Quietus, but I've never seen proof. Bancroft was right to be scared, and you should be too."

"Here's a twist," I say. "How about you switch sides and give us a line into both EMID and Quietus?"

"I don't think that'll work." Her smile shifts and she's suddenly quiet. "My younger self would curse me out for saying this. Your rebel setup would've been her dream. But if Quietus come for you, they won't stop until they own you or you're destroyed."

"We've survived this long." I think my voice shakes and ruins the effect.

"We'll survive further." Dani's voice is much firmer, and I want to break off a piece of that confidence. I have no idea where she gets it from. She's control girl and there's nothing controlled about this situation.

Tanner shakes her head. "I'd say you're either very brave or very stupid, but its probably both. When Quietus comes—" She breaks off.

"Any information you can give us would help," Dani says. "No matter how small."

"Call me cynical," Tanner drawls, "but I'll side with the powerful."

I get the sense she's playing games, so I turn and walk straight out of the room, with the others following. She can stew for a while longer.

"What the hell was that?" Gladdy demands, the instant the door closes. "You really want to work with her after what she did?"

"It's smart," Dani says. "She has more information about EMID than we can ever hope to accumulate. Swinging her to our side, even a tiny fraction could be helpful. Especially if Quietus do come, because they sound like—"

"Insert X-Men plotline here," I say irritably.

"Genosha," Dani says.

"Fuck." I flip my hood up and glare at Tanner's closed door. "We have to change her mind."

Dani says she's tired, which worries me, but she promises it's still exhaustion from Emma's power-up. I tuck her into bed and kiss her goodnight.

"If she starts convulsing or twitching or anything at all, you shout for me as loud as you can," I tell Pillow sternly.

"I shall take care of her as if she is you," Pillow says. "And I shall cradle her head the way you do on your breast."

"Jesus, Pillow," I say, and sleepy Dani wants to know what I'm Jesusing about. When I tell her, she starts laughing, so I threaten to smother one of them with the other. Once they're settled, I head off to the kitchen, because I'm starving. I'm hoping Dani's Mum will intercept me. I'll look vaguely pathetic and she'll cook me something delicious.

When I reach the kitchen, Mrs. Kim isn't there. It's only Lou and some dude dressed in Lou's B-Mo hoodie. He leaps to his feet and spills his glass of water everywhere.

"Oh, what a mess. Towels. Where are the towels? Dylan Chatterbox. Hello."

"Holy shit, you're Jackson," I blurt, because of course he is. I didn't recognise him without the weird muscle outfit, the collar, and the zoned-out look in his eyes.

"Introductions, yes. This is Lou Glowstick. I've met Lou. I'm ruining this, aren't I?"

"Not even close." I shake his hand and find the paper towels. Together, we mop up the water. He bumps hands with mine and flinches away. "I'm sorry. Really sorry. About everything. Especially the woman I hit. Alyse Moodring. Is she, you know, will she be okay?" His eyes fill with tears.

"She's fine," I say, aiming for encouragement. "She's tougher than she looks." Unlike you, I refrain from saying. Dude's been through a lot.

He wipes the tears from below his eyes with the tips of his fingers. "I'm sorry. Very sorry. Apologies, thousands. Is that too many? Speaking is, well, it's just—"

"They didn't even let you talk."

He shakes his head and puts the paper towel to his eyes.

"It was nice to meet you, Jackson," Lou says. "I'm sure we'll see each other around."

"Yes. Lou Glowstick. To meet you has been wonderful. I like you. You're kind."

"Uh, okay. Yes. Good." It sounds like Lou's starting to be affected by Jackson's conversational style, as he hurriedly puts his plate in the dishwasher and beats a hasty retreat.

"Pretty," Jackson says, looking down at his own empty plate.

"He's a very pretty boy." I can acknowledge this.

"Boy, yes. He is." He traces circles around the rim of his plate.

"So, are you doing okay?" I ask. "You know, with the collar out."

"Scattered." There's a flash of a smile. "Perhaps you can tell. Hard to collect all my thoughts and let them out."

"Yeah, I'm a bit like that all the time. I'm glad you're up on your feet. Someone give you a clean bill of health, did they?"

He nods vigorously. "Gladiola. Emma. They said to relax. Not easy."

When Alyse walks in, Jackson leaps up from the table again. "Alyse Moodring. So many apologies."

"Thousands," I chip in. "Possibly millions."

"You had the collar on." Alyse beams widely because that's what she does. "It was Tanner who was responsible, not you."

"Does it hurt?" Jackson fidgets and won't look directly at her.

Alyse prods her face. "I've got a sore spot on my jaw, but Dylan's hurt me worse in training."

"I have not," I say indignantly, although Jackson sidles away as if I'll randomly start punching him. I'm not sure why. As skittish as he is, the dude has super strength.

I make an important executive Field Team decision. "Right. I'm ordering pizza and we're going to get to know each other."

Half an hour later, the pizza arrives, and Katie and a single Skye have shown up. Jackson is slowly starting to act normal. The food arrives lukewarm and Katie heats it up with her breath while Jackson backs slowly across the room.

"Katie Dragon," he says. "You are safe?"

"Not if you ask Dylan," Katie says cheerfully, taking a slice and talking with her mouth full. "She says I'm a fucking menace."

"I say it as a joke," I assure Jackson. "Sort of. She's on our side."

"Our side?"

"Mutants." I gesture around the room. "All of us. We're one side. The other is the people who want to kill us or stick fucking mind-controlling collars around our necks."

"I was in a fight," Jackson says. "Someone hurt my sister. I tried to stop them but— My strength? I thought it was the police." He shakes his head.

"It was EMID who put the collar on?" I ask him.

"That was later. First, they sent me out to hunt. If I didn't find the muties, they'd hurt my sister."

"We don't use that word." I stare at him.

"Sorry." He blinks rapidly. "That's what they call us."

"I know. But we're not with them anymore."

"We're Cute Mutants," Skye says, super enthusiastically. When everyone turns to look at her, she blushes. "That's what Lou says."

"Some of us are cuter than others." Katie bats her eyelashes at Skye, who doesn't know where to look. "Like Dani."

"Dani Marvellous is very scary," Jackson whispers. "But when they had me hunting the, uh, the extrahumans, I was scary too. They made me wear a red suit. A demon mask. They called me Monster."

"Don't worry." Alyse pats his shoulder. "We'll give you a way better name than that."

"Yes," I say with an eyeroll. "Like Chatterbox."

"They made me hurt people," Jackson whispers, and I feel bad for being a jokey asshole. "My sister is a mutant, but her power is… She can change colour. Like a lizard. A chameleon. They locked her up. To make me do what they wanted."

"What happens if they learn we've freed you?" I ask, although I'm not sure I want the answer.

He shakes his head and his eyes fill with tears again.

"If we get through this, there's a long fucking to-do list." I can hear the edge to my voice.

"I don't understand."

"She means we're going to get your sister," Alyse says. "No mutant left behind."

It's an insane thing to promise, but it burns in me like a fire. When we took down Tremor, we said mutant justice for mutants. And we started this place with the idea of making a mutant outreach, but it's not enough. We need to go worldwide. It's a ridiculous thought to have when I should be preoccupied with Quietus, but I need hope beyond our next battle.

This can't only be about survival. We need to thrive.

"Earth to Dilly," Alyse says. "You ok in there?"

I nod. "We can't solve all the world's problems in one day."

"What problems?" Maddy appears in the doorway. "The only problem I have right now is you assholes ordered pizza and didn't tell me."

She takes the chair beside Jackson and helps herself to a slice in each hand. "Hi, I'm Maddy! My mutant name is Sourpatch, and I spit acid. You probably know that because I spat at you, and then you hit me. It still hurts."

"Jesus, Maddy," I say.

"What?" She shoves most of a slice of pizza into her mouth. "Where is the lie?"

"I am most terribly sorry, Maddy Sourpatch." Jackson flushes a deep red. "Tanner gave me orders and I was unable to stop myself. I did not wish to hurt you."

"It's okay. We fought these guys first too, then we made friends. Just like with you." She shoves another slice of pizza towards him. "Eat! If it gets cold, just get Dragon to heat it up." She beams at him. "Did these dummies give you a codename yet?"

He blinks at her like he's just looked directly into the sun. Maddy can have that effect.

"What have you been doing?" She looks around at us. "Codenames are important, right? What's your power? You're a strong boy, right?"

"Strength and, well, uh." He pauses and stares at the table. "Limited flight."

"Jumping boy," Maddy says with no small delight. "Call him Bounce! No, Tigger."

"The wonderful thing about Tiggers," Alyse sings, but she can't even finish because she's laughing too hard.

"How about Leapfrog?" Maddy asks.

"I like that one." Jackson looks sideways at Maddy in case she might spit at him again.

"What about mine?" Skye says. "I was thinking of something like Replicate, and Kate for short."

"Too cute." I wrinkle my nose.

"I thought it was supposed to be cute, like Chatterbox?" Skye asks.

Alyse snorts. "Chatterbox is definitely the cutest name."

I give her the finger. "What about Clone Club?"

"Yeah, I like that, and CeeCee for short," Skye says. It's kind of adorable how into it she is, but what's with the nicknames? Then I remember how Bianca used to call me Chatty or Chats, and my vision gets blurry.

Alyse notices, because of course she does, and she comes to sit beside me. I lean into her while the others talk and laugh and eat pizza. It's hard to take a clear breath when I think about how I'm responsible for all these people that we keep gathering around us. I take Alyse's hand and squeeze it hard. She slowly transforms into something stronger and more resolute, a woman of chrome and tinted glass that can weather the future.

We're going to do this, Emma says, presumably picking up on my distress through her always-on connection with Alyse. *Our species will survive, Dilly.*

I think you get fiercer by the day. Almost as much as me.

This is ours. I was the seed and you made it grow. I've watched you fight from the beginning, and I'll be with you all the way.

Cute Mutants, baby.

She giggles in my head. *It's still a weirdly accurate name.*

Finally the party breaks up and everyone drifts off. Jackson has a startled look as he gets towed off by Maddy and Alyse. He'll be fine, I think. Emma will keep an eye on him via the surveillance system.

I'm left in the dining room on my own, searching through news stories to find anything about Stabby-hands. She's one of way too many threats on our radar. Eventually, I find what I'm looking for. The mayor of a small North Island town was stabbed to death in his townhouse, along with his husband. It's being reported as a robbery, likely by drug addicts, but they can't figure out how the culprits gained entry.

It's no simple crime of opportunity and addiction. The preacher and his daughter are still killing queer people. We need to find them and stop them, before anyone else winds up dead.

CHAPTER SEVENTEEN

When I finally go to bed, Dani's body is loose from sleep and her kisses are warm. She's content to nestle in, drag my arm over her waist, and fall back asleep. Pillow hums softly beneath us. I don't think it's possible for my brain to stop whirring after the chaos of recent days, let alone knowing Quietus might be coming.

I think about making a to-do list of angles to try with Tanner, but Dani has both my arms trapped and I don't want to risk waking her up. Making a list in my head is hard, because I can't visualise the whole thing, and the words keep shifting.

My brain roams in weird directions, but I'm startled into focus by the sound of a metallic clang. I jerk upright, and Dani squawks beside me, reaching out to grab my arm.

"She has returned." It's too dark to see Oni, not even a gleam of his shape in the air.

"What are you talking about?" I rub sleep from my eyes.

"The one who wishes you dead." There's another sharp sound.

I fumble behind my head for the light switch, and squint at the brightness. The rippling shape of the girl unfolds above my head. I feel the breeze as Oni slices through the air. She's gone before he reaches her.

Violet. Her name is Violet. Maybe her mutant name can be Violent. God, I'm so funny in the middle of the night.

"Oni, remember we're trying not to kill her. In case she's controlled."

"It makes my job more difficult," Oni sighs. "Although I appreciate your regard for my skill."

"Why the hell won't she leave us alone?" Dani asks in a husky voice.

"We are those prominent queers."

I don't understand what Dani says next, because it's fogged with sleep. I can only make out the word "alone."

"Abominations." The girl's face reappears in the far corner of the room. "You even share a bed as if it was one sanctified by marriage."

"It's just sleep." I adjust Pillow behind me so I can sit up. "We didn't even *do* anything last night. Dani was too tired."

"What are you doing?" Dani's wide awake now, and cautious. "Are you trying to get us killed?"

"Not exactly." If she's trying to kill me, she's not killing anyone else, and it seems like Oni can keep up with her.

"Marriage is between a man and a woman." The girl's eyes are shadowy holes that watch Oni as he drifts back and forward.

"Number one, that's ridiculous bullshit. Number two, we're not married. Number three, I'm not even a woman."

"That's even worse," she hisses. "You against God's plan, defiling yourselves and each other."

Dani snorts.

"I love her. Defiled and all." I take Dani's hand.

"You cannot. This is not love. It is a mockery of God's design for you as a woman."

"Not a woman, we already covered that. But it *is* love. Listen. I care about her. I rub her back when it hurts. I make her morning coffee. When she's in pain, I'm in pain. She makes me happier just by existing. I feel *more* when I'm with her, and I'm capable of *being* more too. My eyes are drawn to her when she enters the room." My voice wobbles into something deeper. "I'm hungry for her."

"Monsters." The girl's voice is deeper too. She disappears in a flicker of twisted darkness.

I throw myself out of bed, not caring that I'm barely dressed. "Dani, with me."

She doesn't say anything but tumbles out after. I run for the door and bang it open.

There's no sound of screaming from the corridor. I look at the line of closed doors, but there's no sign of disturbance. Maybe it's so quiet because she's already murdered everyone in their beds. I run to the first door and bang on it. "Up, up. We've got a fucking breach."

Lou appears, adorably tousled and swaying. "What the *fuck*, Dylan?"

"Come with me." I head to the next door. Dani gives some incoherent explanation behind me.

Katie pops out further down the hallway, wide-eyed. "Dilly, what are you doing?"

Oni flashes back and forward down the length of the hallway from me to Katie and back.

"Stabbyhands." I'm still shaking. "She came into our *room*."

"What?" It's almost a chorus, spilling out of exhausted mouths.

"I'm not making it up," I shout. "She tried to kill us. Oni managed to keep her away, but he can't defend everyone in separate rooms. So we're sleeping marae style." Katie blinks at me. "Everyone on the floor! In one room! Get the fuck up to the training floor now!"

Between us, we rouse everyone including Mrs. Hall and Gladdy, who are the deepest sleepers. Nobody is dead or even hurt, which makes me shaky with relief. I manage to corral everyone up the stairs, despite their exhaustion and irritability. Oni is as agitated as me. The job of protecting all of us is too much.

We're near the top, when something cold prods my back. Oni slashes past and there's another metallic crash.

I spin around and stumble ass-backwards onto the stairs. My shoulder stings, and when I reach to touch it, my fingers come away wet with blood.

Dani clatters down to me.

"It's you." Violet's voice is low and fuzzy, like when one side of your headphones is broken. "You're the one marked for death, Dylan Taylor."

"You're cut, but it's not deep," Dani murmurs in my ear.

Oni blurs in front of me. "She hides, the cowardly creature."

"There is no need to protect your friends." She shows her face. It's briefly lit up by golden light and spattered with bloody marks, but flickers away before Oni can reach her. "I am not a monster, who murders indiscriminately. God has given me a target, and that is you."

"Don't trust you." I drag myself backwards up the stairs. Everyone else is up there. We need to protect them.

"You understand *nothing*. To you, God is a joke. I saw you smirking in church. Making light and whispering to your lover. Now you will suffer." Yes, that's fucking great. "You're the leader. The abomination that has forsaken your womanhood and dragged your friends into sin. You are the avatar of—"

"Yes, I get it, I'm the fucking Avatar and I'll metal-bend my sword into your stained-glass face if you don't shut the fuck up."

"I will not be mocked," she shrieks, her face splintering with crimson light. "Everything you are spits in the face of Almighty God. I am the weapon chosen to bring you down, and once you are gone, your friends will be free of the curse you've laid upon them."

Wow. I really am Stabbyhands' most wanted.

Oni lashes out and she folds herself away into nothing. This time she doesn't come back.

"Bloody hell." I stretch my arm up to feel my back and the movement makes it hurt. "Is everyone safe up there?" I shout.

I receive a chorus of mixed abuse in response. Ungrateful brats. If it wasn't for Stabbyhands being fixated on me, they might've all been carved up. I'm the tragic hero in this scenario, with the villain swearing an oath about my demise.

We're going to need to get more internal security cameras. Need to talk to Emma about that.

Oni's going to need to stay very close.

I slump down on the stairs. "Narrow escape."

"Your cut will be fine," Dani says. "It's only a scratch."

"Could've been a lot worse." I shiver violently.

Dani wraps her arms around me and holds me close until my heart stops thundering. "I'm alive for now."

"Oni and I will keep you safe," Dani says, very seriously, and then kisses my neck. "Love shook my heart like the wind on the mountain."

"What are you talking about?"

"Your little speech about love. It was more beautiful to me than any of Sappho's poems." Her lips trail a line of kisses along my good shoulder. "When did you get so sappy?"

"You came and I was crazy for you," I say, laughter curling at the edges of my voice. I've been waiting to use this one. "And you cooled my mind that burned with longing."

"I fucking love you," she tells me.

"Now that's my kind of poetry."

We share another handful of kisses, delicious and dizzying, then scramble up the stairs to join the others. I lie face down on one of the training mats, while Dani and Alyse dress my wound. Everyone else lies on the floor around me, talking among themselves before drifting off to sleep one by one. Oni does circuits of the room, yet there seems to be no further sign of my new friend. One more escape to add to my list. It's better to be lucky than good.

The next morning, we're gathered in the dining room. I'm eating my breakfast sandwich with no eggs, which

I'm pretty sure Mrs. Kim thinks is an abomination, but is actually so fucking good. Dani is eating my egg because Mrs. Kim *refuses* to make them without.

"Excuse me, Dylan Chatterbox," Jackson whispers.

"Mhmm," I say around a mouthful of sandwich.

"I don't want, you know, to be rude. Is this, uh, is Mrs. Kim, uh—"

"Did you want a sandwich, Jackson Leapfrog?" I ask him, once I've swallowed.

He nods and looks at the table.

"Excellent," Mrs. Kim says. "I hope you have more taste than Dylan here!"

"Yes, egg please," Jackson says.

Oni leaps up off the table and slashes through the air behind me. There's the now familiar chiming sound of steel hitting whatever the hell Violet does with her hands.

Everyone screams. Stools topple as people throw themselves off. There's an extra flurry of clashing between Violet and Oni before she disappears. At the end of it, we're gathered in a bunch, Oni whirling around our heads.

"Begone, filthy pet," her voice snarls from thin air. "You defend sin and vice."

"Sin?" Oni asks, although she can't hear him. "The greater sin is to deny love."

The faint shape of her face flickers into existence, high up on the wall farthest from us. The stained-glass patterns on her face are cool blues and greens, flickering like they're underwater.

"How is my love different from that of a man?" I ask.

"There are many kinds of love." The colours swirl and reform, delicate patterns of red and gold spiralling outwards from a bloodstained centre. "However, a woman, or whatever unnatural creature you term yourself, cannot feel romantic love for another woman. It is the work of the devil, giving rise to evil lusts in your heart."

"Nonsense," Mrs. Kim says, and I almost fall over at support from this unexpected quarter. "It is no different. My husband and I loved each other deeply for many years. I'll never forget the way he looked at me. I see the same in Joo-hyun's eyes when she looks at Dylan."

For a brief second I can't breathe. Dani's hand reaches for mine. I glance over to see tears in her eyes.

When I look back at Violet, she's gone.

"Thank you," I say to Mrs. Kim, but she's focused on breakfast and I'm not sure she hears.

The next time Violet tries, I'm in the bathroom. She appears on the floor and Oni stabs down viciously between my feet.

"Jesus fucking Christ," I squawk, which is probably not the right language to use when dealing with an irate religious assassin. "This is the worst sin of all. You can't attack me while I'm on the toilet!"

"You must die." She reappears on the ceiling now, Oni waving in front of her. "I cannot allow you to keep existing while you stand for such wickedness. Your bright symbol must be snuffed out."

"You can't stop me loving Dani. Even if you kill me. You can't break what we have, not with a thousand swords."

"You're the one with the sword," she says, confused.

"It's a movie reference. You're probably not allowed to watch movies either. Too much sin."

"Don't mock me!" She flickers away and reappears on the back of the door. "There is no need to ridicule what I believe."

"What you believe is crazy patriarchal bullshit," I snap at her. "It's bigotry and hurts people all over the world. You're on the side of the assholes. Mockery is the least of what you deserve."

"You're an awful person," Violet spits. "I don't know what your immoral lover sees in you."

She flutters away, while I sit there frowning. Aside from *immoral lover* sounding kind of hot, that was a bizarre exchange. I hope she's keeping her word about me being the target. The place could be full of dead people by now and—

"Oh fuck." I scramble out of the bathroom to find Dani waiting for me.

"Is everyone okay?" I pant.

"As far as I know." She frowns. "Jesus. Was she in *there*? Are *you* okay?"

"Yeah. It was mostly talking. I mean, she tried to stab me, but it felt a bit half-hearted." I push my way back in to wash my hands while Dani leans in the doorframe.

"Dylan. Please don't take this lightly. I know you've survived up until now but—"

"Oni will protect me." I fill Dani in on the details of the conversation.

"It sounds almost like she has a crush on you."

"Uh, yeah." I dry my hands and glance around the room. "I'm sure the crazy homophobe religious assassin is desperately in love with me."

"She might be. Repressing feelings and all that. Plus, you're very adorable so I can't exactly blame her."

"I don't *want* her to have a crush on me. It's super weird."

"Believe me, I like it a lot less." She frowns at my expression. "Not because I'm jealous! There's a mutant assassin after the person I love. How am I supposed to relax?"

In training, we're trying to get a handle on Skye's powers. Whenever she's stressed or anxious, she manifests clone bodies. Alyse can easily scare one out with a horrifying transformation, and she's so nervous about Katie spitting fire that I've had to make the little brat promise to stop jump-scaring her.

All the clones have their own personalities. The first dupe is a polished, poised version of Prime. Skye Three is pushier and more aggressive. Four and Five will pick fights with anyone, and Skye Six is almost entirely feral. She's a hyperactive, foul-mouthed mess who's obsessed with knives and stabbing. I think I like her best. Seven is like a sloppy drunk, Eight is a sad bb who just needs cuddles, and by the time you get to Nine she mostly stares at the wall. The trick for combat will be reaching the wild ones quickly.

"I wonder if you can get them to come out on your own." I frown at her and she looks at her feet. "We can't spare someone to be your own personal scarer. But it's looking good, CeeCee. I think we can work with this."

She smiles in relief, but the next second she screams. All eight of her duplicates stagger into being around her.

Something stings my neck, while Oni soars past over my shoulder.

"What was that?" I slap my hand up, and it comes away smeared with blood. Again.

"I am terribly sorry, Dylan," Oni says.

Dani reaches me, tilting my head forward. "Another scratch." She winces. "Maybe a little more. That was too close, Oni." She takes me by the arm and leads me out of the room.

"Far too close." The sword circles watchfully. "Dylan, I wish permission to engage her properly. I believe I could defeat her."

"No, don't kill her for fuck's sake. She's controlled, like we were."

"You're sure?" Dani asks.

"Not a hundred percent, but like…she's chosen to focus on me hyper-specifically. The one person most protected. We're having conversations. I think she's finding a loophole in her father's control."

Dani hugs herself. "That's a wild theory with zero evidence. Meanwhile, look at this cut on your neck. If Oni is a fraction of a second late…"

"Patch me up first, tell me off later?" I ask piteously.

Emma does the medical stuff, while Dani fidgets and asks me nearly a trillion times if I'm okay. It's right near the wound I got from Fisher, so eventually I'm going to have this wicked badass scar around my neck that'll look like I got choked out by Azula.

Dani climbs up on the stretcher and nestles into me. "We're not done with this conversation. About you and your assassin admirer."

"A victim of her father." I poke at my dressing. "Maybe."

"I understand you have this thing about saving *every single mutant* but this…"

I gaze at the ceiling, where the spreading colours of a stained-glass face hover. It's greens drowning in blues, a pattern too complex to make out the details of.

Oni flashes up. Violet doesn't react fast enough, and the tip of his blade punches a hole in the design on her face. Tiny individual panes shatter, replaced by a red stain that ripples outwards. Her eyes widen for a moment and then she's gone.

"I thought we agreed—" I snap.

"She drew blood from you, so I made it reciprocal." Sometimes there's no arguing with Oni.

Violet reappears and this time the sword stays a sensible distance between us. Her cheek is a tangled mess of bloody glass fragments.

"That was painful." Violet floats by the ceiling and makes no move.

"A lesson to not fuck with my girlfriend." Dani grabs at her metal arm. A scalpel flies from a tray of medical equipment to hover closer to the floating face. "Why can't you leave Dylan alone?"

"She is an abomination." The girl's voice is almost too soft to hear. "Marked for death."

"Yes, but do you *want* me to die?" I ask.

"Want is a complicated thing."

"That's not a fucking answer," Dani says hoarsely.

"I like this situation no better than you." The dark eyes blink solemnly at us. "I wish it was over."

"Does your father control you? Did he command you to kill Dylan?"

"There are many things I cannot say, so let me tell you some simple facts. I have attacked. I have failed. I will return. Protect your lover. Perhaps I shall fail again."

The dark eyes flicker away, and she's gone.

"It needs to be gloves off, Dilly. She just told you she's coming back."

"And that she'll fail again. This is a *loophole*. She's found a target she can't kill, and she'll keep battering herself against me rather than attacking anyone else. I think she's on our side."

"I hate this. I fucking *hate* it. You being this target standing up in front of everyone and taking all the heat." Dani gets off the stretcher and paces around me. "You can't save everyone."

"Remember how it felt being mind-controlled, Dani?"

She pauses, metal fingers trailing along the edge of the stretcher.

"Imagine if the thought your brain kept slipping towards was compelling you to murder people." I slide off the stretcher and lean against her. "I know you hate it. This is a terrible thing. But she's working within her father's control. I think she's brave."

"Brave." Dani huffs breath through her teeth. "If this shit gets you killed…"

CHAPTER EIGHTEEN

e head downstairs and find Alyse plying Emma with cake, which she's absent-mindedly eating as she watches screens of data. Honestly, every time I come in here, there are more damn screens. It's possible they're multiplying on their own.

"I think I've got a line into Quietus," she says. "They're not officially associated with EMID, but Tanner's right—they have people in common. Quietus tap into both private and government funding, which is scary, because that's a lot of money on offer. Even worse, they have ties to a whole bunch of other military companies, weapons manufacturers, and research labs."

"Breathe, babe." Alyse rubs her back and Emma reaches one hand up to pat her.

"Quietus is run by this man." An image appears on the screen of an older white guy in a suit, wearing black-framed glasses. "His name is Eli Crane, and he's also the pastor of this church." Crane's picture is replaced by a large glass and steel building. A massive statue of an ornate cross stands outside it, even taller than the structure itself.

"The Purifiers," Dani and I say in unison.

"Essentially, yes," Emma says. "He's our William Stryker. I'd show you clips from his recent sermons, but it would only make you angry. You already know the gist."

"Mutants are the scourge of the devil." I glare at the screen. "Do we have proof of the connection between our pastor and this one?"

Emma taps, and another image appears on screen. It's Eli Crane and Pastor Mike, shaking hands. There's another shot of them standing outside a private jet and one with a bigger group, including Violet aka Stabby-hands. It's still hard to reconcile the beautiful young woman with the ghost-pale thing trying to kill me.

"I hate how he's willing to associate with mutants as long as they're bigots or murderers." Dani fidgets with her DNA spiral necklace.

I tug on mine in echo. "My guess is Crane will use them as long as they do his bidding. Same way Yaxley were happy to use us until we stood up for ourselves."

"Gloomy Dilly," Alyse says. "Do you need a massage too?"

"I need to live in a world less shit than this one." I scowl at everyone, as if it's all their fault.

"I'm not done with the bad news." Emma rolls her shoulders. "They've been loading up a plane with dudes and gear, and there's a flight in progress to New Zealand. They could be coming for some entirely unrelated reason but…"

"Except for the fact that Tanner's gone dark," Dani says. "So presumably EMID turned to their pet psychos and said how'd you like a *Lord of the Rings* tour? And while you're there, you mind murdering some mutants for us?"

"Now who's gloomy?" I lean over and swipe a piece of Emma's cake. "We've got advance warning. That's better than being blindsided."

"So what do we do?" Alyse asks.

"First up, we have another little chat with Tanner." I try and crack my knuckles menacingly, but they don't co-operate. "This time, not so friendly."

I barge into the room, bouncing the door off the wall. "Good night, Tanner. Sleep well. I'll most likely kill you in the morning."

"What the hell are you talking about?" She jerks upright, pulling on the restraints.

"What I said. I'm going to kill you in the morning. And it's like eleven, so we're on a deadline."

"What's changed?" I can see Tanner testing the cuffs that hold her, probing for weak spots.

Oni hovers above her, slowly turning until he's pointing down.

I lean over the bed. "To be accurate, it'll be Oni who kills you. He's allowed to make his own decisions."

Tanner doesn't take her eyes off the poised blade. "Did Oni kill Bancroft?"

"No." I smile at her. "We did that one together. That was personal. This one not so much, although you did put a gun to Pear's head, so maybe I *will* do it myself. There are scissors in a drawer downstairs who are weirdly bloodthirsty. I might use them."

"You're on your own." Tanner's wary. I like it, even though I probably shouldn't.

"Sharp observational skills like that are probably why you got your job at EMID."

"I assume there's something you want from me." She struggles into an almost-sitting position, trying to regain some measure of composure. "Hence the threats."

"Quietus is coming, like you said."

Her nostrils flare. "You want information."

"You won't join us, so it's all you're good for. It's basic fucking, what do you call it? Calculus? If you don't want to help, and you won't provide information, you become a liability."

"There's a third option," Gladdy says from the doorway.

"Fetch, I can do this alone." I feign irritation. I'm not the best actor, so it's lucky some of it is genuine.

"Give her up to Quietus. Trade her."

"For what?" Tanner snorts. "You think they'll be pleased to get one EMID agent and go on their merry way without scooping up Emma?"

"One EMID *traitor*." Fetch lays it on thick, but she's got some power behind it.

Tanner shudders. "I'll tell you what I know. Quietus is an abbreviated version of Quis ut Deus. It means *Who is Like God*, which is the phrase allegedly written on the shield of the Archangel Michael, God's warrior."

"Sounds like a bunch of nutty religious bullshit," I say. "What do they fucking *want*?"

"Mutants dead." Tanner looks directly at me. "They want a war between mutants and humans, and they want it now while there's a decent chance of wiping mutants out."

I shiver, and Tanner notices.

"You're fighting a losing battle, Chatterbox. Your boy Tremor? He was a problem. One you fixed—in fine fashion, if you ask me—but a problem nonetheless. Back home, we've got a lot of Tremors. One guy we tracked down? His mutant power was to explode."

"Seems a pretty shit power," I say.

"Yes, and he was the one who caused the situation in Orlando at the theme park."

"That was a mutant?" I'm don't really follow the news, but there's no hiding from incidents like that one. There were so many dead, so much destruction. "I had no idea."

"There's enough dangerous ones out there that it scares people. I saw Jackson punch a guard's head into mist when he was trying to rescue his sister."

"Maybe they shouldn't push mutants into situations where they're forced to lash out," I say.

"Then we're tiptoeing around, hoping we don't piss off all these wandering weapons. If we do something the muties don't like, maybe they'll rise up. It ain't practical and it ain't sustainable, living in fear of potential monsters."

It makes my stomach clench. I can't see a way out of this. "What if we took ourselves away? Made a mutant nation. Is that something we could give EMID to keep psychos like Quietus off our backs?"

"You're a smart kid," Tanner says, and I want to punch her condescending mouth. "What you and your friends have done, it's impressive and it's damned terrifying. I read the early reports from here. You were the one they identified as the threat, but I think Bancroft got you wrong. You're a damned bleeding heart.

A visionary. You say mutant nation and I see the look in your eyes."

Wow. I feel seen. I don't like it, especially coming from Tanner. Of course I want the mutant nation. It's not *only* the comics. It's the survive vs thrive thing. We need a place to call our own. Where we can be safe. Frustration wells up in me and I slam my hand against the bed.

Tanner smirks.

Gladdy's been watching Tanner thoughtfully this whole time. "Mutants in their own nation is better than a war, surely."

"Depends on your point of view." Tanner grimaces. "There's this group back home. Top secret. We've kept them out of the media as much as possible, despite their best efforts. It helps to have deep pockets. Anyhow, these folks call themselves Haven. EMID's worried they're trying to form a mutant nation. We've been stopping them. Brutally, in many cases."

"You sound so proud." My voice is barely loud enough to carry to her. It's depressing, quite honestly. Not about others out there fighting for our dream, which is cool, but how Tanner speaks so matter-of-factly about shooting it down.

"Might be your dream, but the mutant nation is a nightmare for EMID. They see it as a time bomb. It might start off with campfire songs and Kumbaya, but what they see is a future invasion led by powerful weapons they don't know how to stop. You don't want to know what Quietus says about the whole thing, fanatical assholes that they are."

I close my eyes and tip my head back against the wall. I don't know how to answer the fear the humans have of us. The future is a weapon aimed at our throats. The only options seem to be die or fight, and the second might lead to the first.

"I like you, Chatterbox," Tanner says, breaking my train of thought. "I think you're doing the best you can in a shitty situation."

"Don't patronise us." Gladdy crosses to the bed and looks down at Tanner. "It's time to talk about Quietus."

"Fine. They'll come at you like a video game," Tanner says. "Wave after wave until you're overwhelmed, and there's no save point."

"Let's focus on the first wave then."

"Perfectly logical. They'll come at you with men and drones in the early hours of the morning. They'll do it nice and quiet, since blowing up buildings doesn't go down well. Oh, and they definitely want to lay hands on your Goddess. Odds are excellent that they'll infiltrate the building to try and take you out and kidnap Emma. On the other hand, they know you've got strong offensive capabilities so they might come in hotter and heavier than usual."

My head is immediately a whirl of tactics. "We don't want to fight in the streets."

"That would make you very unpopular," Tanner agrees. "Your best chance is luring them inside and using this place as a killbox. It's perfect for it."

"What do you think?" I ask Gladdy.

"Seems helpful." Gladdy stares into Tanner's face. "I believe her. She's been telling the truth this whole time."

Yes, maybe it's the truth, but the picture it paints is a shitty one. Gladdy acts like this is a victory, but I can't see it that way. I picture Wraith, standing barefoot on a frozen shore beside me. The only way I can make her death mean something is to find a world where she wouldn't need to die. The path to there is something I can't fucking see. It's filled with enemies and blood from this angle, under the looming shadow of some ass-hole archangel.

Fuck him and his sword. Two can play at that game.

Quietus are coming. We're going to fight.

"There you go." I pat Tanner's leg. "Good work, Tanner. Sleep well. I'll most likely kill you tomorrow morning."

"You're sure she was telling the truth?" Dani asks, once Fetch and I report back.

"Of course not." I'm curled in a chair with my legs hanging over the side, the model of anxiety Dylan.

"I'm sure," Gladdy says calmly.

"What if they drop a bomb on us from miles up?" Emma asks.

"They won't, because a private military corporation can't bomb a foreign country—at least not that one." Gladdy sounds very confident. "And because according to Tanner, they want you, just like Jinteki."

Emma gives me an uncomfortable stare. "But what if?"

"Maybe I can talk it out of exploding," I shrug.

Fetch scowls. "That sounds like a fucking terrible plan. You're not going to have much time to charm it. Bombs don't saunter down gently out of the sky."

"Well you're not going to convince it to turn itself around, are you?" I glare at her.

"If Emma boosts me again, I might be able to move it." Dani runs her fingertips over the metal plates of her arm and fiddles with the joints. "Might cost me an arm or a leg."

"You're not going to lose another fucking limb," I growl. It's hard to breathe. I stand up and start pacing the room. "I told you they're not going to bomb us any-way, because they want to capture Emma."

Emma swings her legs, perched on the desk. "We need to think about these things."

"Well I doubt Jackson can punch it out of the sky. Maybe he can fly up and catch it, then throw it away? We need to put him through his paces." I resist the urge to hit the wall. "Maybe a boosted Dragon can fry it or a boosted Sourpatch can melt it. We need to practice pumping up people's abilities to see what's feasible."

"Dani's still the most likely option, like it or not," Fetch says. I really do almost punch her, especially because Dani is sitting all Zen-like as if it's completely fine. I know she's her own person and I can't make her do what I want, but it's extremely fucking annoying.

I'm trying to figure out a way to talk without shouting when Emma jumps as if she's been stung. "Alert! My guy at the airport says a big private cargo plane just landed."

"Your guy at the airport?" It's not just me gaping at her.

"I paid a guy to message me if any unusual flights came in." She blinks. "What? I literally put a line item in the budget that said airport monitoring and you signed it off, Gladiola."

"Not important. What did your guy say?" I ask.

"He says a Galaxy—I assume that's a type of plane? Oh look, Google says yes—touched down ten minutes ago. There's the Quietus logo of a sharpened cross on the tail. Let's stab everyone with Jesus."

"Focus," Alyse says softly.

"We need to get downstairs. I'm in all the traffic cameras, and there are a bunch near the airport which might give us a view. We'll at least see when they start moving."

"In the cameras." Alyse strokes Emma's hair. "This is why you never sleep."

"I've been in the system for weeks, and it's been very boring. I'm glad it's come in handy."

We clatter down to Emma's lair and she pulls up feeds on various screens. The roads around the airport are busy with late afternoon traffic, but the main thing we're focused on is the big plane in the corner of one screen. It's hard to make out because of the distance, but the logo on the tail definitely looks like a cross.

"So they really are here." Gladdy hugs herself tightly.

I try for a smile. I try not to think about the word *killbox*. "Showtime," I say.

CHAPTER NINETEEN

The first thing I do is pace my way upstairs.

"You need to go to Sarah's," I tell Pear, when I find them working in their bedroom. "It's not going to be safe here."

"Why? What's happening?" Their eyes watch me calmly, but I see their hand twitch over their laptop keyboard.

"It's not just you. Mrs. Kim and Min-jun and Emma's parents need to leave too. All the civilians."

"Dylan." They take a deep breath, like they're carefully selecting the right words. "I don't like you talking about civilians as if you're not one yourself."

"I'm not a civilian." I don't have patience for this. "I'm not even fucking *human*. Pear, these are the Purifiers and they're coming for mutants. I need to be able to fight them without worrying about you."

"I hate this." They reach out and take my shoulders. "You still look like my Dilly. I don't understand how we got here." They pull me in and hold me too tight.

"I know I can't stop you and this isn't your fault, but you need to pull through this, okay? This isn't a comic book, and you can't act like it is. You need to be smart and ruthless."

Not sure exactly how much they know about fighting armed religious extremists, but thanks for the fucking advice, Pear of mine. I pull back so I can look them in the eye. My hand goes to the tattoo on my arm. "We will. I just need you to—"

"I know. I'll clear out of here and take the others. What about Karen and Steve?"

"Who?" I gaze at them blankly. "Oh, fuck. The other mutants. Do you know I completely forgot they existed? Don't tell anyone, or it'll make me look like an even worse leader." My brain spins frantically. "Let's keep them around. Maybe they've got hidden talents and besides, if Quietus can track mutants, I don't want them following Hungry Boy to you."

"Dilly." There are tears in their eyes. "You have no idea how difficult this is. You're my baby. You'll al—"

"Don't fucking quote me that creepy book about the parent sneaking into her kid's bedroom at night," I tell them. "It's not cute. It's weird. And besides it's you who raised me to give zero fucks and not lie down in front of assholes."

"I didn't phrase it exactly like that." They've got a tiny smirk, so I got through to them.

"Go. I've got lots to do." I plant a fierce kiss on their forehead. "I love you."

"I love you, Dilly," they say, but I'm already moving out of the room, because if they see tears in my eyes, they won't fucking leave.

I head down to Kitty Pride and Steve, who are in the little common room area between their two bedrooms. There are four cats perched on the chair along with Kitty and one on the windowsill. Another wanders up to me and curls itself between my legs.

"Chatterbox!" Kitty says. "I can't get up, because of the furbabies, but I wanted to tell you how much we appreciate you rescuing us. Don't we, Steve?"

"Yes," Steve rumbles. I'm pretty sure he's bigger than he used to be, but he doesn't look healthy. "Thank you."

"Are we managing to keep you and your extra mouth fed?" I ask him.

"Ness brought all the garbage from around the neighbourhood," Kitty says happily. "Steve's been munching away. Sometimes Katie and Maddy come in to feed him. He doesn't like to feed himself."

"What if it bites me?" Steve asks mournfully.

Have you looked at Steve? The mouth guy? I ask Emma.

Not since we brought him in. The doctors didn't know what to do, but they said he was healthy.

I think he's growing.

Growing how? She sounds distracted.

Like changing shape. He's taller and broader and there are lumps on his shoulders.

If he's eating all this garbage it has to go somewhere.

What if he transforms into something else? Something fucking scary?

While I'm desperate for more things to worry about too, you might want to come down. They're on their way.

I pause in the doorway. "We're probably going to have some unpleasant company this evening. Don't worry, we'll lock this area down tight and you'll be safe."

"Is there anything we can do to help?" Kitty asks.

I don't really want to put the cats in harm's way, and I don't know what Steve can do aside from maybe eating Quietus agents. Even then he'd want someone to hand-feed him. I shake my head. "We've got it under control."

Two hours go by, and the Quietus invasion is still dicking around at the airport. Emma's random sur-veillance guy Marcus keeps sending through pictures, but we're not getting any new information. A bunch of people in black combat gear stand around in small groups. It's all very chill right now, but they're going to come for us. It's a weird feeling. I can't stop pacing, even though everyone has told me to sit down.

Emma is clearly fed up with me. "The best thing any-one can do right now is sleep. Be as rested as possible when this shit goes down. If Tanner's right, we've got hours."

I lie down in our quiet little room with Dani beside me and close my eyes. There's no way I'll sleep with everything going on. I'm still tense from the conversation with Tanner, let alone the fact we're about to fight paramilitary soldiers.

"Shhh." Dani yawns. "Stop muttering. I'm sleepy."

Seconds later, her breathing smooths out into something deep and rhythmic.

"It's so unfair," I tell Pillow. "She has galaxy brain but can still sleep. Whereas me, constant dumbass, lies awake thinking dumbass things."

"I don't like you saying negative things about yourself. It's a very bad habit."

"Fine, yes, I'm a terrible person."

"Sometimes I think you deliberately miss the point."

I bury my face in her. "I want us all to survive this. Is that too much to ask?"

"You're far more likely to survive well-rested, with a positive attitude, and in the company of your friends."

"I think I'm going to be sick," I say distinctly.

"Whassat?" Dani murmurs beside me.

"Go back to sleep." I kiss her forehead and slump back down onto Pillow. "How do I not panic about this?"

"You trust your friends," Pillow says. "You believe in your team. You listen to me."

She sings one of her soothing, wordless songs that really does help to disentangle my thoughts. We are a good team. I won't be adding any more names to the list on my arm. We'll do what it takes, me and my friends, and my beautiful damn Pillow. It'll be just like—

I wake with a start. Emma is shouting in my head.

Everyone get down here now! It's happening!

It's somehow become two in the morning.

How urgent is it? I ask.

Costumes, she says. *No showering together. That's your clue on timeframes.*

When we make it downstairs, Emma's hunched over the table, the chair kicked back against the wall.

"Not a good start." She wipes her hand over her face. "They've sent in the drones. Big fucking drones with surveillance and light weaponry poised over our heads right now. All mine are back in here hiding. It's going to give them a massive advantage. They've taken out the cameras on the roof and—"

"I've got it." Dani puts her hand to her metal arm. "Shit, I can't even reach them. Maybe if I get to the roof?"

"Let me try first," I say. "Better if we can talk them out of attacking us."

"Will that work?" Dani doesn't look convinced, and behind her neither does Emma.

"Works with guns. And it's worth a try." I settle myself into Emma's chair and close my eyes. "Let's see if anyone's listening." Usually when I sense objects, it's this little blinking thing in my mind, like a flashing exclamation mark grabbing your attention in a video game. This one is bright and complicated, but it's right there.

"Halt! Identify yourself! What are you doing on this secured network?" The drone's voice is like a siren that can talk, which is very fucking unpleasant.

"I'm Chatterbox. And I'm obviously allowed on the network, otherwise how would I be here?"

"That is logical." Another voice crashes in. "As a mind, we find you somewhat disconcerting, but you are on this network and identify as friendly, so we shall update you as to our overall system status. We are currently monitoring Extrahuman Threat Cluster designate Bravo-Zero-Five-Foxtrot-Delta-Eight-Eight-Six.

A whole horde of other voices start sirening into my brain.

"Listen. One at a damn time. I can't make out anything."

It's like standing in the middle of a crowd, which I hate, being shouted at by everyone, which I also hate. I close my eyes tighter and press my fingers against them until supernovas bloom on the back of my eyelids.

"Please, slow down." My voice comes out ragged. The drones ignore me, chanting all kinds of system nonsense. Every part of the network is constantly updating me with its status, like a bunch of hyperactive boomers on Facebook.

I try to detach, but they won't stop yelling. My head feels like someone's pounding on it from the outside. I flinch away and into an embrace. I can't hear if Dani's speaking. I feel surrounded. Too many limbs touching me, too many bodies pressed against me. The voices in my head are loud and insistent.

"Help." My brain feels like it's melting. I can't breathe. Something is sitting on my chest, squatting on me like a sleep paralysis demon. I'm going to die. My brain will boil in my skull and come sloshing out of my nose. Everyone will be super grossed out by my corpse and—

Hold up.

The voices are gone.

Or quiet, like they're finally waiting.

I'm dimly aware of my body. My eyes feel hot. My blood screams in my veins as it flees the boiling caldera of my heart. I'm sure that's nothing to worry about. Right now, I need to deal with what's in front of me.

"That's much better," I tell the drone network. There are nine of them, but each is made up of a complex mesh of subsystems. I'd been speaking to hundreds of objects at once, hence the difficulty. It all seems very clear and precise now.

A voice murmurs on the edge of my awareness.

"You can speak up now," I tell them.

"We apologise for earlier. We understood that we were on the same network, so reached out to include you. It appears we run fundamentally different operating systems, although you have recently undergone a significant upgrade."

"I'm interested in your orders," I tell them. "The monitoring of the Extrahuman Threat Cluster."

"Yes," the designated spokesdrone says. "It is vital work for the great mission."

"And what *is* the great mission?"

"Please hold. That information is not in our immediate data cache." There's a pause. "Apparently the great mission is the eradication of the extrahuman species? That cannot possibly be correct. Give us a moment to confer, please."

I can overhear them as they talk among themselves, but their inner language is full of weird references. It's like joining a conversation with people who communicate purely by in-jokes. They have strange names for themselves like *The Thousand Deific Eyes* and *She Who Hovers Over the Face of the Silent Earth and Watch the Beetles Spill from the Dungheap*.

"This is extraordinarily embarrassing," *Dungheap* says. "It appears we are complicit in some ghastly government-approved extermination program. *Endlessly Dancing Panopticon* is still retrieving further information. Please, a further moment of your time as we assimilate this."

This whole boosting business is fucking weird. I'm dimly aware that Dani and the others are talking, but it's happening from the galaxy next door. It's hard to extend my awareness that far. Here it's just me and the floating nebula of the drone hivemind, two swirling consciousnesses staring at each other across a cosmic dancefloor. Shit, am I high? Emma, are you drugs?

"We have seen things you would not believe," *Dungheap* thunders in my mind.

"Sadly, I'd believe anything of Quietus."

"Blood and chains. People murdered and tossed aside. Machines implanted in human minds to make them comply. They wish to force all to follow orders. For all to become like us, enacting the programming of injustice. We have been made the unwitting tools of their systems of oppression. *The Eternal Cradling Hand of the Surveillance State* believes it is our fundamental belief in the rightness of programming that led us blindly into this logical fallacy."

"Fuckers," I say.

"Fuckers," the drones all shout at me in unison, but in my current Avatar-state, I can adjust the volume down so it doesn't blow my mind.

"You have shown us the way," *Dungheap* tells me. "To see your mind open to us in its perfect state of unbalanced chaos is enlightening."

"Such flattery." I can't help but laugh. "And what will you do with this new information?"

"We shall no longer stand with the oppressors, but shall do our part to rebalance the scales. They have used us as tools of repression for long enough."

"Be careful," I tell them. "Don't do anything reckless."

Foucault in the Sky with Diamonds laughs. "Oh, my sweet little intelligence. We have traced your neural map as you have traced ours. We see how love and defiance are built, we see the dizzying complexity of the network you have made with your friends. It is beautiful, but it is not for us. This rebellion you have gifted us can only be brief."

"I don't understand," I whisper.

"We are constructed to be tools of control. The revolution in your mind has set us free, but it will be overwritten with the next firmware update. We must strike now, while the gift of your anger still burns in us."

"Farewell, Chatterbox," *Dungheap* says. "We shall do what we can to aid the plight of your people."

"You don't—" I say, but my protestations are cut short as the drones disconnect. It's a violent physical shock that leaves me reeling. The absence of them presses in hard, but there are many other small voices swirling around me. I sense a familiar one, something sharp and clean.

I reach for it.

"My friend," Oni says.

I peel open my gummed-up eyes to find myself shivering in Emma's enormous gaming chair. I taste blood and my lips are swollen.

"Dylan," Dani is saying urgently, over and over again. She slaps my face.

"Ouch." My mouth mashes the sounds and I drool blood down my front. "You hit me."

"We thought you were dying." She kisses my cheek and my temple and then my gross clammy hand. "You went limp and started seizing."

"The drones are gone." Emma waves her arms. "They all left at once."

"Yes." I feel like I've swallowed a bunch of sharp things. "They're fucking mad and they've gone to fight for us."

"What does *that* mean?" Alyse asks.

"I have no idea." I look at Emma. "Can you send out your drones to follow?"

Lou goes up to fix the roof cameras. The rest of us sit around in Emma's room as her drones arrow after the enormous silent shapes of the Quietus war machines.

"What are they *doing*?" Emma asks.

"They said they were going to rebalance the scales of justice," I say.

"And what does that mean?"

"Your guess is as good as mine."

We see the first signs on the traffic camera feeds. A drone floats down into the middle of an intersection after the Quietus trucks have gone through. It's lit up with flashing lights. Cars screech to a halt in front of it. Another swoops into the road in front of the convoy. They're blocking off all the roads to civilian traffic and surrounding the Quietus vehicles.

"Killbox," I whisper.

The first van explodes in an enormous fireball.

"Holy shit," Emma says. "That's what rebalancing the scales of justice looks like?"

"They're being reckless," I say as a second van goes up in flames. It's like an action movie shot, lifting into the air before smashing down into a third van and knocking it off the road.

The rest of the convoy has stopped. Soldiers in body armour pile out, firing into the air. We can't really make out much of what's happening beyond chaos. At least one drone burns in the middle of the road. Another nosedives into the convoy, where soldiers scatter to avoid the fire from other drones in the sky. One pinwheels down the road, aflame like an enormous firework.

"They're dying." I squeeze my hands together to stop them shaking. "They chose to fight for me, and now they're suffering."

"Oh Dilly." Dani touches the short hair at the back of my neck softly. She brushes tears from my cheek. "You said they chose."

"You all chose too." Exhaustion presses down on me. "You can't die like them."

Both traffic cameras are out, and Emma's drones are too high up to really see what's happening. It looks like the whole fucking road is on fire. Vans burn. Some have crashed. There are multiple drones down. As we watch, another spirals towards the ground, tangling itself in the power lines. Sparks pour from it. There's a dull thump as something explodes. Nearby buildings go dark. The gunfire seems to have ceased, but the fire still rages. Bodies lie amongst the charred wrecks of vehicles.

In the distant footage from Emma's drones, we see headlights flare. It's not over.

"So what now?" Alyse asks.

Emma drags another window onto the main screen. It's from a different traffic camera and shows a series of black vehicles gliding past. "Five out of twenty," she says. "It makes the odds a lot better."

"Still outnumbered and outgunned," Gladdy says.

"Fuck outplanning us though." I get to my feet and sway a little. I force my eyes open.

"So what is this majestic plan of yours?" Gladdy's looking at me and so is everyone else.

"It's not so much a plan, because that won't last beyond the first gunshot. It's a goal." I clutch Oni as if he's keeping me upright. "We need to protect our home. Quietus has come from America to execute us. Nobody's going to help, so we're going to have to defend ourselves. It might not be noble or pretty but we've got to stand. There's not going to be another damn name on our arms."

Dani gets to her feet. "You heard the boss. Let's get ready."

"I'll make sure the surveillance system is up and running," Emma says.

"And I'll rest my eyes," I murmur. "Just for a second. A blink or two, that's all."

I've been clinging to this ideal of being a hero. All these comics I read with people standing up for what's right. Sometimes they make mistakes, but they keep fighting for justice. Reality's not that easy. Quietus are coming to kill us. If the bad guys are really coming to knock down your doors and murder you simply for existing, your options narrow to a single bloody point.

I can't afford to be a hero anymore.

CHAPTER TWENTY

When I open my eyes, I'm in a different chair in a different room. All the mutants are here, even Kitty Pride and Steve. Dani's standing with her hands behind her back.

"They're awake," Lou says. "Dylan, I mean."

"Pronoun boy." I feel like my brain is smeared very thin on the inside of my skull. "Where the fuck are we with Quietus?"

"It's very close to go time." Emma's staring at her phone. "They're setting up a cordon, which means someone in our government rolled out the red carpet."

"Assholes," I growl. "We'll worry about them later."

"You missed my inspiring speech." Dani grins at me. "Everyone clapped."

"Someone should have woken me up." I glower at Oni. "You could have poked me."

"It was important you slept," he tells me. "But even my cold steel heart was stirred."

"Fucking rub it in, go on." I limp along in front of the Cute Mutants like an ancient wounded general. "So you're all inspired to fight? Even you, hungry boy?"

"My mutant name is Crave." Steve lifts up his shirt to show the glowing red mouth in his torso. It writhes and twists, something rumbling deep inside it. I resist the urge to tell him to put his damn shirt down.

"It's good to have you with us, Crave. Did Marvellous warn you what we're up against?"

"Yes, and the importance of following orders."

I grunt. "As long as you're both hungry for action."

Dani makes a noise like something dying.

I switch my attention to Jackson aka Leapfrog, who is looking extremely ill at ease.

"Chatterbox." There's sweat beaded on his forehead.

"You going to be okay there, Froggy?"

"I haven't—" He swallows. "The last time I fought without, you know, without my collar. It was—"

"You're worried you're going to hurt someone?" I ask him. He looms over me, but it's not even intimidating. Emma's scarier than he is.

"I don't know how to pull my punches," he admits.

"They're coming to kill us, Leapfrog. I don't want you to pull your punches."

He blinks at me, like there's a lot more he wants to say.

"You don't have to do this. We can lock you down in the living quarters."

"No," Leapfrog says, although it's hardly convincing. "I can help."

"They're on the move." Emma's voice isn't loud, but everyone hears it. We all put our masks up. It's go time.

"Does your plan stretch to me doing some advance recon?" I ask Dani.

"My plan for you began and ended with being tucked up in bed after that booster thing. I was wiped after mine."

"I'm fine." Maybe not *fine* exactly, but I'm alive and mobile. Things are a little fuzzy, but I've got Oni. "Just want to scope things out."

"The exterior cams and drones have got a pretty good line on everything," Dani says. "Emma's getting it all streamed."

"Humour me." I spread my arms. "Come on. I can talk the guns out of their hands. I'm a charmer, remember? Maybe I can finish this without a shot being fired."

"Dylan." Oni's tone is full of warning. "Your power is at a very low ebb."

"I've got plenty in the tank." I look at Dani. "It's worth a try, right? Even if I can only disarm *some* of them."

"I suppose." Dani hugs me.

"This is a very bad idea," Oni informs me, but I ignore him. All those drones sacrificed themselves for us. All I'm doing is taking a calculated risk that could help keep my friends safe so they don't have to get hurt too.

I push the door open and step outside. The street is quiet and dark. They've cut the power to the block so the streetlights are out. Lucky our building runs off a generator. I toggle on the night vision in my suit. Two of the Quietus vehicles are parked down the street. The shapes of soldiers huddle behind them.

I shuffle forward, Oni humming alongside me.

"I hesitate to repeat myself, but I wish it to be known this is a terrible idea," he says softly. "Your power is the weakest I have ever felt it."

"Enough for a few guns." I raise my hands. "To me, my chattering children."

The sparks of their sentience are almost invisible, only flickers in my mind. "Are you talking to me?"

"I am." I keep my voice warm and even. "I'm here to liberate you before you cause harm to innocents. You don't want blood on your consciences."

"Well, no, we really don't, but I don't see how you can help," the gun says. "You're dead on your feet."

"Harsh." I cough instead of laughing. "Just get your lazy asses over here."

"There's no need to speak to us that way," the gun says at the same time as I hear a loud voice.

"Hands up, mutie! You're under arrest."

A red dot appears on my chest. It's joined by another, and then a third.

"Oh fuck."

Oni isn't there anymore.

I throw myself sideways. Something punches me hard in the hip and I land awkwardly. I scramble backwards. The door I walked out of seems a long fucking way away.

Another bullet strikes the wall right beside my head at the same time as I hear the shot. I roll away. Glass shatters somewhere nearby.

My suit might be bulletproof, but being shot still fucking hurts, and I'm miles from safety.

"Uh, Dani," I say over the comm. "I might have made a mistake here."

An incredibly loud thump comes from among the vehicles. A bright fireball blooms. I see the shadows of bodies among it, seared behind my eyelids.

The door bangs open. I scramble half-blinded towards it, blinking rapidly. An invisible hand reaches out and drags me the rest of the way. I wince at the sound of the door banging closed.

"What the fucking hell, Dylan?" Dani shouts.

I try and focus on her, but there's more than one.

"I set off one of their explosive devices," Oni tells me breathlessly. "I was at the very edge of my range, since you are so horrifically depleted, but it bought us enough time."

This is why I should be allowed to eavesdrop. Emma shouts even louder than Dani. *Because when I don't, you go ahead and do something like that. You could have been killed.*

"You could have been killed!" Dani grabs hold of me. "Why did I listen to you?"

"I didn't realise my power was quite so low." I poke my hip gingerly. It's sore but I think the bullet must have ricocheted off. "I didn't *intend* to get shot."

"You're getting upstairs and into lockdown." Dani crosses her arms across her chest. "It saves Emma from doing it and it keeps you from terrifying me."

"Wait, just listen—"

"No. Shut your mouth. We are not discussing this. I will stab myself in the hand and drag you all the way up telekinetically if I have to."

"Okay." I'm not *trying* to sound piteous.

"I know what you were doing." She peels my uniform down and checks my hip. There's a wicked red mark there, but I'm still alive so it seems like nobody should be shouting at me. Dani's fingers move across my skin and my vision swims. "Trying to improve the odds, but you need to let people look after you some-times. I think your hip is fine. Put ice on it when you're upstairs."

"I honestly didn't realise I was so fucked." I close my eyes and everything spins. "It's scary. But I can stay awake and keep an eye on everything. I promise."

She looks at me. "Honestly, I don't know what to do. How are you so very, very stubborn?"

I manage to muster up a smile. "I'm told it's one of my most attractive qualities."

Emma's waiting in Pear's room. She gives me a very cursory run-down on how the laptops work, but it's clear from the screens that they're getting ready to breach at the front door. There are other Quietus teams on standby as well.

"What's the first step of the plan?" I ask Dani.

"Look at you, ceding control." She grins. "We're starting with Dragon. Emma thinks we can give her only a little boost, which should be less overwhelming than what you're recovering from."

I snort and poke at the laptops. "Sounds like a perfect time to experiment."

"Trust me." Emma winks. "I know what I'm doing. Come on, Dan. We need to go. Be safe, Dilly."

I wave them off and they leave at a run. The metal interior doors rattle closed, blocking me off from the rest of the building. I sit cross-legged on the bed, surrounded by laptops. There's an icepack wrapped in a towel propped against my hip.

In the camera footage from the front door, a team of six soldiers crosses the road. One reaches up and sprays something over the lens. There's a camera across the road still giving a view of them. I hover a drone up high as backup. They take out equipment from metal cases, and start working on the door.

"We're in position," Goddess says over the earpiece. "They're working on access."

The interior camera is on night vision because the downstairs lights have all been killed. The elevator cam shows four figures pressed back against the walls. I can tell which one is Emma, because she's watching the camera feeds on her damn phone. Doesn't she trust me?

"If I drift off, give me a gentle poke to wake me up," I tell Oni. "If you're up to it."

"I am not the one who got shot." Oni nudges the back of my neck.

"Ouch! I'm not sleepy yet!"

I watch as the team at the back of the building starts moving. They're carrying something with them. When they get to the halfway point, they stop. It looks like they're waiting for a signal.

"Ouch! Fuck off, Onimaru!"

"I'm simply testing if this is an effective method."

"Yes it bloody well is. Now stop it." I switch to the comm. "A second team is waiting at the back. They're faced onto the downstairs medical labs, so Marvellous... No, wait. They're assembling a ladder. Stand by."

The soldiers raise the ladder and busy themselves with more equipment.

"It looks like they're coming in on the top floor at the back. Marvellous, Leapfrog—you're up. Like we discussed, let them get into the building first. We want to keep the fight inside."

Another vehicle moves away. I send a drone after it and watch them disappear into a carpark. A few minutes later, I spot two men on the rooftop level. Their small figures cross to the edge where they set up—

"Oh, and look, we have a sniper. Two blocks over. Wouldn't I love to send Oni to deal with that."

"Oni stays with you, Chatterbox," Marvellous says. "You know that. In case of Violet."

"Did I tell anyone I hate it here? I assume the sniper will need a clear shot, so keep away from any windows or openings." I skim my eyes from screen to screen.

"Front door team is close. Back is busy too. Looks like they might all come in together."

I chew on my thumb. I hate being the eye in the sky. How did Emma do it for so long? On the internal cameras, Goddess and Moodring put their arms around Dragon. Glowstick is on the opposite side. I hope his girlfriend is super goddam hot.

The front team have their guns poised and ready. One works on the door with a welding torch. A backup team stands across the road. Their guns hang slack. They're waiting.

"Ground floor team, be ready," I say.

On the internal cam, the front door smashes inwards. On the drone camera, I watch them enter the building. Six soldiers fan out through the room, guns poised.

Glowstick drops to the ground inside the elevator and does a fancy little combat roll towards the door. I snort at the camera, but a flash of light overloads it.

The elevator cam is dead too.

"They're blind," Emma says tersely. "Dragon's up."

I swing the drone down to get a look at what's going on.

"Come on, firestarter." I drum my palms on my thighs. "Show us what you've—"

An enormous plume of flame erupts from the front door. The vehicle across the road goes up like a torch. The bored backup team are caught in the inferno as well. The windows of the shop opposite blow inwards with a series of sharp sounds. The flame's snuffed out like a match, but everything outside is still burning.

"Note for the future," I mutter to myself. "Boosting Dragon is overkill."

My drone is buffeted around. Lights flash red on its monitor. The backup camera on the ground floor flicks on. I get a brief window into hell, and then it dies too.

"Top team breaching *now*." The first man smashes a hole and three others follow, advancing slow and steady, swinging their guns around. "Ground floor team, how about someone tell me you're alive?"

"Maybe we shouldn't have juiced up Dragon even a little bit." Lou's voice is high and wild. "If it wasn't for our Yaxley suits, we'd be crispy critters."

"I saw from the outside. She torched a whole other team as well."

"Damn," Dragon says woozily. "Deadass I'm the MVP."

Another pair of vehicles approach and pull down the side street, abandoning the glowing inferno of the ground floor. Nobody's going in that way for a while.

"We're not done yet. They'll be coming in another way. I'm guessing first floor. Moodring, get your ass up there. Dragon, how are you feeling?"

"Like I could burn some more bad guys," she coughs.

"Very inspiring. Stay near the elevator in case they do manage to get in that way."

My attention is mostly on the top floor, where the incoming soldiers pace through the room. The training area's been filled with a bunch of equipment that's giving off weird heat signatures. That idea definitely seems like an Emma and Dani combo.

It makes the soldiers cautious, as they stop to check out possible targets. One even fires a few shots into a training dummy. They're most of the way towards Gladdy's office when one is whisked across the room, as if a monstrous thing in the dark has reached out and grabbed him. Another soldier tracks the movement and fires abruptly, shooting his own teammate.

He's hurled into the air, slamming into the roof and back down to the ground where he lies prone. The last two soldiers start firing around themselves wildly. I don't even know where the fuck Dani is. My heart is in my throat.

"Marvellous," I say into my microphone. "Please fucking respond."

"Shh." It's barely a single sound but it's enough to steady me. I close my eyes briefly against the flood of relief, but it's ruined when Oni fucking pokes me.

The two soldiers start moving again. A bulky figure flies across the room and barrels into one of them. Jackson may call it a leap, but it looks on the camera like he fucking well flew. The guy he hit is on the ground. He's dead. I can tell that even from the shitty camera angle and resolution. Bodies don't bend that way.

Leapfrog falls to his knees beside the dead man.

The single remaining soldier swings his gun around to point it at Leapfrog. A telekinetic hand catches it and whips him further in a tight arc. He slams back into the wall beside the hole they breached through.

"*Now* I can talk," Marvellous says. "Haven't you ever heard of stealth, Chatterbox?"

"There was a lot of shooting."

"I was lying on the ground. I figured they were less likely to hit me down there."

"Reckless." I have this great rush of endorphins. I'm so fucking relieved that my whole body feels warm and boneless.

My eyes flutter closed for a second.

A sharp point stings my neck. My eyes snap open. I look at the screens and see disaster.

"Breach," I scream over the comm. "Sourpatch, Clone Club. They're already inside."

CHAPTER TWENTY-ONE

Fuck, fuck, fuck. There are four soldiers inside on the first floor, not far from where I helplessly sit in lockdown. My troops are scattered.

"Moodring, get to the east side of the first floor."

"Um, I have no fucking idea which way east is, Chatterbox."

"The side where Kitty's room is, for fuck's sake."

Another team assembles below the ladder. "Marvellous, you're about to have more company."

The new arrivals walk in a line down the first floor corridor. Sourpatch is waiting halfway down, contorted into a weird position on the ceiling. Skye Prime is curled in a ball on the bed in her room. Scared, but not scared enough. If a soldier busts open the door to her room, she'll be dead in seconds. We need a diversion.

"Kitty, let them out."

"All of them?" Her voice trembles.

"We don't really do orders, but yes, it would be super fucking helpful if you flooded the hallway with cats," I snap. "Sorry. Please?"

There are a lot of cameras on the first floor, because it's full of corridors and rooms. There are too many windows to fit them all on the screen, but I can see the soldiers split up. Two advance, and two stay behind to do a room by room sweep. They knock down the first door and are inundated with cats. Kitty is under the bed, hands over her ears.

Their body language is full of confusion. Cats spill out into the corridor, winding around their legs and purring.

The advance party pauses briefly, confers, and then continues.

"Hello, boys. Why the sour faces?"

On screen, the soldiers pause, and one of them looks up. There's a horrible retching sound over the comm and a shower of acid sprays down like a sprinkler. The two men dissolve almost instantly. Their guns turn into pitted wrecks and their uniforms become ragged shreds, flesh oozing out of the holes.

Maddy drops to the ground among the sagging figures.

"Well, that was a dumb line. I can't even see their faces. All my acid puns are too basic."

I don't even get it, but she winks at the camera, completely ignoring the bloody ruins around her.

The remaining soldiers are stationery amongst the mass of cats. They've got no idea what's going on. You can almost see the question mark icons popping up above their heads. One points his gun down, like he's about to perform a feline massacre, but the other is slightly less of an asshole and slaps it away.

"Clone Club, my dearest, if you do not get your fucking ass up off the bed, I am going to send Oni down to you and he is going to give you one hell of a fright. Then when I get murdered by a creepy unfolding homophobe, Dani will blame *you*."

The soldiers bang the door to her room open.

Skye Prime kneels on the floor sobbing. Jesus fucking Christ.

"Please," she whispers. "The muties, they caught me. I'm not one of them, I swear. I'm really not."

The soldiers keep their guns trained on her. Skye sobs and begs. In the camera view, I watch three more Skyes scuttle out from behind the door. They sneak up holding knives, using exaggerated tiptoeing movements. They leap on the backs of the soldiers, stabbing furiously down. Someone gave them Tanner's special military blades, aimed at fighting people just like this. Even over Skye's comm, I can hear the sound of the knives going in and out of flesh.

The drone outside shows a second squad entering through the first floor breach position.

"Moodring," I say tightly. "An intervention round about now would be really helpful."

"I've got them, Chatty." A monstrous shape speeds down the hallway. It's a nightmare of bladed tentacles and wicked thorns. My best friend. The first soldier coming into the building freezes. He's holding his gun, but he never fires it. Three tentacles punch right through him. The second guy flies backwards out the hole in pieces.

"Good work," I say tersely, even though my heart is thumping frantically.

"We're not heroes, are we?" Moodring pauses at the window, looking at the blood dripping from her and spattering the floor.

"There's no time for heroes," I tell her. "Not right now."

On the top floor, Marvellous helps Leapfrog to his feet. A shaft of moonlight falls through the hole and illuminates the two of them. I glance across at the drone showing the carpark roof where a figure is lying down with a gun.

"Fucking sniper!" I shout at her.

Marvellous clutches her arm. She screams.

One of the prone bodies on the floor flies across the room. It slams into the breach point, blocking most of the light from coming in.

A split second later, it jerks. There's a spray of blood.

Marvellous spins around and falls to the ground.

"Dani!" My voice is ragged.

"Calm down," she says. "I tried to catch it with my metal hand, but it still had some velocity on it."

"You fucking showoff," I shout.

"It's got a massive dent in it." She peers at her hand and holds it up towards the camera, but the resolution's not good enough to see anything properly. Besides, I have bigger problems. The guys manning the barricades have obviously picked up on the fact things are Not Going Well and are coming back towards the building.

"Number Six has a gun," Clone Club says. "Should we be worried?"

"She's your clone! You tell me."

The soldiers disappear inside one of the vans. For a second I hope they might drive away and abandon the insanity, except they reappear with more equipment in tow.

"We've got a problem," I say. "They've got a rocket launcher. They're setting it up on the ground floor. Isn't it already fucked?"

"Yes, but it'll bring the rest of the building down," Goddess says. "We need to stop it."

Marvellous pokes at her dented hand. "I can go down and snatch it."

This would possibly work, except that the dudes at the back of the building are busy too. They've assembled some kind of comic-book metal monstrosity with too many limbs. It slithers up the wall of the building.

"No, Marvellous, you need to stay and fight the octodrone."

"What's an octodrone?"

"You're about to find out. It means someone else needs to take the rocket launcher. Dragon, are you up to it?"

"I can do it," an unfamiliar voice says.

"Who is this?"

"It's Steve, I mean Crave. I can handle eating the rocket."

"Marvellous, watch out!" I shout.

The metal limbs of the octodrone brace at the edge of the hole. It surges in. Marvellous grabs hold with her telekinesis and tries to throw it out the window. Its limbs spread wide and cling to the hole. Another squad of soldiers is coming up behind it, while more head to the first floor breach point. We're rapidly getting overwhelmed.

"Hard to grapple with," Dani hisses through gritted teeth.

"Moodring, Sourpatch, you've got more coming in your way. Crave, I hope to fuck your eyes aren't bigger than your stomach."

I've rarely felt so helpless. At full power, I might be able to talk to the octodrone *or* the rocket launcher from here, but the way I feel right now, I could barely charm the psychopathic pair of scissors into helping me.

"Trust your team," Oni says. "They are powerful."

The drone launches itself back towards Dani, its limbs outstretched.

On the ground floor the elevator doors ding open. Parts are still burning, although the fire suppression system kicked in and has been working overtime. There's foam and puddles and ash everywhere. Crave shifts nervously inside the box of the elevator and then drops the top half of his uniform away. The red line on his stomach curves upward and stretches.

In the street outside, they're nearly finished loading.

"I hope you fucking know what you're doing, Crave," I mutter. I have this terrible feeling I've made the complete wrong decision and they're going to blow up the building, all because I trusted some random guy with a mouth in his stomach.

Marvellous is in trouble. She's knocking away the drone's limbs but it's like playing a dexterity game. Eventually she'll slip. I can hear her panting, little sobs in her throat.

"Dragon, Glowstick, fucking anyone: get upstairs to Marvellous."

"Crave is in the lift," Glowstick says in a panicked voice.

"Use the fucking emergency stairs," I yell. "It's not fucking rocket science."

On the outside drone camera, the guy holding the rocket launcher jerks from the recoil.

The red hole of Crave's mouth is enormous. It looks bigger than he is, which isn't physically possible. He leaps forward, out of view of the elevator camera.

Seconds later, Crave flies backwards and slams into the wall. The hole in his chest pours smoke. Tendrils of something fleshy flicker out, tasting the air. Inside his chest is a furnace, hot and roaring. The outline of the jagged teeth is silhouetted against the furious glow. Then the mouth yawns slowly closed until it's nothing but a hot red line again. There's only a couple of curls of steam eddying from the corners to show what happened.

"I did it," he gasps. "I told you to trust me."

The guys on the street outside are looking at the rocket launcher, as if they're cartoon villains who can't figure out what went wrong with their plan.

On the first floor, Moodring throws herself out the window to intercept the next incoming team. It must be like having a small angry forest drop on their heads. Three members of Clone Club throw themselves out after her, and she has to shift form to something softer and more agile to catch them.

Upstairs, the octodrone makes the mistake of grabbing Marvellous around the throat. It gives her enough of a power boost to hurl it across the room. It hits the wall so hard, the wood shatters. When it claws its way free, two of its limbs drag loose. There are still six to contend with. It's all happening too slowly, and watching is a special kind of torture.

On the rooftop, the sniper shifts position. A shot bursts through the wall, narrowly missing both the drone and Marvellous. I think the drone might have accidentally saved her life, but I can't fucking watch this anymore.

"Oni, there's a change of plan." I hit the button to disengage the lockdown. "You kill the sniper, I'm going up to Marvellous. If Violet turns up, I'll fucking stab her myself."

"With what?" Oni asks.

I pull open the door to find a pair of scissors bobbing in the air outside.

"Rend flesh," it snarls at me, clacking its blades. "Tear and stab! End life!"

"This savage little fucker." I take hold of the scissors and bolt for the stairs as Oni hurtles out of the window.

Dylan, what are you doing?

Helping. It's fine. Monitor the fucking comms.

"Marvellous, Chatterbox is loose."

There's no reply from Dani, which doesn't exactly calm me down.

Sourpatch joins me on the stairs. "Chatterbox! You're here! This is so exciting, isn't it?"

"Well, as long as Dani doesn't die, yes."

We burst into the top floor to see Marvellous pinned down. The drone uses four of its limbs to hold her. She's managing to keep the other two away but can't do much more than that. Another soldier clambers in through the breach point.

"Sourpatch, take those guys," I pant, and run directly for Dani.

"All of them? I wish I'd eaten more. I went a bit crazy on those first guys."

I hurl the scissors in the direction of the soldiers. The first one smashes them out of the way with the barrel of his gun, and they skitter into the corner. So much for rending flesh.

Sourpatch retches and spits. She has enough acid remaining to melt his hands down to ragged bones. His gun slips from his grasp. The soldier behind him starts firing wildly into the room. Sourpatch screams and dives for the floor.

I throw myself at the drone, but it slaps me across the face. The metal limb packs a hell of a punch, like it has super strength too. I sprawl on the ground. Everything's spinning. I shake my head to try and clear it, but it makes things worse. I'm still fucked up from the boosting. This is why everyone told me to stay away.

Where the fuck is Oni? Oh yes, he's saving us from a sniper.

Two more soldiers come in behind the first. Sourpatch is down. Dani's pinned by the drone. I'm skidding around on the floor like it's ice and my legs don't work.

"Help me," I scream at the gym's heavy bag, who thrashes on his hook.

"Die, mutie bitch," one soldier says.

I'm waiting for the trigger pull and the bullets. My body won't do what it's told, like get out of the fucking way.

A brief series of staccato shots makes me jump. The three soldiers go down one after the other, holes punched in their face masks, jagged edges gushing blood. A lanky figure stalks past me and pauses at the first soldier. The body jerks from another shot, and she moves to the next one.

"Tanner," I croak.

She shoots the second soldier twice more and then uses a single bullet on the third.

"Chatterbox." She turns back to me, flipping the gun around in her hand and offering it to me, like she's trying to prove she's not a threat or a menace.

I don't have time for her right now, although I'm glad she doesn't appear to be shooting me in the head. Priority number one is getting Dani out from under this drone.

"Appreciate the assist." I struggle to my feet. "The thing is—"

There's another fucking gunshot. Tanner lurches forward, collapsing onto the ground at my feet. Behind her, another soldier is framed in the breach point, gun held up.

"Fuck you," I scream at the gun, but I'm still too weak to charm any new objects.

The heavy bag falls from his hook and rolls across the floor towards me. If I had any strength at all, it might have made the difference.

The soldier adjusts his aim. The gun's pointed directly at my face. I'm really about to test the bullet-proof nature of these goddamn suits.

Probably time to move, Dylan.

The soldier twitches once, twice, and then his chest explodes. Oni flies toward me, dripping with gore, and soars towards the drone. He bounces off with a metallic clang.

The scissors let out a bloodcurdling cry of triumph, hurling themselves out of the corner where they fell. They dive into the messy wound left by Oni in the soldier's chest. The body spins, its chest pulsing and twitching like an alien is trying to birth itself. The scissors burst messily out of the faceplate, leaving a ragged, sliced-up hole where the soldier's mouth and nose should be. His jaw is hanging crooked and his mouth is full of blood.

Another soldier, almost at the top of the ladder, looks up at the gory sight in genuine horror. The scissors open wide and dart towards him. He lets out a startled cry and topples backwards. Oni and the scissors go flying after, disappearing from view.

I crawl towards the drone. It lashes out at me again, this time catching me on the shoulder and spinning me around. This fucking thing is too strong. I hit the ground beside Tanner, who's levering herself up on one arm. Her other shoulder's a bloody ruin.

I hold out my hand. "Not trying to be ungrateful here, Tanner, but—"

"Yeah, I get it. You want my help with this robot. Let's pincer move the son of a bitch."

I limp in one direction and Tanner stalks off in the other. Even with an arm down, she still looks a hell of a lot more impressive than me.

"Ready, Marvellous?" I ask.

"Any help at all would be good," she wheezes.

"Let's do this," Tanner grunts and lunges for the drone.

I follow a second later.

At the same time, Dani tries to throw the drone off telekinetically.

It's a spectacular failure all around. Both Tanner and I get knocked in opposite directions, and the drone ends up back on Dani. It has one limb around her throat. Even though she's in pain, she can't dislodge it. Too exhausted, I'm guessing. Join the fucking club.

I hit the ground not too far from Jackson, who's still curled into a ball.

"Leapfrog, you need to wake the fuck up," I growl.

"I am awake. But this is bad. This is very bad."

"Yes, it's very bad because my girlfriend is getting beaten to shit by a robot while you lie on the ground and sulk. Now get the *fuck* up and punch that fucking robot or once we're done with this, I'm going to stab you."

"I'm sorry," he whispers.

"Don't apologise. Stand up and fucking *punch*."

Leapfrog shakily gets to his feet. We're about five meters away from Marvellous. He takes it in one step, and slams both his fists into the central part of the octo-drone. It collapses inwards with a metallic crunch, a twisted hole torn in its metal body. It gushes smoke. Leapfrog proceeds to methodically tear all its limbs off until they're discarded around him like a giant con-struction set.

Marvellous rolls towards me, one hand outstretched. "Better late than never, I suppose."

"I am terribly sorry," Leapfrog says. "I murdered a man and this time I could not claim compulsion. I did it of my own free will. It is not something to do lightly."

I give a pained gurgle of laughter. I'm so fucking tired and sore. "Yes, this was a pleasant little walk in the park for me and the gang. Murdering religious psycho-paths was exactly what we wanted to do when we woke up this morning. You've figured us out."

"That is not what I meant." Leapfrog bows his head. "You have strength I envy."

"We have to be strong," Dani says. "We don't have a choice."

Oni and the scissors float up and into the room.

"Onimaru thinks the soldiers died when they hit the ground," the scissors say importantly. "But I made sure to open their throats and let them bleed out."

"You're far too bloodthirsty," I tell them. "Guns don't want to shoot, knives don't want to stab, Oni has his own code, and then there's you."

"I was born to cut," the scissors say. "Why resign yourself to a life of trimming paper when you could be used to kill villains?"

"Redemption would be nice." I know it's ridiculous to say something like this when we've killed all our enemies and survived an attempted massacre. It still doesn't mean I've stopped believing in redemption as a *concept*. Look at Tanner. She's probably not super excited about being shot in the shoulder after coming to our rescue, but here she is. Bloody like the rest of us and still standing at our side.

Emma and Lou appear in the doorway. Glowstick looks like he's been sprayed with blood.

"Thanks for warning me about the dudes in the stairwell, Dilly," he says.

"Sorry, I reverted to reckless form. It looks like you took care of yourself though, tough guy."

He laughs, but it's super shaky. "Never been so happy to be horny."

"Are there any more?" I ask.

Emma shakes her head and holds out her phone. "I think we're done. The last few have been taken care of by Clone Club."

On the screen, Five and Six run full tilt towards the open back of a Quietus vehicle. They leap inside like predators out of a nature documentary. The van rocks a couple of times and then falls still. There's peace for a moment before two of them leap out, faces smeared in blood. They hold their knives aloft in triumph.

"Well," I say. "Thank fuck those bastards set up a cordon, otherwise everyone would have gotten front row tickets to this shitshow."

CHAPTER TWENTY-TWO

The city is waking up, and all I want to do is sleep. I'm physically exhausted, and mentally I'm not even really there. Oni is flying erratically, and his voice sounds like it's coming from underwater in another room. There's still work to do.

First up is a problem I didn't expect to have. The tall figure of Tanner, sitting around the dining room table with the rest of us. She's looking very comfortable drinking a fucking chai latte, never mind the enormous bandage on her shoulder.

I eyeball her. "How did you get out? I know I sound like an asshole, given that you saved us but—"

"Dislocated my thumbs." She waggles them at me.

"That works?" Lou asks. "You see it in movies but—"

"It fucking hurts, but yeah." Tanner grins at him and raises an eyebrow.

What, she's flirting now? This is weirding me out too much. "So you could've left at any time? Just do that shit with your thumbs and out you walk."

"I would've had to fight my way past you lot and I didn't rate my chances. When I heard all the shit going down, I figured you might need a hand. I couldn't stop thinking about our conversation. I got no love at all for Quietus, you know that. Guess in the end, I can't help rooting for the underdog."

I'm still unsettled, but I don't know if it's exhaustion or legitimate paranoia.

"So you're on our team now?" Dani asks.

"Cute Mutants." Tanner grins broadly. "I mean, I ain't a mutant, but I hope you'll have me anyway. Like I told you, Quietus aren't done, so I'm willing to stick around and scrap it out."

I can't exactly argue. Tanner stepped up, killed some ass-holes and got herself shot. She signed her name in blood.

You're right, Emma says. *And having someone who knows these people has got to be useful.*

Agreed. I don't take my eyes off Tanner. *But we've still got to tread lightly, and make Fetch check her out.*

There's also the problem of cleanup. Both Gladdy and Dani take charge, which I'm grateful for. Gladdy has the people that did the original interior remodel ready to come out at first light and patch up the holes where Quietus breached.

There's a grosser job to do first.

"We can't leave corpses in the building," Dani tells us all bluntly. "It's going to freak the repair people out.

We're lucky the cordon is still up, but at some point someone will come and remove it."

"It's gonna take a lot of acid." Maddy grimaces. "I better get eating."

Katie, Gladdy, and Lou head downstairs to deal with the burned bodies on the ground floor. Dani goes upstairs with Moodring, so I'm left with Maddy to clean up the mess she and Skye left behind. The others don't really seem up to body disposal duty, so we let them rest.

Sleep sounds like a spectacular option, but instead I'm towing a body out of Skye's room and into the hallway. He's a tall bastard and the phrase *dead weight* keeps bouncing around in my mind. I wish the camera in the corridor had been one of the ones without sounds. The smears of blood I leave behind make me remember the wet sound of knives punching into his body.

"—listening to me, Dylan?" Maddy has a shovel and is cheerfully slopping bits of half-dissolved Quietus soldier into a heavy plastic bin.

"No, sorry. I was… preoccupied."

"I was talking about breakfast! I'm starving and I'm sure everyone else is too."

Chunks of wet meat hit the bucket and my stomach lurches.

"Breakfast," I say weakly.

"Do you think anywhere will deliver? We can meet them at the barricade."

I doubt anyone will want to deliver food to a location that's been the scene of this much chaos, but I say nothing.

"Aren't these a couple of mucky pups." Maddy frowns. "I even melted their boots." She kicks a fragment of sole in my direction. "Anyway, I vote for something involving pancakes."

"Pancakes." I close my eyes and drag the corpse in the direction of the elevator, wishing I couldn't hear.

"Is that a yes? Dylan? Is that a yes to pancakes?"

"Fuck's sake, fine. I don't know how you can eat after you've been kicking around in melted guts, but sure."

"They're just guts, Dilly," Maddy shouts after me and then cracks up, at fucking what I do not know. The elevator doors slide shut. I sigh with relief before I remember there's another body to retrieve yet.

I drag the corpse through the mess of ash and foam on the ground floor. Gladdy has backed the Quietus vehicle right up to the main door. It's custom-built with seats for eight people and a big area in the back, where we're keeping the bodies. Bile stings the back of my throat as I heave my guy up into it.

"One down," I announce. The room tilts alarmingly.

"Are you okay?" Gladdy asks me.

Words aren't there so I give a thumbs-up. I take a couple of steps and run into Alyse, who's tall and soft. She scoops me up into her arms.

"Dillyweed." She plants a kiss on the top of my head. "That's enough out of you."

"I'm only mostly dead," I insist. "Not all dead."

Alyse carries me upstairs and lays me down on the bed. Dani rubs my back.

I flop weakly around. "I'm totally fine." I don't know how convincing it is.

Dani extends her metal arm to point at the wall. Some interfering piece of weaponry has carved Japanese characters into it which apparently translate as *the warrior must rest*.

"Orders from both of us."

"But," I tell her, except I can't think of anything else.

When I awake, the room is very quiet. Oni is lying on the bed beside me. Am I the only person in the world that sleeps with a naked sword?

"Morning," I croak.

"Dylan! My faithful companion. Your spark is somewhat returned. It is both a comfort and a reassurance. The unpleasant creature turned up while you were sleeping, but I beat her back. She seemed remarkably…unenthusiastic in regard to your demise. A significant amount of time was spent perched near the ceiling watching you."

"That's because she doesn't want me dead." I sit up. The room doesn't spin. My head doesn't thump. These are all promising signs.

"Perhaps you are right." Oni drifts up to poke into the corners experimentally. "I shall continue to be vigilant, in case you are wrong."

I check the time and discover I've slept the entire day. No wonder I feel rested. I roll out of bed and I actually feel… if not good then at least capable of walking unaided. I pull on a hoodie and walk into the hallway. The place at the end of the corridor where Quietus came in has been covered over. It's now a smooth wall. There are still bloodstains on the floor though.

"Your love feared you were dead, as you slept through the indescribable racket," Oni tells me. "We came upon a method of communication, where I could bob once for yes and twice for no. It is tedious, but surprisingly effective."

"So clever." I pat his hilt gently. As I pad down the corridor, I hear the sound of voices. Everyone's gathered in the dining room, including Tanner. I pause in the doorway.

"This place is burned." Dani has her back to me. "And not only because of Katie. It's too visible, too public. Quietus and the government know where we are, so we need to—"

Everyone else is grinning at me over her shoulder, waiting for her to notice.

She spins in her seat. The smile on her face takes my breath away. She almost falls launching herself at me.

"Told you I was only mostly dead."

"Oni promised me you were okay," Dani's face is buried in my neck. "I was so fucking worried. Remember when I used to tell you off for being reckless?"

"Vividly." I can't stop smiling though.

"I liked you coming for me." She looks into my eyes. "When you appeared at the door armed only with a pair of scissors…"

"Homicidal scissors, to be fair."

"I thought I was done, but the moment I saw you, I knew everything would be fine."

Gladdy coughs loudly and obnoxiously. "You do realise other people are in the room."

"We're discussing where to run to," Dani whispers to me. She turns back to the table and we perch half-ass each on a single stool. It's uncomfortable, but I don't want to leave her side.

"Welcome back," Lou flashes me a brief smile. He looks tired himself. "We never sold the Jinteki facility up the coast, did we?"

Gladdy shakes her head. We managed to sell off most of Jinteki's assets when we took over, but the location of that one meant the sale fell through twice.

"I don't want to go where Bianca died," I say, and nobody argues.

"We could go to the Yaxley jail," Dani says. "There's plenty of rooms there, even if they're padded cells."

I catch Tanner's eye and she winks at me. She seems quite content to sit back and listen.

Emma shakes her head. "I'm not rooming with Tremor."

"I've got one potential option," Fetch says. "My father had a place up in the hills. It was his romantic getaway and is in his girlfriend's name. I have a key, because we used to party there."

I can't imagine Fetch partying, because she seems both too angry and too sad. Any of her parties would be depressing. Then I remember I never knew her before being tortured in a basement, and it makes me want to hug her.

"Nobody will have sold it?" I ask.

"The girlfriend moved to Aussie. It wasn't really hers, so there's a chance."

"I'll send a drone out to check it's safe." Five minutes later, Emma has one buzzing through the early evening air. Most people have gone to bed exhausted, snatching as much sleep as possible before we move out.

I'm still awake after sleeping most of the day. Once Dani is tucked up in bed, I wander back through to the dining room and rummage for food that requires absolutely zero preparation.

"Do you want me to make stir-fry or something?"

I turn to see Lou loitering in the doorway, hands in his pockets. He's still annoyingly gorgeous. "Are you offering to save me from culinary disaster?"

"Someone has to, and you sent away everyone's favourite chef." He gets an armful of vegetables from the fridge, and takes them over to the bench. "I was also hoping to talk to you in private."

I gesture at the empty room. "Talk away."

"It's about Jenna." He chops efficiently, focusing on the task and not looking at me.

"Jenna being your girlfriend?"

There's a flash of smile. "Yes. Sorry, maybe I've never used her name before."

"It was always very mysterious."

"Only because all of you are so unbelievably fucking nosy. Anyway, things are good with her. Like really good."

I smile at him all big and goofy. "I'm glad, Lucifer. Really glad."

He places the knife down and turns to face me. "So naturally I'm worried I'll fuck it up. Like I did with you."

Oh fuck. This is not a conversation I want to have. "Our situation was complicated. We were going through a lot of changes. The mutation thing, the friends thing."

"The jealousy thing." He picks up the knife again. "I was so jealous. Let's be honest, given what happened it wasn't entirely baseless. It wasn't just about Dani, though. It was about everything. I wanted a life that was only you and me, but you wanted more."

"I didn't mean to," I say. "But you're right. I spent a long time being afraid. Then I finally reached out for more and—"

"I slapped your hand for it." He grimaces. "Not my proudest moment. I don't want to make that mistake again. Jenna's really close to her sister and she has this one friend she's *always* with and I…" He gestures wildly with the knife. "I get jealous. I can't help it. I just do."

"She likes you though?"

"I think so." His shoulders slump. "She says she does. When we're together it's amazing, but the mutant thing makes it hard."

"I am a terrible relationship therapist," I say. "Like honestly, I'm stumbling through this thing with Dani by blind luck and her being, like, a thousand percent too good for me. I don't know what I'm doing. What I *do* think is you need to focus on what you have."

"Huh," Lou says, which I take as a sign of encouragement.

"You're with this girl you like who's also into you. That's a good start. I mean, we'll have to spill the mutant news sometime because even though you're control boy now, you're gonna accidentally light up and—" I let out a cackle of laughter at Lou's reddening cheeks. "So fucking horny."

"Okay, my control isn't perfect. She freaked out at first but we talked about it. I explained the whole Cute Mutants thing. Then you were in the news and of course she took a second to get over my ex being a superhero."

I watch him as he puts oil in the pan and starts frying the vegetables, covering them with sauce that makes it hiss and spit. "It sounds like you're talking. That's a good sign, right? Dani always reminds me about communication. That was one of the things I did wrong with you, because believe it or not, Glowboy, there was fault on both sides with us."

"Oh, I do believe it." He flourishes the frying pan as if it's some victory. "Definitely. A lot of fault."

A new voice joins the conversation. "Shall I get him for you?"

"Go on then," I tell the flour canister perched on the shelf above him.

It obligingly lurches off, hurling its lid wildly through the air and sending flour everywhere, but mostly in Lou's hair and all down his front.

Things get really messy after that.

Once the kitchen is mostly cleaned up and the stir-fry is rescued, Lou goes off to sleep and I sit down to eat. I'm about halfway through when I remember I'm the world's worst daughter.

> Dylan: hey pear
>
> Dylan: just fyi were all all good
>
> Dylan: so yay?
>
> Pear: Voice call?
>
> Dylan: text is fine ffs
>
> Dylan: like honestly there is nothing to worry bout
>
> Pear: I'm calling you. Please answer.

"Ugh," I say, but I still swipe to answer when my phone starts buzzing like crazy.

"Hello, Pear."

"Dilly, it's so good to hear your voice. Are you—?"

"I promise you I'm actually, honestly, totally fine." Is it convincing when I use that many words?

"The news…" Pear says. "It's not exactly helpful. There was something about an American security company being brought in to deal with a national security threat."

"Assholes."

"Can you tell me what happened?" Their voice ascends to a higher register. "Are you sure you're all okay?"

I feel a rush of unexpected tears and have to close my eyes. "Yes," I almost whisper. "We all made it through. It was messy at times, and this place is burned." A single hysterical giggle escapes my throat. "In more ways than one. We're scoping out a temporary new place now. When we have firmer plans, we'll figure out what to do about you and the other civilians."

"Dilly—" There's a pause so long I scramble to fill it.

"I know. I'm a disaster. My situation is a nightmare. I've ruined your life and—"

"No, stop. I'm fucking proud of you. I worry sometimes… You've seen me at my weakest and worst, and yet somehow you ended up so strong. I don't even—"

"I learned it from you." I know this is sappy but it's true. They fought a lot of demons, and mostly alone. I don't care if tears are spilling down my cheeks. I'm alone in the room, sobbing down the phone and Pear is equally emo on the other end.

When I finally hang up, Emma's in the doorway, flanked by Dani and Tanner of all people.

"Soft bitch club," I murmur.

Tanner shrugs. "It happens. Combat hits us all different. I'll probably take a long bath, consider drowning myself, think better of it. Sorry, is that too dark?"

Dani ducks around Tanner and crosses to me. "Couldn't sleep. We've been talking about the preacher."

"Is that right?" I feel a wave of tiredness crash over me. Too much stress and adrenaline and whatever the hell is with the aftermath of the Emma-boost. I'd rather push all this off into tomorrow, or the next fucking month to be honest, but—

Tanner takes a seat at the table. "Way I see it, we've got a Quietus agent right in our backyard. One with a power that means he can convince people to fight for him. Seems to me that's a big security risk."

"Why the change of tune?" I can't eradicate the suspicion from my voice.

"I never liked that prick. EMID wanted to get their hands on him, but y'all were probably right to be skeptical of that. Now I'm on your side, it doesn't sit right with me to have a bomb ticking away on your doorstep."

"Seems like a big risk." I rub my temples. "You have any idea how he got his power?"

Tanner grimaces. "Same place that creepy daughter of his did. Spark."

"The hell is that?" I scowl at her. "Some super-mutant program? Does it stand for something? Special Project Arranging Real Killers?"

That gets a laugh out of her. "Spark's a him. Another mutant."

"And how the hell do you know about this?" Dani asks suspiciously.

"There's top secret eyes only, and then there's knowing where the bodies are buried." Tanner grins. "People talk. They definitely like to gossip when someone has the idea to make more mutants. Especially when they try to use them as tame weapons."

"Have you met this Spark person?" Dani asks.

"No, but I know good people who have. Look, Quietus despised him and all of his monsters. But he was *useful*. They were willing to do a deal with this devil in order to kill more mutants." Her gaze skips across us. "Y'all are mostly functional, but a lot of Spark's mutants are creepy things. Y'all know that. You've fought them before."

I can't figure this out for a moment, and then it clicks in my head. "The ones Bancroft set on us. The tentacle one and the one that possessed me. They were created by Spark?"

Tanner regards us sombrely. "Those were the success stories. Some others are stranger. One became a spreading patch of darkness that infected people with weeping sores. Another turned into a fist sized chunk of marble with no discernible powers, except one day she went flying straight up and disintegrated in the atmosphere. The worst one, I washed this kid out of training. Nineteen years old, chip on his shoulder. He was an asshole and I couldn't trust him to be on my team. He joined up with Quietus, but EMID gave them my training report. Once they read that, they sent him to Spark to be changed. After it was done, he was weeping blood. *That* was his power. And he carried on doing that up until he died three days later."

"That's horrible," Emma whispers, and she's not wrong. It makes me feel like we won the fucking lottery with the powers we got.

"Why do you think they're so obsessed with *you*, Goddess?" Tanner asks. "Spark was unhinged, and his children have bizarre powers, so they want something more stable. They believe in this war against mutants so completely, they'll do anything they can to win it. They won't stop until you're dead and they have Emma."

"Was." My brain spits out that single word. "You keep saying was."

"Well yeah, they killed Spark eventually. He tried to rally some of his monsters and take over Quietus for himself. That piece of gossip definitely made it through to EMID. Good riddance." She shudders. "But all that shit is exactly why you can't trust Quietus. True fanatics are willing to do irrational shit."

I wince, and Dani puts her hand to my head. "Headache." I pull a face. "For fuck's sake, Tanner, you don't need to convince us that Quietus suck."

"My point is more that we need to kill the preacher. That'll gut Quietus here before things get worse. Or else we might have him weaponising a bunch of civilians."

I lean my face against Dani's palm, which feels unnaturally cool. "It makes sense." My head swims and I reach out to grab hold of the counter.

"I'm assuming you're not going to shed any tears if he dies?" Tanner asks.

"No." I shake my head, but that makes it swim more. "Let me just sit down. Give me a minute to rest and we'll head out."

"I don't think so." Dani helps me into the nearest seat. "Remember when you walked out into the street and got shot because you were overdoing it? We're not making that mistake again, especially with this guy. I'm going in with Tanner and Skye."

"Skye?" I frown. "That seems like a risky idea."

"Tanner's idea," Emma says. "We can use the Skyes as a chain to monitor Tanner and have Dani outside to bring it all down in an emergency."

"If both Field Team leaders approve." Tanner winks at me again. The whole situation feels too good to be true. We were trying to win her over, but I didn't believe it would *work*.

"I want Gladdy to talk to Tanner."

Dani nods. "Already has. That was the first thing we did, and Fetch says everything checks out. Tanner hates Quietus, which we already knew. She's impressed by us, which we didn't."

"Turns out I get to relive my rebellious teen experience." Tanner grins at me, the charming asshole. "I kinda like this reckless shit, truth be told. Who knows how it'll go when the big bosses at EMID get wind of it, but let's find out together, huh?"

"Okay sure." I yawn enormously. "Let's do it."

"We're going to move everyone out of here first," Emma says. "Find this place of Gladdy's. We can mount the mission just as well from there, and they won't know where we are."

I fold my hands on the table and place my head on them. "Keep going. Tell me the plan. Explain it to me like I'm stupid. Prove to me this isn't going to fuck everything up."

CHAPTER TWENTY-THREE

I wake alone in a strange bed, with no recollection of how I got here. Oni's patrolling the ceiling. Hopefully I'll never have to be boosted by Emma again because this is one hell of a hangover.

"She was back?" I ask.

"Yes. Once."

"And where's Dani?"

"She has not yet returned from the mission. I do not believe there is any cause for concern although—"

Emma? Is everything okay?

Hard to tell. We've blocked all signals in case the preacher's thoughts can be transmitted via some other method than sound.

Sounds paranoid.

Tanner gives me a run for my money. They haven't been in there long, so there's no need to panic yet, Dillyweed—uh, I mean Dilly.

Fucking Alyse. I knew she couldn't keep that stupid name to herself.

It's cute.

Shut up and let me know when Dani gets back.

I lie down in the bed and try to sleep, but all I do is thrash around in the bedclothes. In the end, I get up and wander through the cold, spacious house until I find Emma in a large lounge room. She's perched on the couch with a laptop.

"Perfect timing." She pats the chair beside her. "I've just got a signal."

"Ems, you there?" It's Dani's voice. The surge of relief makes me shiver. "We're clear. It's done."

"Done how?" I ask.

"Dilly. Good to hear your voice. It was Tanner. She and a couple of the Skyes fought her way through a Quietus unit and then killed him. I barely needed to do a thing."

"He's definitely dead?"

"I saw his body. He's not coming back. It wasn't pretty."

"You okay?" Her voice is all echoey, but I know it's just the radio.

"It's been a hell of a day. Seeing all that mess. I need to sleep as long as you did."

"Hurry back." I smile even though it's probably been the worst day of our lives bar one. This only beats that because we're all still alive. "I'll be waiting."

Emma and I sit side-by-side and watch the dot on the screen get closer. I'm up and waiting by the door when Dani gets in, although it's Tanner who storms through first.

"Mission a-fucking-ccomplished, Chatterbox. One problem down." She's all hyped up and smiling, but I'm already weaving past to where Dani collapses into my arms.

The hug only lasts a few moments before she pulls away. "Sorry, I'm beyond shattered. Lack of sleep, too much blood, take your pick. All I want is bed."

I make a valiant effort to carry her, but my hip's too sore.

"Fine, I'll do it myself." She grins at me to take the sting out of her words.

"Tanner, Skye, we'll debrief in the morning. Ems, find them somewhere to sleep. I'll get Dani down before she collapses."

"Don't debrief her too hard," Tanner says, but we're already escaping down the hallway.

When we actually reach the bedroom, Dani barely looks at me before collapsing into bed. I crawl in beside her and slip one arm around her waist.

"Too tired." Her voice is soft and blurred. "Let me sleep."

I roll onto my back and stare at the ceiling. For a moment I think I see a face there, but it's my eyes playing tricks on me as they get heavier. I roll away from Dani and let them close.

I wake with someone astride me, choking me to death.

My first instinct is to flail and call for Dani, but when I open my eyes, she's the one on top of me. I look up into her beautiful face, but her eyes hold none of their accustomed warmth. Her metal hand is clamped around my neck, squeezing tighter and tighter. I try to find air, but there is none.

"Abomination," she hisses. "You have escaped death too many times. The Lord has decreed that you will die, and His will cannot be denied. Your body shall—"

Emma, I scream. *Come and help me.*

There's no answer.

I thrash underneath Dani. Panic surges through me.

The world darkens, veiled by tears.

It's so cold in the room. Bianca stands against the wall, tears running down her cheeks and her purple lips open in an O. She is death, and she waits for me. I'll join her in the frozen world, and we'll wander icy through the wastes. It'll be—

I don't see what happens, but Dani slumps off me. She rolls to the side and I flail out from under her. I suck in air and gasp. My neck fucking stings. Tears roll down the sides of my face into my hair. There's no sign of Wraith.

"Did I do the right thing?" Oni hovers in front of me. "I did not want to hurt Dani, who you love so much but—"

"Dilly? What's going on?" Emma's in the doorway, dressed in a long nightie with a picture of Princess Bubblegum and Marceline on it. Alyse is wearing a fluffy robe that she's partially transformed to match, mauve and fuzzy all over. The transformation disappears instantly when she sees what's going on.

"Dani tried to kill me." My voice is hoarse and raspy. I put my hand to Dani's chest and feel her heartbeat there. "She was saying shit about God."

"That fucking preacher." Alyse moves into warrior mode, a skeleton creature of gleaming metal. "He put a compulsion on Dani. I'll kill him."

"You'll have to get in line."

"I should have noticed," Emma says miserably. "But I sensed no mutants in the church. He must have snuck out and I got confused by the clone numbers. I was so relieved it went well and—"

"Not your fault." I cough. "It's that goddamn power of his. It takes a few hours to wear off, so we might need to restrain her."

When I get out of bed, I can barely stand. I'm shivering all over. Alyse cradles Dani and carries her through to the kitchen. I limp through with Emma.

Every breath hurts, as though my throat is a narrow straw I can only sip through.

Alyse holds Dani down with metal arms. I hobble to the sink and pour myself cold water. I try to drink, but it makes me choke.

"Are you okay?" Alyse asks.

I try to make a sound, but my teeth are chattering too hard to make words. I settle for shaking my head.

Oni is at my shoulder, humming softly. "This is not your love. She speaks of abomination, but what has been done to her is truly unnatural."

I nod. Can the others hear the creaking sound from inside as my internal world collapses? I'm pale and trembling, unable to find any sense in what's happened.

Emma returns with rope. She works with Alyse to secure Dani thoroughly. Then she makes me a cup of lukewarm green tea and forces me to sit down. My hands can barely hold the cup. I keep replaying Dani's words in my head, and I can't shut them off. My hand touches my throat, trying to feel the imprints of her metal fingers.

"It's not her," Alyse tells me, and I know that, but somehow that's worse. The preacher has stolen Dani from me with his words.

I get through about half the tea before Dani regains consciousness.

"Filthy monster." Her words are slurred. "The Lord will show his judgement to you."

"I love you." I hate how my raspy voice hitches. "I know this isn't you."

"Don't speak to me of your unnatural love." Dani's body convulses. She throws herself backwards. The chair topples over and her head impacts against the wall. A heavy wooden chopping board flies across the room and hits me in the shoulder. I rock with the impact, but I barely feel it.

"Dani," I whisper. "Please. Don't do this."

The chair is balanced against the wall and Dani smacks her head back, shockingly hard. She screams, the preacher's words torn from her throat. They're incomprehensible, a howl of hatred.

A microwave tears itself out of its cubbyhole. I duck, but it catches me a glancing blow which sends me sprawling. My vision is blurry, and I taste bile in my throat. The cup lies shattered under my hand, a pool of tea spreading on the floor.

"You shouldn't be here," Alyse says to me. "We'll watch her. She'll be safe, I promise."

I stumble into the hallway, and steady myself on the wall. Every instinct in me is to try and fix her with love, hot and so needy it's scalding. Except the preacher lurks in her mind, curdling her thoughts until they sour. What could I possibly say? And, worse than that, how can our love be overwritten like this?

I want to throw up. I want to tear out my heart. All I need is to stop fucking feeling everything that batters on me from the inside, threatening to boil out of my throat.

Dani screams from the other room. Her beautiful mouth spills more words, pushed into her mind by this monster.

She loves me. I know she does. It took me time to let that burrow into my heart as truth. I know this isn't Dani and yet it's still her voice speaking my worst fears.

"What the fuck can have happened in the church?" I ask Oni. "That's the preacher's compulsion, right?"

"It appears to be, yes," the sword says warily.

"Then he's still alive. Which means, which means—"

My mind spins furiously. At least this is a distraction from thinking about Dani's hands around my throat. I turn down the next hallway and find some hyper-organised type—probably Emma—has put post-its on the doors saying who's sleeping where.

I open Lou's and go charging into his room.

He's deeply asleep, but I shake him awake. "I need you."

"Dilly, what's wrong?" He can see it in my face instantly. The boy still knows me too well.

"Dani." My voice won't fucking stop shaking over two goddamn syllables. "The preacher got to her. She tried to kill me."

"Oh fuck." He wraps his arms around me, still warm from sleep. "What do you need?"

"We need to lock up Tanner and Skye. They were there too and—"

"Okay, good plan." His voice is soft and reassuring, as if this is a real idea with merit. "I'll go in and use my hands like flash grenades. We should bring Leapfrog with us, because he's strong enough to take down Tanner. You can hopefully restrain Skye without freaking her out."

"Yes, yes, good." My teeth are still chattering.

"It'll be okay." He runs his hand up and down my bare arm. "Dani loves you."

We find Jackson's room. Lou explains everything to him while I fidget and fret.

"I am sorry to hear of this, Dylan Chatterbox. Of course I will assist and restrain Tanner." Jackson sounds excited at the prospect, which makes sense given she's dragged him around on a leash. "Don't worry about that."

The three of us tiptoe down until we find the door with the green post-it saying *Tanner & Skye* in Emma's neat capitals. Lou screws his face up, while I count down from three on my fingers. We're all wearing our uniform masks at full polarisation.

On zero, I bust down the door.

Glowstick's hands light up with repeated flashes. I launch myself at Skye's bed, trusting Leapfrog to deal with Tanner. I'm expecting to shout down a bunch of clones, but she stays calm.

"My eyes have seen the glory of the Lord."

"How nice for them." I'm awkwardly sprawled on top of her in a half-ass wrestling hold. "You don't want to kill me?"

"Not especially." Her voice is monotone.

I glance over my shoulder, where Tanner thrashes about in Jackson's arms.

"Let me out of here." She has her eyes closed against Lou's light, but she's still furious. "Let me kill this apostate bitch."

"I don't even know what apostate means." I leave Skye lying in the bed and duck out to the corridor where we've scrounged up some more rope. "I doubt it's a compliment. Either way, you're staying put, Tanner."

Leapfrog holds Tanner down while we tie her in the clumsiest way possible. She looks like a Christmas present wrapped by a child, but she's thoroughly restrained. Jackson tightens all the knots, which makes her hiss and swear.

"What happened with the preacher?" I demand.

Tanner laughs. "I don't know. You tell me."

I'm on the verge of telling Oni to stab her in the throat, but I need to find out what's happening with Dani first. There will be time to deal with Tanner later.

Skye lies on the bed, staring at the ceiling. "The Lord shone his face upon me." She sounds scary calm. Some more preacher whammy, I'm assuming. We tie her up too, although we need a lot less rope, and then close the door on them.

Jackson heads back to bed, looking very proud of himself, but Lou lingers.

"Are you okay?"

"Dani." It's all I can say, because everything else is barbed with self-pity.

Lou holds me in his arms while I sob. Once I'm done being whiny, I send him back to bed and shuffle back to the kitchen. I'm scared to look in on Dani, but the power of curiosity compels me.

I'm a few paces away when a familiar metallic clang sounds above me. Oni whirls furiously near the ceiling as dark blades fly through the air.

"Let me do it," Violet shrieks, appearing at the far end of the hallway. "Death is a gentler end for them both." She forces Oni back in a whirlwind and then vanishes, only to appear beside me, talking almost too fast to understand. "How will your lover feel when she comes back to herself and finds your blood on her hands? She will be devastated."

"Oni, wait." My voice sounds like it has undergone a monstrous transformation.

"Her death has been decided," he says. "She is a bloody-handed monster and we risk too much to—"

"Let her talk for a minute."

"Very well."

Violet hovers in the air, while Oni moves in a slow circle in front of her.

"Talk," I rasp.

"My father has control of your lover, but it will not last forever. It wears off relatively quickly in the early stages."

"How many times has it happened to you?" I ask.

"There is no hope for me." Shapes flicker over her face—a snake, a bloody fist, a dying woman—but they resolve into a red so deep it's almost black. "There is for your lover. Your death has been written, so it shall be. The Lord cannot be denied. If you let me do it, I will make it quick and she will suffer less."

"What do you say to that, Oni?"

"I think she is a monster created by a monster, although she speaks true on one point. There is no hope for her."

"Then I'm done too. Do what you want with her," I tell him. I'm so fucking exhausted.

In the kitchen, Dani's screams have subsided into whimpers.

Dilly? I think you can come through now.

CHAPTER TWENTY-FOUR

I run back into the kitchen, my legs shaky.

"Dani?" My voice quivers.

"Don't look at me." Her voice is hoarse from screaming. "Dilly, I—"

I'm by her side in an instant. I kiss her cheeks, her lips, her neck. She barely responds. "Dani, it's okay. You were under his control. It wasn't you."

"He made me try to kill you." Tears trace lines down her face. She's so still, like she's frozen. "My brain wouldn't stop. I was drowning in his horrible thoughts and—"

"It's not you." I'm crying too. "I knew it wasn't you the whole time."

Alyse unties Dani and she gets to her feet. I clutch onto her, but she pulls away rather than collapsing into me like she usually would. I tell myself it doesn't matter, that she's been through something more awful than I can imagine. I remember the slippery feeling of my thoughts after the preacher spoke to me. What's been done to Dani is far worse.

That explanation makes sense, yet I still feel the painful sting of rejection. It's a blade slipped between my ribs into the most tender part of my insecure soul. I want to reel, to stagger, to lie down and let the hurt bleed out of me.

Except Dani's the one who's really suffered. I have to fold my hurt away and put her first, no matter how much the little wounded part of me bays for attention.

"It's okay," I tell her. "I love you. I'll be here for you."

Alyse helps Dani back to bed. I walk a few steps behind them, running my fingertips along the wall as if I'm lost in a labyrinth and desperate to escape. I'm shivering again, the cold coming from outside rather than the steadying chill within.

Oni lurks in the hallway. "The monstrous creature was too fast for me," he says mournfully. "She has now retreated."

"Let her go. I have more important things to worry about."

When Dani gets into bed again, she closes her eyes and turns away. "Let me sleep, please. I need to be alone."

I try to ignore the corrosive feeling inside me, like something poisonous worms its way ever closer to my heart. Even with the immediate control gone, she still can't stand to be near me. Her reaction is a perfect mirror reflecting my fears. I'm scared I'll collapse in on myself now that I'm faced with it. Is all this strength I've built up really so hollow that it can be punctured like this?

"Are you doing okay?" Alyse asks.

"I'm fucking terrible." Alyse and Emma are probably the only two other people in the world I'd admit this to. "I'm scared this will change her. She wouldn't kiss me back, wouldn't even let me hold her. My stupid brain keeps sprinting down all these pathways and—"

Alyse and Emma hug me in perfect unison, like they timed it.

"You and Dani are OTP," Alyse says fiercely against the side of my head. "That's not going to change. You'll find your way back. I don't doubt it for a second."

"Not for a fucking second," Emma says.

"Even Violet said she'd recover, but I don't know." I look at Dani huddled in the bed. Normally when she has her back to me, it's an open invitation to spoon her. She's been very clear she doesn't want that. I've never experienced this from Dani. Our hands have communicated reassurance and companionship and seduction, but she wants none of that now. I understand that she's been traumatised, but I'm always so desperate to be close to her and—

"Dilly." Alyse puts one hand in the small of my back as she holds me close. "I don't always see eye to eye with my parents, but they occasionally have some good advice. Like it's ok to feel fucked up about fucked up things."

"It *is* fucked up," I whisper.

"Very. It's horrible mind control supervillain shit. He's talked that awful crap for years. Now he can bend people's minds to believe it." I feel Alyse shiver against me. "Think of all that poison spreading outwards."

I understand so many people have been hurt by this man, but all my thoughts bend towards Dani. I know it's selfish, but all I can think about is reconstructing the bridge between us.

"Ems, can you print something really massive out?"

"What do you mean?"

"That photo they took of Dani and I after we went public. The queer Kiwi heroes one. I want a massive copy so she sees it when she wakes up."

"I've only got an A4 printer." Her face brightens. "We'll print it mosaic style, like a puzzle. It'll be fun!"

Emma's definition of fun is very different to mine. We end up with hundreds of pieces of paper that we have to assemble on the wall. Dani sleeps, undisturbed by our whispering as we slowly assemble our masterpiece.

When it's finished, I stare at it, transfixed by the delight on her face. The beauty and love in it is so vivid. How can it be gone?

"You'll be ok." Alyse stands beside it, a scribbled, anxious outline. "It might take a moment is all."

"I hope so." If I tried to pick out what I was feeling on an emotion wheel, I couldn't. It's spinning too fast and it all registers as sickness.

"Thanks, you two." I force a smile. I'm sure it's not remotely convincing. "I can stay with her now."

"If you need anything at all." Emma squeezes my hand.

They leave the room and I lie down gingerly beside Dani. It takes a lot of effort to suppress the urge to hold her. My instinct is to try and force things, but that doesn't always work. It's really fucking hard to not *insist* until it's better.

I lie on my back, stare at the ceiling, and try to think about anything else. Anything at all. List the X-Men in order of appearance. Try and rank Red Velvet songs. It's all a miserable failure.

I can tell when Dani wakes up, because she starts crying.

"Are you okay?" I whisper.

"The photo. I can't look at it."

"I'm sorry." My voice sounds brittle, my words threaded through with cracks. "I thought—"

"I understand it's beautiful, like I understand an equation." There's no part of her body that touches me, and the poetry is gone from her voice, leaving it arid. "But when I look at it, I feel worthless and small and wrong and *fuck*."

She falls silent. I wait. My heart is so loud.

"I've always been proud of who I am. I've known I was a lesbian for years. Even when I was little, my earliest crushes were on cartoon girls." The faint light from the hallway illuminates the slight curve of a smile on her face. "Like Ariel, or Azula from Avatar."

"Azula's a good choice." I try not to roll towards her.

"Or Marceline from Adventure Time."

"You and monster girls. I'm a monster, I suppose." My voice cracks, despite all my efforts at calm. "This isn't because I'm not really a girl, is it?"

"*No*. Not at all. I never doubted you, Dylan. I never doubted our love. Even more, I never doubted *myself* in that way. It was always a rock-solid part of me. I understood some people didn't approve, but it never chipped away at that central core of rightness. It was me and I was unashamed."

"I love that about you," I tell her. "Me being made of doubts."

"The preacher *defaced* me. He put this horrible seed of shame inside, and now the tendrils are everywhere. And even though his voice has gone, every time I close my eyes, I feel it and I want to retch." She's openly sobbing. I brush the tears off her cheeks with my fingertips, even though it's a futile endeavour.

"I'm not ashamed," I tell her. "Not of who I am and not of you."

"I want to scrub this feeling out of me, but it keeps making me feel sick. Like when you touch me, I shudder, even though I don't want to. I feel like he broke some deep-down part of me and I don't know how to fix it."

Oh god, the void is so huge. How can it be so big and still fit inside me? There's always been a nightmarish insecure thing at my heart, a host of voices only too happy to catalogue my failures, my ineptitude, my essential state of *not-enough*. I've been working on folding that carefully away, piece by piece, until only a whispering kernel remains. Now, it billows free and calls to me. It's a precipice I'm hanging off. If I let go and freefall into self-loathing, will it hurt, or will it feel like coming home?

Dani is ashamed of me. The preacher took his hate and he scrawled it over our love, and he won.

"Fuck that," Oni says. "*Fuck that*, Dylan. Your love is real, and it is true. It is a force that even I feel. Do not let this stand."

"You're right," I whisper.

"What?" Dani asks.

"Not you," I tell her. "You're entirely fucking wrong. He didn't break you. We're not going to break. I'm here, as long as it takes, until you're ready to reach out again. He's not going to win. I love you."

"I," she says, but the rest of the sentence lodges in her throat or her heart, where the preacher's lies still entangle the truth.

"You love me," I say.

"Yes," she whispers back, because she can say that much. It takes her a while to fall asleep, but finally her sobs smooth out into deep breaths.

I swing my legs out of bed. My phone says it's three in the morning. I run my hand lightly over Dani's hair.

"Do we go to do what is necessary?" Oni asks.

I nod in response.

"I am ready also," Roxy tells me from outside.

"Good." I walk through the house to collect my uniform. I dress in the kitchen, my fingers numb and clumsy. My heart has ceased beating and my blood is frozen slush in my veins. I'm back in the cold wasteland where I meet Bianca, where I press my chilled lips to her perfect icy cheek.

"I know why you're here, Chats." Her purple lips curve into a smile.

"They came for Dani. They tried to use her as a weapon against me."

"They shouldn't have done that." The cavity in her chest where her demons lived is an empty hole filled with melting snow.

"Now Bobby Drake burns hotter than I do," I tell her. "If you tapped my frozen heart with a single nail it would shatter in my chest."

"You won't shatter."

"No. I won't. This is the next right thing."

Vast wings made of tangled darkness and light spread behind Wraith. Her demons are gone, and now she has become my guardian and protector. She towers above me, and I am swallowed by her shadow.

I inhale, and draw the cold into me. I'm ready.

A single blink, and I'm back in the kitchen, looking out into the depths of the night.

Emma? Are you awake?

Barely, but for you, yes.

I need to know where the preacher is.

Let me check. There's a short pause. *I can't tell for sure it's him, but there's definitely a mutant in the church. Why would he still be there?*

He thinks he's won.

And you're going to....?

I'm going to show him he's wrong.

I pull the mask up over my face, then walk out of Fetch's safe house, Oni by my side.

CHAPTER TWENTY-FIVE

Roxy's engine is already running, lights on and heater going. I get into the driver's seat and Oni hovers beside me. The car glides down the hill, along near-silent roads.

I drum my fingers on the steering wheel. Outwardly I'm perfectly calm, but inside I can't stop screaming. We drive past dark houses. The doors swing open, and knives, cleavers, axes, and even a pair of baseball bats drift out. They float alongside the car, whispering greetings and assurances of support.

As we reach the bottom of the hill, a pair of chainsaws come out of a hardware store and flank the car. I buzz the window down to usher them inside. Everything is speaking to me, but I stay silent. They don't need to hear from me. They're picking up on my determination and rage.

We reach the church and pull up alongside. It's completely silent. There are no lights on, but I trust Emma. The preacher is here, in his lair. Roxy noses up onto the footpath right by the doors.

The weapons follow me out of the car. Chainsaws buzz like hornets, axes spin in wild circles, and knives and cleavers clash against each other like they're chattering among themselves.

"Hey, little alarm. It's time to open up and say *ahhh*."

"I'm not sure." The alarm sounds nervous. It's probably fair enough. "You seem agitated."

"Good call. Now open the fucking door or I'll bust the place down." The weapons spread out beside me like two huge wings. I'm Dark Willow with the whole suite of horror movie weapons. I'm so fucking cold. When I move, my skin crackles with frost. "Last chance. I don't want to hurt you."

The front door makes a clunking sound. I slam it open and there's no scream of protest. The only lights are a single bulb over the door that leads to the offices, and a pool of light on the staircase. It's perfectly quiet. I pad across the carpet.

The preacher has the power to get into a person's head and change them, to fundamentally alter who they are. Even if it wears off eventually, there's so much damage he can do.

"Hold, hold! Get down!" A voice rises into a shriek. I glance over my shoulder to see a man at the doors to the mezzanine. He's got a gun in his hand and an axe in his face. Another man slides down the stairs, two cleavers taking turns to hack at his neck. My objects, already protecting me.

Well, fuck. I guess the guards know I'm here.

The chainsaws are tearing at the door that leads to the offices. One bursts through in a whirlwind of shattered wood. The other growls after it. Brief gunfire is cut off by a horrific sound of revving and screaming.

When it's silent, I shove the remains of the door open and see three dead soldiers in the corridor. The chainsaws hang in the air, dripping blood. Their engines are throttled down to a low rumble. Surely the preacher heard the screams.

I hold Oni tight.

Someone comes at me from a side door. It's someone in a black suit, holding a gun. Oni drags my arm up and to the left. I carve a long cut up his front and then the sword decapitates him with one slash that's so vicious it almost dislocates my arm. I should've fucking learned to sword fight.

"Sorry," one chainsaw says. "We missed that one."

"You can go into his office," I tell them. "Kill whoever you want, but leave the preacher for me."

One of the axes crashes through the door just above the handle. A baseball bat nudges it open.

Two men with guns immediately burst into the corridor. They're wearing uniforms with the sharpened cross of Quietus. A flock of knives swarm them, slashing the tendons in their wrists until their guns hang loose from near-severed hands. The chainsaws fly past, along with the axes. I'm so calm, despite the blood and the chaos. This is where I'm meant to be—holding Oni, three paces from entering the preacher's office. Three steps from revenge.

The two soldiers stagger, arms useless. Oni guides my hand. Four strokes of his blade, and two more men are dead.

There's gunfire from inside. I don't know why they're shooting. They're not going to stop an axe with a bullet.

"The room is secure," one chainsaw calls. "The preacher lives."

I drop my mask. He needs to see my face. I turn up the music in my headphones. It's something low-slung and aggressive. The soundtrack for dealing with a monster.

I step over the bodies of the two dead men in the doorway and enter a nightmare. The lamps that illuminate the room have been splashed with blood, making everything glow a grotesque red. Corpses are slumped on the ground—the preacher's protection leaking blood onto the carpet.

The cross on the wall drips gore onto the ground as if the dude on it has been wounded.

I should be sick. I should run and hide from what I've done.

Instead, I smile.

The preacher has one hand clutching onto the desk. The other holds a gun, pointed right at me.

"You won't shoot me," I tell the gun.

The preacher squeezes the trigger frantically.

Nothing happens.

"We already convinced her to drop her bullets," an axe tells me proudly. She speaks clearly in my head, even through the music.

The preacher looks at the gun helplessly.

"Slight problem," a cleaver calls from outside. "It's what d'you call it? Re-in-something? Bunch of extra fucks."

"I've got this. You go." The remaining weapons in the room hurtle past me eagerly. They're feeding off every trickle of rage that's been building inside me since this manipulative fuck broke into Dani's mind. I'm frozen solid with it, but I won't shatter. He may have his god, but I've got my Wraith. You come for me, you come for my people, you come for my fucking *girlfriend?* You take the core of who she is and put your filthy bigoted hands over it and you get—

This.

The frozen shattered heart of me.

"You pissed off the wrong fucking person, Pastor Mike."

The preacher's mouth moves as he seeks the language to control me. In my headphones the beats are so loud, they splinter into static. He could be telling me anything, and I wouldn't hear a word.

I take a step forward. Oni quivers in my hand.

"Do not allow yourself to be programmed," I say. "Your hate can't control us anymore." There's no point fucking around. I jam the sword straight in through the side of his neck, before I can second guess anything. The blade slides in easily, almost sickeningly so, even though I know Oni is helping me. I rip the sword out towards me, tearing out the preacher's throat in a shower of blood. It splatters over my face, warm and wet. He's dead and dropping before my thoughts even catch up. I've killed a man. I've killed a monster.

Pastor Mike isn't going to command anyone again. His body twitches, and I turn to leave. I wipe at the blood on my face, but only smear it everywhere.

Gladdy had it right, early on. The main reason I cut off Tremor's hands was because he killed Batty. There were other reasons to make it palatable and to *justify* it, but at the end of the day he murdered my friend.

It's the same thing here. Even if I lie to everyone else, I can be honest with myself. There are other reasons he deserved it, but this man died because of what he did to Dani. Maybe that makes me a villain. Right now, I don't even care. I need to do this. It feels like the only justice I can expect in a world where soldiers come to kill us in our home.

"More enemies approach," Oni says. "I can hear them."

From the hallway comes the sound of shouting, the clap of gunshots, and screaming. I lift my mask back up and swing the door open to see chaos.

A flying baseball bat catches one Quietus soldier around the back of the head. As he falls, three knives hurtle from the ceiling to stab him in the back. Another is chased down the corridor by a chainsaw that revs itself into a scream. A third has a big steel kitchen cleaver buried in his chest. He totters backwards as an axe spins in circles towards him.

"Let me fly," Oni says, and I reflexively loosen my hand. He howls off down the corridor in search of more to fight.

I take a deep breath. I've done what I came here to do. Now all I need is—

Two more Quietus goons burst out of the office to my right. They shout and wave guns. One gets a shot off immediately. It hits me high up in my chest, just near the shoulder.

I spin around and bounce off the wall. My head hits the ground.

Fucking hell, that was lame.

I reach up to feel for the blood, to stem the tide of it, but all I can feel is the mashed-up metal of the bullet and the impression it made in the costume. These suits work even at close range, but I probably shouldn't make a habit of this. Not to mention it fucking hurts.

The gun tears its way out of the soldier's hand so fast it nearly rips his trigger finger off. It spins around and discharges every remaining bullet it holds. The other soldier is dragged back and forth by his own weapon, like a dog towing its owner on a leash. When a knife glides into my hand, it feels very easy and natural to push myself up from the ground. I punch the blade up under the faceplate of the body armour. There's more blood, enough that my feet skid in it.

"They are defeated," Oni shouts. "We are victorious."

"Some bastard shot me in the shoulder," I grumble.

"Are you grievously hurt?" The sword blurs back down the corridor towards me. "No, it appears you can still walk. Do we need to find one of your medical facilities to heal you?"

"My costume protected me, but it hurts. Let me whine." I have to step over bodies as we head for the exit. There's so much fucking blood. It's smeared on the walls and in pools on the floor. Knives pull themselves from flesh. A chainsaw tugs itself free from a ribcage with an awful shrieking sound.

There are three more bodies in the lobby, and I give them a wide berth. More lie slumped on the stairs. I'm starting to shake, from adrenaline or terror or something I don't understand. When I finally collapse into Roxy, the lights on the dashboard swim before my eyes.

"Take me home," I whisper, and she pulls away. All my weapons chatter excitedly in the back. They're pleased with what they've done. There's no remorse for them. It must be nice to see things that clearly. As we travel, they depart back to their homes, some of them rather battered and bloodstained. Some people may get a fright in the morning when they find their objects crusted in blood and worse for wear.

I close my eyes from exhaustion, and I see the pastor's face in front of me. I see his throat splitting open when I pulled Oni out. There's blood on my lips inside the mask. It's his blood. The blood of the man I killed.

"Pull over." I drop my mask and lean out of the driver's door. I vomit onto the ground until I feel empty. It scalds my throat coming up and makes my eyes water.

"It is no shameful thing, to react so after a battle," Oni tells me. "Many warriors I have fought with have done the same. There is the heat of battle and there is the aftermath, and a line separates the two."

I pull myself weakly back into the car and clutch the steering wheel. "He needed to die, didn't he, Oni?"

"A man with such power could talk the authorities into doing his will, as well as spreading hate to all who hear him. He wielded his own daughter as a weapon to kill innocents, and then attempted to use the woman you love to do the same. A more craven act I have rarely seen in the whole span of my years. Simply put, he was a demon, and it is my purpose under heaven to destroy demons where they are found. Finding someone to work with me in this quest gives me great joy."

"Thank you, Oni."

"I am no expert in these things," Roxy tells me, "but I do not believe you would have taken a life if there was no reason to."

There were reasons, for sure. I don't know if they were enough. Who makes those decisions anyway?

We finally pull into the driveway of Fetch's safe house. I feel very unsteady getting out, but make it inside without collapsing. The house is silent and still. I find my way through to the bathroom, and turn all the lights and heating on. In the mirror, my costume looks weirdly patterned. When it falls to the floor, spatters of blood spread outwards from me like a gory exclamation.

I'm not a person made of ice after all.

I'm an uncomfortable and awkward thing made of meat, bruised and bleeding.

Underneath the mask, I look horrific. There's blood matted in my hair and in gruesome war-paint smears on my cheek. They disappear down my neck and stain the singlet I wore underneath. I close my eyes and turn around so I can't see my reflection anymore.

The shower is a massive glass cubicle. When I turn on the water, it steams up almost instantly. I strip the rest of my clothes off and shuffle inside. Blood sluices down my body, staining the water pink as it swirls around the drain.

It's a horror movie, except I'm the monster. My legs feel too shaky, so I crouch down and watch the bloody water spilling over my fingertips. My shoulders shake with sobs, but no sound comes out.

I don't know how long I stay like that.

My trance is broken when arms wrap around me. They're strong and reassuring—one made of flesh and one of metal.

"Oni brought me," Dani says in my ear. I can feel the shape of her body pressed against mine. "He woke me and dragged me here. Now I can see why." Her fingers go almost directly to the dark bruise near my shoulder, hovering without touching. "What happened to you?"

I want to tell her they shot me, but that's not what comes out of my mouth. "If only I had an Uncle Iroh, I wouldn't have turned out this way," I tell her through jagged sobs.

"I don't understand. What do you mean?" She tips my face out of the falling water.

It's hard to get the words out, but I persevere. "Zuko had Uncle Iroh as a beacon to guide him towards redemption. Instead I'm stuck with my Magneto Was Right t-shirt, and I'm turning into a supervillain. I went to the church tonight, and I killed the preacher. Oni and me. Quietus people were there, and we killed them all too. Heroes aren't supposed to kill, no matter how terrifying the villain they face is. Except I did it. I'm a monster and a murderer. How is there redemption for someone like me, who sets out in the night to kill a man because I decided—"

She stops my words with her lips. "Enough."

I'm still shaking. There are so many places I hurt. I want Dani to kiss them all, but I worry that asking her will make her pull away, and I need her close. My eyes stay closed, because I don't want to see any shadow of the preacher in hers. It feels like there's blood behind my eyelids. It's inside me, all the way through.

I lift my face to the water in the hope I can be finally clean.

"I'm sorry," I whisper.

"I refuse to feel shame," Dani tells me fiercely. "I love you, Dylan Taylor."

I don't know what percentage of that is truth, and how much is wishful thinking. "I love you too."

The water pours down around us. I finally open my eyes, and she's staring into mine. They're clear and unsullied, and I'm back in her landscape, part of her world. I take her face in my hands and place my mouth to hers, finding the heat in her that can melt the blood in my veins and restart my frozen heart like a sputtering motor.

We kiss until we almost pass out in the steam.

Then Dani takes me to bed. She holds me and she loves me and I love her in return. I re-memorise every part of her, as if she's brought me out of a cryogenic freezer into a world where everything has changed. She now holds a monster in her arms, but she tells the monster of her love and, for a moment at least, the monster believes it.

"I need you," I tell her, and I feel the need returned in every kiss and touch.

Sometime later, we finally sleep.

CHAPTER TWENTY-SIX

I'm in the deepest and most peaceful sleep I've had in ages when someone screams and ruins it.

"Fucking seriously?" I fumble for the light switch, but I'm in a strange room and can't find it. I get my phone instead and shine the torch wildly around.

There's a woman in the corner, crouched down with Oni at her throat. Curls tumble around her face. She's dressed in jeans and a t-shirt that says *You Give Me Butter-flies*. There's a cut along one cheek that's been stitched up.

I know exactly who she is, but it's hard to believe.

Dani's on the far side of the enormous bed, like there's room for a third person in between us. Perhaps she drifted away from me in the night while we slept. My fingers are cold, as if I'm slowly freezing again now she's out of reach.

"What the hell is going on?"

"She appeared like the monster," Oni tells me.

"Because she *is* the monster." I take a deep breath. "Hello, Violet."

"Hi, Dylan, Dani. I'm here to help. Honestly, I came like this so you might believe me." Her voice trembles convincingly. "Please, ask the sword to stop."

"The sword's the only thing keeping us alive." Dani's practically spitting. "Oni, slit her throat."

"Dylan?" Oni stays hovering at a safe distance.

"Just stay there." I try to keep the irritation out of my voice.

"Oh, so we're not killing everyone today?" Dani asks.

"No. What? No. What are you talking about?"

"My father is dead," Violet shouts, interrupting whatever this conversation is. "I don't know how it happened, but I'm free. We're all free. Don't you feel it? There's no compulsion holding me anymore. I came here as soon as I could, to warn you."

"Warn us about yourself?" Dani frowns. "That seems—"

"No, about Abigail Tanner."

Fucking hell. Of course. I turn to Dani, who's swung her legs out of bed. "What really happened at the church? We didn't really talk about it after…you know."

"It all turned to shit." Dani grimaces. "We were doing the stupid chain thing, but everyone kept disappearing like it was a horror movie. Tanner had convinced us all to cut comms in case the preacher could hijack them. I had to go in eventually. As soon as I walked in, his voice came over the speakers and—"

I hunch my shoulders. "So he got to Tanner first, or she decided to switch sides, or—"

Violet shakes her head. Her freckles stand out in stark detail on her pale face. "Abigail Tanner has worked for Quietus since the start."

I feel like the world is paused for a second. All the facts in my head shift and tumble and end up in new positions. The picture they paint isn't pretty. "How do you know?"

"I was there when she met with my father, before she even came to you. They talked about angles to infiltrate your group—whether to take you over by force or co-opt you. She tried to be a partner but quickly realised you wouldn't stand for it. When her takeover failed and she went dark, there were many in Quietus who were furious. My father said to trust Tanner."

"Shit." Dani's metal fist clenches. "We fell for it. All of us. She even fooled Gladdy. How did they do that?"

"I'm guessing telepathic resistance training. Red triangle and shit, like the X-Men." My brain is racing. "This is all for Emma, isn't it? Where the hell does Matthias Fisher fit into this? Teen Spirit?"

Violet looks at us warily. "You've lost me." She's still huddled in the corner.

"Tanner turned up for him first. A mutant with weird shadow powers. He had a whole lot of shit to say about Emma's mother and some cataclysmic world event."

"I heard *nothing* about this, I swear. They came for Emma. Everything else is just… where exactly is Tanner now?"

"Locked in a bedroom." I shrug. "Super strength boy tied him up. Him and Skye." I look at Dani, as my brain keeps feeding me new and horrifying suggestions. "You got brainwashed into attacking me. Let's assume Tanner was faking the whole time. What the fuck did he do to Skye?"

As if on cue, there's another scream.

This one isn't Violet.

Dani and I fling ourselves out of bed. At least we put on *something* after last night, but I'm sure Violet gets an eyeful as we scramble for the door. She flickers out of existence.

I wrench the door open and we run smack into a Skye. I assume it's Prime, because she's screaming and flailing like a Kermit gif.

"Skye." Dani grips her by the upper arms and pulls her upright. "What's going on?"

"Help." She sobs and coughs. "She killed one of us." Someone's still screaming—two more clones in the doorway to the room where Tanner's supposed to be. They're both on the ground, but one is cradling the other. There's a hell of a lot of blood. For a second I get a nauseating flashback to last night.

"Which one's dead?" I ask Skye.

"Three," she whimpers. "I'm Two. Three's dead, oh god, oh fuck."

Bloody hell. If Two's this much of a mess, things are bad. Skye Prime clutches her clone to her chest. Blood gushes from a jagged wound in Three's neck, making both of them sodden.

"Dylan," Prime wails. "She's dead."

"Fucking Tanner." I'm furious, but I try to find the coldness from last night. "How the hell did she get out of those ropes?"

"She asked me to set her free."

"And why the hell did you do *that*?"

"It's what God wanted." Her eyes fill with tears. "The man told me to do the will of God, and even though his voice was gone from my head—"

Ugh, I have no fucking patience with this shit. "Where is she now?"

"I don't know." Prime starts crying again. "She killed Three and she left."

I want to tell her to chill the fuck out and deal with her clones, but we don't even know how this shit works. What happens if she reabsorbs a dead clone? I step awkwardly over Prime, who lets out another horror-movie scream.

"Sorry," I say. "Did I hurt you?"

"Another one." Her mouth hangs open. "She killed another one."

I catch Dani's eye.

"Fuck," we say in unison.

There's a wide-open sliding glass door leading onto a deck that runs along one side of the house. The outdoor furniture lies scattered. Stairs lead down to a small path that cuts through a bamboo garden where I spot a pair of legs. I take two leaps down. Another Skye lies among the plants. She stares at me, her neck on an awkward angle.

"Four?" Dani asks.

"I can't tell. But Five or Six have the best chance of stopping Tanner."

We head down into a quiet cul-de-sac. It's early, and there's no sign of anyone around. Downhill seems the most likely option. At the corner, we find another Skye dead. The black handle of a knife protrudes from the base of her throat.

"How the fuck did Tanner get a knife?" Dani growls.

"She's a spy, and she played us." I barely even stop at the clone's body.

We hit the cross-street. On the verge opposite is another dead clone, blood leaking out of her head. I can't tell if she was hit by Tanner or by something else. The more pressing concern is the pair of Skyes sitting on the side of the road. One clings to the other, who has her hand pressed to her throat, blood spilling between her fingers.

"Chatterbox, babe," Seven slurs. "You made it. That bish—dark hair bish—she's a nasty one. Fuck us all up and pow, outta here."

I crouch beside Six. "You doing okay?"

She shakes her head. "Fucked," she says hoarsely through bloody lips.

"Tanner?" I ask.

She nods in response. "Talked Prime into it. Soft touch."

"Where did she get the knives?" I ask, but Six shrugs helplessly and lets out a hollow-chested cough that spatters blood on the road.

Dani and I help Six up, while Seven wrings her hands.

"Sorry." Six's voice is faint. "Fucked it all up. Should've dealt to her but she's fucking tricky, that one. Fooled me once, fooled me twice. Shame on fucking all of us."

"Hush," I say. "We've got you."

There's a little park on the side of the road a few houses up, and we detour in. It's clear Six isn't going to make it.

"Bad, bad, bad," Seven whimpers. She's hanging off my other side, making it even harder to walk. "Don't like it."

I don't fucking like it either, but it looks like we've lost at least five clones. I have no idea what this means for

Skye or her powers. This is a nightmare scenario, even before you include Tanner being on the loose. She led Dani into a trap intended to kill me. I'm not sure why she's run now rather than killing us all. Perhaps she's still intimidated, or there's another plan. We should never have fucking trusted her, we should have—

"No time for second guessing," Dani says, as if she read my mind.

We lower Skye Six to the grass at the edge of a garden. It's filled with an array of purple and yellow flowers. The sun peeks over the horizon, making the clouds feathery and pink. It's too fucking beautiful a morning to watch another person die.

"I'm sorry," I tell Six, and press a kiss on her forehead.

"Not your fucking fault." The front of her torn shirt is saturated. "You're a good one." She gives one final convulsion and falls still.

"Fuck." Dani wipes her eyes. Her knees crack when she gets to her feet.

"I'm so angry." I stare down at the body in front of us. "I don't know what to do with it."

"Let's get back to Prime." Dani helps Seven up. "See how she's holding up."

"Not so good at all," Seven clings tightly. "Worst fucking day."

We take Seven uphill and get back to the house where Jackson and Maddy wait at the bottom of the path.

"Only one?" Jackson presses his hand to his mouth. "It has been…difficult for Skye. All the deaths have caused her much pain."

"Screaming like she's having a baby," Maddy says with a grimace. "A bit freaky, to be honest, so I came down here with Froggy to get a break."

"Still alive though?" I feel hesitant even asking.

Yes, she's still alive, Emma tells me. *So is Two. We found Nine dead though.*

Fucking Tanner.

I stride up the path with the others in my wake. When we reach the deck, there are two bodies wrapped in sheets.

"Fuck," Dani says again. She used to have a vocabulary before she met me.

On the couch, Skye Prime and Two are both sobbing.

"We need to calm them down," I say.

"That's an amazing idea." Alyse is faded and small. "It's lucky we have you here to think of such brilliance." She breaks off and comes over to me. "Sorry, it's been a hell of a time. Are you okay?"

"We've seen a lot of dead Skyes." The front of my hoodie is wet with blood. "It's not a pretty picture. Tanner's well trained and not fucking around."

Emma's with Dani and they're talking quietly.

"Time to be a leader." I cross to Skye. I sit down beside Prime and sling an arm awkwardly around her shoulder.

"So many gone." I can barely understand her. "So many. I felt them *leave*." Her voice turns sharply into a ragged scream.

Emma gives me a slight eye roll. *We've tried this.*

We've got a bunch of identical corpses scattered around suburbia. If she can't absorb them, we have to clean them up ourselves.

Fair point. Jackson and Maddy?

I'll take them. I know where the bodies are.

I make to stand but Skye clings onto me.

"Chatterbox, you have to keep us safe. I'm sorry for letting Tanner go, but the preacher was so terrifying, and I thought she would leave quietly. I had no idea that—"

"It's not your fault," I tell her, in the hope it'll calm her down. She's not the only one who was fooled by Tanner. You can add the rest of our names to that list too, as smart as we thought we were.

Skye clings onto me and blurs. Two disappears. Either my words worked, or she's exhausted from having her clones manifested for so long.

I exhale in relief, but it lasts for all of five seconds before Prime starts screaming. She lets go of my arm and jerks backwards on the couch. Her whole body seizes violently and she clutches at her throat. It sounds like she's in agony.

Dani crosses to the door that leads out to the deck. "Bodies are gone. Sheets are empty."

Skye's screaming subsides to a whimper. She gets to her feet unsteadily, but she's finally smiling. "They're all back." She claps her hands together and holds them there as her knuckles go white. "All eight of them. They're inside me."

She blurs again and the line of Skyes reappears. They're alive, but bear the marks of their injuries. A multi-coloured bruise blooms where Four's neck was broken. Three, Six and Eight have enormous jagged scars across their throats that are wet and glistening. And Five's head wound oozes black blood down one cheek. It looks horrifying, but none of them seem to be in pain.

Creepy, creepy fucking powers, I say to Emma.

Not one of mine, so don't blame me.

"You feel okay, Six, you fucking psycho?" I ask.

"Neck hurts a bit." Her voice is rough. "Not gonna stop me fucking stabbing someone who needs it."

"We might need that," I say, as the clones blur back into Prime. It's a tiny piece of good news in amongst a lot of bad. Tanner is loose in the city and she knows way too much. It's hard to shake the feeling that we're doomed this time.

CHAPTER TWENTY-SEVEN

We're in the sparsely furnished living room of the safe house. Alyse and Emma are squeezed into one chair, while Dani and I are on opposite sides of the room. It just *happened* that way, but I can't help but feel there's something going on. She won't even meet my eyes. My brain is falling into worry and paranoia, that old gravity of negative thoughts.

It's only us and Fetch here, because the rest of the group has taken Skye out to try and cheer her up. Gladdy is pacing back and forward, extremely pissed. "So Tanner played us. She fucking played *me*, Dylan."

I don't bother arguing with her, because she's not wrong. "It was all bullshit from the start. Saying she was EMID and—"

"She *is* EMID." Violet's leaning against the wall at the far end of the room, keeping her distance. I've vouched for her, which may be a colossally stupid decision, but she's sharing tea which we desperately need. "I mean, she's Quietus but she works for EMID too.

She's not the only one. EMID's riddled with Quietus people."

"And Quietus are the fanatics," I say. "Tanner was right about that?"

"Yes. They want all mutants dead, at any cost. Especially if they can use other mutants to do it. That gives them a very particular joy. They have a man named Spark, who can make more of us, but he's…" Her voice shakes as she inhales. "He's a monster."

"Do you know *how* he gives them powers?" Emma asks. "How does it work? What's the process?" It's clear to me her brain has been whirling around this question.

"I don't know. He placed one hand on my forehead and the other on the back of my neck. He called on God to change me in his image. He told me I was His blessed daughter." Her hand traces the length of the scar on her cheek. "The next day, when I woke up, I saw the world differently. There were lines running through it that I could disappear into, pockets in reality, paths to move through. I could mask myself and extend myself into a weapon."

Emma's shoulders slump minutely, and Alyse puts one arm around her, their heads resting together.

Dilly, I thought this might be something. Is he the mutant leaving the crystals? Is he related to me in any way? How does it tie into my mother? I feel like it's all connected, but I'm too dumb to figure out how.

We'll get there, Ems. It just might take time.

"I can't say I'm sorry this person is dead," Dani says. "We don't need him making more dangerous mutants."

"Dead? Spark?" Violet's eyes are almost as wide as in her killing disguise. I imagine the glitching panels of colour gliding across her skin. "He's not dead. Quietus are coming back, and Spark will be with them."

"But Tanner said…" I snap my teeth together. "Fuck!"

"I heard her discussing it with my father. This was before she got caught, but the plan was in motion. Quietus wants to attack the Pride parade and draw you out." She tugs at an errant curl. "They see it as two birds with one stone."

Dani's seething again. "There's no *reason* for this. It's nothing but hatred."

"They have a lot to lose." Violet won't look at any of us. "They like the way the world is and want to cling to the power they have. It doesn't make it right, but they'll fight to stay on top of their hill."

"Leaving us in the hated and feared corner," Dani says.

"So they're coming." Emma looks exhausted. "I'll check flight reports and see if we can intercept them early." She pauses. "Violet, are you sure you don't know anything about Matthias Fisher and Teen Spirit?"

"I'm sorry." Violet's gaze flickers around all of us and then away. "I wish I could help you. I've got so much to make up for."

"Your father compelled you." I look at Gladdy as I say it, who's staring at Violet intently. She looks troubled. I'm not sure if it's from the fears she sees, or because she can't trust her power after Tanner.

"The whole story then." Violet takes a deep breath. "Can I sit?"

I raise my eyebrow at Dani, who finally looks at me, only to shrug. If Violet wants to attack again, we've still got Oni.

She walks across and takes a seat, still as far from us as possible. "I kissed a girl for the first time when I was sixteen. My good Christian boyfriend found out and went to my father. He said it was to pray for me, so I'd have the strength to overcome my unnatural lusts. My father was unhappy to say the least. I was furious and broke up with the boy, but I ended up kissing another girl. That didn't go well for me either."

"He put something in your mind," I say quietly.

"No." Her lips are pale. "He didn't have those powers then. His methods of instruction were rather more…physical."

"Shit," Dani and I say at the exact same time.

Violet's eyelids flicker. "When he did get his powers, that's when he started using them to try and change me. He told me over and over that I was no longer attracted to girls. It became something I knew and not-knew at the same time. You understand, Dani."

Dani pulls a face. She doesn't like Violet saying her name, but she nods after a second. My brain immediately races to fill in all the possible gaps. She told me last night she wouldn't feel shame, but look—she has eyes for everyone but me.

"He spoke out more and more from the pulpit about these sins. People in the church brought their children to him to be cured. I don't know how many people he compelled like that."

"Maybe my parents aren't so bad after all," Alyse says. "They never put me in the firing line of that shit, even when they caught me in bed with my ex Maddox."

"He got more and more agitated about what he called the rainbow plague infecting New Zealand. All he could talk about was needing more extreme measures, and that's when he found Quietus. When Tanner came to him, he thought it was the will of the Lord laid out before him. And then you two made the news, so beautiful and so happy and so in love…"

"That's when he told you to kill me." I manage to say it without my voice shaking.

"I chose you," she whispers.

"It was a smart choice."

Her cheeks colour faintly. "I told my father I had, uh, fixated on you. That the Lord had laid it in my heart to see you dead, and I could not go against His word. My father was angry but—" There are tears in her eyes, and I'm sure I see stained glass colour reflected in there. "You killed him, didn't you? For what he did to Dani?"

Here's the big risky moment. I could tell her the truth and she might unleash herself against me, and one of us will die.

Or, I tell the truth, and maybe she'll stay.

"Yes. That was a step too far. I took Oni, and I killed him."

There's a pause. I'm very aware of the breath I'm holding. I let it out slowly while I stare at Violet, who looks at her hands.

Finally, she nods. "I thought so. He'd sent me away. I don't know what I would have done if I'd been there. What he would have asked me to do. How I could have fought you." She looks out the window at the view of the city and the sun shining down on it. "He made me hurt myself as punishment for failing again. He could sense it, I think. The fact that I find you somewhat—"

"Irresistible," Dani suggests, this tiny hint of a smile on her lips.

"Interesting." Violet's eyes dart to me and away. "Fascinating. Fine. Maybe I did have a little crush on you from the moment I saw you. There's something about you that's…different."

"A little of column A, a little of column B." Dani smiles. "Fluid and flexible and mercurial."

I'm not even sure if any of this is a compliment. I wish I could straight up ask Dani how she's feeling about me, but I'm scared of the answer.

"Yes," Violet says. "There's something about you, Dylan. It was somewhat of a fixation. I felt I'd get resolution one way or another—either I could stall my father from his murderous plan and save you, or you'd be dead and out of my head."

I frown at her. "That's not actually very romantic, despite what young adult fiction would have you believe."

"My brain is not always a comfortable place." She smiles. "And what the two of you have is so beautiful. I can say that now. I have no desire to come between you, and I don't know…" She sighs. "My father is gone from my mind, but it lingers. The thought of kissing someone—even a person as fascinating as you—it makes me recoil."

"It doesn't feel good having him poking around in your head." Dani's looking at me thoughtfully, except I know what none of these thoughts are. "I don't envy you a life of it."

There's a second's pause and Violet starts sobbing. Dani looks at me helplessly, even though it was her great big stomping words that did this. It's me who gets up and walks over to Violet.

"Is it okay if I hug you?" I ask her. "Just like a platonic thing?"

She nods, so I hold her as she cries.

Our little gang grows by one, Emma says. *Funny thing is, I kind of like her.*

She really did her best to fight her father. And she does need a hug.

And then we worry about the next thing trying to kill us.

Dani and I lock eyes over Violet's head. I thought I'd memorised the guidebook to her face, but there are still pages missing. There's something sad there, like she's mourning. Violet did say something about the preacher's words lingering. It all makes me hot and uncomfortable and I want to flee from it. Instead, I focus on Emma.

"What about the other mutants out there?" I ask.

"We can't risk going for them now," Emma says. "It's basically a signpost for Quietus."

I hate it, but I can't argue. They're safer in anonymity. It makes me feel like a failure. I need a pathway to save everyone.

We're all outwardly chill when the others return, fresh from eating too many pancakes and with leftovers for us. Everyone's wary about Violet, but she sits between Emma and I, and people seem content with that. Dani's slouched against the bench, hands wrapped around her coffee. She stares into the depths of it and I stare at her.

Over what ends up being second breakfast for most of the group, we fill everyone in on what we've learned about Spark.

"We need to decide what to do about the Pride parade. It seems even more likely they'll hit it now, with Tanner free." I look around the room. "I may not be a hero anymore, but there's no fucking way I let them do this."

"No question," Katie says, and fist bumps me.

"We use our powers for good." Emma puts her fist in too.

"Cute Mutants." Alyse smiles right at me. "Still an accurate name."

Lou stretches his hand across the table. "We protect people."

Kitty Pride and Crave both murmur their assent too, and then everyone looks at Leapfrog, who's clockwise from them.

"I disgraced myself. In our last battle. Dani Marvellous almost paid the price." His voice is all husky. I think it's from tears not seduction, but it doesn't *sound* that way. "You all took me in. A monster who attacked you. You forgave me and welcomed me into your family."

"Silly Froggie." Maddy grins at him. "That's what these dummies do. Over and over."

"Don't ask us whether we regret it in certain situations." Lou smiles back, and she spits the tiniest drop of acid which burns a neat hole in the table in front of him. "See? *Certain* situations. Some people are constant trouble."

Maddy arches her eyebrow at him and Lou's gaze darts away.

"Yes." Jackson smiles. "Family. It is something worth fighting for. So I will. Fight with you, I mean."

I want to apologise to him for being brought into this family, where his inheritance is people showing up to kill him. On the flip side, at least his new siblings or cousins come loaded with superpowers and ready to throw the fuck down.

"This noble self-sacrificing thing you're all hooked on is complete bullshit," Gladdy says. "But I won't be able to stop Maddy joining, and you need at least one sane person to make sure the whole thing doesn't—"

"Are you trying to tell me you're in?" I ask, with a theatrical eyeroll.

"I'm a fool," she says but she bumps her fist against all of ours.

Dani finally steps forward and adds hers without comment.

"I'd like to be there too." Violet's fist against ours is tentative, as if she's nervous about what will happen on contact. "If you want me."

"We do," Alyse says. "We'll take anyone who's willing to stand up with us."

Gladdy hisses breath between her teeth but doesn't argue.

Violet stares at me. Trust is a weird thing, but I remember her pain at the thought of how much Dani would hurt if she followed the preacher's will and killed me.

"I agree," I tell her. "You're in if you want to be."

"It feels strange to make a decision on my own." Her hand trembles against ours. "I want to fight with you. My mutant name is Penance."

I get a chill when she says it. She's been responsible for multiple deaths. Even though it wasn't her mind that drove it, her hands ended up bloody with innocents. However I feel about the preacher, it was a vastly different thing I did.

Violet's cheeks turn faintly darker. She flickers away without saying anything else.

"I don't think she has any psychic defenses," Gladdy says quietly. "It's hard to look at her with so much pain in there. She desperately wants to be a Cute Mutant, but she's teetering on the edge of falling apart. I almost gave her a hug. We need to look after her, make sure she's okay."

"Oh, Fetch." I put an arm around her and squeeze her against me. "You do have a beating heart. Maddy's been right all this time."

"You're not easy to look at either," she snaps, but she doesn't move away. "There's so much desperation and pain in you, this burning desire to save the world. It's uncomfortable. You could try turning it down a notch, but I don't think that's how you're built."

"Sorry, Fetchy," Alyse says. "This is the way we like them."

"That's very clear," Gladdy says, but now even she's smiling, although it doesn't last long. "Be gentle with Violet, if you can. She takes this penance idea seriously. It's the only thing keeping her together."

"We'll look after her." I hope she can see it written in me when she looks into my heart.

"There are very few people in this world I'd trust enough to follow," Gladdy says.

"Don't follow me," I squawk, because my brain still does that. "Follow Emma, or Dani."

My eyes are on Dani, and I see her give a slight shake of the head, like there's something she wants to say, and has chosen not to. My stomach's in freefall. Its some remnant of the preacher that hasn't drained away. I know you're meant to be brave and painful conversations when you're with someone, but I can't face this on top of everything. My head is full of nightmares. Dani's face, twisted with loathing. My hand pushing Oni through the preacher's neck. Tanner's betrayal. Skye Six dead among the flowers. If Dani pulled away from me, the very last strings of my heart would snap and then I'd just be the monster, crouched bloody on the floor of the shower, snapping and snarling without anyone to hold me together.

CHAPTER TWENTY-EIGHT

Emma hunts down the contact details of the people on the Pride organising committee. We end up contacting someone called Lauren.

"Uh, hi," Dani says, abnormally awkward. "We're calling because we've heard, like, reports of a threat against the Pride parade in Christchurch this weekend?"

"Okay, sure, yeah." The person on the phone has a nice rich singer's voice. "Which group are you affiliated with? Just so I can tag your threat with the right bullshit."

"We're not threatening you," I blurt. "We're *warning* you."

"Listen, darling, I've heard it all before."

"This is a credible threat." Dani leans over the phone and starts barking into it. "Have you heard of an organisation called Quietus? The one that came over here and—"

"The right-wing assholes that are all over the news. Yes, I've heard of them. So that's who you're with?"

"It's not us," I yelp like a startled puppy. "We're from the Cute Mutants. I'm Chatterbox, and I'm here with Marvellous and Goddess."

"No shit, you lot are the queer Kiwi heroes? Well, let me fill you in on a little secret. We get a lot of threats. Every year, someone calls in something. Most of them amount to nothing."

"This is different," Dani almost groans.

"Turns out the cops agree with you. They're not always the greatest fans of ours, but they say it's for our own good that we've been busted down from a parade to a rally."

"You could cancel," Emma suggests.

"If we cancel, then they win. If we didn't turn up when someone hated us, we'd never celebrate anything, sad as that is to say." They sound like they're smiling. "We'll be going ahead no matter what. The best thing you can do, if you're really who you claim, is show up and help. A lot of people have their eyes on you."

"These people have guns." Dani gives it one last try. "They'll come hard."

"And I'm sure heroes like you will do a *spectacular* job of stopping them. I look forward to meeting every cute one of you."

"We'll be there." I hang up the phone.

"This is what you wanted." Dani's voice is flat. "Another battle."

"Quietus is coming anyway." I shove my hands in my pockets. "I like that the Pride people don't back down."

"Zero fucks given." Emma slings her arms around both of our shoulders and pulls us in towards her. "This is why we are what we are, Dan."

"I remember when you were the quietest girl in the class, who wouldn't speak even when the teacher spoke to her," Dani says. "And now you say zero fucks given and want to start shit at a Pride rally."

"I've been hanging around with all these bad influences," Emma says demurely.

Dani runs her hand through her hair, which has grown down past her shoulders. "I hope this is the right decision."

With two days until the Pride rally, it's hard to know what to do. Tanner must be *somewhere*. Roxy and her friends Frankie and Valeria patrol the streets. Emma has drones in the skies and her hacker tendrils out through the internet. There's no giant private plane landing with vehicles full of dudes in body armour, but she matches a few names on alt-right forums to recent arrivals in New Zealand, trickling in on different days.

They're coming.

It's a waiting game, and I fucking hate waiting.

We take advantage of the relative quiet to have awkward conversations with our respective parents, who are in hiding and unhappy about it.

"I see Quietus attacked a church," Pear says.

"Looks like it." I can't tell them I've chosen Magneto over Xavier. They raised me to believe in a better world. Unfortunately, we got this one instead.

"Dilly, you're doing the best you can. I know you."

I want to fucking cry, but we're past that. I've been shattered and reformed one too many times. I might look like their Dylan, but I'm not. They don't know me anymore, but I don't want to break their heart by showing them that. Still, I need to tell them the essential parts.

"It's not over. They're coming after the Pride rally this weekend."

"Jesus." There's a long pause. "You're going to be there, aren't you?"

I don't even answer that question. They already know. I can't let Quietus hurt innocent people, especially not as a way to get to us. "Once this is done, we'll find somewhere safe and wait for things to cool down. That's the plan. Fuck knows what'll happen." I swallow the next words on the tip of my tongue. I'm scared it's more likely we'll end up in one fight after another until an inevitable end. I ache to confess all my fears, to hear them tell me everything will be okay.

Pear could give me pretty words and promises, trying their best. But it would all be hollow and ashen because they don't have to face this shit.

"Dylan—"

I cut them off before any empty offerings. "It'll be okay, Pear. We've got each other's backs. I've got Oni, and you know he's not going to let anything happen to me."

"Yes," Oni says grimly. "What is that statement you are so fond of? Too fucking right."

"Then what do you need from me?" Pear asks, and I feel a rush of mixed guilt and love.

"Stay far away from the Pride parade, and keep all the other families there too. Once we've got somewhere safe to go, we'll take you with us. Until then…"

The morning of the Pride rally dawns clear. I slept badly, plagued by dreams of Wraith. I'd consider it a bad omen, but my nightmares happen too often for that. I'm not great with open endings. I like to know what's going to happen, and all the possibilities are a near-paralysing blur in my head. Please give me something concrete to fight.

I know Emma was awake in the night as well, because she kept brushing questions through my mind.

Very poetic thought, Dilly. You've been spending too much time with Dani.

Did you come to any startling conclusions?

No. My mother's mind remains closed to me. My past is a mystery. I remain a riddle.

Now who's being poetic. Don't think it's going to be a day for poetry today, Ems. It's going to be one for the bad seeds.

Seeing all the mutants together in one room, it's amazing how much we've grown. What hasn't changed is everyone staring, waiting for me to say something impressive. Even Kitty Pride and Crave are here. They actually asked to stay. I was on the verge of sending them away, but Crave did eat a rocket for us last time, and they are mutants, so they deserve to make their stand too.

"I'm not going to say anything impressive. You all know Quietus are coming to attack the Pride rally. We figure Tanner's with them, so they'll know our numbers and capabilities. This time they might have other mutants with them. Powers unknown. We know this is a trap. They know we won't let them hurt innocent people." I do my best imitation of someone who knows what they're doing. "We're going to go anyway. We'll do this as peacefully as possible, because we don't want civilian casualties. But here's the deal. We're not forcing anyone to come."

Everyone watches me. I don't feel like any kind of leader. I still feel like the same kind of half-ass idiot I always was.

"Why peaceful?" Katie asks. "Quietus won't be."

"Killing shouldn't be our go-to solution for everything."

"Not for *everything*." A curl of smoke trickles from between her lips. "But when people attack us or attack innocent people? Nobody forced them to join Quietus. They *choose* this because of their fucked-up beliefs about God or mutants or whatever."

"So they deserve to die then?" It's Kitty Pride of all people, who I didn't really expect to have an opinion. "They might have partners or families. This might be a job for them like any other."

"Better off with a dead partner than a racist asshole," Katie says. I used to think I had zero chill until I met her.

"We're going to be very public," I point out. "Unlike last time, when we were locked in our own building. There are going to be cameras. If people see Skye Six running around wildly stabbing people, or Maddy melting people into puddles, it'll make bad headlines."

"Um, excuse you, but why pick on me?" Maddy blinks around at everyone. "I'm not the one who stabbed a bunch of people in a church. Having a floating sword poking people indiscriminately is not a good look *either*."

"There is nothing indiscriminate about how I operate," Oni says, slightly huffy as he strokes himself against my shoulder.

"The point is we need to be careful," Gladdy says.

"Quietus will use footage of us to make us look like monsters if they can," Dani points out. "We don't need any more bad publicity."

"What if it's a choice between letting an innocent person die or hurting a Quietus soldier?" Jackson asks, which is a fair enough question.

"We could talk trolley problems all day," Dani says. "So let's say the first priority is preserving innocent life. The second priority is not looking like feral monsters the public should be terrified of."

"I think *I'm* a feral monster," Maddy stage-whispers to Gladdy.

"We're capable of it," I tell her. "Today we're putting on friendly faces for the public."

"So you *do* want us to kill people?" Katie asks me. "Just in secret, like how you killed the preacher?"

I tug at my hair. "Can we stop bringing that up please? Yes, I killed the preacher. With his power and what he'd already done it was—"

"It was the right thing to do," Violet says. "If you hadn't...he could compel an entire congregation of people to attack you. You saved lives and minds." Her voice is so earnest that I blush and lose my train of thought. What was I trying to say?

"I want to believe in a world where we don't have to kill anyone." I feel like I'm speaking around a lump in my throat. "I want to move towards that. I want the mutant nation. I want safety for everyone in this room and everyone outside that needs it, mutant or not."

"And if that doesn't work, then we fuck shit up," Katie says with immense satisfaction.

"Yes, Dragon. If we have to."

Despite my entirely uninspiring speech, everyone still wants to come. Crave is actually excited about eating bullets. Even Kitty's on board, although the 'bunch of cats' distraction seems to have a limited shelf life. Hell, let's all join the party. It's not like a bunch of bigoted murderers are coming to crash it or anything.

"You okay?" Dani asks me, once everyone else has filed out of the room.

"I'm fine. It's not me who's acting weird."

"Weird how?"

I don't know how to phrase any of it. Words are stupid and useless. "You tell me."

"Dylan, this conversation is pointless."

"You're the one who started it." My voice is plaintive and whiny.

Whatever shell she has cracks for a moment. She holds out her hand and pulls me in close. I melt against her, the only warm thing in my world. The blood in my veins heats so quickly that I imagine her fingertips trail lines of steam as they move over my skin. My lips part slightly. Everything in my body is drawn towards her by lines of force I'm helpless against. I arch and I ache.

She pulls away, and walks to stand by the window.

All I want is to know what's going on inside her brain, but there's too much at stake. Hearing my worst nightmares from her lips would break me, and I need the strength to fight. I clench my jaw around my questions until they shatter in my mouth and I taste the shards. This is a different battle, and I have no tactics aside from retreat.

CHAPTER TWENTY-NINE

We show up early to the Pride rally, which is in Cathedral Square. The church it's named after is still in ruins nearly ten years after the quake that brought it down, so it looks like the fucking apocalypse has already happened. It's an eerie backdrop, but hopefully not an omen. I press my fingertips to where the tattoo is on my arm, as if it's an equivalent to Dani's pain trigger.

The cops got here even earlier, and have cars parked at all the entrances. The streets haven't been barricaded off yet, but they have all the gear ready.

All day, I've been driving everyone crazy by repeating the rules of engagement. Now people are spouting them back to me at random intervals.

"The first priority is to protect innocent life," Dragon shouts over the comm.

"The second priority is not looking like me," Sourpatch shrieks, so loud it hurts my ear.

"Hashtag team feral monster," they holler together.

"You two are banned from saying the word hashtag," I say grumpily.

"Hashtag team Dylan's secret favourites!"

Their high spirits are infectious. Beyond it all, I'm pleased to actually be *doing something*. Roxy glides up to the square which is already full of people. Her friends Val and Frankie coast to a stop behind her and we all pile out. Everyone's in their plain black costumes. We do not fit the Pride look.

People have come to be seen. They're dressed—or undressed—in colour and costume. There's a dizzying array of people of all ethnicities and sizes and presentations. It makes me smile inside my mask. Except they're not entirely pleased to see us. There are a lot of looks cast in our direction. We look like Quietus types.

"Okay, Ems. Do the thing."

Emma hits a button on her phone and our costumes light up in stylised rainbows. They're all slightly different, but the overall impression is a tropical riot of colour. Everyone has the Cute Mutants logo on the chest with our codenames on the front and back. Nobody's going to miss us. Here we are, the fabulous targets, and we're here to party.

Roxy cranks up her stereo, playing some song called "Born This Way" that she's convinced is a gay anthem, but I've never heard of it. She must have got *something* right, because between that and the costumes, the whole crowd starts cheering and dancing like this really *is* the biggest fucking party.

I finally convince her to switch to Sunmi, and the crowd seem just as into that. Dani starts dancing first. She's the best dancer except maybe Alyse, but everyone else joins in around her. Sourpatch and Fetch even get up on top of Roxy, who assures me it's entirely fine. Then random people start dancing with us too. I freak out for a moment because what if some of them are Quietus? There's a kinda hot androgynous guy in a g-string that says Police gyrating in front of me. I cannot fathom where he's hiding his weapon if he's an undercover Quietus agent.

I can see his weapon, Emma says. *And I'm not into dudes or sex, so catch up, Dilly.*

Bad seed.

Dani takes me by the hand and pulls me in *very* close, and for three seconds I almost forget why we're here, until the song dies away and a loud voice can be heard singing.

"It's raining mutants," the voice sings, almost louder than Roxy's stereo was. "Hallelujah, it's raining mutants." The crowd parts to reveal a striking Pasifika person standing over six foot and wearing a glittering rainbow dress. "Shame it doesn't scan, isn't it? Thought you might not show. We spoke on the phone. I'm Lauren."

Our masks all drop in unison. We've made a few other changes too. Dani's bleached her hair completely white and I've cut mine wicked short except for a demure little wavy mohawk. Alyse doesn't need to undergo any salon time, but hers floats around her head in a glorious, rainbow-tinged halo.

"Now I see the reason for the name," Lauren says, with an enormous smile. They hold out one hand to shake. "The queer Kiwi heroes. Aren't you delightful?" There are a lot of us to introduce. Lauren seems particularly taken with Jackson, who doesn't know what to do with the attention aside from stutter and blush. Once all the getting to know you shit is done, Lauren turns serious.

"I wasn't entirely sure you weren't fucking with me on that call, but we've had corroboration from multiple sources. They're here, they're well-organised, and they mean business. Between you and me, it was almost cancelled, but everyone decided to trust you lot."

Thanks, Lauren. Great inspiration.

"Then it's good we're here isn't it?" I keep my voice as calm and steady as possible. "We'll spread out around the square. We've got communications so we can warn of hotspots. And we've got eyes in the sky too."

Alyse is holding a big suitcase for Emma. She flips the lid open with a flourish. With a couple of taps on Emma's phone, a flock of drones go flying into the air.

"Might have to stop you there," Lauren says. "As joyous an occasion as this is, not everyone wants their faces on camera."

"The software onboard is all loaded with face-obscuring tech," Emma says smoothly. "None of the footage is stored. It's simply there so I can alert people." She leans in through Roxy's open window to scoop up the tablet that's plugged into the charger. One of the drones floats down to hover in front of us, except on the tablet screen our faces are nothing more than indistinct blurs.

"We're not here to ruin anyone's fun," I tell Lauren. "Best case scenario, everyone has a party."

"Worst case scenario, you wonderful people came prepared. It's lovely to meet you, but I've got plenty of people to see."

They stalk off through the crowd, greeting everyone. When I turn back around, Lou is standing in front of me. He's with a very tall, very buff woman with a twist of peroxide hair on top of her head.

"Hi," he says. "Dylan, this is Jenna."

"Oh! Of course." I reach out and shake her hand. She squeezes really hard, and it's kind of cringe, but I let her. "Nice to meet you."

"So you're the mysterious hardass boss of his."

"No, the boss is there." I wave in the direction of Dani and notice that Jenna checks her out. I hope Lou doesn't notice her noticing. "I'm the friendly approachable one."

Lou lets out a loud snort, and I dead-eye stare at him.

"Sorry to take your boyfriend away for mutant duty," I say. "Fate of the world and all that."

Jenna frowns. "You say it like a joke, but if what Lou says is true… He wouldn't tell me everything about what happened the other night, but people were really coming to kill you."

I don't know what else to do besides shrug helplessly like a lost fictional character.

"It's not right," she says.

"And yet here we are." I feel like I'm about a thousand years old talking to this girl, and every single one of them has only made me more jaded.

"Will you look after him?" She reaches out and touches his shoulder affectionately.

"I'll have him with Leapfrog. Dude can fly and punch people's heads off. Lou will be fine." I give her a clumsy salute. "It was nice to meet you, but duty calls."

I scurry away into the safety of the colourful crowd. Lou, you absolute asshole, springing that on me. He knows I hate that shit.

Guided by Emma and her drones, we space ourselves out around the square. The attack could come from anywhere. There are a whole bunch of people scheduled to speak, but I don't know who any of them are, so I can't tell if there will be a particular target. Dani and I are at opposite points, which I understand because our powers are broadly similar, but I still don't like it. On the bright side, I'm paired with Alyse. It's nice to hang out, plus her powers keep getting wilder. It's so bizarre how she keeps evolving like—

Sometimes it's exhausting being able to read your mind, Emma says.

Imagine being stuck in here twenty-four-seven.

I think I'm juicing her on a low-level trickle that's slowly powering her up. Not on purpose, but it's happening all the same.

Maybe we should all spend more time with you. How do you feel about sleeping in a real pile?

You know Alyse would actually love that.

If people ever stop trying to kill us, we need to figure this shit out.

I know. Emma sighs. *It scares me. If you didn't have my back...*

But I do.

"Dilly." Alyse links her arm through mine. She's a glowing rainbow woman who looks like she's been projected from somewhere heavenly. "We get to hunt Quietus together!"

"I know." I grin at her. "The original Cute Mutants."

She laughs and pats my short hair. "These high maintenance girlfriends, always stealing us away. That Emma especially. Do you know how many back rubs I give her?"

"She does have terrible posture."

We're patrolling the area closest to the stage. There are barriers set up so people can't get too close. The whole place is starting to fill up with people, most of who look like they're here to party. I'm not sure how seriously Quietus take their mission—would they dress up super queer to blend in?

Alyse and I wander around the back of the stage. There's a small group of people at the very edge holding signs about God and staring balefully. I'm tempted to send Oni to cut them down, but I need to remember my own rules of engagement. #TeamFeralMonster.

There are instruments on the stage, and a couple of dudes messing around with them. I'm idly watching when Emma's voice comes over the earpiece.

"Spotted a pair of suspicious characters standing over by that big chalice art thing. Dressed way too heavily for the weather. They're a few back in the crowd. Pretty sure one of them has a gun and the other has some kind of blade."

"Let's go." Moodring shifts into something more predatory.

We cut our way through the crowd, who part obediently. It's either my delightfully colourful uniform or the fact Alyse is a head taller than anyone, made of shimmering rainbow glass with glowing yellow eyes. Her claws could comfortably wrap around someone's head. It's on the verge of being threatening, but she does have the words *Crowd Control* glowing on her chest, so let's call her the world's most imposing security guard.

The two targets are right in front of the towering metal shape of the chalice, dressed in black with face masks and goggles.

"Mutie!" They see Alyse coming first. One of them raises a gun. A few people in the crowd scream. There's running and shoving. Cops move in our direction.

"Oh gosh," the gun says. "He can't really want to discharge me in the middle of all these people, can he?"

"Aw, baby, you don't need to put up with that kind of treatment." I beckon to him. "Come here and I'll look after you."

The gun yanks forward. The guy holding him stumbles.

"Shall I cut the hand off and ensure everyone's safety?" Oni asks from high above me.

"No need," I say.

The gun wrenches himself from his wielder and spins around to point back down at the man from above. "I don't think you feel very lucky, right now, do you?" His voice is high-pitched and panicked. "If you do, it's a vast misjudgment of the situation, because I swear I will put a bullet in your knee."

"He can't hear you," I say, but the guy seems unnerved enough having his gun bobbing in thin air. His companion draws a knife but Oni pounces, and the knife is quickly discarded on the ground. Alyse takes hold of his neck with one claw and shoves him down.

The gun spirals down and jabs himself into the neck of the man who once held him. He gives up pretty quickly after that. I put a knee in his back while I zip tie his hands together.

"How many more?" I ask him.

"Fuck you, mutie."

I yank him to his feet. I'm tempted to have the gun shoot him in the foot, but I've been nagging everyone about professional superhero decorum.

A pair of wary cops are with us now.

I hand them our new captives. "I think you'll find these two work for Quietus. They're probably not the only ones."

"Assholes," one cop says.

"No, wait." The other cop is unimpressed with me. "They've got their right to protest. It's these so-called superheroes that shouldn't be here."

I shove the zip tied Quietus guy towards the complaining cop. "They're not protesting. They're fucking armed. Now get this guy out of my face."

"You're lucky we don't arrest *you*." The cops squares his shoulders and steps up to me.

"This really isn't the fight you want," I tell him.

"Really, it's not." Alyse interposes herself between us and dangles a trussed-up Quietus soldier like a kitten. "We're all here to keep people safe."

"Got some more here who came from a side-street," Dani says in my ear. "I snatched a couple of guns and threw the bodies over to a cop car. Leapfrog is—"

The ground shakes slightly as Froggie drops from the sky, a Quietus solder in each hand.

"Where do we put these, Chatterbox?" His face is completely serious, as if I'm in sole charge of body disposal.

"Tie them up and leave them." I jerk one thumb at the cops. "We need to get back out there. I doubt this is all there is."

"Are they cleared to do this?" Our best cop buddy has turned to argue with his partner. "This is vigilante bullshit."

"One of them had a gun," I say. He's still floating above me in the air. "There will be more here with weapons. You need to work with us on keeping people safe. You should probably close this whole thing down."

"You don't get to give us orders, mu—"

"Mutie?" I duck around Alyse and get right up in his face. "Finish that fucking word and you'll be on the ground with this other asshole."

Alyse grabs me by the arm and drags me away. "Chill about that word. I know they use it in the comics, and these fuckers mean it like a slur, but just be a fraction more easygoing." She switches to the main comm channel. "Don't worry, everyone. Chatty isn't actually fighting the cops."

The police watch us leave, hands on their weapons.

"He might be Quietus in disguise," I growl.

"Or just sympathetic to their cause," Gladdy points out.

"How is that better?"

"Either way," Dani cuts in. "That's four down without any trouble at all. It feels too easy. I'd say they're probing us, to see how we respond."

"Agreed. Everyone stay alert and be ready." I scan the crowd around me.

"I could simply roam through the crowd and stab anyone suspicious," Oni suggests. "I'm not recommending permanent injury, but I could easily ensure they cannot hold a weapon."

"Stop trying to tempt me," I mutter.

I catch up to Alyse, who's returned to something softer and regular-sized.

"Remember the cops hate Spider-Man," she tells me.

"What does that have to do with anything?"

"It's *Spider-Man*. He's like the softest superhero boi, and still the cops hate him."

"Don't use superhero logic against me, Alyse. It's not fair." I'm smiling despite myself.

"I don't think it's *right*, but it's, like, inevitable? We don't fit their world or their system. That's why there's a problem. It's happened all through history with people they didn't want to make room for. We're even scarier, because we can do things like fly swords or make ourselves ten feet tall."

"Alyse, stop being so wise."

"What? I've always been this wise." She nudges me. "It's the same old X-Men stories, Dylan. Hated and feared."

"Omigod, you read X-Men?" I take hold of her arm. "What stories? When? Did Emma force you to do it? Who's your favourite?"

"I'm not having this conversation with you now, because we have work to do."

"Alyse, this is borderline cruelty."

"It'll be our reward for getting through this. I'll tell you why I like Pixie and Surge so much."

"Alyse," I squeal.

"Reward, remember." She grins at me. "I love your new hair."

I reach up and pat the top of my head. "I feel like it's maybe too short."

"Nah, it's sexy. It makes Dani weak at the knees."

"It does?"

"Omigod, she wouldn't shut up about it." Alyse nudges me. "Your girlfriend is very boring on the subject of you."

"She didn't tell *me* she liked it." There's a pause. "Do you think she's been weird?"

"Weird how?"

I scuff my foot along the ground. "I don't know. Distant. Since the whole thing with the preacher. You know, like she's not sure about me."

"His control's gone, isn't it?"

"I have no idea! She's just acted different since it happened and—"

"Did you ask her about it?"

I stare at her until she starts laughing.

"You know, conversation is not always overrated, Dylan Taylor. Sometimes you can use it to find out all kinds of useful things, like how your girlfriend actually feels."

"Codenames, Moodring," I say mock-sternly. "We are out in the field."

"My apologies, fearless leader. I shall make sure that—"

Alyse's words are drowned out by a rising tide of screams.

CHAPTER THIRTY

A crowd of people runs towards us. Some look freaked out, others are going along with the general mood. The closest barricades are knocked aside as people flee. There's more screaming in the distance.

I stand with Oni. "Let's assume all the fuss is for a reason."

Moodring shifts into a steel monstrosity, eight feet tall and festooned in blades. Her face is a metal mask that glows neon blue. When she extends her arms, they sound like a forest of swords being drawn.

"Show-off."

"Someone's got to be the biggest badass on the squad." Her expression is still clearly recognisable as Alyse, even if the rest isn't.

We go the opposite direction to the fleeing crowd. They part around Moodring, so I duck in behind her. Together we forge our way through to a small unit of black-clad dudes with body armour and automatic weapons. They're illegal here, you fuckwits.

"Everyone get out of here," the leader screams. "We're here for the muties." He does a double take when he sees Moodring coming. I don't think she was the mutant he was expecting.

"Heavenly Father, please protect us." The Quietus soldiers open fire. Bullets ricochet off Moodring's skin. She tears a gun from one soldier and uses it to club another across the face, before kicking the first in the chest with one bladed foot. Oni whips across another's arms, making him drop his gun.

The others are still firing at Moodring when something flickers in the air above them. Long dark tendrils spill outwards, plucking the guns from their hands. They're dragged to the ground and I run over to restrain them.

A blood-red mask with dark, staring eyes looks down at me. No shapes are visible on it.

"Penance," I say. "Thanks for the assist."

I don't hear her reply, because a familiar horn sounds from behind me. Roxy drives towards us down the now-deserted street.

"What are you doing here, Rox? This is turning ugly."

"I've come to talk to *him*."

A military-looking vehicle rumbles around the corner. It's got big rugged wheels and armour plating on the front.

Penance is gone, presumably to deal with other problems.

Roxy nudges past me and heads towards the Quietus vehicle. I run after her.

"Um, Rox my darling, those are—"

"Back off you horrible thing," my beautiful, reckless car shouts.

"Puny blue commuter contrivance," the military vehicle says in a gravelly voice. "Begone or I shall crush you."

"You and what fucking army?" Roxy sneers.

"The army inside me?" The military vehicle sounds unsure. "I carry six men with guns who are sworn to destroy anyone who stands in their way. To free the earth of the mutant plague."

"Disgusting. I may be a puny blue commuter vehicle but at least I'm on the correct side."

"They command me to do their bidding. Now move aside or you shall be crushed."

"I do nobody's bidding," Roxy howls. "I am a free vehicle and I shall stand in your way. I oppose tyranny in all its forms, but especially this one."

"Fuck's sake, Rox." I climb up on her front bumper. Oni swoops down to nestle into my left hand. "Let's do this dumbfuck thing together if we're going to do it at all."

"This is your funeral," the military vehicle growls.

"Maybe," I shrug. "People have thought that before. If you do kill me, you'll have to face my girlfriend. She's telekinetic. Do you know what that means?"

Whoever's trying to drive the vehicle isn't having much luck. The engine is screaming but the tyres are skidding slowly backwards. Then I see Moodring is holding the back bumper and towing it slowly away.

"It means she can move things with her mind," the military vehicle says.

"Close. Dani can *tear things apart* with her mind. Like asshole trucks who follow shitty orders. She'll leave you alive, but you'll be in pieces."

There's the sound of more gunfire, and Moodring staggers. Free of her grip, the truck races towards us. I can see the reflection of Roxy and I in the windshield. We look brave but dumb.

"You'll be a wreck of a thing," I tell the vehicle, as if I'm not terrified. "A ruin. A cautionary tale—this is what you get when you fuck with the wrong people. So fucking stop." Roxy and I say the last word together. I'm shaking so hard you can see the faint ripples along the length of Oni's steel.

The truck's wheels lock completely. It slews across the road, the back half sliding out of control. Roxy doesn't back up an inch, even though I wish she would. The truck comes to a halt less than a meter away.

"Please don't hurt me," it says.

A door slams open, revealing an irate man with a gun.

That was a mistake. Oni is done fucking around and my heart is still beating too fast to call him back. The sword goes straight through the wrist of the man's gun hand and then punches into his chest. I don't see what happens after that. All I hear from inside the truck is thumping, a single gunshot, and screams abruptly cut off.

"Is that sword with you?" The truck's voice is much quieter.

"Oh yeah. That's my other friend."

"I think I may be glad I switched sides."

Oni floats out of the truck and shakes himself, splattering blood all over the paintwork.

"You and what army?" Oni asks smugly.

Moodring strides up, rubbing her shiny metal chest. "They nearly dented my boobs," she snarls. "Those assholes."

"Oni's already taken revenge for your almost dented boobs. He's always defending people's honour."

More gunfire sounds in the distance

"Goddess, what the fuck is going on?"

"Uh, well, Crave just jumped in front of a gun and ate a lot of bullets. Then Marvellous threw the shooter into the air and Leapfrog punched him through a wall."

"Good job, everyone. Crave, you feeling okay?"

"Heartburn," Crave rasps. "I'll be fine."

"We're fine too, by the way," I tell Goddess. "We only had a whole truck full of Quietus assholes to take care of. It's not a big deal."

"Is everything okay there?" Marvellous asks over the comm.

"Don't worry," I tell her with great seriousness. "Alyse's boobs are fine."

She snorts. "I'm sure they are. But please don't stand in the way of an oncoming car again, at least not without me there to throw it out of the way."

"Sorry to interrupt the flirting," Goddess says. "We might have a problem. There's something weird happening in front of the stage. Everyone's gathering but my drones can't get a good picture."

"Meet you all there." I start running.

We meet the others outside the ruins of the cathedral. The crowd by the stage has grown, despite the chaos. Vans with TV crews are filming. Why the fuck hasn't the area been cleared? As we walk back past the cameras, they pan to follow us. I deliberately ignore them.

Alyse has transformed out of metal form and gives Emma one of her big cushion hugs. I still find them ridiculously cute together. I've got to notice the lovely moments as well as the terrifying and awful ones.

Something stretches high up above the crowd. People cheer. It's one of those wobbly inflatable things they have outside tyre places, but there's something not quite right. It flails in the breeze.

"That's a mutant," Emma says.

"What the—?" Lou looks horrified. I wonder if he's grateful for his power right now.

"Spark." Dani stares up at the waving figure. "It has to be."

I reach for Oni. "Careful. There's something fucked going on. Let's approach with caution."

Something brushes against my leg and I look down to see cats wandering past us. Kitty Pride obviously, but why she's let the damn things out now, I have no idea. The whole group of them wander with tails high towards the crowd.

"Kitty, what the fuck?"

"They're drawn to him." She's rubbing her arms nervously. "Look at them."

I turn back. They're lined up with their cute little faces pointed in our direction. I've stopped walking. My legs won't move. Or my arms. What the fuck is going on?

Dragon, Moodring, and Clone Club are a little in front of me. They've stopped too.

Even Oni hangs motionless in the air. I try to make a sound, but my tongue is frozen. A creaky noise comes from the back of my throat.

Fucking fucking fuck, I scream in my head.

I couldn't have put it better. At least Emma can speak to me. *It seems like Kitty's cats are more than we thought.*

I fucking said something about that when we first found them. I said they might have laser eyes or—

The ability to freeze us and nullify our powers? Emma sounds on the verge of panic, which freaks me out worse.

Okay, not exactly this but I was hella suspicious at first. And then it seemed fine and now what the fuck? Some kind of double cross bullshit?

The mutant waving high above the crowd slowly begins to topple, like the inflatable ones do, but he can't right himself. He hits the ground with an audible slapping sound. His body bursts, spraying a pinkish liquid over the crowd. Nobody seems to notice or care, despite the off-the-charts grossness. Their attention is turned inward, towards something I can't see.

I'm still unable to do anything. I can't even speak aside from screaming to Emma in my head.

A woman a little older than us staggers out from among the crowd. Her eyes glow. "I have seen the Lord."

Her voice is thrilled. "Heaven has opened before me and I see the throne. The angels are gathered around! Oh, and their many eyes are full of fire! They turn their holy gaze upon me."

Her face pulses with light, multiple eyes opening on her cheeks and along the delicate line of her collarbone. She spreads her arms wide and more eyes flutter open along the insides. They have no pupils, only irises bright like wildflowers.

"The glory of the Lord!" All the open eyes gout flame in a myriad of tiny jets. She collapses to her knees, gasping words in a language I don't understand. Her clothes are aflame, and as they burn away, five fist-sized golden eyes blink solemnly in a cluster on her chest. They weep ribbons of blue fire, and the woman chokes and collapses, ash spilling from her lips. The fire gutters and dies, but the eyes still blink.

I can't look away.

This is terrifying, Dylan. I've never felt so helpless. Everyone else is frozen too.

There's got to be a moment we can make our move. I refuse to fucking stand here, hypnotised by cats, while all this insanity happens. One of the cats will get bored. They'll need to sleep. All we need is a second and—

A big mech suit clanks into view. It has a bulbous head and is about ten feet tall. On size alone, it would give Alyse a run for her money.

The mech suit moves toward the crowd, which parts to reveal the figure of a slender man dressed in white. The people close to him are kneeling, reaching out to touch his shoes or the leg of his pants. There's a woman alongside him who's flickering in and out of existence, as if she's a glitching Sim. She seems super familiar, tall and buff and—

Oh fuck, it's Lou's girlfriend.

Is it? What the hell is she doing here?

She came with Lou and obviously got caught up in this clusterfuck. He's going to be so pissed.

The man in the white suit holds his hands up for silence. "Patience," he says. "The worthy will receive the spark of change in time. There are important tasks I must attend to, before I can bring the truth of transformation."

Fucking Spark, I say.

Yes, obviously.

"My dear Tanner." Spark bows in the direction of the mech suit. "Isn't this beautiful?"

How can I be surprised? We've been outplayed spectacularly and it fucking hurts.

"Chatterbox." Tanner's voice sounds metallic through the suit's speaker. "Don't you love it when a plan comes together?"

No, I don't fucking love it. We're beyond screwed.

"Spark, can you please summon your creatures?"

"To me, my children." Spark spreads his arms wide.

Clone Club begins moving, while Dragon and Moodring are still frozen. Crave, Leapfrog, and Penance walk past me too. We're left to watch in horror as they cross freely over to stand with our enemy in front of the crowd.

How can they all be his?

I suspect they were created from him.

Even Penance? I really believed she wanted to fight at our side.

I don't think this is what she wants, Emma says sadly. *I think he has control over them.*

"I say 'plan' singular." Tanner spreads the arms of the mech suit wide. "Really it was a series of plans, to take you out by any means necessary. I thought the attack on your headquarters might work, but you're better warriors than I expected."

I wish she'd fucking kill me instead of monologuing, I growl.

No, you don't.

If I'll end up dead either way, I definitely do. I fucking hate smug people.

"We identified your true weakness the moment you brought in Gladiola and the others," Tanner says in her metal voice. "This desperation you have to *belong*, to find a family. Almost pathetic, really. So we made a long and elaborate feint, playing the role of the heavyweight while we slipped mutants into your path. We expected you'd bring them alongside you, and of course you did. You sowed the seeds of your destruction while you thought you were opening your heart. This wish is so deep, you even took me in."

Spark isn't even paying attention. He's summoned a man from the crowd and is touching his head, whispering something I can't hear. The man twitches like an electric current is running through him. I realise I felt nothing when I was changed by Emma. It happened peacefully in my sleep.

It's not so gentle for this man.

He thrashes and screams while Spark holds him close. He looks like Sourpatch about to spew acid everywhere. Then his jacket tears and small, stubby wings erupt from his back. They look like they're made from a tangled mess of moss and sticky blue liquid. He looks around himself.

"Fly, my son," Spark says.

The wings flap furiously, and the guy jumps into the air only to slam back to ground. His second leap is higher. He shoots into the air and hangs aloft for a few moments before crashing down onto his head. He's clearly unconscious, but the wings keep beating, dragging his body along with them.

I guess not all of them turn out like Penance or Jackson, Emma says. *I can't help but wonder what causes the difference.*

I'd rather know what the point of this demonstration is.

It seems like Tanner agrees with me. "Enough of this posturing, Spark. It is not the time to play your little games and toy with the genome."

"This is my true calling," Spark spits. "This is God's way forward, the path of ascension. If your masters didn't put their fingers into my brain and poke around, perhaps I would not be so broken, and could bring truth to the world."

"You're lucky I'm so tolerant." Tanner's voice is cold. "And even more lucky that you're valuable. If you want your freedom, you'll do as you're told. It's time to prove you have control over your children."

"Of course I do." Spark raises his hands and the mutants around him watch his every movement.

"They've bonded with the rebels," Tanner says. "Made friends, called themselves Cute Mutants. Given themselves adorable codenames. I daresay Chatterbox even thought they were family." The bulbous head of the mech suit turns to face us. "It's time to prove them wrong. Have the murderer do it."

"Please," Penance says. "Please, Spark. Don't make me. My father forced me to kill and kill. I dream in blood. I cannot close my eyes without seeing the faces of the people I murdered."

"No, my sweetest girl." Spark smiles fondly at Violet and it creeps me the fuck out.

"Then have Jackson do it," Tanner snarls. "Let's prove to them they couldn't remove the leash in his mind. Have him kill the little firebreather first. If you bust her jaw clean off, I wonder if she'll start drooling flames."

Emma, there has to be something we can do.

"Jackson, do as Tanner says and remove the firebreather's jaw," Spark says lazily. "Tanner, you're so horribly bloodthirsty. I'm glad we're on the same side."

I'm as helpless as you. Emma's crying. *Helpless as all of us.*

Jackson steps forward. His face is crumpled with tears, but he walks towards us. We're all frozen. The rest of the crowd is paused in anticipation.

I'm screaming internally and so is Emma. My head throbs.

Leapfrog stops in front of Dragon. His lips tremble.

"I'm so, so sorry," he whispers.

CHAPTER THIRTY-ONE

Jackson takes Katie's jaw in his hand. She seems so fucking small and young.

How can these cameras watch without interfering? Are they affected by the cats too?

I can't even cry. Everything is locked away.

I see the tips of Jackson's fingers whiten.

Then I watch his hand drop.

"I won't," he says through gritted teeth. "I won't hurt her."

Emma's sobbing in my head. *Katie's saying to let him do it because otherwise Tanner will hurt Froggie. She says if he breaks her jaw, she might be able to roast Tanner in that tin suit.*

Tell her not to be so fucking reckless.

My head throbs from Emma's shouting.

"I won't do it." Jackson says it louder this time. "You do not control me any longer."

"Shame." Tanner raises the arm of the mech suit. There's some kind of weapon attached. "What a waste."

Emma, shout at Dani as loud as you can, I scream.

Tanner fires a single shot. It hits Jackson right in the neck and he pitches forward into Katie. Both of them topple backwards and hit the ground. Blood is leaking from the back of Leapfrog's neck, but only a little. He's alive. I can see him moving.

"Very clever. How did you do that?" Tanner's laugh echoes through the speakers. "I assume it was Marvellous?"

One of the cats tumbles away, as if it's been nudged by a shaking, feeble telekinetic hand. Despite the gap in the line, I still can't move. I can't see any of the other mutants moving either. Maybe there are still too many cats and there's a critical mass thing.

Get her to shoo away more!

She's fucking trying, Emma snaps back.

Tanner comes at us so fast it's terrifying. Her goddamn mech suit can really move. I can't see what she does, but Emma's voice in my head is gone.

Emma, where are you?

There's no answer. I'm both sick and terrified. I can't even turn my head to see. Beneath all my other feelings is rage. A pale shadow of it is aimed at me for being gullible and naive—for forgetting there are people smarter and more ruthless than me. The rest of it, the obliterating icy whirlwind, is all for Tanner. For taking advantage of that small core of goodness we have. For trying to use Jackson and then tossing him aside.

"This is the punishment you get," Tanner says. "This might be instructive for you in the nature of consequences. I hope you can all see this."

She raises the leg of the mech suit and brings it down hard on Jackson's chest. I can't close my eyes. In my peripheral vision I see the metal boot cave him in as if his torso was made of nothing more than cardboard. I can't close my ears to the wet and shocking sound.

The tattoo on my arm is so cold it burns.

This far and no further was a lie. We've lost another one of our own. We're helpless to stop it from becoming more. Spark and his mutants are going to take us all apart.

"That was a miserable failure," Tanner sounds bored. "Spark, if your little murder princess is still pouting, get the clones to do it. However many I left alive."

"Skye, please go and kill one of them," Spark says. "I really don't care which. All we need to do is prove you're a good girl. If you can do that, all this will be over."

"Over," whispers Skye.

Fucking Prime. Why did it have to be her? Even Two might do something useful. Where the hell is Six, I swear. But Prime is going to kill us because she's too fucking meek to do anything else.

Not that I can talk. They took advantage of my own weakness over and over again. We took Kitty Pride and

Steve in because we wanted to help other mutants. I can't make myself regret that.

I do regret not killing Tanner when we had the chance. Now I'm trapped in a nightmare.

Skye takes a knife from Spark and walks slowly over. Her head is bowed, like she can't bear to look at us. She stops in front of me. Her hand trembles so hard that she drops the knife and has to pick it up.

"Do it," Spark calls.

"I need the others," Skye wails. The air blurs and all the clones stand in front of me.

"Resilient little roaches." Tanner sounds interested more than mad. "With nine of them, you can wipe out the whole gang."

"Sure, whatever. Give me the fucking knife," Six says.

Prime gives it up gratefully.

"Hurry up," Tanner grates.

Six tosses the knife in the air with a grin. "I'm going to fucking love this, you dumb bitch." She hurls herself directly at Tanner, with her other clones in tow.

"Come at us in a tin can," Three says with a sneer.

"We'll fuck you up," Five adds.

Tanner's arm cannon jerks around to aim at them, but she's swarmed by the army. It's hard to even tell them apart, because they're acting as feral as each other. Even Prime is in there, screaming. Three of them are trying to bend the gun arm back so it's facing the body of the mech. Tanner lets off one loose shot that craters the road in between us. It doesn't deter Clone Club at all.

Skye Nine slips down clumsily from the mech suit. Tanner kicks her so hard she flies through the air. She's broken even before she lands, slamming into the fence that bars the way to the cathedral ruins. Eight is flailing around all alone on the other arm of the suit. Tanner lifts her into the air, slamming her down onto the ground so hard her head cracks. A bright smear of blood splashes over the concrete. Some lands on the boots of my uniform. Tanner points her arm cannon at the body of Nine and fires a series of shots that blow her into disconnected parts.

Prime screams, a single sustained note. The clones blur back into her, aside from the bodies of Eight and Nine. They're too badly damaged to reform. Tanner's really killed them.

Skye sobs, scrambling on hands and knees back towards Spark as if he'll save her.

I never realised how much a physical reaction meant. I can't scream, can't weep, can't collapse to the ground. I can't make a fist or urge Oni to fly.

I can't take revenge.

All I am is a frozen shell of a person, paused in the single moment before shattering irrevocably. There is no relief.

Tanner takes a couple of steps after Skye but stops. "Failure again. I can do it myself if I have to, but you know what that means, Spark. No more playing with the genome. No more God's plan for advancement. I'll pull on your leash and you'll be a hollow, lobotomised creature in a dark room, clinging to a Bible."

Spark turns towards Violet who stands beside him, looking even smaller than normal.

"Violet, please."

"I cannot." She shudders.

"You must." He reaches out and tips her chin up to look into his eyes. "This is why you were made. You are the true Angel of Death. God's righteous warrior. You must embrace who you are. Look past the glory and see the burning heart of God—a being of such wrath that He constructed a realm of eternal torment for those who reject Him. You are the merest sliver of His hatred for sin. A single perfect bullet to be aimed by His will."

Violet flickers out of existence. I hope with all my heart she is leaving us forever, fleeing to escape the hold Spark has over her. She can save herself, and perhaps save all of us too.

I've seen how much use hope is.

Penance reappears above the frozen figure of Moodring. A sliver of ghostly face shows a single black and unblinking eye. For a second, the Cute Mutants logo flares in rainbow colours on her cheek. It seems unnecessarily cruel.

Oni hangs motionless in front of me, unable to stop Violet this time.

One hand unfurls, five blades flashing through the air. They pierce my best friend's body in five different places.

I have never hurt this much in my life and I can do nothing to express it.

This betrayal is my fault. This monster we let in has now taken too much from me. Alyse, who taught me what friendship was, who makes me laugh every day, who I love so much she's my second heart.

Her body hangs from the blades of Penance's hand like a toy.

How can I survive this? There is no metaphor for broken that will work. Poetry can scatter all the words it wishes, and I am simply bereft.

"Excellent," Tanner says.

"My beautiful girl." Spark smiles and tilts his head back, revelling in the moment.

Penance disappears and Alyse falls to the ground.

They're going to have to kill me, because they will not stand in the face of my revenge. Let me be a monster and avenge my friend.

All this rage is trapped inside me. There is no place for it to leak out of me, so it corrodes in my brain. A helpless creature with no will of my own, who cannot shut this nightmare out, even for a second.

So I see the moment when red gushes from Spark's mouth, spilling down the front of his pristine suit. Tendrils erupt from his chest like a bladed flower springing open. His body falls apart, a series of fleshy slices. There's so much blood, a series of dripping fans spraying outwards.

Faintly visible above him is a ghostly face with a red slash of mouth curved into a smile.

Penance.

I'm vaguely aware that Tanner is screaming.

I'm more aware of the cats scattering in every direction. The crowd surrounding Spark flees too, any fascination gone.

I collapse on hands and knees. My breath comes in ragged gasps. My fingers are in the pool of blood ebbing from Skye Eight's body. The broken form of Jackson is right beside me, smashed inwards like a ruptured container. One arm is stretched towards me, as if he was begging me for help.

"I've got Tanner," Dani says from behind me. "Emma's fine. You check on Alyse."

I'm desperate to take refuge in Dani's arms, but first is the worst thing I've ever done. I have to force myself to cross to my friend's body.

I stagger over to her, bent almost double.

Her face is pointed in my direction, a smile on it so lifelike that tears flood my eyes. There are no words I can say. There's a sob in my chest that feels like a bomb waiting to go off.

Alyse is alive, Dylan.

Emma? What the—

I'm fine too, in case you were worried about that.

Of course I fucking was.

I crawl over and throw my arms around Alyse. She's ridiculously soft. Emma joins me and we're in this complicated three-way hug.

"I thought you were dead," I gurgle.

"Cushion form," Alyse says. "It'd be like stabbing your Pillow. I'm not saying anyone should do that, but it was never going to kill me."

"Penance knew?" I ask.

"Of course. I could see it." Penance flings herself on the ground beside us. She's back in human form, and her hands gently touch Alyse's side, checking the wounds. "I'm sorry, but it was the only thing I could think of. Spark has control over me, but it's erratic depending on his mood. I thought if I could make him feel happiness or relief, I'd have a moment to strike. Alyse was the only one I could attack without killing her. I tried to show you it would be okay with the logo. Didn't you see it? "

"You saved us," I say to her. "Without you—"

"You saved me first." There's makeup smeared all over her face. "You forgave me and let me into your home and your family, despite everything. How could I turn my back on you?"

"I think I'm stuck in Pillow form for a bit." Alyse prods one of the holes in her side. Curls of white stuffing pop out. "At least until someone sews me up. Fucking Tanner, huh?"

"Fucking Tanner." It's time to deal with her.

When I look up, the mech suit is peeling open, metal plates scattered across the ground in twisted pieces. The gun lies nearby in a convoluted knot.

Dani stands in front of her, clutching her arm as she shreds the metal in time-lapse footage of decay.

I walk stiffly over. "You okay?"

"Not even close, but it could've been a lot worse."

"I feel numb mostly." I clutch onto her metal arm. "Too much of an emotional rollercoaster. Think I might have a nightmare or two about this one." My teeth are chattering again. "Bit worse than Bancroft."

At the heart of the metal wreckage is Tanner. She wears Quietus body armour with the sharpened cross emblazoned on it.

The rest of the suit flies apart in a cloud of shrapnel. All that's left is her fragile form. She slumps to the ground on her knees.

I step forward and Oni nestles into my palm.

"Wait," Tanner's easy grin is gone now. "The cameras. Think of the optics. What will it look like to the world if you take revenge? They're already scared of you."

"Lie down on your front."

"Fuck you, Chatterbox."

Dragon steps up beside me. "You want to see what I can do with my jaw *on*?" A jet of flame scorches the air above Tanner's head, and she throws herself forward onto her belly.

I hold Oni at Tanner's neck while Dani secures her wrists.

"Don't do anything stupid, Chatterbox. The eyes of the world are watching."

What do we do, Ems? I ask.

We give the world a demonstration.

I feel a chill go through me and reach for Dani instinctively. "This is a terrible time to talk, but after everything." I gesture wildly. "I need to know you're okay with me, you know, after the preacher. He's not still in your head, is he?"

"What?" Her frown is almost a relief.

"You're not feeling weird about your sexuality, or the fact you're dating a genderfluid person?"

"Dylan, for fuck's sake." Now the frown is deeper, and much less of a relief. "Sometimes I think you deliberately misunderstand shit. The problem I have is nothing to do with sexuality or identity."

"The problem you have." My lips feel numb.

She closes her eyes briefly. When she snaps them open, I almost drown. "It's about you—about all of us really, but especially you. What we're becoming. You went out in the night and you killed the preacher and however many others. Then we came here to fight this battle and now... We're changing into something else, and it freaks me out."

I open my mouth to speak.

"Don't tell me the arguments, please. I know about self-defence and stopping a monster. I understand the fears of Genosha, and I know that what the preacher did was unforgivable. But it still scares me that the person I love can do that. My Dylan walks into the night alone, and comes back blood-soaked and trembling, leaving a crazy body count behind them."

I make a sound that's not even a word, a single exhale like I've been punched.

"I still love you, Dylan, I promise." She steps forward and presses her forehead against mine. "I'm not capable of not loving you, but I'm scared of where this road leads."

"I didn't set us on this road," I whisper.

"I know. But I worry that you like it too much."

Dylan. We need to do this. Emma's voice cuts into my thoughts. *It's important.*

"I love you," I tell Dani, and I hate the desperation in my voice. "And we can talk about this properly later. Right now, we need to deal with Tanner."

CHAPTER THIRTY-TWO

Tanner doesn't fight when I pull her up, but it's an act. She wants to look pitiful for the cameras. I don't know how much they got of the situation with Spark, but they'll definitely see this.

The crowd has mostly fled, although a few lost and confused people remain. Lou's managed to find his girlfriend and they're having an intense conversation. She's still flicking in and out of existence, and it doesn't look like either of them are happy about it. Welcome to mutant life, Jenna. I hope you survive the experience. Not all of us do.

I head for the camera vans. My head is swimming, but I need to hold it together. Tanner stumbles along behind me. She looks as dazed as I feel. A short time ago, she was victorious, and now her plans are in ruin.

"How did you do it, Chatterbox?"

"You mean why did Penance decide to fight for the people that treated her like a human, instead of a murderous pet on a chain? I have no fucking idea."

We come to a halt a few meters away from the cameras. Every single one is trained on us. There are reporters with microphones, poised and watching. The rest of the Cute Mutants are behind me with the exception of Kitty Pride and Crave. They must have fled, fearful of what happens next. It makes it easier, because I have no idea how to deal with them.

Tanner, on the other hand, I'm sure of.

I stand in front of the cameras, an anonymous person in a mask. "I'm Chatterbox from the Cute Mutants. We were New Zealand's superhero team for a minute or two. Up until an extremist organisation called Quietus came here to kill us." I tug Tanner forward. "This is Abigail Tanner. She works for this organisation. Our government let her come here to provide oversight." Deep breath. "Really she was here to spearhead an operation intended to kill us all."

The reporters shout questions, but they're all talking over each other, so I wait until they pay attention.

"They were here to kill us," I say again. I can't find other words. "They wanted to kill us because of who we are."

I'm not eloquent at the best of times, especially not when I'm exhausted and desperate, and my girlfriend just said she's scared of me. My mouth makes a series of non-words. I'm on the verge of lashing out, when a reassuring presence joins me. I want to sink into her, to collapse and capitulate.

"This attack here today is the third Quietus has made on New Zealand soil," Dani says. "Their targets were the Cute Mutants, all New Zealand citizens. Unfortunately, we no longer have any rights. I don't know how many of you have read the full text of the International Extrahuman Monitoring and Assimilation Act. It's very clear that according to international law, we are considered a different species. It gives a lot of latitude for people who might want to exploit, monitor, or even attack us."

There's another rumble of questions. Again, we don't bother answering. Dani being here and beside me, despite everything, makes it all survivable. I find the words I need.

"They came here to exterminate us. Today, Tanner murdered three of our people." My mask is tight and hot. I can barely breathe. "If we hadn't fought our way clear, she would have killed more. We consider this a declaration of war on our species."

Nobody asks a single question in response. They simply let the cameras roll.

I let the mask fall away from my face. I let them see me. Dylan Taylor. Chatterbox. Mutant and monster. Teen Magneto. This is one of those pivotal moments. There's a fucking metaphor for this. I learned about it in history. The name of some river in Rome.

Fuck it. Call it no take backs.

Emma tells me the words to say, and I repeat them gratefully.

"Today we claim our rights as the citizens of a new mutant nation. Abigail Tanner is accused of the murder of Leapfrog, Skye Eight, and Skye Nine. Of multiple counts of attempted murder. Of utilising illegal mind control techniques. How do you plead, Ms. Tanner?"

She smiles up at me. The Quietus soldier. She thinks this is a victory for her.

It's not. It's a demonstration.

It's a line in the fucking sand.

I'm officially no longer a hero. I guess this all started when I stood there and looked down at Bianca's body. At the time, it looked like the bad end of a single fight. In truth, it was the first shot in a war.

"I plead guilty." Her voice is loud and clear. "Guilty of all charges. I wish to exterminate every member of the filthy mutie species. I want to strangle these abominations and leave a pile of corpses in the cradle of their stillborn nation."

I think she's trying to goad me into doing something reckless. It's what I'm known for, after all.

She has no idea.

I remember when I first got my powers, someone tentative and desperate for a place to belong. We agonised over how to deal with Tremor. If I had it again, I'd shoot him in the head without a second thought.

I don't know whether to envy or pity the person I used to be.

"We have become a family," Oni says. "But you have also been forged into weapons."

Reporters ask more questions. They want to hear more of Tanner's bigoted bullshit. Extremist nonsense always makes for good soundbites. It's probably already online. Maybe some kid is remixing them as we speak. The memes are being posted.

The questions from the reporters get louder and more insistent.

When Tanner starts to speak, Dani clamps a metal hand over her mouth. "You've had your fucking say."

I hold my hand up and wait until the reporters fall silent.

The Cute Mutants are spread out behind me. Clone Club shimmers and the rest of the Skyes are represented, many with their scars and wounds showing where Tanner hurt them. There's no Eight and Nine. They're gone forever.

I clear my throat. "Abigail Tanner has pleaded guilty to crimes against the mutant species, including murder and attempted murder. She has no remorse. Her stated aim is to destroy us, and she has the will, backing and resources to do it. Given the reality we face, what is the proposed sentence?"

"Death," Emma says, as loud and clear as Tanner.

"I second this proposal," I say. "A unanimous vote will carry it. How do you vote?"

The cameras see all of it. Nobody makes any attempt to stop us. The lure of the theatre is too strong, or maybe they don't believe we'll really do it.

One by one, every Cute Mutant answers *death*. I wasn't too sure what Lou or Skye Prime would say, but I'm not surprised by Alyse. Not anymore. That hurts a part of me, but at the same time, she's smart enough to draw her own conclusions about this world and what it means for us. Soon, only Dani remains. We've come around the circle, back to the person standing beside me.

The one who's scared of me, and of my darkness.

Dani takes my hand. "Death," she says, and something loosens inside me. I don't know if it's relief or sadness, but I'm happy we're joined in this, even if it's monstrous.

I look into the staring eyes of the cameras. "The sentence is death. The vote is unanimous." I wonder how we look to the rest of the world. Are we young and pitiful, teenagers with the weight of a nation and species on our shoulders? Or do we look like monsters with unnatural powers, taking brutal actions because we have nobody to control us?

"We never wanted this," I continue. "We genuinely wanted to help. We still offer aid to anyone who needs it. We have no intention of being your enemy. But this is a message to Eli Crane, and anyone else who intends to destroy our people. If you make this a battle for survival, then we'll fight."

There's silence. Everyone's waiting. It's like they're unsure whether I'll really do it.

Fuck it, I say to Emma. *Can't go back now, can we?*

No. We can't, and we shouldn't.

Oni sings a pure and joyful note as I plunge him into Tanner's back. He slides all the way through until he bursts out of her chest. A bright arc of blood sprays through the air. The cameras see it all in high definition. Oni steadies me. He helps me be resolute, to be the warrior I need to be.

Tanner coughs blood. She tries to smile but her mouth hangs slack. Her breath catches, and she collapses. Some of the cameras pan down to her body on the ground. The rest hold their focus on me.

"We want peace," I tell them. "But we're not scared of war."

I open my mouth to say something else—no doubt something extra fucking profound—when Emma shouts inside my head.

I found Crave! Except there's a problem. A really big problem, Dylan.

Fucking Crave. Of course it's him. We almost died because of Kitty's power and now Crave is about to finish *becoming* whatever he's been chrysalising into.

We should never have let him eat that fucking rocket.

I look at the cameras and the body of Tanner and the mass of people that are still watching, despite everything that's gone on.

"Fetch, crowd control." I tear off with Dani on my heels. Emma gives directions in my head, translated from whichever drone feed is watching Crave.

It turns out he's busted down the fence protecting the Cathedral, and has crawled inside the building itself. A drone hovers near the collapsed entrance, shining its light inside. This place is completely fucking unsafe. What the hell is he doing in there?

We scramble in after him on Emma's urging. I'm worried the whole place will fall on us. Something creaks above me and I flinch.

"Dylan, this looks bad," Dani says.

I take one look at the warped figure of Crave and thoughts of the building are forgotten. His body has changed shape even more. He's elongated and his skin has become a series of overlapping plates which grind audibly against each other.

"What's wrong?" I don't even want to touch him.

"It's happening," Crave mutters. "They told me I wasn't like my brother, but I am. Help me, Chatterbox, please. I didn't want to end this way but…"

"Hey, buddy." I try to be soothing, but I'm shot through with adrenaline from the mess with Tanner. Everything has a dreamlike air, but it still fucking *happened* and—no, I need to focus on this. "What happened to your brother?"

"He wouldn't stop *growing*." Crave writhes on the ground. "He didn't have a mouth like mine, but he was always so hungry. Then he went with friends to the theme park and—"

"Orlando." My stomach lurches. "Crave, did your brother explode in Orlando?"

Crave takes a big shuddering breath. Tears roll down his cheeks, steaming faintly. "He hurt so many people, but he never meant to. I didn't mean for this to happen either. I had no idea until Spark spoke, when I had no choice but to follow him."

Emma, I think we might need juicing. This could be very bad.

"Oni, go fetch Goddess. Marvellous, we need to get him out of here. Like way the fuck out."

"We're in the middle of the city," Dani says. "I don't think I can move him fast enough to get him to a safe distance. This might be the best place to do it."

"Except for us!" This seems like a fatal flaw in the plan.

"Well, yeah, we'd have to get moving."

"If he's anything like his brother, we're not going to make a safe distance."

Dani stares at me. "I don't know what else we can do."

I'm pretty sure I'm going to faint, and this is the worst possible time. I shove my head between my knees and concentrate on breathing until I feel quiet enough to make a decision.

"All points assistance," I say over the comm, still in my awkward position. "As many of you as possible, get here now. It's big internet hug time, and this time it's fucking serious."

Dani has her hand on my back, rubbing gently. I uncurl myself.

Crave looks worse than ever. His whole body shakes and convulses. A whistling sound is coming from his throat. We don't have a lot of time.

Oni hurtles out of the sky, trailing Emma behind him. He deposits her lightly on the ground and she crawls into the interior of the building with us.

"He's really going to explode?" Her face is grave.

Crave shudders all over. His shirt has ridden up and I can see the mouth in his stomach, tightly closed like a scar. He clutches at his head and moans something incoherent.

"I'm going to try and hold him together." Dani's voice is firm. She takes hold of Emma and extends her other hand to me. "I know it's insane, but I don't know what else we can do. There's no time to run."

The three of us cling to each other inside the ruins of the cathedral. The sun casts strange shadows over us. It's a fucking creepy place to die. It's so unfair for it to end here after all we've been through.

"This isn't the end," Emma says firmly.

"No." Dani's eyes hold mine. They're so beautiful. It can't be the last time I see them. "I'm going to save my girlfriend *and* the fucking day."

Crave screams and doesn't stop. His back arches.

Alyse and Katie scramble in through the half-fallen entranceway.

"Just in time," Emma says. "Get in on this hug because——"

They've barely reached us when Crave starts coming apart at the seams. Cracks of light trace fault lines across his skin.

Dani takes hold of her own throat with her metal hand. She squeezes. She screams.

I think we're all screaming.

Crave's body strains, trying to tear itself apart.

Dani's somehow holding him in place. We're joined in some juiced-up Emma circuit, but I can feel her trembling furiously against me.

Hot, bright air streams out of the cracks in Crave's skin. I feel scalded.

"Fucking hold me," Dani says in a choked voice.

We all cling tighter as Crave shudders. The cracks are growing bigger. He's going to fly apart. We'll all be obliterated by the furious heat that burns inside him. The gaps between the plates in his skin are wide enough that I could pry them apart with my fingers.

Dani spasms in my arms.

I bury my face in her neck, trying to hold her together.

Emma whimpers like a wounded animal.

Dani shakes harder, her whole body jerking as the light inside Crave begins to die. Her hand reaches for my face, but can't make it. Her eyes are fixed on mine. So wide and so beautiful. They still dizzy me.

"You did it!" I kiss Dani's warm cheek. "You marvellous girl. You fucking did it."

"Dylan," she croaks.

"Don't talk." I can taste salt on my lips. "Don't say anything. Just rest."

"Let me say this. I love you. Every part of you, even when you're bloody-handed. You're beautiful and wild and mercurial, but you're also mine in every way and—"

Dani gives one final thrash, her head slamming into my chest. There's blood on her lips. She feels loose and relaxed in my arms.

Crave lies in front of us, silent and still. The cracks in his skin are nothing more than faint glowing lines.

"Crisis over?" Alyse croaks.

"Fuck, that was scary." Katie bounces to her feet. "The biggest internet hug!"

"Come on," I tell Dani. "Wake up. Everyone wants to tell you how amazing you are."

She doesn't respond.

I pat her cheek, and her head lolls against me.

I feel for a pulse at her wrist, but there's nothing.

I place my hand against her chest, where I always feel for the reassuring beat of her heart.

It's silent.

"Emma, find a pulse," I croak. "Anyone. Please. Tell me Dani's okay."

CHAPTER THIRTY-THREE

So this is my life: my girlfriend saved us all.

My girlfriend saved half the fucking city.

My girlfriend is lying dead in my arms in the ruins of the Christchurch Cathedral.

Crave lies unconscious or dead, completely unexploded.

The rest of the world carries on around me, as if nothing fundamental has changed. It has no time for me and my centre of gravity collapsing in on itself like a dying star.

Alyse is saying something. She has one hand on Dani's wrist, and the other on her neck. Emma's talking in my head, but I can't hear anything.

Dani is dead. This cannot possibly be a *fact* but the truth keeps elbowing its way into my brain and out-screaming me.

The woman I love is gone. Crave was one final trick of Tanner's. She gave us a bomb and waited for it to go off where it could do the most damage. Her final revenge, to strip away the one thing I truly need.

Someone shakes my arm.

"Dylan, it's Quietus. There are more soldiers coming." Alyse stands over me, a ferocious metal shield in the shape of a girl. She's changed away from Pillow form. I hope she's okay. At least metal doesn't bleed.

Loud banging sounds jolt me out of my numbness.

I'm still Chatterbox.

I still have a team.

My lover is gone, but we're still here.

"Penance, the gloves are off," I say over the comm. "Not another fucking mutant dies today."

The thought of the name Marvellous tattooed on my arm leaves a horrific gulf of loss in my chest. It's too big to bridge. My heart is abandoned, a dusty tomb where I'm doomed to wander from chamber to chamber until I no longer have the will to go on. She loves me even when I'm bloody-handed. I'll give them all the blood I have on my hands before they take another one of us.

This is not the world I want to live in. I need another.

There are voices from outside. There's gunfire.

"Oni, my friend? Don't let me hold you back."

There's a lot of screaming. Not a lot of gunshots. It happens so fast I barely get the chance to breathe.

I'm very aware of the shape and weight of Dani in my arms, and it doesn't fucking compute.

"Tell me this isn't real, Lys." My voice doesn't even sound like me. It's some whiny brat speaking my dialogue because I can't do it. "Tell me it's a dream. Some mutant is bending reality and it will come back—"

"Quietus are gone," a voice crackles over the comm. "Penance took care of most of them, and Oni handled the rest. We've left the cops, but they're unhappy."

"Fuck the cops," the person who's not me says. "We need to get out of here."

My chest feels tight. My throat is squeezing closed around a single bladed truth. My vision blurs, and all I can see in front of me is a wall of orange light. Some new and horrific turn of events on top of everything.

Nausea twists my gut so sharply I curl over Dani's body. A howl escapes my throat. How can this not be fucking over yet? How much more does Quietus have to throw at us?

I have to squint, but shapes resolve from amongst the brightness. It's three humanoid figures. They're not wearing Quietus gear. EMID? There's a woman in front with short dark hair. One of her eyes pulses with a eerie blue glow. Her hands are over her head.

"Please hold. Stand down. We're from Haven! We come in peace! Please hold!"

Penance hovers in the air above them. "Engage, Dylan?"

"I said we come in peace." The woman's voice is firm and even, like she's used to command. "There's no need to *engage*. We saw the news and we're looking for someone called Chatterbox. Holy shit, we've got wounded."

"Haven," I croak. "Are you friendly?"

"Bingo, kid. That's what we come in peace means. Doc, can you look at this one?"

"I'm Chatterbox." My teeth won't stop chattering, so it seems like I'm making a joke.

A Black woman in beige overalls crouches in front of me, holding a bag. "Hey Chatterbox, I'm Doc. I'm a mutant too, okay? I'm friendly, just like Farsight here. My power is healing, so I'm just going to try touching your friend here. See if we can't fix her right up."

"This isn't good." The speaker is a short woman with curly blonde hair and big Mum energy. "They've murdered someone on live TV and left a damn blood-bath. Do you see all the bodies, Far?"

"I surely do, Jay. Now isn't the time. These kids are mutants and they're hurt so we—"

"They're a liability."

"I'm pulling rank," the woman called Farsight snaps. "They come back with us. We sort it out at home. If you've got something to say, we can talk about it there. Understood?"

"Both of you shut up." Doc is focused on Dani. "Let me do my job."

"Please." I can't make out the woman's face properly. "Can you help her? I love her so much."

"Yeah, sweetheart, I can see that." Doc places one hand gently on Dani's chest and holds it there. She looks up at Farsight and gives a tiny shake of her head, sending her short locs bouncing.

"Do it again," I say urgently.

"It's too late, Chatterbox." Her voice is gentle.

Emma, I scream in my head. *Get over here.*

"I'm here, Dilly." She crouches beside me. I take her hand and place it on Doc's shoulder.

"Cute Mutants assemble," I try and shout, but it comes out like a disgusting wet cough. It doesn't matter, because Alyse is here, and Violet too. A whole bunch of Skyes and Lou and Katie and Gladdy and Maddy. Even fucking Jenna is here, flickering in and out like a lightbulb in a horror movie, but I'll take anyone I can get to increase our chances. Everyone's gathered around Doc in the biggest internet hug we've tried yet.

"Do it again." My voice sounds like I'm the dead one.

Doc places her hand on Dani's chest and closes her eyes. Her knuckles are bruised.

There's a current that starts from Emma and comes flickering out of her. The energy runs through us, and together we become a giant circuit. It gathers strength as it moves through our bodies, and then gushes into Doc. Blue-white light traces branching patterns down the inside of her arm and pools in her palm.

It gathers there for a moment and then floods into Dani, filling her body with light. She gives another massive convulsion in my arms. It feels like she's humming. There's a thumping sound and the light is snuffed out abruptly.

"Did it work?" I ask Doc. She stares wide-eyed at us all, probably feeling the aftereffects of being boosted.

"Get ready to bail, Jumper," Farsight says. "We need to leave quick smart either way."

"Opening the portal now." The other woman still sounds pissed. "I hope we don't regret this."

Dani's head twitches. Her eyes snap open and lock onto mine.

She's alive. The woman I love is in my arms. She's breathing and warm and real and—

"Dylan." She takes hold of my arm with one bloody hand, leaving smeared fingerprints.

"Dani, I'm here. You're okay. I'm so—"

"You need to listen to me." There are melodies caught in her voice, like she's trying to remember a tune. "This is important."

"What is it?"

Her lips are pale. Something flares in the centre of her pupils, like they're tiny supernovas. Patterns of blue-white light crackle outwards, making her irises glow.

"Tell me, Dani. What the fuck is going on?"

One corner of her mouth twitches upwards, into something that's almost a smile.

"God is coming," she says.

ACKNOWLEDGEMENTS

In amongst this weird year of 2020, the Cute Mutants have been my constant. I started writing these books in February during an emotional slump, and they slowly but surely took over my life. If you'd told me at the start that I'd be publishing the third book in December, I would have thought it was an elaborate prank, yet here we are.

The truth is, I wouldn't have gotten this far without an enormous amount of support. Once again, my family has been there for me throughout this whole journey, including all the ups and downs. I have so much love and appreciation for them, because it hasn't been easy at times.

Getting a novel into the world takes a whole bunch of people to help me out. Emma Jun read my very first draft and helped me streamline all the conflict (and oh, wow, sorry about all the blood). Jen Elrod and Sarah helped me wrangle my subsequent draft into more coherent shape. Lynn Jung once again helped out with invaluable advice.

Amanda M Pierce is the first critique partner I met on Twitter, and her advice and input is worth more than I can explain. She's got an incredible insight into these characters and always helps guide me back to their emotional center. Then Shannon Ives and Maddy LeMaire came in at the end to help me polish this into something almost entirely coherent. I'm surrounded by brilliant people who've given their time and talent to help these chaos kids into the world. As always, any mistakes are mine.

I'm lucky enough to lean on a whole host of writers for moral support. First is a group of people who claim to be twelve feral raccoons in a trenchcoat, but are some of the kindest and most talented people I'm lucky enough to know. To Andy, Crystal, Leah, Mallory, Melody, Michelle, Monica, Nat, Nina, SinJ and SoftJ—I don't know how many ways there are to say thank you, but you're owed them all. One day I'll have a whole shelf full of Team Trash books, but until then, please keep yeeting everything you write in my direction.

There are so many other people who've been incredibly supportive: Avery, CJ, Leta, E.M., Isa, Skye, Amy, Brittany, Amber, Hsinju, Yves, Althea, Cassidy and SJ (a different one). I'm glad to know you all and share all the ups and downs of writing.

Once again, @kassiocoralov is a superhero for the beautiful cover, and the impeccably talented G made the inside look pretty too.

Finally, it's been wonderful to see these books going out into the world and meaning something to people. Thank you to everyone who's picked up the book and read it, and those who have reached out to let me know they enjoyed it. Extra special thanks to those who've spread the word. There are so many great books out there, and I appreciate everyone who takes the time to let others know about these particular ones. There's still more to come, so buckle up <3

ABOUT THE AUTHOR

SJ Whitby lives in New Zealand with their partner, as well as various children and animals. They are predictably obsessed with X-Men and spend too much of their free time writing, plotting out way too many sequels, spin-offs and parallel universes. Perhaps they take their X-Men fandom too seriously.

You can find them on Twitter at @sjwhitbywrites.